I0682101

Just Walk

TRUTH! the series: Book Two

T. Randall Jones

Lvolution Books
Charlotte, North Carolina

ISBN: 978-0983336112

Released 2011, Revised May, 2013

Cover model photo by: Toni Jackson

Cover model: Shanika Latimer

For information visit

www.Lvolution.org

Acknowledgments

For all that I have done, or ever will do that is good,
to God be the glory!

To my family, my God-given purpose is to write;
but the thing that makes the work all worthwhile is your enduring
love, PATIENCE and support.

To the men and women by choice,
or divine intervention, who inspired this work,
I pray that you can hear my heart.
I used to say, 'I don't understand',
and now that I get that I don't have to, I do!

This book is dedicated in Loving Memory to

Harriett Burch Redic Bell

Miss Harriett's life was a walking testimony of love and courage.
Her smile and generous spirit will forever be missed;
her legacy never forgotten.

A word from the Author…

WARNING: A small portion of this book contains specific references to abuse and / or sexual violence that may be difficult to read. I sincerely apologize to anyone who is caught off guard, hurt or offended by these passages. I promise I would not include them if I didn't feel very strongly as an artist that they are relevant to the character development and plot. If you wish to avoid reading them, these passages are marked *** well in advance, and then ### immediately after (so you don't miss too much).

This book, as well as the other novels in *TRUTH! the series*, also contains detailed accounts of actual sex, tastefully written, I'm told; and no, I have not marked those passages (Ya Nasty...). We're all grownups; or at least we should be....But if you are not, PUT THIS BOOK DOWN!!!

Oh, and sometimes there's some cussin'. See above...

And finally, there are references to scripture, including one or two interpretations that one might find, depending on one's raising, offensive, inaccurate, or occasionally, just plain blasphemous. (Hmm. What to say?) ...

TRUTH! the series is a collection of stories about, but not exclusively for, the LGBT Faith community. I am a Christian, and a lesbian, and an artist. I am not a pastor, and do not claim to be either a theologian or biblical scholar. The opinions, beliefs, and views expressed in this series are those of THE SPECIFIC CHARACTERS, not necessarily by me, the author.

With all that said, I do indeed hope that the characters, relationships and themes in these books inspire discussion. And I encourage you to mark the pages and reference them in your interactions with your book club members, partners, church family, friends, acquaintances; and when and wherever appropriate, your children. If you find any part of this book, or the others, encouraging or uplifting, or I dare to dream, worthy of passing on to someone else, then my prayers have been answered. I've found my purpose! I feel profoundly connected to each and every person who reads these stories... and GETS IT!

Thank you and God Bless!

Tia

1

THE ELEVENTH COMMANDMENT

*T*he instant that she sobered up, the initial shock of Kevin's news wore off, and reality set in, Gabrielle began to unravel. She'd been thankful that Ethan was with Kevin's parents for the rest of the summer, but terrified that, without him there, depending on her for food and transportation, but mostly looking after her, she would not survive until he came home. But she'd been too shaken, shattered, perhaps just too prideful?, to call anyone she knew for help. She hadn't been joking when she told Kevin that her own mother would probably say, 'I told you so'. She genuinely believed that to be true. She had a few longtime friends; but she couldn't face them, certainly not after the bitchy way she'd always, not entirely discretely, looked down her nose at them, and judged their relationships as being less fabulous than hers.

Losing her famous and talented and beautiful and nice husband to man was bad, but it wasn't, surprisingly, the worst. Just hours after Kevin left, she knew that, if she wanted to, she could survive without him. She had, after all, been living without him for all of their eight year marriage. She didn't even need his money. With Kevin in New York working and on tour, she'd actually turned her career into a hobby, diving head-first into all aspects of entertainment management, publicity and personal representation. She had creative and active gifts of her own, but never had the drive or desire to be in the limelight. While she'd always been told that she was talented enough to have a career of her own in the theater, she found the most satisfaction in supportive roles. She enjoyed helping people achieve their dreams and reach their potential. And while money wasn't the most important thing to her, she was good at what she did, so, she had plenty of it. She didn't actually need Kevin for…anything.

So, no, his announcement that he was, had likely always been, gay and had fallen in love with a man, was not the worst thing that had ever happened to her. The worst thing was the reality that he didn't have to tell her. He didn't have to divorce her. He'd been living in New York for thirteen years, and pretending to be gay for nine of them. He only saw her when he came home to see Ethan, when she came to New York for his events, and for family holidays and vacations. For nearly ten years, she'd practically been his mistress, anyway. They could have gone on forever like that. He could have done that for her. And if the truth ever came out, she'd have had a right to be angry! So, what hurt the most, was that, 'despite his being a homosexual', Kevin was honest and good enough to tell her the truth, before anything horrible happened; before anyone, but her, could be hurt! He claimed to love her, too much to live that kind of lie, but not too much to push 'his urges' aside and stay with her? He valued her friendship, trust and respect, but 'not her love'? He was concerned for their son, but not the humiliation she'd suffer when the truth came out? Kevin Rivers was a star. People were going to find out that he left her to live some 'alternative lifestyle' with an openly gay man! "Who does that? What kind of woman gets left behind and cast aside for a man, and a shameful, filthy life? Why didn't he love me enough to make 'him' his mistress for a while? Fine, I know that's ridiculous. But, why didn't he love me enough to just stay? Why didn't he live in fear of losing me, and tell his stupid gay crush that he wanted to screw him, but he loved me and couldn't bear the thought of a life without me? When did I stop being …everything to him? When did I stop being beautiful and special and worthy of his love and devotion, at any cost? Why wasn't I…enough?"

And for forty-eight solid hours, those and other questions played over and over again in her head, until she realized she had to stop them. Being solution-oriented, she sought the most expedient, most effective way to simply quiet the noise. Suddenly, her usual glass of red wine wasn't potent enough. Sure, she could drink enough that she got drunk and it dulled the pain momentarily. But The Voices never really stopped; they just got sleepy. When they woke, they were angry, and not at him, but at her! Being mostly alcohol to begin with, they, The Voices, weren't affected the same way some people are by spirits. They, The Voices, weren't more honest and relaxed, or candid. They weren't even fun and lively, like her fermented-grape-induced personalities. They, The Voices, were belligerent, and antagonistic, and destructive and mostly…just plain mean. And they, The Voices, told her that she wasn't good, or special, or pretty, or deserving enough to be anything to anyone as special and as good as Kevin Jerome Rivers. And they, The Voices, told her over and over and over again, that the world would be better off without her. So, she continued to feed, and water them, until her cupboards were bare. And as she scoured her liquor cabinets, polishing off party leftovers, icky sweet things she'd received as gifts and only pulled out to be polite, and the very last of a very expensive bottle of scotch she'd kept in the house for her father, they, The Voices, began to take over; until they finally remembered the cases of champagne she'd just purchased as gifts for her clients, seized control of her cell phone and located her assistant's number.

"Sh-shel-eee!" Gabby somehow stammered, slurred and screeched her assistant's name all at once. "Bring it. You know where we put it…in that thing behind the thing… You know Shelley, the thing!"

"Mrs. Rivers?" Gabby's assistant never called her anything other than Gabby, unless, and on the very rare occasion, Gabby seemed upset or agitated. That typically only happened about once a year, usually around her anniversary. But that was in March, and it was August. "Mrs. Rivers, are you okay?"

"Don't call me that! What the hell is wrong with you? You don't call me that! You call me, 'Gabby' or 'Gabs'… Ooh, 'member that time I landed that AAA baseball team and you had everyone in the office callin' me 'G-Money' for a week? That was fun. You make me smile, Shelley; and you give the best nicknames. You must really like me. Ya know, no one else has ever given me a nickname before. He never called me anything special… just 'Gabby', or 'Gabrielle', when he was mad at me. He was mad at me a lot. Why was he always mad at me, Shelley? He doesn't love me, Shelley. And he's a gay. Did you know that? I did. I prolly shoulda told 'em, huh? Did you find it?"

"I don't know what you want me to look for, G-Money, but I'm on my way." Shelley stared wide-eyed at her girlfriend and pointed to the phone while she looked for her jeans.

"No, I'll come there, I was on my way in anyway." Gabby spun around looking for her keys.

"No, Gabby, it's Saturday, and it's the middle of the night. You stay right there. I'll find it, bring it and I'll be right over. Don't leave, okay? I'm gonna need you to let me in. Are you dressed?"

Gabby actually pulled the phone away from her ear to look down at herself, and saw that she was actually wearing her wedding dress. "I am dressed! I look like a princess! It's kinda big, though. When did I get so skinny? Do you think I'm too skinny, Shelley? Do you think that's why he doesn't love me? But, all those other women are even skinnier. Oh, yeah... Well, maybe his stupid, dummy-dumb boyfriend is a big fat fatty, and that's what he likes. I could have gotten fat, too, Shelley...if he'd asked me to."

"You're not too skinny, Gabs; you're perfect, just beautiful." Gabby had actually gotten 'scary thin' in the last year, but Shelley thought better than to point that out.

"What do you know, Shelley? How are you suddenly the expert on beauty and why men like fatties?"

Shelley tried not to laugh out loud, as she fastened her seatbelt and handed Tiana the keys. "I don't know, Gabs; I just know that you're very, very pretty... and well, since it's four o'clock on Saturday morning, I can say out loud, 'super-hot'."

"Hey!" Tiana whispered and shook her head laughing.

"See, now you sound like one of those people... like one of the gay... Only a lesbo would say something like that..."

"Gabby, I've worked for you for four and a half years. How do you *not know* I'm gay?"

"Oh my God! You too?! What is wrong with you people?!" Gabby screamed before hurling the phone across the room and shattering it into pieces.

When Shelley and Tiana arrived ten minutes later, they found Gabby curled up in a ball on the floor, wearing her too big wedding gown, which was smeared with blood from a cut on her hand. She'd been running around the house smashing pictures, and then immediately picking them up, apologizing to them and clutching them to her bosom. Her usually picture-perfect hair was a tangled mess, she appeared to have made herself up and then had second thoughts, so there were wild streaks and smears of liner, shadow and lip-gloss all over her face. And, in her limited experience, Shelley thought her boss smelled like a homeless person would: a mixture of pee and either very cheap or large quantities of very expensive booze.

"Oh my, God." Shelley whispered and tried not to cry. She barely recognized her boss and mentor as the discarded princess-bride, vandalizing her own modern-day castle. As her employer, Gabby was awesome: demanding, supportive, fair and generous with her time and attention. Personally, she was very private, speaking only of her husband and son in broad terms, never details. She knew that 'Rivers' was Gabby's married name, and her husband's name was 'Kevin'; but she'd never met him, and would never, even if her life depended on it, have guessed that he was the 'Kevin Rivers' of Broadway. There'd actually been, over the years, rumors among the assistants about his actual identity and occupation. But, after failing to put the pieces together, and deciding that she actually liked Gabby too much to pry into her intentionally private life, Shelley finally gave up and let her fantasy that he was some manner of international spy take root. As she looked around Gabby's living room at the images of the actor alone and with his family, she more than once had to hold down her urge to scream, 'but spies don't leave their wives!' Nothing made sense, least of all, the sight and smell of Gabrielle Nichols Rivers in a broken heap of white satin and lace on her own Calamander wood floor.

"Hi Shelley!" Gabby lifted her head and actually smiled at her friend. "Did you find it? Who's this?"

"No, Gabs. I told you, I'm not sure what you wanted me to bring; but I was worried about you, so I rushed right over. This is Tiana. She drove because I ran out of the house without putting in my contacts."

"Oh, okay... I don't wear contacts. I have perfect vision, absolutely perfect..." Gabby's voice and thoughts trailed off, as the younger women picked her up and looked for the nearest shower. She continued to mumble, as they tried to remove her blood and booze stained gown and waited for the water to warm just a little. As the lukewarm water began to slowly take effect, Gabby began to remember bits and pieces of the previous forty-eight hours. "My life was perfect, Shelley, just like my eyes. I had a perfect, perfect life...but he said it was a lie...and he's leavin' me to be a gay..."

"I know, Gabby. I'm so sorry. But you're going to be okay. We'll get you cleaned up and tomorrow everything will be just fine."

"Nothing will ever be perfect again. Hey! You said you're a gay, too! My daddy says gays are horrible, sinful people. You are so fired, Shelley! ...Thank you for washing my hair... You're really nice... and your lesbo friend is pretty... okay, you're not fired... but you'd better not tell my daddy..."

2

FUBAR

*W*hen the male therapist Tiana referred her to gave her a list of women's support groups, Gabby did absolutely nothing but complain. "Why do they all have to be so far out in the middle of nowhere?" In her newly cantankerous state, to Gabby, anything out of Uptown, even Southend, was 'the middle of too damn far'. "And why in the world are there so many of them? I guess I should find some consolation in the fact that I'm not entirely alone in my misery."

Having narrowed the two-page, double-sided list and various web links down to the three least intimidating options, she finally settled on a twice-weekly meeting of racially and socio-economically diverse women, between the ages of twenty-one and forty-five. She sat quietly in the uncomfortably large circle of women, in the vast open space of a converted warehouse, just outside the old industrial heart of Charlotte, North Carolina.

"Hi, My name is Gabby." She offered when it was her time to speak. She didn't want to be there; but her time was valuable, and she wasn't going to waste it by just sitting there. Besides, after her DUI and the attack on the Chinese food delivery guy ten days earlier, the judge warned her that her only options were to 'find help immediately, or do time in the county jail'. And she didn't look good in orange.

"Hi, Gabby." The rainbow of women answered.

"I'm not sure why I'm here. My therapist 'suggested' I find a support group; but there are surprisingly few support groups for women whose husbands didn't cheat or give them fatal diseases, but suddenly left them for men." Awkward chuckles and smiles sprinkled the room. "If anyone has a problem with me being here, I completely understand. It's just that, after watching a documentary about...women in your situation, I sort of thought this would be the closest fit." Gabby explained without an ounce of judgment in her voice.

"HIV isn't fatal; and exactly what situation do you think we're all in?" Lindsay, a pretty but haggard blonde asked, as she slowly sat upright in her folding chair.

"I-I thought that this was a group for women who'd contracted HIV from their cheating husbands..." Gabby said apologetically, as she felt her face grow hot.

"And your husband didn't cheat..."

"And you don't have HIV..."

"So you think we have what in common, exactly?" Cheryl looked skeptically at the casual, but impeccably dressed woman claiming to be her sister.

"That the men we loved and trusted and thought we knew, turned out to be gay... All you hear about these days is 'brothers on the DL'. I just thought that must be how..."

"My husband is a very straight intravenous drug user. He'd been clean for ten years when he lost his job and, after a year of looking for work, decided his heroine-induced, hazy-days-of-yore were much more appealing than life as a stay-at-home dad." Lilly, the pierced and tatted redhead chuckled to keep from crying. "I actually thought he'd been going on interviews again for the last six weeks, before he died of an overdose."

"My boyfriend's, 'ex-girlfriend' contracted HIV from her new fiancé, who supposedly got it from one of about a thousand groupies on the road; and go figure, he'd never stopped sleeping with her." Gabby looked at the young woman, Tracie, who could have been her daughter or younger sister, and silently prayed a prayer of 'Thanks' that Kevin had indeed stayed celibate while they were in college, and faithful throughout their marriage.

"There, but for the Grace of God, do I go..." She whispered softly. "Is he a famous musician?"

"No, basketball player." Gabby got a cold chill and quickly ran through her client list in her head. She consoled herself, for the time being, that none of her athletes had been recently engaged or...disengaged.

"Well, my former husband is one of those secret-dick-sucking-likes-it-up-the-ass mother-fuckers; and I think they all deserve to burn in Hell! Serves their nasty asses right! God don't like that shit!"   A nervous, former trophy-wife returned from chain smoking outside to interject, and glared at Gabby, while patting her foot anxiously.

"Wait a minute, Valerie. If HIV and AIDS are God's punishment for homosexuality, what's your sin? Never mind. Yours is probably that you're just plain hateful. But, what's mine?" Yasmine, a pretty, twenty-eight year old, Latina asked quietly and waited, as though she honestly expected an answer.

"I can't blame anyone but my damn self." Elaina, a stunning brunette, who Gabby was certain she'd seen somewhere before, smiled and shook her head. "My therapist calls me a 'serial-monogamist'. Throughout high school and college, I always had a boyfriend. But, I could never find 'the right' boyfriend, so I had a different boyfriend every three months. I slept with almost all of them, eventually. I always started out with the best intentions. I insisted he wear a condom in the beginning; but if I thought I was in love, 'this is the one, we're going to be together forever', I just made sure I was on the pill and, otherwise, just made myself available to him. The most ironic thing is that I don't think I'd ever really been hurt by a man before. I was the one who always left, or said it wasn't working. I never felt betrayed or cheated on. Most of the men I dated were really good to me. I almost got married twice. But something would always happen, and I'd end it because 'it didn't feel right.' As it turns out, I'm a lesbian. That's why my relationships with men didn't work. But, I had it so much in my head that 'sex comes first and the rest of it comes after that', that I couldn't figure it out, until I really sat by myself for a while. I took a solid year and didn't date, men or women; I didn't even flirt. I just worked, worked out, and went to church; and I got to know me. And then one day, I just walked into the bathroom, looked in the mirror and said, 'Stop playin' you're gay.' And I never looked back after that. But by then, I knew just enough about HIV /AIDS that I started to get paranoid. I used to think that it was a gay man's disease, so I was safe because my boyfriends were always 'certifiably heterosexual'. I finally got tested, mostly so I could just breathe easy. It, and the five tests I had after that, came back positive. The good news is, I've never been sick a single day; but the hard part is, I have to tell anyone I'm even remotely interested in that I'm HIV positive. Initially, women are like, 'oh, that's okay'; because they think they can't get it from another woman. But, when I explain that that's not true, that, yes, it's harder to transmit woman to woman, but it is possible, they back away. Lesbians don't like to wear clothes to bed, let alone condoms. So, I finally figured out who I am 'sexually' and I'm condemned to this 'sexless lifestyle.' And it is absolutely no one's fault but my own."

"I'm so sorry. You all must think I'm an absolute... bitch. I have no business here..." Gabby stood to leave.

"Gabby, wait." Tamika, the group's facilitator stopped her before she could get to the door." You are welcome here. This group is for any woman who needs to share her experience and hopes to gain some understanding and peace from hearing someone else's. We don't all have HIV; we obviously were not all betrayed the same way you were. The thing we do have in common is that we've each reached a point in our lives, some of us earlier than others, when we desperately need the support of other women to deal with some major, life-changing events. I don't know about yours, but my pastor couldn't handle the kind of reality I was trying to live in five years ago; and my therapist couldn't cover enough ground in one hour a week. I found out I was pregnant and HIV positive when the results of my rape kit came back. That was five years ago. I'd just graduated from college, I was still a virgin, and about to marry my high school sweetheart. In the blink of an eye, I went from feeling like my life was just about to begin, to it being over. Period. All I could do was sit in rooms like this and listen and cry, all day, for a year. I had to, to keep from leaving this life completely. But with the help of these women, some who've come and gone, a lot of them just like you, I made it through. Today, I have a beautiful family, a career more fulfilling than I ever dreamed possible, and a condition, not a disease, that is undetectable, but, yes, incurable. I'm actually thankful for this tie that binds me to the hundreds of truly amazing women, most of whom, I'd never have met, otherwise. If someone had turned me away, because I didn't have the right disease, contracted in the right manner, I wouldn't have survived even one day."

Gabby watched the young woman in awe through her tears and sat back down. "Thank you for saying that." She smiled softly.

"I just feel so foolish. Everyone thinks I'm fine, because that's what I keep telling them. That's what I told him. But I can't breathe. I don't know how to function anymore. Before he told me, and decided to act on, what I already knew, I had the perfect life: a stunning, superstar husband, one brilliant, talented and obedient child, the nicest home in the most exclusive neighborhood, world travel, shopping in New York, Paris...It was a picture perfect life. And when he told me... what I already knew... I had to face the fact that it was over. How was I going to explain it to people, my parents, our friends, those nosey heffas in my church? How could I possibly live through that kind of ridicule? So, I told him to 'take the kid and go!' Sure, I did it in a way that only I could do it, with a smile on my face... and a back-up plan tucked away in my hand-crafted, Italian leather handbag! I was going to fix his sorry ass! He wasn't just going to leave me and run off and be happy with some man, just because he thought he was in love, and think that I was just going to take it. He was going to pay. When I killed myself in the most glamorous and scandalous fashion imaginable, and told the world that it was all his fault, he was going to look like a monster; and then no one would love him, and he'd finally know what it felt like... to not be loved. But I couldn't just say all of that, right? I had to set it all up. And he thinks he's a great actor! Ha! They should give Oscars to jilted first wives! I was fucking brilliant. I even cried a little...just enough that he wouldn't think I was just pretending to be okay. And then I sent him off to live his little faggoty life with his perfect, pastor, musician, if David were carved out of dark-chocolate perfection lover!" Gabby grew quiet again for a moment.

"Gabby, how long ago was that?"

"About two weeks ago."

"Okay, so you're still very much alive, and beautiful, by the way; so what happened to the plan?" Elaina tried not to giggle.

"Ha! I remembered all the shit I'd done to him since we were six years old...the seduction, the manipulation, the lies. I remembered that he had always been my very best friend, and I have known our whole lives that he actually is gay! I only tried to convince him that he wasn't by sucking him into *my* fantasy of a life. He'd even come close to getting away once..."

"Wow. How'd you get him back?"

"I got pregnant... Don't look at me like that! I love my son. He is the best thing that's ever happened to me. In fact, he has saved my life more than once. I just can't seem to figure out what it's been saved for? It can't be so I can buy more shoes, but that's the only thing that gives me any pleasure. I can't imagine that there could be anyone else out there for me! I had the perfect life and the perfect husband; and he left me to be with a man. It doesn't matter that he's gay. He's loved me my whole life. It is of little consolation that I manipulated him throughout our whole relationship. This shit hurts; and everyday... still, I feel so empty... and so ugly... But, I realize that I can't check out. I can't do that to my baby... and to the rest of the people who still love me... But it's so hard, and I'm so lonely... The prospect of dating again is absolutely terrifying, and now, for completely different and horrifying reasons, thanks to y'all. I'm just not equipped for this! I was raised by a Baptist preacher, who is apparently, according to my shrink, flawed... and a mother who never expressed a singular thought or opinion of her own... about anything, except what I should wear, study or buy, or what sorority I should pledge. My life is... oh my God! What's the expression?"

"FUBAR?" Lilly, the inked redhead offered.

"What does that mean?" Gabby considered the suggestion.

"Fucked Up Beyond All Recognition."

"Yes! Yes, it is. My life is FUBAR."

3

CHANGE THE SCENERY. CHANGE YOUR LIFE.

"*I*'m not running." Gabby said, as much for herself as for Dr. McNair, her therapist. He nodded and waited as he watched her weigh her options. In her initial assignment to list all of the reasons she had to live, she'd declared that, aside from her son, the one thing she had going for her was her career; but even that was becoming tiresome and unfulfilling. She'd always planned to start her own firm, and after ten years in the industry, she actually felt like she was ready. Well, it wasn't so much that she was ready, as she could not handle working for a large corporation in her current state, regardless of how liberal and accommodating the management was. It was all she could do to return phone calls and meet deadlines for things and people she'd already committed to. She just didn't have it in her to play politics, or pretend she were still concerned about growing the organization. Having returned to work medicated, one month after her legitimate and humiliating nervous breakdown, she was focused, to the point of annoyance. With the help of some intensive psychotherapy, she'd managed to view her marriage and impending divorce with clear vision, new perspective and an honest examination and acceptance of her own accountability. But her healing, although more progressive than any Dr. McNair had seen, left little emotional energy or tolerance for any other aspect of her life. So, even as she tried to work remotely, she could not hide the fact that every memo, email or conference call she encountered thoroughly pissed her off, even the ones generated by her own staff. "I just don't have it any more," she admitted, as she explained the latest incident involving a stapler, some very harsh words, and a tearful, gay male intern. "I can't shake the feeling that everyone around me is incompetent...except Shelley." Gabby was careful not to unjustly inflict anymore negative criticism on her loyal assistant and confidant. Shelley, along with Tiana, had been at her side ceaselessly through what the three woman would come to refer to as 'FOA', the 'Fall of Arcadia'.

"She's almost the only thing keeping me there. She's covered my butt for weeks. She's had to smooth over so much crap on my behalf that they'll practically have no choice but to fire her, if I leave. I've got iron-clad non-compete and confidentiality clauses built into my contract. There's no way they'd trust her not to help me take my clients with me. Not that I would try to."

"So, with those clauses in place, you couldn't work for another firm or start your own anyway?" Dr. McNair knew the answer; but he also knew the solution involved her terminating their sessions. And while, he'd been thoroughly professional, he could not help being smitten. He was himself newly single, and even though he couldn't date her, he did enjoy his sessions with Gabrielle.

"Actually, I could, if I started my own firm in another state and didn't actively pursue any of the firm's clients for at least five years." Gabby rolled her eyes.

"That sounds reasonable, doesn't it?" The Harvard Medical School graduate flinched just slightly as a fantasy bubble burst in his head, then returned to his role as supportive, unbiased, caring professional.

"It would, if I hadn't spent the last ten years building up the most impressive client list in sports management and marketing history for them! There's practically no territory left to cover. I'd be starting from scratch."

"But you've done it before..." Dr. McNair had quickly assessed that the devastated woman he'd met little more than four weeks earlier was indeed capable of accomplishing anything she'd set her mind to. He hadn't told her yet, but he did not expect that he would be treating her for very long, regardless of whether she stayed in Charlotte. In his professional opinion, she was mentally and emotionally very healthy and, in the light of day, and sober, honest, on a level that made her much more equipped to deal with change and adversity than anyone he'd ever counseled. She was a force of nature. He did, however, hope she'd continue to speak with someone about her 'troubling' parental and relationship issues. While he was certain she was out of the woods in terms of her mortal safety, he noticed immediately, and advised her as gently as possible, that perhaps she might not have gotten into her current predicament, had she had healthier role models for dating and relationships.

"Oh, don't you worry about that! My sex life is none of your business, Sir. I'm never having sex again; so there's no reason to date. And since I'm never going to date or have sex again, my deep-rooted 'daddy issues', hurt at my mother's emotional detachment, and desensitization to all things romantic, brought on by my thirty-year witness to their loveless marriage, are inconsequential to our meetings. Now, if you will redirect your eyes and your thoughts away from my breasts and out of my bedroom, and ever-so-kindly sign off that I'm 'no longer a public menace', I'd like to get back to what's left of my life." Gabby waved the 'release from court-ordered psychiatric counseling' in a notably non-threatening, but deliberately flippant gesture.

Dr. McNair just smiled and nodded, as he reached for the form, wondering if he could lose his license to practice medicine for writing, 'Mrs. Rivers is a beautiful, brilliant, only mildly psychotic, ball-busting, man-hating bitch.' The handsome, metrosexual psychiatrist, with baby-doll lashes, framing mesmerizing almond-shaped brown eyes, beautiful hands and prematurely gray hair, recovered from the unsolicited sting, gave the lady what she wanted, and sent her on her way; but not before sharing a healthy dose of playa's psychology: "Gabrielle, I'm signing this form because there is nothing clinically wrong with you. In fact, you are as close to perfection as I have ever seen; and I'm saying that as a man, not a doctor. I have absolutely no doubt that your ex-husband was a good man, who simply happens to be gay, because only a gay man could leave you; and you're too healthy to still be mourning the loss of a fool. It's going to take time to heal your broken heart, and faith in God to restore your trust and courage to love again. But if you continue to attack every man you encounter, ignore your own emotional needs, deepest desires and inexplicable insecurities, you will indeed become the thing you actually fear most: a lonely, abandoned, inaccessible, Independent, shrewish, Angry Black Woman."

"Thank you, doctor." Gabby stood to leave and waited for the man to stand or hand her the form. He took an excruciatingly long time to do both, and Gabby felt her face get hot and her knees weaken slightly. "Who the hell does he think he's talking to?" She tried not to think too loudly, for fear he'd hear inside her head. She just wanted to get out of there, away from his stupid, smug, sexy, smile and kind, knowing eyes; out of his office, with the fake Ivy League degrees and expensive, sturdy furniture. The scents and sounds in the room, that she'd first observed as innocuous at best, were suddenly assaulting her, and she feared she'd vomit or pass out, if he didn't give her the damn form soon so she could leave. Just as she thought she was about to fall, he stood, with the form still down by his side. She tried to take a deep breath without looking phased by his insight...or his voice, and closed her eyes in a long blink to compose herself. When she opened her eyes, his long, outstretched arm, with a rolled sleeve, revealing a part of a tattoo (Philippians 4:13 and an eagle?), held the key to her freedom, and she snatched it and fled, quickly and quietly.

She waited until she was safely inside her car to finally let go and sob for the first time in three weeks. He was right, and she hated him for seeing her and throwing rocks at her armor. "What the hell kinda doctor talks to people like that? ...Fine, I'll stay in therapy, but it won't be with him!"

The next day, Gabby gave her notice at Tillman and Phar. They accepted her resignation, but not her notice; and, as she expected, ordered her and her assistant off the premises immediately. Gabby would receive all of her commissions and bonuses, totaling roughly, three-million dollars; and Shelley, a healthy severance package. Out of guilt, and a larger sense of duty, Gabby offered her a position with the new firm she'd be starting immediately in Atlanta, complete with a twenty-five percent salary increase, paid moving expenses, company car, four weeks' vacation and domestic partner benefits. Shelley accepted and Tiana was coming with her.

Having settled in within a month, Shelley made it her first order of business to find Gabby a local, female therapist. Gabby was starting to look more and more like her old self; and having seen her below rock bottom, Shelley realized perhaps, what looked like 'normal' for Gabby wasn't necessarily 'well'. Shelley saw what Dr. McNair had seen, that she'd been hiding behind a mask of perfection to protect herself. But Shelley had also seen her boss vulnerable and realized that, that woman was even more beautiful and worthy of protection, and a whole life of her own.

4

JOYRIDE

Gabby stood in front of the mirror, wearing moisturizer and a thong, staring at the twelve outfits she'd packed for the three-day weekend. "What does one wear on a second date with a lesbian?" She giggled and answered her own riddle. "Stilettos and a weight-lifting belt? Stop it! This is not a date! Nicole Vanderpip is not marriage material! She's a distraction. Granted 'a super-sexy, kinda bitchy in the hottest way, distraction; but a distraction no less. And this is not a date. You're just going out for drinks, maybe dinner... and some dancing. We haven't even kissed, yet... Oh my God, Ga-brielle! You want to! No I don't! Oh, yes you do! Okay, fine! I want to know what it feels like, what all the fuss is about. 'Gay' is the 'new black'. And if you're going to be curious... Hell, what did the girls tell you? 'Go big or go home!' A super-producing, Broadway legend, who's also the most powerful lesbian in New York is as big as it gets."

Gabby decided to ere on the side of slutty-chic and went with skinny jeans, a loose, but plunging, black silk halter top, and the Manolo stilettos Nikki sent her from the Spring show she missed the previous week. She pinned her long curly hair up loosely, highlighting her swanlike neck. Her silky, natural curls were often mistaken for a weave, perhaps because of their contrast to her dark complexion, at least in Georgia where she grew up. She'd been across the country and around the world, and was told wherever she went how beautiful she was. She'd tried modeling once, but, at just five-one, she'd only been able to do catalogue work, and then only if she'd stayed skinny. But she grew up on cornbread, collard greens with bacon fat, fried chicken and sweet tea. She learned early that food was good, and 'nobody wants a bone, but a dog'. "What an ugly expression", she sighed to herself as she admired her butt in the full-length mirror. "Whatever. I look good!" And she did. At thirty-two, she looked and felt more beautiful than she had at twenty-two, or any time before.

Still, she had to remind herself that she was attractive and desirable. It took a long time to get back here, to feeling good. After a season of letting the wrong men pick her, she'd used her feminine wiles to land the perfect husband, and all that got her was... divorced. "Hell, it should have been annulled." She'd long since stopped pretending that her marriage to Kevin had ever been real. She loved him; but somewhere deep down, she'd known he was gay when she came to New York. There wasn't any other reasonable explanation for the emotional distance between them, if she believed everything he'd told her about his life at the time... and she did believe him. She also believed he loved her, but they should have just stayed friends. "But then Ethan might not be here... Damn it! Stop it, Gabby! It's been a year! He's not coming back, and you don't want him to! Just move on... please. Please, God, help me to just move on." The phone rang, forcing her to turn away from the minibar.

"Hey, Gorgeous. I'm downstairs. Are you ready, or should I come up?" Gabby was uncharacteristically nervous, and not particularly anxious to leave the security of her suite; and thought for a moment that she could change a few more times while Nikki had a drink there, but thought better of it.

"Nope. I'll be right down." She checked herself out in the mirror again. "Not bad." She pressed her palms against her nipples in a lame attempt to conceal, at least for the moment, that she wasn't wearing a bra. She reached for her makeup bag, put it down and smiled before applying lip-gloss, slipping it in her pocket and turning out the light.

Nikki waited in the lobby. They greeted each other awkwardly, with a loose hug and cheek presses. Nikki would have liked to simply kiss Gabby 'hello' the same way she would any friend she'd meet for drinks, shopping or dinner in New York. But she knew her date would die before being seen kissing a woman, even in Manhattan. Image was important, especially to the publicist-daughter of an ultra-conservative Southern Baptist preacher, even if that preacher was up to his eyeballs in a sex scandal of his own.

"Where's your car?" Gabby stood outside The Plaza Hotel

looking for Nikki's Mercedes.

"Oh, that old thing? It sat in my garage for a year and then I gave it to my nephew as a graduation present."

"Gary must have had a stroke!"

"He didn't speak to me for a week! It was divine! It's his fault, though. He's never seen me drive. I don't drive. I drink." Gabby laughed out loud and looked at Nikki as if she'd lost her mind. "This is me." Nikki glided to the farthest rear door of a super-stretch Hummer.

"And how many other people are we pickin' up tonight?" Gabby asked as the driver shut the door behind her.

"Just you, Dear. I require two things at all times: luxury and privacy. Stretchy affords me both." Nikki put her hand on Gabby's thigh. She let her hand rest there while she considered the beauty and simplicity of Gabby's favorite jeans., before turning to pour drinks. "To Deuteronomy 22!" She lifted her glass.

Gabby made a mental note to look up the reference. She was fairly certain that was the chapter that forbade the wearing of garments made from two different kinds of cloth. This chick is nutty and going to Hell! She suddenly felt out of her league, or at best, like a hip-hop video vixen. I knew coming to New York 'just to hang' was a bad idea. She thought. 'Go, have a little fun. Be wild for once.' What the hell are you going to tell to your clients when you end up as the opening story on *TMZ* next week, draped all over 'Karen Walker'? New York City is no place for the former president of the Atlanta Chapter of Preachers' Kids for Christian Modesty! She tentatively took a sip of her drink and scanned the den of inequity on wheels for emergency exits.

But what happens in Nikki V's limo stays in Nikki V's limo, and it only took about an hour and two apple martinis before Gabby's handkerchief of a top was draped delicately across a buttery-soft, hand-stitched leather seat. They'd both known they'd go at least that far when they met. Car-shopping with Nikki's business partner, Gary Sheppard, proved to be all the foreplay either of them needed. Besides, Gabby had the advantage of having heard about Nikki from Kevin for years. He'd described her affectionately as an 'angry, ultra-feminine, man-hating, dyke, with a string of broken-hearted starlets that went back at least two decades'. She'd made it very clear, at least to her peers, if not the starlets, that she was not interested in commitment, just fun. And for Nikki, 'fun' meant 'sex with beautiful, usually straight, women'.

Gabby closed her eyes and let her hands fall to her sides, not really sure what to do with them. There were no whispers of surprise or protest as Nikki caressed and kissed her perfect breasts. Gabby did not reach for Nikki's hands to stop her as she slowly unbuttoned her jeans and slid her hand inside. But Nikki did gasp at what she found. The Black American Princess and Stanford MBA had shaved for her first 'non-date' in over a year. And on the list of things that turned Nikki on 'preparation' was right up there with 'impeccable grooming'. She rubbed gently and determined that it was not dumb luck, rather an invitation, so she lingered a while. She moaned softly against Gabby's soft belly and pulled her hand away so she could remove the jeans. She rested the heel of Gabby's foot on her shoulder as she unbuckled the ridiculously expensive sandal, kissing the petite ankle. She slowly pulled the cotton away and revealed a thick, but shapely leg. She ran her hands down either side of it, from the hip on the outside and the very top of the inside, letting her knuckles brush the dampness of the black thong, and down to Gabby's tiny foot, sucking each elegant toe slowly. Gabby gasped softly. Nikki continued until Gabby lay completely naked and stretched across the backseat of her limo with her eyes closed.

Nikki sipped her drink and watched Gabrielle. She considered whether to continue when she noticed the car had stopped. Gabby had made no move to reciprocate, not even an exploratory hand. This was usually the point in an encounter where the ingénues attempted to prove their worldliness and versatility. Nikki realized how boring those little girls were, as she watched Gabby with absolute delight. Gabby had nothing to prove to Nicole. She was a stunning, accomplished woman, seeking some safe excitement and just a little break from the drama of her otherwise full life. She was content being adored for the first time in what must have been a solid decade. Of all the things Nikki had to offer, an attentive ear and a safe place for her new friend to let her hair down were the most valuable.

"We're here, Beautiful. What do you want to do?" She

asked softly. Gabby opened sleepy eyes and looked at Nikki before flashing a wicked grin. She slowly slid her hands up her torso and clutched her own breasts, pressing her thighs together as she squeezed her nipples. "Damn." Nikki whispered to herself. She pressed a button on the intercom that called to the driver, forty feet away. "Mark, just keep driving, and cancel my reservation, please. We're not going in."

"Yes, ma'am."

Nikki knelt on a pillow on the floor of her car. She was still fully dressed in a tight A-line skirt, silk blouse and equally impractical shoes. Thick sheets of straightened brunette hair hung softly and brushed Gabby's face as she moved to kiss her mouth. Gabby moaned softly and let her hands fall away again. Nikki took control of the manicured hand with its short natural nails and slid it down the curvy body it belonged to. Nikki kissed Gabby deeply until she began to masturbate on her own, first with one hand, then both. Nikki sat back and watched her from her position on the floor, and slowly unbuttoned her own blouse enough that she could reach inside it. She slid her free hand under her skirt and inside her panties. She watched Gabby for as long as she could before closing her eyes and surrendering to Gabby's sounds and her own touch.

Mark, the driver, took Stretchy and the girls on a three-hour tour of the five Burroughs, while the Broadway barracuda and Georgia goody-two-shoes bonded over drinks and heavy petting. Despite Gabby's curiosity, Nikki's experience, and the excessive amounts of premium alcohol they consumed, they easily stopped at kissing each other and touching themselves.

"I'll have to tell Kevin the rumors about your sexual proclivities are exaggerated." Gabby teased with Nikki's head in her lap, completely at ease for the first time in two years.

"You'd better not! I paid good money for those rumors." Nikki quipped.

"So you don't do more with every new female lead?"

"You mean, do I go down on perfect strangers who work for me? Uh, no. That's tacky... and disgusting. Don't tell anyone, but I have to be in love to... go there."

"Really?"

"Think about it."

"Yeah, that does make sense."

"Yeah... "Nikki pulled Gabby's leg so that it wrapped around her and rubbed it.

"Ew." Gabby thought more about the rumors.

"Exactly."

"But...Whatever. Damn, you're hot!" Gabby giggled.

"Well, it takes a lesbian super-nova to know one." Nikki reached up and tugged on one of Gabby's tousled spirals.

"Oh, I'm not a lesbian."

"Oh my God, you're as confused as your damn ex-husband! Fine, you're not gay. Hey, let's call Gary and bet him a house in The Hamptons that you are!" She laughed.

:Oh shut up! I'm just horny. That was the most turned-on I've been in years; but I like men. I like the relationship."

"You like relationships with men?" Nikki thought it would be mean to remind Gabby that she'd never had a successful one. And not that she minded being mean in the name of truthfulness; she just thought it would be exceptionally inappropriate while the woman was naked and otherwise vulnerable.

"Yes. I like the balance and the designated roles. I like knowing that there are 'men things' and 'women things'. I like the things that men do for women, and I like the expectations that come with defined gender roles. I wouldn't know how to be in a relationship with a woman. Don't judge me! It's the way the world works and has worked for a thousand years! Boring and straight are perfectly normal things to be."

"Ha! Is that what your daddy taught you?" Nikki poked at her friend. She'd become a sounding board for Gabby as the accusations against her father began to go public. The once popular sorority girl found herself sisterless again for the first time since undergrad, as even women she'd gone to church with for nearly thirty years began to distance themselves from her and her family. Nikki stepped in and reminded Gabby that she was not her father, and his mess was no reflection on her at all. Nikki knew something about surviving scandal and holding your head up while the world threw rocks at you. Gabby talked for hours about not knowing who she was if any of what was said about her father were true. He'd been the creator of her entire system of values. She didn't even feel confident that her faith was genuine, and not just another of his manipulations. Nikki agreed with Gabby's therapist and didn't necessarily think that was a bad thing. She continually challenged the younger woman to think for herself and use what was happening as an opportunity to re-evaluate every aspect of her life.

Gabby found that it was easier to re-evaluate some things than others. For instance, she was able to cease her judgment of other people because, on a very basic level, she really did believe that all people were created equal in God's eyes. And it was no stretch to accept that Kevin loved her, but his heart's desire was to love and be loved by a man. She even understood Shelley and Tiana. She enjoyed their friendship, and rooted for their relationship, as she witnessed the challenges they faced as an openly gay couple. It was harder for her to extend that kind of understanding to herself. It was okay for all of them, her new 'queer' family; but being that different, living so far outside of what she'd been raised to believe was right, was the opposite of acceptable for her. She hadn't considered whether that was a standard she'd set for herself or another limit that had been placed upon her. Nikki agreed that unless or until she fell in love with someone who challenged that thinking, it would not change ... and that was okay. Gabby didn't have to be gay, or even whole, for Nikki to like her. Despite the preconceived assumptions that she was a 'gold-digging, manipulative bitch, who'd trapped an award-winning superstar into marrying her', Nikki found Gabrielle Nichols to be an interesting, intelligent and kind woman, who was every bit as powerful and magnetic as her former husband. Nikki spent her work-life surrounded by divas and professional liars. She put just as much effort into filling her personal life with good and real people; and in the quiet places that people assumed did not exist for her, she regularly gave Thanks for her select group of close friends. In the last year, Gabby had become one of them.

"No, that's not what my daddy taught me, Smarty. It's just what I've seen, what I want. Everyone has an image in their head of their true love, and a list of qualities that they're attracted to. It's not wrong, it just is. The image in my head of the person I'm meant to be with is of a man, and the qualities that I find most attractive in a partner in relationships are masculine."

Nikki continued to be amused. "I hear you, Nichols, but have you considered why fifty percent of marriages end in divorce? Perhaps the rules and expectations that modern women have for men and relationships aren't really practical. What if you're missing the person you're supposed to be with because you've got your mind set on the wrapping, not the person inside?"

"Nikki, you do not want me." Gabby said gently.

"I'm not talking about me, Sweetie." She reached up and tweaked Gabby's nipple. "I'm saying keep your mind and your heart open... and your eyes closed. I suspect someone really wonderful is waiting for you; and he might be a man, but..."

"What?"

"I think you're awesome, and I don't want you to miss your blessing, searching for the perfect package."

"Who *are* you?" Gabby smiled down at Nikki and rubbed her cheek.

"Your new best friend."

"Okay." Gabby smiled as she ran her hand through Nikki's hair and let it rest on her breast.

5

I Kissed A Girl

"*I* swear, Liz, if you say it, I will leak your client list to Perez Hilton!"

"First of all, you, your clients and mine all know that you're not 'A List' until you're in therapy and *have been outted by* Perez Hilton, so thanks. And second, say what?"

"'I told you so!'"

"Gabby... You know I'd never say that to you. And, I'm not a fortune teller, but being able to predict the outcome of everyday situations, based on the information given, is simply what I'm trained to do." Dr. Elizabeth Keaner tried to remain professional, and did her best to put on her therapist hat. She'd already crossed one line with her patient. She was exceedingly, and she feared inappropriately, fond of Gabrielle; and secretly looked forward to their weekly sessions. She spoke in her own state-mandated sessions about her guilt, and even suggested that perhaps she should refer Gabby to someone else. But to her relief, Liz and her therapist agreed that, since Gabrielle was not depressed or at risk of hurting herself or anyone else, and was only seeking clarity from a neutral source about the turn her personal life had taken since her divorce, there was no need to make her uncomfortable or undo any progress she'd made. So every Tuesday afternoon for almost two years, Liz started her day by reminding herself that Gabrielle Nichols was her patient; she was her doctor, and their ninety-minute sessions, despite the fact that she'd begun preparing for them as though they were, were not the best dates she'd ever been on. It also helped her to remember that she was herself happily married for nearly twenty years to Seth, her very best friend, and father of her five children. As Gabby kicked off her shoes and curled up on the loveseat in her office with her usual glass of red wine, Liz looked deliberately at the family photos on her desk again, to bring herself out of the recurring fantasy that involved the two of them running away to some secluded, clothing-optional utopia.

"You told me that it was possible that, since every man I've ever been attracted to is gay (or an ass), that I am likely a lesbian, or at the very least, bisexual." Gabby's expression was a mixture of defeat, disbelief and distain.

"No, Gabrielle, I suggested that you do some thorough introspection about your needs and personality, as they pertain to your dating experience and selection criteria."

"I've got an MBA from Stanford, with a minor in Psychology, Liz. That's shrink-speak for 'get a clue, you're a dyke!'" Gabby pouted and Liz laughed out loud.

"You're also delusional. Remind me to write you a script before you leave. Seriously, that is not what I meant... entirely. Tell me what's happened."

"I kissed a girl... and I liked it." Gabby spoke the song title, ironically unaware that the song existed, as Liz tried to keep a straight face.

"That doesn't have to be more than simple exploration. You said yourself, you've had limited dating experience. It's actually more unusual that you spent six years in California and haven't kissed a girl by now. Was this girl someone you could be serious about?"

"Actually, she's not a girl at all. She's a woman, a goddess, actually."

"So, you're attracted to her?"

"Yes. I have been since we met, but..." Liz waited patiently, while Gabby took a sip of her wine and paused for a long moment. Her private musings about Gabrielle aside, she was surprised (and impressed) to hear that Gabby could step outside of her comfort zone to find herself in a position where something like that could happen.

"We did more than kiss... but, that's not the point. I'm just not a lesbian. I like men. I like the relationships. And I like sex with men."

"You've stated that on more than one occasion. But something made you go out with this woman."

"We're friends. I like her. I love talking to her. I felt safe... and I was more than a little drunk..."

"Do you think you did more than you might have, had you been sober?"

"No. I felt completely in control. And it didn't go as far as it could have. That's my point. I'm crazy about this woman. She is smokin' hot. She makes me laugh. I respect her intellect. I even find her..." Gabby's thoughts trailed off.

"What's missing?"

"I don't know. I think I don't want to think of her as anything other than a friend. The mere concept of having a girlfriend is just ridiculous."

"Interesting word choice..."

"What? 'Girlfriend'?"

"No. 'Ridiculous', the definition of which is 'worthy of causing ridicule'. Are you concerned what people would think?"

"Of course not! ...Well, I don't think so. I don't know, Liz. I think it has more to do with my own sense of comfort and normalcy. A casual fling is one thing. It was fun, an experience I can say I had; but I don't think I love women like that."

"So, how did you leave things."

"We're friends."

"So why are you so upset?"

"Did I mention that I really, really, really liked it?"

"Oh, good grief."

6

GENDER DYSPHORIA AND THE FAMILY DYNAMIC

*F*or Veronica Anne-Alise Reynolds, gender identity wasn't so much a condition of birth as it was a series of choices. The beautiful third child, born to loving, attentive, working-class parents, wasn't like most little girls. Nor was she much like many of her trans brothers and sisters. In the beginning, Ronnie didn't hate her body, feel trapped inside it, or spend every waking hour dreaming of trading her femininity for more rugged and manly parts. She didn't think about her parts at all, until she was forced to. But when forced to point to some environmental or nurturing factor, she did, after extensive self-examination and counseling, attribute her gender identity to one person, her father, David Reynolds. David and Ronnie shared an uncommon bond. While it is completely common for little girls to adore their daddies, and she did, Ronnie's adoration of David was something else. Their admiration was mutual, their friendship was profound. David was a contradiction to the African-American patriarchal stereotype, and would never regard either of his exceptionally pretty daughters with chauvinism. He didn't look upon Ronnie's halo of dark curls, dimpled chin, and emerald green eyes and see 'a girl child'. When he looked at his baby, he saw what he saw in her siblings, 'a beautiful creation of God; a gift to him and her mother and the world, with limitless potential, and a mind of her own'. It wasn't long before Ronnie recognized the fair, honest and godly man; who took her and her brother fishing, and made breakfast on Sunday before church, and never yelled, even on the rare occasion that he was truly and justifiably angry, as the most wonderful person in the world. Ronnie loved everything about her dad, even, and sometimes especially, the way her mother looked at him. And it was just fine with David that, as soon as she was able to articulate the difference, Ronnie made it very clear that she didn't want to marry a man just like her father, she wanted to be one.

Just Walk

Marietta, Georgia - 1980

"So...have you finally decided what you want to be for Halloween, Veronica?" Annette Reynolds looked hopefully at her youngest child and braced herself.

Ronnie paused for a moment. "What are you, Daddy?" she asked beaming up at her father. The four-year-old knew her dad's job was important, just not what it was called.

"I'm a Crisis Management Specialist." David smiled back at his baby.

"Do you wear a suit?"

"Sometimes. But mostly I wear jeans, work boots, rain gear and a hard hat."

"Well, when do you wear a suit?" The image in Ronnie's head of her dad was of him in his Sunday best, as he was then; and she hoped that her portrayal of him required that she get to wear a suit and tie and shiny shoes, too.

"When I need to get people's attention and I can't use my bullhorn." David smiled to himself. His silly description of the part of his job he did the best, but enjoyed the least, made him feel better about the meetings he'd be attending the next few days. He loathed the endless days immediately following the 'official conclusion' of a natural disaster or accident. But, it was his responsibility, as an officer of the National Disaster Recovery Agency, to report his department's progress to local, state and federal government officials. Bureaucrats loved to sit far, far away from the mud, power outages...death and personal loss and devastation, and point out what could have been done differently. But David was fearless, level-headed and effortlessly authoritative; and the first person in his position to not be fired, after four category-five hurricanes in as many years. Like it or not, he was as effective in the boardroom as he was on the ground. As he watched his tiny daughter, he realized those meetings were necessary to bring clarity in the worst of times; and despite his anxiety over them, they usually did end well. It was just like Ronnie to, somehow, remind him that there was an upside to every situation.

"Okay! I wanna be Daddy! I'm gonna be a kwisis man-a-ment specialist!" David laughed and Annette sighed.

"Oh, honey, I thought you wanted to be an actress like Sophia Loren or Elizabeth Taylor?" Annette would have settled for a famous blonde... or anything more gender-appropriate.

"No, Mommy. I wanna be like Daddy. He helps people put their lives back together."

"I know that Veronica." Annette ignored the pride she felt for her children's father, and instead focused on the disturbing and ever-increasing resistance to all things feminine that had become her daughter's passion. "Baby, why don't you want to be a movie star? Sophia and Elizabeth are beautiful, and they have pretty, dark hair, just like yours. I think Libby's gonna be a beautiful ballerina this year!" Libby frowned and picked up her pace to walk even farther ahead of her family. She hated Halloween; but at ten, she'd already weighed the options and decided she'd rather wear a stupid tutu than listen to her mother's nagging about being a lady.

"Yeah?" Ronnie's eyes danced, as she considered her mother's suggestion.

Annette grew hopeful. She'd been trying to kill two birds with one stone, by finding some use for Libby's old pageant gowns, and hopefully, getting Ronnie to look like a little girl for at least a couple of hours. But on the eve of her favorite holiday, she would have even settled for last week's plan to be a television anchorman. She kicked herself for not jumping on that band wagon. At least, she'd have been able to make Ronnie be an anchor *woman*. Problem was, at the time, she couldn't think of any. *"Really, Veronica? How am I going to spin 'she went as her daddy' in the family newsletter?"* But Annette knew there'd be no changing Ronnie's mind, now that she had her dad's support; so, like most things (she imagined) the two of them teamed up against her on, she tried to grin and bear it.

"Can we cut my hair for Halloween? I'm gonna need to borrow Neal's funeral suit, too." Her older brother heard his name, looked up from the pirate costumes, and just as quickly, looked away and giggled. That Ronnie was one weird little kid.

"No, we cannot cut your hair for Halloween!" Annette was about to lose it. She stood in the aisle staring down her little girl, who stared back with her chubby arms folded; her decision made and, her mother knew, final.

"How about we get you a wig, Chipmunk?" David offered just in time, as always. Like Libby, he actually found Halloween a little annoying too; but not so much that he'd take the fun of it away from his wife. Still, if Annette insisted on celebrating the ridiculously Pagan ritual, he was at least going to make sure his children were heard, and their opinions respected.

"I guess that will work." Ronnie conceded. So, David scooped up his daughter and put her on his shoulders, as they walked through the party supply store in search of a tiny afro wig.

"I'm not saying that Veronica's feelings aren't real, David; I'm saying they're not normal. I think she has this thing called 'Gender Identity Disorder'." Annette stabbed at the page of a book she borrowed from the library, with a freshly tipped, hot pink fingernail.

"It doesn't matter whether you think you've found a name for it, Annette. Ronnie's a happy, well-adjusted seven-year-old kid. In fact, the only time she isn't happy is when you're going on about what's wrong with her. There is *absolutely* nothing wrong with Ronnie. And I really don't like the idea of you searching for diagnoses like there is. Not telling you how to do your job, but couldn't your time be better spent *with* her?"

"She never wants to be around me! All she ever wants to do is run around like a wild little... ...."

"'Tomboy?' I think the word you're looking for is 'tomboy'. Right now, Ronnie doesn't like to do girl things or wear girl clothes. It's no big deal. Neal's an actual boy, and that didn't stop you from spending time with him. You did lots of things with him."

"I knew what to do with Neal. I bought him trucks and building things, and enrolled him in a different sport every season. Boys are easy...You said, 'right now'; do you think there's a chance she'll grow out of it?"

"Maybe, but it shouldn't matter, Annette. And I have to say that it bothers me that it matters so much to you. Ronnie's our child, our baby – the last one we're ever gonna have, by the way – and I would think that, as her mother, your love for her would be unconditional, that she shouldn't have to dress like or act like anything that does not feel natural to her. She's an amazing kid! Why is it so hard for you to see that?"

"I do see it." Annette closed the book, folded her hands in her lap and looked up at her husband like a scolded child. "I know she's kind and brilliant and athletic and funny... but she's also beautiful... like 'pageant-queen' beautiful... That combination doesn't happen every day, and if she's not careful, she'll squander it all away, just to be defiant! A smart, talented BEAUTIFUL WOMAN can do anything in this world; but a plain tomboy with a 'great personality' will have a hard row to hoe! Look at Rosie O'Donnell!"

"Who?" David resisted the urge to laugh at his wife. He was getting annoyed; but she was funny.

"Rosie O'Donnell, you know the comedian, actress, talk-show host..."

"Yeah, I do. That's my point. So do you, because she *is* successful, even if not by your standards... Seriously, Honey, you sound positively psychotic. Look, I told you this when Libby was little, you can't live our children's lives for them. Having daughters, however beautiful they may be, isn't your license to relive your tiara-filled glory days. If you're not careful, you're going to push Ronnie away."

"Like that would be different. She already hates me."

"No, Ronnie thinks you don't like her because she's not feminine like you and Libby. She hears the things you say, Annette. They're not helpful. You need to stop pushing."

"I hear you...Okay, I'll try." David looked skeptically at the mother of his children. He wasn't convinced. "I promise I'll try, David."

"Thank you."

7

SMOOTH

*R*onnie was tall for a girl, five-ten, by age thirteen; and she developed early. The boy in her loved towering over boys her age, but she was none too happy about her curvaceousness. In fact, she was mortified when she could no longer hide her breasts and hips under layers of loose fitting t-shirts and baggy jeans. But her best friend, Shawnee, the pretty dark-skinned girl who lived two doors down, was pleased as punch.

"Are all lesbians this handsy, or is it just you?" Ronnie giggled as she wrestled to control Shawnee's hands while they made out, fully clothed, on the couch.

"Who says I'm a lesbian? Where'd you even get a word like that?" Shawnee teased. She kinda already knew she was a lesbian. She was just shocked to hear her super-shy, conservative, best friend speak so scandalously.

"Um, you're a girl, and you're like tryin to get all up in my girl...iness... I heard my mom and Tasha's talking about Miss Kelly."

"Our troop leader is not a lesbian!" Shawnee giggled between kisses.

"If getting busted kissing some woman in her jeep, before our last meeting qualifies, oh yes she is!"

"Cool!" Shawnee reached up to Ronnie's breast.

"No, not cool." Ronnie held her hands, still enjoying the kissing part. "I think they're gonna get her fired."

"Yeah, that would suck. Wait a minute, aren't troop leaders volunteers? Well, look on the bright side. It's almost Summer, we only meet during school anyway."

"Great." Girl Scouts was the only thing Ronnie enjoyed about being a girl. She imagined she'd enjoy Boy Scouts even more, but she surrendered that battle eight years earlier, when she settled for being a Daisy. At least some of their activities weren't stupid, and the ones that were, she just ignored. Still, she felt bad for her troop leader. Miss Kelly was the coolest grown-up woman in the world. Maybe it would all blow over, and by the time the school year started again, no one would care that she was a lesbian. Always one to stay positive, Ronnie tried to redirect her attention to her favorite after-school activity, and not think about the onset of Summer. It was a struggle. Exploring with Shawnee was fun; but, between the Georgia heat, the wardrobe assaults and the boredom, Summer had become her least favorite season. And because Ronnie inherited her stubbornness from her mother, Annette was beginning to dread the swimwear and short-shorts season as well.

Ronnie heard her mother's Ford F150 pulling into the driveway and quickly lifted off of Shawnee and straightened her shirt, a green plaid, short sleeve button-down she borrowed from Neal. Giggling, Shawnee fixed her hair and pulled down her t-shirt. Annette Reynolds floated in, smelling like gardenias and loaded down with packages. "Hi, Shawnee. How's your mom?"

"She's good, Mrs. Reynolds. She said to tell you 'thanks again for the job tip'. She wants you to come over for dinner when she's not working."

"Tell her she's more than welcome. I'm really glad it worked out. Veronica, you wanna give me a hand here?" Ronnie stared at the bags from The Limited, Ann Taylor, and Macy's and rolled her eyes. Nothing good ever came of her mother's unsupervised marathon shopping expeditions. "There are more things in the truck."

The teenagers retrieved the bags from outside and tossed them on the table. With each item her mother pulled out, Ronnie grew more and more irritated. "Can I please just go shopping by myself? I can't wear any of this stuff. I don't wear dresses."

"I don't understand, Veronica. You have such pretty legs! If I had legs like yours, I'd never wear pants."

"I'm sure your legs are fine. You should definitely wear this." Ronnie held up a modest two piece bathing suit by her pinky, and made a face at Shawnee. "Now these I can use." She plucked out a pair of swimming trunks, obviously purchased for Neal, and took off toward her bedroom, with Shawnee in tow. As Ronnie snatched the trunks the tower of folded summer clothes tumbled from the kitchen table into a heap on the floor. Pretending not to notice, and leaving her mother alone to pick up the things she bought, without regard to who she was, or even what she might like, was the closest Ronnie had ever come to being openly disrespectful; but it felt good, and the message was received.

"You are not wearing those swimming trunks to the beach!" Annette yelled after them just before the door slammed. She sat in a chair with her head in her hands, staring off into the distance, before bending to pick up the clothes. As she gathered the things she'd spent the entire day picking out, after weeks of research in *Seventeen Magazine*, a single tear turned into a flood; and by the time her husband and son arrived home from work and basketball practice, she was sitting on the kitchen floor clutching about a thousand dollars' worth of the season's hottest looks for teen girls, and sobbing. Down the hall, in her bedroom with Shawnee, Ronnie was equally distraught.

"Wow, she's still really clueless, isn't she?" Shawnee looked at Ronnie as she lay on the bed staring at the ceiling.

"You thought I was lying?"

"No... hopefully, just exaggerating a little bit. Hey, at least your mom can buy you nice things. My mom has to work two jobs just so we can pay the rent. I'd be a girly-girl to get a whole new wardrobe every season."

"Hmph... Hold on." Ronnie got up and quietly walked back down the hall. She could hear her dad speaking gently to her mother. The clothes had been separated into piles, one for her and one for Neal. She grabbed the largest pile, the one with all the pinks and purples and flowers sprinkled throughout it, shoved it all into the largest bag she could find, and tiptoed back to her bedroom. She emptied the bag on the bed, picked out a mini dress and tossed it to her pretty friend. "Try it on."

"This is never gonna fit me." Shawnee giggled and shook her head. "You're like six feet tall and I'm barely five... not to mention fat."

"Don't say that. You're not fat, F-A-T... you're P-H-A-T" Ronnie made a rude gesture indicating Shawnee's curviness.

"I thought you hated boobs."

"Yeah, on me... On you, they're awesome. Com'on try it on. Lem'me see."

"Fine, but turn around."

"Why? I'm a girl. You're a girl; and I've seen you naked a hundred times."

"Yeah, but not lately."

"Fine, I'll close my eyes." And she did, while the petite, chocolate covered beauty tried on dresses and skirts and girly jeans, shorts and halter tops, and finally, the solid white tankini. Ronnie adjusted the straps on the tank and the ties on the bottom, so that it fit perfectly. She tried to ignore the way seeing her best friend like that made her feel. Sure, they'd been kissing a lot lately, but they told each other they were just practicing. They weren't 'like that'. They'd never even touched each other 'down there'. Neither of them wanted to, or so she thought. So, as their 'practicing' escalated all the way to third base, the sound of footsteps down the hall startled them. "What time do you want to leave for the dance?" Ronnie asked calmly, as Shawnee shot upright on the bed. "Relax, they won't come in without knocking - house rules."

"I'm not sure I want to go. It's just a stupid junior high dance, just an opportunity for kids to pair off, you know... boy-girl, girl-boy. I don't like any boys like that, do you?"

"Uh... no. Still, it'll be fun. We can watch...like the circus."

"Okay, I'll try. I still don't know what I'm gonna wear."

"Take this stuff. I'm definitely not going to wear it, and it looks really good on you."

"I can't do that. Your mom bought that stuff for you."

"She bought it for a pretty girl. You're a pretty girl. Besides, she thinks of you like a daughter anyway. She's not gonna let me return it. It's just all going to go to waste. Please take it. I want you to have it."

"I don't want you to get in trouble."

"Trust me, I won't."

"Okay, if you're sure..."

"Positive."

"Wow, thanks!"

"That's what friends are for!" Ronnie smiled and gathered the things into the large bag, while Shawnee got dressed. "I'll walk you home." Ronnie said as she picked up Shawnee's bookbag and held the door open for her.

"I live five steps away."

"I know. I just want to." She beamed, feeling better that something good had come out of her mother's obtuseness. They exited through the kitchen, where Annette was beginning dinner. "I'll be right back. I'm just gonna walk Shawnee home."

"Dinner will be ready in about thirty minutes. Your dad's going to drive you to the dance around seven. See you later, Shawnee."

"Bye, Mrs. Reynolds. Thanks again for everything." Shawnee replied sweetly, as Ronnie led her to the door.

"You're welcome, dear..." Annette watched the Macy's bag as Shawnee struggled to maneuver through the door with it.

"Let me help you with that." Ronnie offered, effortlessly wrapping her long arm around the awkward bag. As Ronnie pulled the door closed with her free hand, Annette turned to the table and noticed that only Neal's clothes remained. She abandoned her pot of homemade sauce and went into Ronnie's room and quickly looked around the floor and in the closet. "That ungrateful little... bitch!"

"Veronica hates me." Annette flopped on her bed in defeat.

"No, she doesn't; but the sooner you start seeing *Ronnie*... and stop bringing home dresses, the happier we'll all be. It doesn't matter how pretty or how expensive, there is nothing you can buy that will make Ronnie look or feel or act like 'Veronica' again... Actually, 'again' is even wrong. Ronnie is a boy, honey. Please try to embrace that."

"You make it sound so easy, David. I don't have a Master's degree in Psychology. I don't understand why any girl, especially one as beautiful as Veronica, would want to be anything else. Can you please make me understand?"

"No. I really can't. But, you don't have to understand to accept. The reality is, if it's not your reality, you don't have to get it. It's really not about you."

David tapped lightly on Ronnie's bedroom door and waited. Ronnie sulked over, opened the door and sat on the bed, without looking at her father.

"I'm not wearing that crap, Dad."

"First of all, watch your tone. Second, that would be hard to do, since you apparently gave it all to Shawnee. And finally, I'd never make you wear anything you don't want to; although, I'm sure it's not crap. But you do have to go and apologize to your mother."

"Why?"

"Because you hurt her feelings."

"Is she going to apologize for hurting mine?"

"How did she hurt your feelings?" David knew the answer. He just needed to give Ronnie a chance to get the words out.

"She won't listen to me. She keeps trying to make me be something I'm not!"

"But Ronnie, Honey...try to look at it from your mom's point of view. Thirteen years ago, she gave birth to a beautiful baby girl, and no matter what you wear, it's hard for her to see you as anything else."

"Then it shouldn't matter to her *what I wear*."

"You make an excellent point. But you're missing mine. I know it hasn't been easy for you to feel the way you do, and live with the 'queen of pink and pretty'; but she loves you, and she's doing the best she can."

"Do you really believe that?"

David smiled, knowing exactly what Ronnie was suggesting. "Well, I know she loves you. And I love you both, and would like for you to still be in two whole pieces, and speaking to each other, when I get back."

"Where are you going?" Ronnie had begun to dread her father's trips, almost as much as Summer. She missed seeing him every day, but mostly, she relied on him to be a buffer between her and her mother.

"Looks like Louisiana."

"How long?"

"Not too long, hopefully. They're watching a tropical storm that might hit Freeport pretty hard; but I'm prayin' for a mild season. By the time you get back from Mona's, I should be back." David felt the tension that was building between Ronnie and her mom, too; and was relieved that Ronnie'd be going to her grandmother's for relief.

Ronnie frowned. "Can I still go to the dance?"

"Not if you don't fix this."

"Will you take me shopping?"

"Did you really give your girlfriend a thousand dollars' worth of Summer clothes?"

"She's not my girlfriend, but yes; and I can't get them back. So, okay, I guess the shopping is out."

David sighed and shook his head. "That was quite a gesture for a non-girlfriend. Smooth. But next time, use your own money. I'll leave some money with Libby. She'll be home for a few days before you leave."

"Thanks. Can I cut my hair?"

"Ronnie, I can only negotiate one battle at a time. Besides, it's pretty cool long, right? Kinda Prince-ish?" David tugged on the tangled ponytail of dark curls.

"Uh, no. But nice try."

"Well perhaps if you comb it... or wash it... or take that hat off every once in a while..."

"Okay, okay... I get it. I just don't have anyone to braid it right now."

"I know. Libby said she'd wrangle you as soon as she gets in. I love you, Chip..." David really did love Ronnie; and he really did make more of an effort to understand her, and respect her identity, than anyone. Still, he could not bring himself to call her 'son'. Ronnie accepted that her dad did get her; in fact, she liked his special nickname for her, even more than 'Ronnie'. Besides, she wasn't entirely committed to the 'boy thing'. She just knew she absolutely was not a 'Veronica'.

"I love you too, Dad." David leaned in for a hug, and was greeted by Ronnie's right hand and a firm man-hug.

"Oh, yeah..." David rubbed Ronnie's head, grabbing her cap on his way out the door.

8

HONEYSUCKLE

*I*f David Reynolds did 'get' Ronnie, he was one of few people who did. To everyone else in the family, but Libby, and her closest friends, Ronnie was still just a tomboy. Growing up a boy in a pretty girl's body was more challenging than one might think. The onset of puberty was, quite simply, 'sucky'; and Ronnie viewed her developing body as a violation (of what she was not entirely sure), at best, and utterly offensive, at worst.

It was bad enough that she just didn't feel like a girl on the inside. She lived every day since she turned twelve in absolute terror of her period starting. Breasts were stupid, at least on her. But worse than that was the fact that she could not hide her body, no matter how hard she tried, from her classmates, or from the men and boys in her extended family. And everyone thought it was okay to point out what a 'beautiful young woman she was becoming'.

Ronnie and her siblings spent most summers with their grandmother, 'Mona'. Mona's son, Scottie, suddenly back home, having lost his wrestling scholarship, after two subpar semesters at a nearby junior college, was just seven years older than Ronnie. He'd always been a bit immature for his age, so he was actually more like an older cousin than an uncle. Scottie was also less accepting of Ronnie's 'issues' than her siblings were. This unique trifecta made him particularly obnoxious.

"What do you mean 'she aint really a girl'? Sure as hell looks like a girl ta me!" Scottie leered at Ronnie, as she played catch with two younger boys in the yard. "I bet the right man could snap her right outta this lil' tomboy thing she thinks she got goin' on. Alls she needs is someone to make her feel pretty."

"Yeah, you're probably right." Neal, didn't mean his sister any harm. He was just tired of talking about her. The youngest and most talented of the three Reynolds children was 'an attention-sucking, ungrateful, twerp'. Couldn't she be satisfied being a pretty girl, and let him have his rightful place as the only son?

Nope. She had to be a boy. Ronnie did everything well, so that meant she was a better boy than Neal was, too.

"Does she have a boyfriend yet?"

"How should I know? Let's go shoot some hoops." Neal abandoned the bushel of tomatoes he and Scottie had picked and were snacking on to grab his basketball.

Scottie sprinkled salt on the sun-ripened piece of fruit and took a juicy bite, smacking as he questioned his nephew. "Ya live wit 'er dontcha?"

"Yeah. She doesn't, I guess. She doesn't like boys, Scottie. She thinks she *is a* boy, remember?" Neal got up and started dribbling his way down the dirt road. Their grandmother's congregation had just built a new church a few miles closer to town. The old church was just down the road and they hadn't removed the basketball goals, yet.

"Humph." Scottie licked his lips and hopped off the porch. Neal looked back. When he saw that Scottie wasn't following, he just kept going. Scottie darted across the yard and intercepted the football as Ronnie threw a perfect spiral to one of the neighbor-boys. "Two-on-two?"

"What, you and me against these squirts? That doesn't exactly sound fair."

"You right." He mussed the hair of one of the younger boys. "We'll split up."

"Pick one." Ronnie was always up for a game.

"Nope." Scottie spat and wiped sweat from his brow. "Ladies first."

Ronnie turned away and rolled her eyes. "I'll take Paul", she said, referring to the smaller and younger of the two boys.

"Okay, les go. Dem azaleas and that fence mark the goals." He pointed from one side of the yard to the other. "We'll kick off." Scottie tossed the ball to his young teammate and ran down field. The little fella could kick; and Ronnie could catch, and run, and cut. Scottie finally caught up with her and pushed her out of bounds, about twenty yards before she reached the picket fence covered in honeysuckle. He didn't seem to care that she was a girl.

"First and ten." Ronnie was barely winded, as she played center to her eight-year-old quarterback. Scottie watched the snap from an angle as the thirteen-year-old, bi-racial beauty crouched low, leaned forward to hike the ball, and quickly spun and took off toward the end-zone. She moved like a gazelle; and Scottie was still distracted by her, when his tiny teammate stopped her two yards short of the goal.

"Second and two." He tried to get his head back into the game. Sure, he was going to let them win, but he didn't want to make it look too easy.

Ronnie adjusted her ponytail. Her mother refused to let her cut the hair that would have come to her waist, if not for her secret trimmings, but instead fell just passed her shoulders. She was just counting the days til she turned sixteen, the magical number her mother arbitrarily attached to her freedom to personally express herself. In the meantime, she kept it braided as often as she could.

Scottie watched as Ronnie huddled with her QB, and then took her time getting him the ball. "Hurry up. I ain't got all day." The unemployed, slacker actually did have all day. He also had issues with waiting and, in particular, waiting on a woman; or in this case, a girl.

"I aint never seen somebody in such a hurry to lose before." Ronnie smiled and strutted. She was pretty quiet, unless there was trash to be talked. Both of their teammates giggled. Scottie's face grew a little more red than it had been from the Georgia heat alone. Paul finally snapped the ball and Ronnie moved to run it in. She could smell the honeysuckle when Scottie tackled her. Paul cheered. From where he stood, she'd made it in. She still hadn't gotten up yet, though; because Scottie hadn't let her go. He wrapped himself around her and groped her through her jeans. She pushed and pulled his hands away, struggling to get free, while he pretended that they were irreparably tangled. Ronnie didn't say anything. What could she say? "Get off me, I'm a girl! And your niece, you piece of inbred trash!" Never. But the more she fought and did not speak, the harder Scottie fought to keep her down there. She was fast and graceful; but compared to the six foot, four inch, twenty-year old man, she was not strong at all. The younger boys looked on, not sure exactly what was happening. They were still having fun. But when Scottie reached under her t-shirts and inside her sports bra, she squealed; not with glee, but in terror, the way a frightened animal would squeal. "No!" She finally wrestled her arms free, elbowed him in the face and crawled away. As she ran across the yard into the house, Scottie lay rolling in the grass trying to catch the blood pouring from his nose.

9

Scissors

*M*ona called out to Ronnie, as she tiptoed passed the kitchen. "I hear a big storm's comin', Ronnie. Did the rain start yet? Ooh, I hope it don't tear up my roses again this year! Will you help me cover them up, please, baby?" Ronnie didn't answer, she just kept moving down the long hallway.

Scottie finally stumbled in a moment later. "Git somethin' for my nose, Mama."

"What happened to you?"

"That lil' brat hit me in the face."

"Who? Ronnie? What were you doing with that little girl that you had your nose so close to her?" Mona didn't wait for an answer. "I told you to leave those children alone, Scottie. Veronica is a young lady; and, despite the fact that you won't get your lazy tail out my house, you're a grown man. You've got no business playin' with her, or the rest of those children, like that. Sometimes I wonder what you're thinking."

"Are you gon' hep me or not?" Mona had walked away to get the first aid kit, but apparently wasn't moving fast enough for her son. "You always goin' on bout those lil' half-breed brats. What? Their shit don't stink cuz dey part nigger? Act like ya care more bout them than you do me or the rest of the kids that came outta ya!"

"Get out of my house, Scott Christopher! I will not be spoken to like that in my own home. I treat those children like they do no wrong, because they've done no wrong. I didn't raise you to be like that. You're a hateful, ignorant, redneck, just like your daddy. I prayed that you'd be different, because he wasn't around; but I've had enough. I want you out of my home!"

"I'll leave when I'm damn good and ready, Mama." He said it real slow, and he meant it. Mona didn't recognize her son in the blood-stained face of the racist bully standing in front of her.

She was afraid of him, had been for years; but she didn't know what to do. He'd never actually harmed her, and anyone that she knew of. He was just mean and ugly. She didn't know how to explain to people that she'd given birth to a monster, or that she slept with her bedroom door bolted at night, for fear that he'd snap one day. But he'd always been nice to his sister's children. She had no idea before that day that he hated them the way he did. If she had, she wouldn't have let him come home while they were there for the summer. But in that moment, she'd heard enough. He had to go.

"Well, you need to get ready today. Your nose is broken. You need to see a doctor. While you're in town, please see about finding someplace else to live."

"Humph. You somethin' else; pickin' those lil mongrels ova your own flesh and blood." Scottie didn't quite get that they were his blood, too. "But I hear you, Mama. I'm gonna git myself togetha an git me a place. I been plannin' ta make a move all summa. You throwin' me out is doin' me a fava, give me just the motivation I need ta git my act togetha an do somethin' I been thinkin' about for a long time."

Mona sighed and tried to smile. "That's good to hear, son. I do love you; but I think it's time you start actin' like a real man."

"Yup, you right."

Mona finished cleaning Scottie's dressing, gave him some money, and left him to plan his new grown-up life. She forgot all about her roses and the storm. She was suddenly very tired and went to lie down. Before she did, she 'broke the news' to Ronnie that her mom had called to say they'd be staying a little longer, and Annette wouldn't be picking her and Neal up until the following week, at the earliest. Apparently, the beginning of the worst storm season in decades had delayed school openings, and consequently, the start of Ronnie's freshman year, into the second week in September. "That's the silliest thing I've ever heard. Folks hear a lil' rain and wind's comin' and they run for the hills. Oh, well... You know my grandbabies can stay here as long as they want to."

Ronnie lay in bed for hours, thankful that 'the worst, and longest, summer ever', would finally be over when she woke up the next morning. She needed to get off that dirt road and back to the suburbs where she felt safe. Her grandmother's house was too big and too old, and for the first time since Libby went away to college, Ronnie missed sharing a room with her big sister.

*** *** *** *** ***

She wasn't asleep when he came in, drunk, with his eyes still black from where she'd clocked him two weeks earlier. Her eyes were closed, and she didn't hear him for the pounding rain and howling wind, or through the pillow she held tightly over her head. He locked the door behind him; and when she finally heard the floor creek, he was standing over her. She didn't scream right away. Why didn't she scream? She bolted upright and, before she could stand, he pushed her back down hard. He pressed his hand against her chest, digging his nails into her breasts, as he held her down with one hand and held a dirty finger to her lips with the other. "Be easy, now, Veronica. Uncle Scottie jus' wants ta make up witcha. I missed ya. I'm gon' make it feel real good." She shook her head, flailed her arms and kicked wildly. She was trying to reach his still injured face, until he punched her in the chest, knocking the wind out of her. "I said be still, bitch!"

Ronnie's mother's brother raped her for what seemed like hours. It was painful, and unimaginably scary; but the way her mind worked, the thoughts in Ronnie's head actually, as if that were possible, made it much, much worse. As much as it did hurt, Ronnie prayed that if she could just hold on, he'd stop and it would be over; and no one would ever have to know what he did to her. She prayed that if she didn't scream and didn't fight (too much), eventually, he would leave. And for a while, she didn't scream, but she cried and she begged him to stop. But he just would not leave; and he didn't seem to care that they were not home alone. What did he know that he thought he could get away with that? He turned her over and sodomized her; and finally, she did scream, not from the fear or shame or even the combination of the actual pain magnified by the voices in her head, but from sheer agony. And, still, no one ran to her rescue. He ejaculated on her and in her repeatedly, as though the evidence didn't matter, as if neither of them would be alive when the sun came up to tell about it...or be held accountable. When it was no longer fun, perhaps because his high wore off, or

47

she no longer cried or moved, he stopped. Scottie stared down at his niece, who was covered in his semen and sweat, and her own blood, feces and tears, and actually chuckled. "You look like shit. Go take a bath."

The sound that came from the broken child on the soiled bed was barely a whisper. "You may as well kill me."

"Why would I do that, babygirl? You're my family." He suddenly sounded again like the silly, playful, not at all evil, uncle she remembered, and used to love.

"I'm going to tell Mona what you did to me."

"Humph. She'd prolly be bout da only person who'd believe you, too. Shame she had a heart attack and died. Hurry up an get cleaned up, now, ya hear?" There it was again.

Ronnie pulled herself off the bed and pulled on her torn t-shirt and pajama pants. It felt silly to be putting on clothes, so...normal... But she needed to cover herself. She needed him to stop looking at her...like that. She moved as quickly as she could down the long hallway to her grandmother's bedroom. Mona was there, sleeping. But when Ronnie knelt by her side and shook her, she was cold, and she did not wake up.

"Nooooo!" Ronnie howled.

"I told ya she dead. Now go an' git cleaned up so I can call somebody to com' git 'er. She's startin' to smell like horse n ass. Oh. Wait. That's you." The demon was back.

Had he always been so mean? Why was he treating her like that? She'd heard someone say he had problems with drugs and alcohol, that that's why they kicked him out of school; but she'd known him her whole life and he'd never been anything but nice to her. "Is this what Aunt Jackie meant when she said he was a 'mean drunk'?" Ronnie didn't consciously know the difference, but by then, Scott was sober.

Ronnie stared at him. He was a real live monster, scarier than anything she'd ever seen in those movies she wasn't supposed to watch. She did what she should have done hours ago and started screaming for her brother. "Neal! Neal! Help me, Neal!" The monster just laughed and started walking toward her. She tried to run, but she was too sore and weak to get away. He grabbed her by her hair, which was matted and caked with filth, but still loose enough to wrap around his wrist.

"Your big brotha aint here, neitha." Her eyes got real wide. "Naw, I didn't kill 'im. He left a note. Said he was stayin' ova Billy's; probly ta git away from you. He thinks you're a freak. Always runnin' round here tryin' ta be a man. You aint never gon' be a man, Ver-on-i-ca. See...I bet ya don't wanna be a man, no more, though, huh? It felt good, didn't it? You want some more, dontcha?" She spit in his face and tried to get away. He punched her in her face; and she fell against the bed where her grandmother lay dead. He wiped his face on her t-shirt and bit her breast through the cotton, before grabbing her by her throat and pulling her to her feet. "I see ya still need some hep actin' like a lady." He knocked her back down and drug her nearly lifeless body down the hall, this time to his room. He tied her to the bedpost and raped her again and again and again. This time, she screamed until no sound would come out of her. Only after she passed out, and he thought he'd finally killed her, did he stop.

###

When Neal came home six hours later, his grandmother was dead, his sister was naked, raped and beaten, and drifting in and out of consciousness. He'd found her in his uncle's room; but otherwise, Scott was nowhere to be found. Ronnie woke up in Atlanta General Hospital two days later, with her siblings and her mother at her side. She said one word: "Scissors."

"What does that mean, Baby? Did someone do that to your beautiful face with scissors?" Libby and Neal just stared at their mother. What the hell did she mean, 'someone'? Was she really questioning who did this?

Libby went out to the nurses' station and came back with surgical scissors. "Get out, Mom."

"Excuse, me? Who do you think you're talking to, Elizabeth?"

"I'm talking to you...and you, Neal. Please. Get out." Ronnie looked at her sister, nodded and closed her eyes. When they were gone, Libby helped her baby sister out of her hospital bed and into a chair; and quickly, because there was no need for ceremony, hacked off Veronica's wavy locks. When Ronnie nodded that it was short enough, Libby completed the transformation by giving her a stylish, but masculine cut. Ronnie smiled slightly into the mirror before she noticed her battered face and collapsed in Libby's arms.

By the time David could get out of Charleston, three days after Hurricane Hugo hit the port city, Ronnie was still in the hospital. The professional communicator, who made his living talking to people and turning chaos into order, had no words when he saw his youngest child. He just held his daughter while she wailed. He stared down at her short curly hair through his own tears. He didn't care what she did to her hair; she would always be his little girl. He'd tried so hard to understand her. He wanted to die. He didn't protect her. He tried not to imagine the details of what was done to her. After she'd cried herself to sleep in his arms, he was gone again.

David drove the eighty miles from Marietta to Macon, Georgia in forty minutes. He used his wife's keys to open the door of her mother's once stately manor home, ignoring the crime scene tape and the signs that said, 'Keep Out'. Inside his daughter's bedroom, the sheets had been removed from the bed, but the mattress was stained with blood. He looked away and left quickly. He walked slowly down the hall to his mother-in-law's room. At first glance, there was nothing there; but as he was leaving...more blood...on the bed, on the wall, and then a small pool and long smear. "He drug her." Back down the hall, past her bedroom, Scott's room, where he'd wasted most of his twenty years...more blood on the floor and on the mattress. The rope he used to tie her to the bed still lay on the floor, where it landed when her brother cut her loose. David checked the closet and drawers. All of Scott's things were still there. There was no indication that he'd ever packed anything; but it looked as though, recently, he left in a hurry, and apparently on foot. Mona's old Cadillac, their only car, was still parked in the circular driveway. "Where would he go? He couldn't have gotten far on foot, and without his stash?" David picked up a backpack full of weed and pills, enough to sell. He dropped it and left the room. He didn't care about that.

David got in his truck and drove slowly down the dirt road,

trying to pick up anything that looked unusual, trees that seemed unnaturally disturbed, a barn that might be used as a hideout. "The old church." He parked one-hundred yards away and walked to the side of the old building with nothing in his hands, not even his car keys. He found Scott right away, sleeping peacefully in the room adjacent to the baptismal pool. At least two weeks' worth of junk food, beer bottles, roaches and cigarette butts littered the church floor. David kicked him to wake him up.

"David. Wait. Don't!"

"Is that what my baby said to you?" David never stopped kicking the younger man. "Did she do that to your face?" Scottie couldn't answer. Perhaps that was for the best. Scott was already going to die, eventually, for what he did to Ronnie. But if David had realized that Scottie's attack on his child had started weeks earlier, in the heat of the summer day, while children watched, he'd have killed him right then and there, instead of dragging him out to the middle of the road and flagging down a deputy sheriff.

"Whatchu got there, boy?" The fat, red, deputy asked David, with his hand resting on his revolver.

"My name is David Reynolds. This is the man who raped and nearly killed my daughter; the one ya'll said you couldn't find..."

"Well, we'll just hafta let the judge be the judge of who did what to who, now won't we? You just sit right d'ere on the ground for a minute. Did you kill that man? He don't look too good." The deputy walked back over to Scott, checked to see that he was breathing and called for an ambulance. Then he handcuffed David, and shoved him in the back of his patrol car.

10
MAN IN THE MIRROR

Ronnie barely spoke to anyone except Libby, her therapist and doctors for nearly a year. She rarely let Shawnee come over after their initial reunion. There was little time for fun, as she was too busy recovering to pick up where they'd left off. In three years, she'd had six surgeries to repair damage to her face and body from where she'd been cut, torn and burned. In some ways, it felt like the recovery was worse than the attack; and when she was finally able to speak up for herself, she'd had enough.

"I don't want any more surgery."

"But Ronnie, honey, the doctor says just one more procedure will make that scar on your face practically disappear." Her mother tried to reason with her. "And if the internal scarring doesn't heal on its own the right way, you'll never have children."

"I don't care. All these appointments and procedures do is remind me of what happened. I don't want to think about what was done to me every six months for the rest of my life. I want to start actually living it."

"But your face... Aren't the scars on a constant reminder?" Annette insisted without an ounce of tact.

Ronnie walked over and stood in front of the full length mirror in her plastic surgeon's office. She started from the floor, and slowly stared at her reflection. She liked what she saw. Her new boots made her an inch taller. She'd likely stop growing before she reached Neal and her dad's six-five, but six-one wasn't bad, considering. At least she was two inches taller than her mom. "Big Bird gets on my last nerve..." She mumbled to herself about the five-foot-eleven inch Annette. Her height was the only physical attribute passed on by 'the blonde bombshell' that Ronnie did appreciate. About everything else: "Oh, how I wish she would just shut the hell up..." She shook her head and squeezed her eyes shut, hoping that when she opened them, she'd look less like her mom and more like her dad. It was a stretch, because, aside from her hair being darker and now shorter, Ronnie was the spitting image, in face and body, of the beautiful, former Miss Georgia. But clothes did help some. Her favorite, loose fit jeans concealed her hips; and she'd gained weight since the storm, so she looked generally fuller, and her breasts less obvious. Her dad's favorite leather jacket was still a little big on her, but she liked it like that. She stared at her face. Still no facial hair, but the Reynolds men had always been clean-shaven. She had her mother's square jawline and piercing green eyes. Everything else was a blend. Her skin was the color of wet sand on a sunny, Summer day; but in the Winter, she was pale with olive undertones. She smiled at her reflection and turned her face from side to side. She saw them. It was hard to miss the scars that ran the length of her left cheek, from her eyebrow down to the side of her chin, and a star-shaped burn on her neck. She'd only seen them for a moment, but Shawnee said they were sexy. Ronnie thought they made her look tough. She turned around and stared at her mother. "What scars?"

11

OH, NO, SHE DI'NT!

*E*ven after the hell she'd been through, Ronnie often mused at how things always seemed to just... work out. The attack, which she came to refer to as just 'Hugo' or 'the storm', actually set her free in many ways. She admitted to Libby and her therapist how much she honestly appreciated what happened to her. She'd never tell anyone but Libby that she was actually relieved that there was enough damage done to her reproductive organs that, by sixteen, she still hadn't gotten her period.

And finally, her mother was off her back about looking and acting like a girl, for a while anyway. It wasn't so much that she understood. Perhaps it was guilt that kept her quiet for nearly three years. And in that time, Ronnie felt free for the first time in her life. By the time her mother stopped pretending to care more about Ronnie's feelings than her own reputation, she'd come into her own. She was confident and independent, and when Annette did push, Ronnie just ignored her. So she stopped pushing, for another while. But as their family counseling sessions were coming to an end, Annette showed signs that she might not ever be ready to let go of her daughter. Apparently, she'd been attending the meetings hoping that the third psychologist she'd taken Ronnie to in six years (they'd started long before the storm) could finally pull her daughter out of the 'phase' she'd been going through practically since birth.

"Annette, it is very important that you listen to Ronnie, when she tells you who she is. She's not delusional. It isn't even necessarily a result of the trauma. You admitted yourself that Ronnie has never been happy as a girl. She's made the decision to let her outside match her insides. As hard as it may be for you to accept, it isn't that uncommon. There is nothing wrong with her; and I assure you that, if you continue to fight her, you will lose your child."

"But, what do I tell people?" Annette looked at Ronnie as

she asked the question for the millionth time.

"Why do you have to tell them anything?" Ronnie tried to be patient, but she'd had enough. She was already 'there'. She'd been there for as long as she could remember. She'd never been 'Veronica'; and the only person who didn't understand that was her mother. She was starting to wonder whether she actually loved her at all. Or did she just need to hang onto the little girl she thought she'd given birth to? Where was her concern for Ronnie, how she felt, her wounded spirit? Did she even care that she'd been miserable, not visibly, but deep, deep down, where it truly mattered, virtually every day of her life 'before the hurricane'; before she finally stopped trying to hide, for no one's sake but her mother's? Was she really less mortified that her own brother had brutally raped and nearly killed her child than she was at the idea of telling her friends that she now had two sons and one daughter? Ronnie'd tried desperately to love and respect her, but she did not like her; and at sixteen, she was seriously considering becoming emancipated. Her father was in prison for attempted murder, her grandmother was dead. Libby was old enough to take over legal guardianship of her, but she couldn't unless their mother was declared unfit. She wasn't unfit; she was just stupid. So, Ronnie agreed to one more session, as much for herself as for her mom. She didn't want to lose her mother. Their last session was her last chance to show Ronnie she could accept... not who she'd become, but who she'd always been. She closed her eyes and prayed for the words. "Mom, what's my favorite color?"

"I don't know, Ronnie... I'm sure you're gonna tell me it's blue, and making you wear pink when you were a little girl is what did this to you. I know you think it's all my fault!"

"No, Mom. I don't think it's your fault. I don't think it's anyone's fault. It's not even Scott's fault. I felt this way long before he touched me. My favorite color is orange, every shade of orange, except florescent and peach. I also like green, hunter green and Kelly green, and especially sage and khaki. But you're right. I have never liked pink, or purple, or yellow. I've never liked dolls, or pretty clothes. I have disliked my body from the moment I needed a training bra."

"But you're such a beautiful woman..."

"I believe you; because you're beautiful, and I know I look just like you. And I wish it made me happy to hear you say that, but it does not. I don't feel feminine. I feel awkward. I don't want to look pretty... I want to look the way I feel on the inside... masculine and strong."

"So, the next thing you'll be telling me is that you're a lesbian." Annette rolled her eyes.

"I don't know if I'm a lesbian; but I am attracted to girls."

"Oh, God, Veronica! Really!" Ronnie stood quickly.

"Mrs. Reynolds!" Dr. Keaner held up her hands. It had taken them two years, but Annette had finally stopped calling Ronnie 'Veronica'. She'd been 'slipping' more and more lately, and Ronnie warned them both that she was going to walk the next time it happened.

"That's it, Dr. Keaner. I'm done. Thank you for trying."

"I guess you really are a man now, huh..." Annette practically spat the words at her daughter; but they were directed more at her husband. She actually blamed him for getting arrested. In fact, not that she would say so to Ronnie, but she hated him more than she hated her brother. David just had to go after Scott, even after she begged him not to. She'd counted on Scott disappearing and turning up dead on his own of an overdose. But David knew that wouldn't really be justice for Ronnie. To have Scott answer for what he'd done to his child, David was prepared to do a lifetime in prison. Annette listened to him, but his pleas for her forgiveness fell on deaf, and no longer diamond-studded, ears. Throughout his trial, and on the few occasions that she visited him, she pretended to understand, even lied that she was proud at how he hunted down justice for their baby. But it was all smoke and mirrors, as away from David and Ronnie, she hissed at what she called 'his choice to rot in prison', and broadcasted his failure to anyone who'd listen. It was of no consequence to her that everyone agreed he'd done what virtually any other man or parent would have, if they'd found themselves in the same position. As far as Annette was concerned, the man who promised to always put God and his family first, abandoned them with one selfish, vengeful act. And worst of all; as if David's actually being locked up with criminals, or her struggling to provide for herself and three children alone weren't enough, Annette could not escape the thoughts that everyone in the town she grew up in would know that her brother was a redneck, rapist, monster; and so she was, by association, and just like they'd always said, White trash. Ronnie's mother didn't have to say any of that out loud; Ronnie felt it whenever Annette looked at her.

Ronnie stopped and held the door knob but didn't turn around. "I can only hope to be a man like my father... instead of a woman like you."

But Ronnie wasn't a quitter and, despite the hurt she felt at her hands, she did love her mother. Besides, she had Annette's car keys; and if she'd left her stranded at her shrink's office, her dad would have broken out of jail to kill her. So she sat in the driver's seat with her forehead pressed against the steering wheel praying for...anything that would make the situation better. "Forgive me, Lord, for my selfish, childish(?) ways. I want to honor her, to make her happy; but I can't. I don't know how to be what she wants me to be, and not be miserable. Please help me make her understand. Please help her to love me as I am. I believe that You do, God! I feel it when I look in the mirror and I see my own face (instead of his). I know You love me Lord, because I no longer dread the coming of Summer, but instead just look forward to the sunshine. Show me? Give me a sign that I'm not wrong. Or, Father God, if I am wrong, show me that, and I promise I will change. I Thank You, Lord for my many blessings, and I ask these things in Your Son's name, Amen."

"Amen." Annette sat quietly down in the passenger seat of her car. She'd been standing outside for some time watching Ronnie pray. She didn't want to interrupt and prayed along with her, hoping both their prayers would be answered, even though she had no clue what Ronnie prayed for. They never talked about stuff like that. Faith and spirituality were David's department. Annette closed her eyes tightly, fighting back tears. She missed him so much. He'd spent so much time away working, that she'd almost forgotten just how big a role he played in their daily lives. It had been three years, and she and Ronnie and Neal were still barely functional. She was tired of being strong. "Well, you know what your dad always says? 'The prayers of the righteous are not forsaken'."

Ronnie smiled and nodded, not really sure if she was indeed 'righteous'. "I'm sorry, Mama."

"Me too, Baby." She squeezed Ronnie's hand before she started the car and drove home.

For the next couple of days, they stayed out of each other's way. Ronnie noticed that her mom, who'd never been particularly religious before, seemed to be praying a lot more than usual. She'd never actually seen her head bowed anywhere other than in church. She didn't think anything of it, remembering what her father said about the time one spends with God being personal, and not something to do for show. Perhaps her mom was just trying to do things differently. By Sunday morning, Ronnie was hopeful that she was. Annette tapped lightly on Ronnie's bedroom door before walking right in.

"Why don't we go to church this morning?"

"Okay." Ronnie pretended that she had actually waited for her to say 'come in', and tried to ignore the feeling in the pit of her stomach that said Annette was acting weird.

She showered and dressed in charcoal gray slacks, light blue oxford shirt (borrowed from Neal) and the tie Shawnee had given her for her birthday. Annette tried to hold it together as a fairer, younger, but otherwise spitting image of David Reynolds settled into the passenger seat. "Just breathe... Remember what Pastor Nichols said... 'This is nothing a little firm parenting and The Word of God can't overcome.'"

"Mom, isn't church the other way?" They hadn't been to their family church since her dad went away, and Ronnie had never been to any other.

"Oh, we're not going to your dad's church."

"Oh."

Ronnie settled into the pew of the small, crowded, Baptist church in the heart of the city. She'd seen commercials for the new church on TV. She recognized the preacher, Rev. Robert Nichols, and tried to shake the feeling that the man made her skin crawl; but it wasn't working. All she could hear was Neal's favorite expression for things that felt...evil: 'something in the water aint clean'. As the man proceeded to preach from Deuteronomy, chapter twenty-two, Ronnie knew she'd been ambushed. She stared straight ahead, fearing that if she looked at her mother, she might burst into tears;

not at what was being said, but that she would actually go that far.... that her own mother would try to distort her faith (because for most of Ronnie's life, she'd seen no evidence that Annette had any of her own) to prove her point. When Ronnie did glimpse her out of the corner of her eye, Annette nodded her head in agreement with the stranger, who couldn't have been speaking to or about anyone else in the small church but Ronnie. "Just my luck," But, Ronnie knew it wasn't luck. After the service, she made a bee-line for the car and waited inside, facing the front door of the church. She watched as her mother stopped and spoke to the man who'd just condemned her youngest child to Hell, knowing nothing more about her than her gender at birth and preference for masculine clothing. Ronnie didn't expect that her mom would thank him, but she did. She knew she'd never speak up for her and say 'perhaps God is more concerned with the content of our hearts than our wardrobe'. But the absolute last thing she expected to see her mother do was smile tearfully as she squeezed the man's hands. Rev. Nichols spoke to her like they were old friends, and before she walked away, they shared an awkwardly long hug.

"Wasn't that amazing?" Annette asked, as though the message for the day had some profound relevance to her or the rest of the world.

"How do you mean?" Ronnie was so hurt she could barely speak, but she absolutely refused to let her mother see it.

"I mean the service. We've been praying for some guidance, haven't we? Well, I've been praying... and there it is...straight from God!"

"Do you really believe that God is concerned with what I wear, or even who I happen to love, for that matter?" Ronnie asked quietly, more out of curiosity than concern. She'd made her decision. She had to get away from her mother for her own sake, and for the sake of their relationship. She later recalled the events of that morning without even knowing if Annette had answered her question. It was a very good question, in the sense that it inspired the kind of dialogue they'd never had before. Perhaps if she'd thought to ask it three years...or even three hours earlier... But on that blistery winter afternoon, her mother's beliefs about the God Ronnie prayed to daily were as relevant, and she suspected informed, as her theories about global warming.

Libby was livid when she heard about their mother's latest stunt. "Crazy heffa!" the twenty-two year old wanted to drive to Marietta and shake the woman she'd begun referring to as 'Annette Grey'.

Ronnie insisted she was fine. "I just need to get outta here, Lib."

"Okay. Do I need to talk to her, or just come and get you?"

"I can't withdraw from school without a guardian, and I'm not dropping out. She's going to have to withdraw me so you can enroll me there."

"I'm on my way." And just that easily, Libby skipped class the next day, and spent the next three days negotiating Ronnie's freedom and transfer of guardianship. Libby talked their mother into letting Ronnie move to Atlanta with her and finishing high school there. Annette told her oldest daughter it was her way of accepting Ronnie; but both Libby and Ronnie knew better. Annette knew she couldn't win. 'Veronica' was gone for good. At least if 'he' was living with 'his' sister, Ronnie wasn't running around Marietta embarrassing her anymore.

12

PEACE IN THE TIMES OF UNILATERALISM

"You promise I don't look stupid?" Ronnie asked for at least the third time.

"You look fine, stop obsessing." Shawnee reassured her, but offered nothing more. To say anymore would be crossing the invisible line they still had between them.

"I'm not obsessing. I'm just trying not to walk in here and make an ass of myself. I've never worn a tux before." She looked in the mirror self-consciously, and adjusted the tie that didn't need straightening.

"You look incredibly handsome." She said dryly. "Now, can we go in already?"

"Thanks, mom." Ronnie was still uneasy.

"Yeah, like you'd ever get that outta *your* mom. Fine." Shawnee sat back in the passenger seat and turned to look at her best friend. "You look really, really, really hot; hot like, if I were into guys at all, I would be so all over you... like that. Actually... nevermind...."

"What? Oh please, don't stop now." Ronnie blushed.

Shawnee looked away out the passenger side window. She'd promised herself she wasn't going to get emotional. Senior prom was just something to cross off the list, so they'd never look back and regret not going. She'd made it through three seasons of protest. She was just wearing that stupid gown, that she saved all year to buy, as a favor to her hopelessly romantic, and until three months earlier, home-schooled, best friend. She was over him / her, whoever the heck 'Ronnie' was those days.

"Trust me, you want me to keep this to myself."

"I'm sure I don't." Ronnie smiled at her sincerely. Shawnee wasn't much into talk about feelings. She just needed to get things out, otherwise, she'd be uncomfortable the rest of the night. Ronnie understood that.

"Don't say I didn't warn you... but the fact that I know

you're actually really a girl makes you so much hotter...That's all."
Shawnee blushed and closed her eyes. She really loved Ronnie, and
she'd really struggled over the years to accept who he was. It was
particularly hard for her because they grew up together. Ronnie
didn't have a problem with kissing and touching before the storm.
Despite what Ronnie told her, Shawnee did attribute the change in
their relationship to Hugo. It had taken over a year for Ronnie to
even look at her; and by the time she was comfortable enough to
kiss her again, she was someone else. She was 'he'. In that time,
Shawnee realized who she was, too. Their time together before the
storm hadn't been just some innocent exploration; she really was a
lesbian. And while the realization of that amused them both initially, in hindsight, it was devastating. Shawnee had no recollection
that Ronnie had always found her aggressiveness icky. She only
remembered that Ronnie made her feel beautiful; and she was to
Shawnee, the same sweet, super-smart, wicked-funny, totally-hot
girl she used to daydream about and play house with. She missed
her first love, and did indeed feel as though something had been
taken from her too that Summer.

"Thanks..." Ronnie smiled at her. She knew what she
meant. "You look beautiful, by the way." She resisted the urge to
reach for her hand.

"Thanks, now can we go inside and get this over with?"

"Let's go." Ronnie walked around to the passenger seat,
opened Shawnee's door and took her hand. As they held onto each
other most of the evening, they each told themselves, 'it's part of
the act.' They danced and made casual conversation with the ballroom full of virtual strangers. Ronnie had only arrived at the school
in January; and aside from her interactions with select members of
the school paper, debate team and student-body government, she'd
pretty much kept to herself. But suddenly, everyone seemed to
know, or want to know, the super-fine 'new guy' and his stunning
mystery date.

They stayed on the dance floor. But when the DJ warned
that he was about to slow things down, they stared nervously at
each other, until Shawnee walked away and stood against the wall.
Ronnie followed her slowly and stood in front of her. Even in
heels, Shawnee had to look up at her. They stood silently watching

the other young couples in various stages of courtship, until Simply Red's *'If You Don't Know Me'* came on and Ronnie held out her hand. Shawnee took it reluctantly and allowed Ronnie to lead her back onto the dance floor. As their song ended, Shawnee stepped away and stared again, silently asking, 'okay, now what?'. Ronnie answered by leading her out of the ballroom and to the car.

They drove in silence back to the tiny but immaculate house Ronnie shared with her sister. She'd have liked to have taken Shawnee somewhere nice, but there honestly wasn't a plan. This wasn't supposed to be happening; but she knew that Libby wouldn't be home, and remembered her sheets were clean. She leaned over to kiss Shawnee before getting out of the car. Shawnee touched Ronnie's face and sighed.

Shawnee stood in front of Ronnie, as she sat on the edge of her bed and undressed her. Ronnie stood to close the blinds and block out the moonlight, to undress in the dark. She kept her tank top and boxers on.

...Ronnie slid as close to home plate as she could under the circumstance, and under the circumstances, she was as satisfied as she imagined she could be. Shawnee, on the other hand, was still stuck somewhere between first and second. She made one final move, sliding her hand up Ronnie's stomach, but when Ronnie tensed and held her hand firmly, Shawnee let out an exasperated sigh, and let her head fall on Ronnie's shoulder.

"I'm sorry." She squeezed Shawnee's hand.

"Don't be. It's not your fault."

"It's no one's fault, Shawnee," she reassured her quietly. "It is what it is. I'm good, trust me."

"But..."

"What's the big deal?" Ronnie really wanted to know. In her limited, and largely virtual, experience as a lover, she'd already adopted the role and attitude of 'giver', and accepted that things would always be that way. Either subconsciously, or perhaps giving considerable thought to her anatomical limitations, she'd shifted the focus of her sexual energy from physical to emotional and cerebral. She imagined that the sights and sounds of the moment, as well as the physical act of pleasing Shawnee, must be just as satisfying as being directly touched or kissed. She was quiet for a long time, as she hoped to herself that she'd reasoned correctly, or perhaps that Shawnee'd fall asleep and forget. When she felt Shawnee's hand creeping up her thigh, she realized she'd be having no such luck.

"You just make it all look like so much fun." Shawnee teased nervously, as she eased her way back down Ronnie's body.

"Fine, but no hands." Ronnie tried to relax. She kept telling herself not to think, 'just feel'... the soft moist kisses, Shawnee's long hair against her skin. She tried to watch, thinking surely she would be turned on by the sight of her beautiful girlfriend... 'doing that'. But she could only see the top of her head. Again, she tried to use her imagination. "Don't think." It started to work. "Just feel." She actually had the presence of mind to try and give back some of what she'd been given. As it started to feel good, she let Shawnee know with a soft moan, so she would stay there. She reached down and touched Shawnee's her hair and her hips began to move on their own... Ronnie screamed. The release was so powerful, almost violent, that it startled Shawnee, but she loved it. She wanted to stay. Ronnie pulled her toward her, but wouldn't let her kiss her. She held her tightly while her breathing slowed and Shawnee returned to the previously forbidden oasis. Ronnie couldn't relax; but she also didn't know how to explain that, despite what her body was telling Shawnee, she wanted her to stop. So, she didn't try to explain. Instead, she let Shawnee pull her further and further out of her head and into...reality. It really wasn't as complicated as she tried to make it. Everything about making love with her girlfriend felt good. It was only her fear, and the manly voices in her head that thought it all a little unnatural, until finally, Shawnee lulled them into submission, and Ronnie slept quietly on her belly.

Ultimately, it was everything the first time is supposed to be: sweet and sincere, a little bit awkward, and peppered with giggles and kisses and promises. By morning, Ronnie had recovered her machismo, was back in provider, hunter-gatherer mode, and cheerfully announced to Shawnee that her favorite breakfast of pancakes, bacon and fried eggs was waiting for her in the kitchen. But Shawnee was afraid to leave the room.

"Com'on. It's just Libby."

"I don't have any clothes, and I am not eatin' pancakes in

my prom dress!"

"Hold on." Ronnie walked over to her dresser and pulled out the smallest t-shirt she could find, a men's large that had shrunk from too many rounds in the dryer, and a pair of pajama pants. She smiled at the way Shawnee filled out her favorite old shirt, and giggled at how the pants dragged the floor. Shawnee rolled them down several times at the waist and stuck her tongue out at Ronnie. "See, perfect," Ronnie said as she pulled Shawnee close, kissing the top of her head.

"Hey, Shawnee!" Libby rushed over to give the little girl she used to babysit a big hug. She was cool and made no mention of the new crop of hickies on her very fair-skinned brother's neck. They talked about school and where Shawnee and Ronnie would be going to college. But Libby was only six years older than Ronnie, and not being able to poke just a little fun at him and his girlfriend was killing her. She held on as long as she could, until the bacon was gone and she was satisfied that the lovebirds had replenished their fluids.

"So... how was prom?" Libby asked, hiding a grin behind her coffee cup. Ronnie turned beet red, as Shawn slowly sank under the table.

"Oh! You're a jerk!" Ronnie shook her head at her sister and suppressed a grin herself.

Shawnee rebounded and slowly surfaced from under the table. "Hey! How do you even know anything happened? We used to sleep together all the time!"

"Yeah, well, I was mostly only speculating, until you just told me."

"Oh." Shawnee continued to blush and buried her face in her hands.

"Seriously, it was only a matter of time. I'm surprised it took this long."

"What are you talking about?"

"Oh please. I knew when you guys were nine."

"You knew what exactly?" They actually asked in unison.

"That you were a boy... and you... were a lesbian..." She pointed at each of them.

Shawnee's hand shot up, and she waited to be called on.

"Yes, Shawnee."

"If you knew she was a boy and I'm a lesbian, how exactly did you figure we'd end up together?"

"Ha!" Ronnie spit her milk out laughing.

This time Libby turned red. "Oh... Whatever... I just knew... see..."

'Future Ronnie and Shawnee' would debate the facts and consequences of the most pivotal event in their relationship for years; but, truth be told, 'The Great Ultimatum' (later known simply as 'GU') and its aftermath were Shawnee's fault...mostly. By their sophomore year in college, they had eased into what Shawnee described to her female friends as a 'normal lesbian relationship'. If the friendship part changed, it was for the better. Ronnie had finally come, almost, completely out of her shell; and except for their major course studies, they were inseparable. Whether it was due to the people-pleasing she adopted from years of watching her father, or her authentically amiable nature, Ronnie eventually yielded to Shawnee in every way, except sexually. It was in the bedroom, living room, shower, backseat, backyard hammock, etc... that she drew the line. Their first time together was the first and last time she'd ever allowed (any part of) Shawnee to venture below her waist. For three years, Shawnee remained silent, because the things Ronnie did with her hands and mouth, she did exceptionally well; so well, she mostly made up for their one-sided sexual dynamic. But after a semester of women's studies and an A+ paper detailing how *'throughout history, women who have been oppressed by patriarchal, chauvinistic societies, eventually find their strength and arise victorious to not only lead households, corporations, and armies of men... but take back their bodies, and more importantly, their sexual independence...'* Shawnee was feeling empowered... Power made Shawnee horny, and before Ronnie knew it, she was back to her 'handsy' ways. Shawnee was also under the false impression that her rediscovered sexual independence had somehow magically been transferred to Ronnie. She really wasn't a jerk...rapist...bully, or any of the other things that later came to her mind (but never Ronnie's); she just mistook Ronnie's increased comfort around her to mean more than it did.

"So we take baths together, sleep naked together for years, and you still don't trust me?" Shawnee was embarrassed, but mostly hurt.

"Shawnee, I've barely tolerated you touching me *above* the waist in seven years. What in the world would make you think I could, all of a sudden, without any warning or discussion, let you do *that*?!" Ronnie was more upset than Shawnee had ever seen her, but still spoke very quietly. It wasn't so much that she was afraid, she was more concerned that the gesture indicated that Shawnee didn't know or understand her. "I thought you understood."

"Understood what, Ronnie? That you're a man? I'm sorry, but you're not. I've known you my whole life, and you are not a man! I know it's my fault for playing along all this time; but I can't anymore. When I look at you, all I see is the beautiful girl I've been in love with since I was seven-years-old. When we make love..." Shawnee closed her eyes and sighed deeply, to keep from crying. She wasn't sad; she was frustrated and she needed Ronnie to feel that. She stood back and looked at Ronnie. She stared for a long time before slowly walking back to her and breathing into her ear. "Why do lesbians have to talk about everything? ...You are... just... so... lovely..." She let her had rest on Ronnie's chest and slide slowly down toward her waist again. She stopped at her navel, and when Ronnie tensed, she backed away again. "It doesn't matter what you wear, Ronnie. This... us... like this... isn't working for me, anymore. I need more. And I wouldn't ask you to change who you are for anything in the world; but perhaps you can help me out. The next time you come at me all GQ, in your Hugo Boss and Perry Ellis, you'd better have something other than that delicate little finger to slip inside me." Having said the thing she'd been holding in for at least three years, Shawnee stormed out into the cold. Ronnie didn't go after her; she knew she wouldn't have gone far. She just sat in the driveway for an hour.

While Shawnee was gone, Ronnie got herself ready. She was, surprisingly, not nervous or anxious. In fact, she'd later remember being eerily calm, as she showered, poured out the wine neither of them was ever going to drink, changed the music from whatever god-awful Indy band Shawnee'd been following those days to classic R&B, and as Teddy Pendergrass instructed, turned out the lights. When Shawnee returned, Ronnie was sitting on the edge of their bed in the dark. Only Ronnie's face and shoulders were visible in the light from the single remaining candle. "I'm so sor..."

"Shhhh... It's okay. Come here." Ronnie pulled Shawnee strongly toward her, but only far enough that she could lean in to kiss her. She enjoyed the taste of Shawnee's tears mixed with her drug of choice, sugarless, raspberry bubblegum. She smiled to herself at Shawnee's constant and endearing quirkiness. She really did love her. She actually trusted her, and did indeed feel safe with her. And as always, she was prepared to give her what (she selectively heard her say) she wanted. She'd always been. She'd only waited so long, because she knew that, from that moment on, for better or worse, nothing would ever be the same.

Ronnie undressed Shawnee slowly, with a new kind of focus. Her kiss and touch were different, more passionate than tender. Shawnee liked it, and whispered her apologies over and over, until Ronnie was tired of telling her there was nothing to apologize for. She finally decided to show her. "Yes..." Shawnee whispered, as Ronnie slowly slid her hand down her body. Ronnie moaned deeply at the wetness, and Shawnee sighed in anticipation of her patient and skillful entry. But when she pulled her hand away and shifted her body against Shawnee's, she felt it. "Huh!" She gasped and tried not to panic. Ronnie hoped Shawnee wouldn't speak, as she watched her face and slowly slid inside her. As she imagined, they fit perfectly; and long after Shawnee's own multiple orgasms, she instinctively and cheerfully atoned for her earlier transgression.

"When did you? Why didn't you? I'm so confused... I'm a jerk! Hey! Why are you so good at that? Have you?"

"Of course not! I don't know why... I guess it just feels right."

"How long have you had it?"

"For a while now... maybe six months..."

"Why didn't you say anything before now?"

"Believe it or not, I thought I was being ...selfish?... presumptuous? You're constantly reminding me, in some way or another, that you're a lesbian..."

"I'm sorry..."

"No. It's okay. I don't mean it like that. It's just that, I always thought that you might not like it or need it, and it would just be about me. But you liked it?"

"Are you kidding? Oh my God!" Shawnee screamed into her pillow, and reached down to give her new best friend a firm tug. "Can you feel that?"

"Yes..." Ronnie closed her eyes and rolled her hips as Shawnee pressed the prosthetic against her previously off-limits 'girl parts'.

The novelty of their thoroughly hetero relations quickly wore off, and as Ronnie suspected, Shawnee gradually reverted back to her naturally aggressive tendencies. Only now, Ronnie's response was less cerebral and much more primal. And while Shawnee did actually enjoy the physical act, she didn't like what it did for their overall dynamic. The seemingly natural and easy balance of power that existed before the GU began to shift; and as Ronnie became more aggressive sexually, she also became more dominant in general. She actually was, and had always been, strong and competent and a natural leader. She was more grounded and mature and emotionally, more honest. She'd been quietly holding their relationship together, ignoring her own needs and the inadvertent assaults against her gender and sexual identity; mostly because she loved Shawnee, but also because it's hard to defend an identity you're not entirely sure of yourself. They'd never had the talk; but Ronnie realized she'd never actually told Shawnee she was a man. And she was pretty certain she wasn't a lesbian. She only knew she wasn't what her mother told her to be. If nothing else, she'd learned from years of therapy that it really was a mistake to try and be something you're not, even for someone you love. If she and Shawnee continued to cling to their labels, or her lack thereof, ultimately, they'd end up hurting each other.

Whatever box she checked (or wanted to) on her driver's license, intimately, at least with Shawnee, Ronnie wasn't ready to submit or be even the slightest bit vulnerable. And Shawnee's welcoming response to the physical manifestation of Ronnie's manhood aside, Shawnee required more reciprocity than Ronnie was able to give. Like a lot of concepts floating around in her head, Ronnie's relationship with Shawnee was... complicated; and although Shawnee was extremely intelligent, she never wanted to talk. So, as Ronnie'd done since they were little, she found a way to present the issue concisely, and in a manner that Shawnee could easily accept. "Shawnee, I'm a dude... and you, my beautiful, dude-like friend, are definitely a lesbian."

"No kidding, Genius!" Shawnee laughed and elbowed him in the ribs. Within a week, they each moved out of Libby's house and into apartments of their own... across the hall from each other.

13

IN THE PLACE TO BE

*R*onnie listened as the other young men in the circle shared their stories, and tried not to stare. He felt out of place. Sure, he enjoyed the camaraderie, and was comforted by seeing other young people like himself; but beyond that, he couldn't relate. His life wasn't a nightmare. Fitting in wasn't a struggle. It wasn't even a challenge to pass or 'go stealth' as Aidan, the group's leader, put it. Ronnie didn't like those terms. He wasn't trying to hide; and had no desire to catch someone off guard. Still, he looked around and felt...safe. The ten young men in various stages of transition immediately welcomed him with open arms. It didn't matter that he wasn't sure of his classification, or that he didn't know anything about hormone replacement therapy (HRT) or binding or any of the other terms they all spoke of with so much authority. He was a biological female who preferred to live, be treated like and identified as, if you must, a man. He was one of them.

"So, what's with the name?" Ronnie asked Aidan.

"Well, you've heard the expression 'walk like a man', right?" The handsome but diminutive fellow tilted his head upward at Ronnie.

"Of course... Oh, yeah... Just Walk... Clever..."

"Is this your first meeting?"

"Yes."

"Wow... congratulations."

"Uh... thanks. What for?"

"You haven't had any help, and you're completely convincing."

"I said this was my first meeting. I didn't say I didn't have help. I've done some research, and I've got a lot of support... my sister and my girlfriend, well ex-girlfriend..."

"Ah, the ex-girlfriends..." Aidan interrupted. "You'll have lots of those. Straight girls don't get it right away. They're so conditioned to being screwed over by meat sacks that they can't think outside the box. They think if you weren't born with it, you're not a real man, and if you're not a real man, she's a lesbian. They're all pretty resistant to that...at first."

Ronnie laughed. "Yeah, that sounds frustrating, but that's not my issue either. Shawn did get that I'm a guy. The problem was, she really is a lesbian." Ronnie smiled and shook his head at the irony. It had been nearly a year since their break up, and he could finally say her name without tearing up. "We're just better off as friends."

Aidan stared at his new hero in awe. No drugs, no surgery, no identity crisis? How was he doing it? Aidan was smart and a natural leader, a real 'alpha male'. He'd been charming women away from their boyfriends and out of their panties for years; but he knew instantly, Ronnie was different.

Every Friday night for six weeks, Ronnie wondered to himself why they absolutely had to go to a straight bar. As Aidan, 'the four apostles' Matthew, Mark, John, Luke, and the quiet new guy squeezed into a booth inside the busiest sports bar in Atlanta, Ronnie vowed to ask the question out loud the next time the topic of hanging out came up. In the meantime, he tried to blend in and enjoy himself; and he did, until it happened again... He took a sip of his tall cranberry juice and shook his head. "Oh, this is gonna get ugly." Aidan was so damn cocky. Ronnie sat in the corner and watched as the stud winked at the pretty blond waiting for her date to return from the bar. He stared some more as he got up to play pool. Aidan engaged in this deadly staring contest just long enough for the girl's behemoth of a boyfriend to return and catch her.

"What are you looking at?" He asked 'Gidget' before fol- lowing her gaze to the stocky, chiseled and tan Aidan, who now seemed to be heavily engaged in a high-stakes game of nine-ball. Satisfied that the pint-sized playa wasn't stupid enough to try any- thing with him actually sitting there, 'The Fridge' returned his limited attention to his trouble-making lady. Ronnie breathed a sigh of relief, but stayed on alert. It would be highly unlikely to escape a night out with Aidan and 'the boys from T-Rx' without one of them needing to flex their new man-muscles. Any one of the five guys out with Ronnie that night was likely to engage in some form of pissing contest; but the safest money was always on Aidan to set things off first, and in the most explosive fashion.

Since joining their group of female to male transgenders (FTMs), Ronnie'd begun researching the benefits and risks of testosterone treatments. The benefits were obvious. Sooner than later, he would begin to look more like a man: his skin would toughen; he'd develop facial hair, his voice would change... Most importantly, taking T was the next logical step for someone planning to fully transition, which he fully planned to do. But he was still assessing the risks. Obviously, he was concerned about the long-term effects. The research was scary, and he'd heard as many horror stories as successes. Still, watching his brothers live out their post-adolescent fantasies, he was tempted. After all, "life without the occasional bar fight isn't really worth living, is it?" Aidan returned victorious from his billiard battle and made his way back to his friends at the booth; but not without flashing one wicked sexy grin at the monster's trophy princess. And this time, 'Bear' was watching. He stood slowly as Aidan approached the table. "Oh, shit." Ronnie thought as the offensive lineman finally reached his full six feet, six inches, blocking Aidan's path to the goal line.

"You got a problem, little fella?"

"Actually, no, I do not; at least not since I embraced the awesomeness that is Aidan Benjamin Crawford. How 'bout you?"

"Huh, the kid's funny." The Greek god chuckled to his goddess. "How come every time I look up you're staring at my girl?" It was a really good question, almost civilized, really.

"Aren't you more concerned with why she keeps staring back at me? Nevah mind. I know, she just needed somethin' better to look at, eh." The opposite of civil.

"Man, you're lucky I can't hit a little kid. Why don't you just run along before you get hurt?" Again, civil... maybe a little insulting, but it almost sounded like genuine concern. His attorney could argue that he fired a clear warning shot before he broke Aidan in half.

"Com' on, darlin' let me teach you how to play eight-ball. I'll even let you use my stick."

"Oh, you're kiddin' me right?" Ronnie practically said out loud as he stood quickly, towering over Aidan, but still needing to look up at Bret. He said a quick prayer before he spoke. "See,

Bridget, I told you Bret here would defend your honor. He was actually quite the gentleman. He didn't even have to throw a punch. And Aidan! Man, you were fantastic! I actually believed that you believed you could get this lovely young lady to abandon her perfect specimen of a boyfriend and run away with you! It was just the right combination of 'Prince Charming' and 'raging asshole'. But clearly, ma'am, you've got yourself a true gentleman here. Our work is done. Guys, the last round is on us. Y'all enjoy the rest of your evenin'." Ronnie put a twenty on the table and spun Aidan around toward the door and gave him a shove. The others fell in behind them laughing hysterically. "No, really, why do we always come to straight bars?" That time, Ronnie was sure to ask out loud through his own laughter.

Outside, the boys were roaring. Aidan wasn't even mad that he didn't get to hit anyone. "Man that was friggin' awesome! Where did you learn to do that?" He leaned against the side of the building as he and all four apostles simultaneously lit up various brands of menthol cigarettes.

"My dad, I guess. He trains people in de-escalation tactics. He goes in when there's been a disaster and people are all outta control, and he has to find the fastest way to neutralize the situation and calm everyone down. He was away a lot when I was a kid, so I used to watch a lot of his training videos. I never thought that would come in handy."

"Well, you certainly got my attention." Suddenly the blond from the bar was standing in front of them with her boyfriend standing guard behind her. "Hi again. That really was pretty cool. What's your name?"

"Ronnie Reynolds" He shook her extended hand too firmly.

"Ronnie, actually I am an associate producer for *The Other World*, and we are in town scouting for our next show. I think my bosses, and fifteen to twenty-four year old girls everywhere, would absolutely love you. Take my card and give me a call tomorrow so we can schedule an interview." And with that, Bridget and Bret were gone.

Ronnie did call Bridget the next day, and the following day he interviewed and was immediately cast to be on the reality show *The Other World - Atlanta (TOWA)*; about an eclectic group of eight young adults living in one giant house with paper-thin walls. Ronnie was the 'too sexy for words, androgynous, peace-making, guitar playing, graduate student that no one knew much more about, but everyone wanted to get to know better'.

14

THIS IS A MAN'S WORLD

*S*ix months after his season on TOWA was over, Ronnie was still recognized and approached for autographs, job offers, and sexual encounters; ranging anywhere from casual, 'right here and right now' to 'weekend in the Hamptons followed by brunch with my parents'. He didn't mind. It's not like the pretty girls who smiled at him and bought him drinks were intruding. After his breakup with Shawnee, he'd done some serious reflection and decided that it was best that he stay single for a while, while he figured things out. Despite what he showed her, losing his first love stung more than he was willing to admit. He wasn't willing to expose himself to that kind of pain again anytime soon. But he eventually realized that he hadn't actually lost her, and he had indeed gained something better. Their friendship, more than that, their mutual love and respect, was far more important to both of them than having their sexual identities tattooed on their flesh forever, and settling down. Once they were no longer a couple, they actually talked; and what they agreed upon most was that gender identity, and in particular, sexual identity, even if not for either of them, was probably more fluid than the world wanted people to believe. For instance, Shawn finally admitted to Ronnie that she too felt, at times, more masculine than feminine, but only on the inside. And Ronnie, reluctantly, now that it didn't matter, acknowledged that he didn't really 'feel like a man', or necessarily want to be one; it was the world that told him he had to choose. So, when faced with the decision practically every day, he chose the most practical option *for him*. He was six feet, one inch tall. He had those scars on his face and neck, that while they didn't make him any less beautiful, certainly went a long way to making him look...ruggedly sexy and...a little dangerous. He was naturally muscular, strong and athletic. And in almost every way that he thought mattered, he thought like a man. He was instinctually chivalrous, and wanted to be provider, protector, Mr. Fix It and make it all better; and he had the tools to be all those things. He looked damn good in... everything but a dress, but particularly a suit and tie; not at all like a little girl playing 'drag-king'. All he needed was a mildly uncomfortable compression garment to hold down his C-cups, and the right single-breasted three to four button jacket. He didn't run out and buy facial hair. His mother's bone structure and dimpled chin, while pretty and feminine on her and Libby, were just manly enough for him. His piercing green eyes would have been effectively seductive on a eunuch; and his perfect curls, dark in Winter, auburn in Summer, were always neat, but long enough to be pulled on, in that way only a man's (or a lesbian's) hair should be pulled. And finally, speaking of pulling... Ronnie preferred to have sex as a man. It would be a while before he realized the downside to having so much power; but, he discovered that he got more than a little rush from the way women responded to him, in and outside of the bedroom.

His stardom, launched by *TOWA*, immediately overflowed out of 'the house' to his actual life. While he'd spent most of that year celibate, with his head buried in books or tied to his computer, stepping into the real world, was exhilarating, and awakened his wild side. The freedom and temptation that came with his sudden and public success actually began to get the best of him. Although he didn't change completely, he did pick up some very bad habits. For one thing, the formerly shy bookworm discovered that he enjoyed having lots of random and casual sex; and as the hottest thing not on stage or screen, it was entirely too easy to come by. Women, and quite a few men, in the studio where he worked as an intern, in the clubs he hung out in, on the occasional train ride home, practically threw themselves at him. His magnetism was hard to explain. Perhaps it was because he was extremely attractive, but also, somehow, disarmingly, unassuming. He didn't walk around as though he knew he was 'all that'. He just *walked*. His swagger wasn't deliberate or manufactured; it was authentic, but balanced by his quick, light-hearted wit, intelligence and genuine kindness. Any woman he set his sights on, as well as most who sought him, was rendered instantly defenseless against a smile that could melt icebergs. And although, he'd come to hate it later, in the beginning, he especially enjoyed the effect his charms had on a particular type of woman: the beautiful, loose, no-strings, except for what favors they

hoped to garner-kind, who only cared that he was a moderately famous, star on the rise, sizzling hot (in a way that even straight men
got it, even if they didn't know why) Man, with a capital M.

So, by twenty-three, Ronnie personified 'It Factor'; and for
nearly six years, his was indeed, for the good and the bad, a man's
world. Not long after his stint on *TOWA,* he'd been selected, from
the hottest of his housemates, who'd also been inadvertently inter-
viewing to be 'the next big thing', as the host of his own late-night
talk show. The same network that produced *The Other World* had a
plan to develop and test talent in the Southeast, and feed them to
the (wolves) national television market. Ronnie never wanted to be
a famous talk-show host, or famous at all, for that matter. He
wanted to help people, to write; and if he could just get back to his
roots, eventually, serve the God who'd saved him 'for something
bigger than a stupid stand-up gig'. He'd just earned his Master's
degree in Journalism. He didn't actually need it; but he enjoyed the
work that went into getting it, and had been advised by his agent
that he'd have a better chance of parlaying his reality show expo-
sure into a real career as a grad student than a journalist.

"I'm not trying to have a career in television." He reminded
Shawn, who'd appointed herself his agent, when he told her about
the show. She was, ironically, qualified, having earned a degree in
Entertainment and Arts Management, while working full time as an
assistant.

"You already have one; you may as well make the best of it
while you're still... well, not ugly... Besides, what better things do
you have to do?"

"I was actually thinking about putting my education to
some use. Or, perhaps..going into social work. I want to help people. I feel like I'm supposed to give back."

"What better way to help people than from a national plat-
form?" Shawn pressed. Having lesser minds to practice on, she'd
become much more talkative, and persuasive.

"I guess you have a point." Ronnie was only slightly surprised.

"Don't I always?"

"Annoyingly... yes..."

15

THE RONNIE REYNOLDS SHOW

"*W*hy doesn't the agency ever send homely, conservative girls to work here?" Ronnie thought to himself, as he made his way to his dressing room. It seemed every week there was a new crop of interns and production assistants. Did they know about each other? Did they know about him? Sex with him wasn't technically part of the job description; but he was starting to wonder why they always seemed to be so well prepared. He watched Belinda from wardrobe. She'd be on her way in any moment. She pretended to pick out ties, while Trevor, his stylist and friend, rambled on about his plans for the new season. As soon as he fluttered away, Belinda grabbed Ronnie's suit and an armful of ties and swayed over. She tapped lightly on the open door.

"Mr. Reynolds, I have the pleasure of dressing you today. May I come in?" Ronnie could only laugh to himself at her choice of words.

"Of course. What fabulous ensemble has Trevor picked out for me this evening?"

"He's mixing things up... Prada with a little Rag and Bone..." The barely legal former debutante draped her excuses across a chair and closed the door. "But first you have to pick your tie." She pointed to her breasts as she approached the desk.

Ronnie smiled at her. "Doesn't it matter what I'll be wearing the ties with?" He played along.

"I doubt it. I bet one of these would go with any...." she tossed the tail of one over her bare shoulder and sat on the edge of his desk.

"You are the expert, aren't you...?" Ronnie accepted the shapely, tan leg being offered to him, but just held it. He wanted to not do that today. He didn't know this girl. All she knew about him was that he had the hottest talk show on television. What did she think a meaningless encounter with him in his office was going to get her?

It was over practically before it started. She kissed him and he slid his hand up her leg. Not surprisingly, she'd left her panties... in her bookbag? Ronnie reached for a condom and spun 'Number 265' around. He gave her an obligatory hair-tossling, as he slid the protective coating onto his ever-ready, way too perfect to be real, but entirely realistic, penis. He pressed her torso against his desk... and wondered if the network meant for him to actually do any real work there... as he slid skillfully into the orifice of the pretty young woman he knew absolutely nothing about. He pounded away at her for eight or nine minutes, until the tops of her thighs were sufficiently bruised by the edge of the desk, before he indicated, by dropping his moans an octave or two lower, that he would climax momentarily. The NYU grad-turned fluffer responded on cue with high pitched oohs, aahs and a rather convincing, 'Oh my God, it feels so good!' Top it all off with a manly grunt, and he was ready for work. 'Belinda 265' turned around without bothering to pull her skirt down, and leaned in to kiss the Emmy-winning stud dejour; but he was done. "Let's try this one." He plucked a tie from around her neck, careful not to actually touch her. "Can you let them know I'll be right out, please?" He asked indicating that, as always, he'd be dressing himself, and would like for her to leave.

"Of course."

"Thank you, Melinda."

"You're welcome, Mr. Reynolds."

Ronnie changed clothes without looking in the mirror. He couldn't. Why couldn't he stop? It wasn't even ... Well, what was sex supposed to be, anyway? Fun? Satisfying? He certainly didn't love those women. He didn't like them. He didn't even know them. He got nothing out of it physically. Okay, maybe a momentary release, but after that, it was always worse than the moments before.

Hours after the best show he'd ever hosted ended, Ronnie sat in his dressing room in the empty studio. Wow. Kyle Rivers-Tye...arrived, on his show! He was as impressive as Ronnie imagined he would be. Was he always ministering to people? Ronnie considered what Kyle asked of him. It seemed foolish for a transgendered person to come out. "We spend our entire lives trying not to be seen as anything other than what we've chosen. Doesn't telling defeat the purpose? Who would telling help?" Ronnie tried to rationalize. He knew he didn't spend a lot of time thinking about God, or anyone other than himself for that matter. Sure, he was convincingly compassionate as a host. He talked a good game when the situation called for an advocate. But his motives were almost always entirely selfish. He wouldn't be concerned with equality, the rights of gays and minorities, if there weren't something in it for him somewhere, whether anyone else knew or not. Even if he was afraid to come out himself, a part of him rooted for his brothers and sisters. He admired their courage, felt their pain... in theory, anyway. "That's not that unusual thinking for a man is it?" He wasn't terribly concerned with fair and ethical treatment of women. Men had it pretty good, and he was part of the club. To really stand up and be heard would signal to the world that he wasn't everything he claimed to be. "I can't do that." But he'd met his hero that night; sat in a chair across from him and his beautiful husband, looked him in the eye and told him he believed in his work, his ministry. When asked what he could do to help, Kyle answered him. It was simple: Stop hiding. 'Tell the world who you are.' Well, at least it sounded simple enough in theory.

"Kyle Rivers-Tye is not God. He's a man with a cause. He fights for the rights of gay people because he's a gay man. Sometimes 'ministry' is just another word for 'agenda'. But you believed he was a wise and anointed man of God, before he asked you to step outside yourself. What is God telling you to do?" Ronnie knew better than to talk to God about coming out. Even in his limited understanding, he knew that the answer would always be to 'walk into the light'.

Ronnie pulled into the garage of his condo and looked for Rachel's car. "She's here," he announced to himself with a hint of disappointment.

"Hi Honey." He kissed her sweetly, as she reached for his jacket to hang it up.

"Hi. How was the show?" She asked casually.

"You didn't watch, huh?" He tried not to sound too disappointed. Rachel had stopped watching every episode of the live show that came on at eleven pm just six weeks into their relationship, even though the show was supposedly what got them together. Rachel had been an early morning news anchor and, one morning between his show and hers, introduced herself to Ronnie as his biggest fan. Despite the immediate 'Misery' vibe he got from her, he played along and... by the time her contract was up, they were seeing each other on a regular basis. He came out to her as a woman after a couple of months, and after a short break up, they were back together and practically living together.

"I'm sorry, baby. I fell asleep." Ronnie casually around the living room. The TV was on, but not on his channel, and a novel she'd been reading lay faced-down and open on the couch. I took a nap so I'd be refreshed when you came home. She pulled him by the hand toward the bedroom.

"Mmm... you do smell nice. I'm just going to take a shower and get fresh myself." He grabbed the black Kenneth Cole bag and locked the door behind him in the master bathroom. Inside he retrieved 'Majic' from the bag, cleaned him up and set him on the sink. He took his time in the shower. He had a lot on his mind. He couldn't get Kyle's words from the show earlier out of his head. Maybe he would be happier if he came out. He emerged from the shower suited up, and opened the door. Rachel was in their bed waiting for him, wearing one of many lacey, G-string thingies he told her he loved. She really was very pretty, nearly perfect really, with a body straight outta Hustler. He watched her ass as she lay on her side with her back to the door, pretending to read. That's what got him. He slipped into bed while simultaneously setting her book on the nightstand and rolling her over onto her stomach. He kissed the back of her neck, as directed by her pulling her hair to one side. He kissed her with his eyes open and noticed the bottle of oil on the table. He reached for it and massaged completely before performing his other nightly duties.

They lay side by side and very still until she rolled over to kiss him good-night. "I've got an early work-out tomorrow, and a late class, so I won't see you 'til this time tomorrow. I'll try not to wake you in the morning; but please don't forget Kam's party Saturday night." She rolled away to go to sleep.

"Rach..." He waited for her to answer; she just waited for him to continue. "We need to talk."

"Really, Ronnie? Can it wait until tomorrow. I'm really tired."

Ronnie thought to himself, "tired from what exactly?" but said, "No, it can't really. I need to tell you something." He reached over and turned on the light.

Rachel sat up. "I'm listening."

"I think it's time for me to come out."

"What? Why? Do you think someone knows?" She looked panic-stricken.

"No, just the people I've told, and my family... but I'm tired of pretending."

"What pretending? You're a man, who happens to not be anatomically correct."

"Thanks," he squinted, his sarcasm completely lost on her. "It's..." He actually meant, 'I'm'. "...more complicated than that, Rachel. I'm a man, but I am also a woman."

"But you said you don't feel like a woman."

"I don't, most of the time. But I am stuck in this ridiculous body. It's getting to be a bit of a hassle...not acknowledging...having to hide my breasts, going in disgusting men's rooms, but not being able to use urinals."

"But you're going to do it right? Once you have the surgery, no one will know the difference. What would be the point of telling people?"

"I think telling people could help someone."

"Who could that possibly help?"

"People like me. People who feel alone and are tortured by the thoughts that they have to hide. This life is hard. I feel like I'm lying to people."

"You're not lying. You're protecting yourself and the people you care about."

"From what?"

"From people who won't understand."

"Why do people have to understand? Whose business should it be aside from mine and yours, and the people like me, and God. And if people who know and love 'people like me' understand that there are more 'people like me' than they realize, life for 'people like me' will, slowly but surely, be just a little bit easier..."

"But if you come out... people will think..." She hesitated.

"What? That you're a lesbian? Who cares. Besides, you're not, I'm a man..."

"Right, but if you come out, you're saying you're something else."

"No, I'm saying I was born a woman, and now I am a man. Do you really care more about what strangers think of you than about my feelings, or the fact that I can help people?"

"No! I'm just not a lesbian, Ronnie. I don't want... people won't understand. How sure are you that you want to do that?"

"It's just a thought I've been playing with. It's not something I've definitely decided to do." Ronnie lied. It was more than a casual thought. He'd been thinking about it for a while, and meeting Kyle had virtually sealed the deal. "I didn't mean to upset you. Get some sleep." He kissed her on her forehead, and she rolled back to her side of the bed.

When Ronnie woke the next morning, there was a note from Rachel:

Dear Ronnie,

I know you too well. If you're talking about it, you've already decided, and I told you, I just can't. I wish things were different. I wish I were stronger. I'll pray that it all works out the way you want it to. Rachel

Ronnie looked around his condo. The few things Rachel had brought there were gone, and the spare keys were on the table. Ronnie smiled to himself. Rachel was sweet, and beautiful, but he wasn't in love. It was time to start living. But first...

16

GET YOUR HEAD RIGHT

*D*r. Keaner actually gave Ronnie a hug. It wasn't a common practice of hers; but when she last saw Ronnie he was barely sixteen years old. The man that stood before her was her proudest achievement as a therapist.

"Wow! Ronnie, I've been watching your show, and I honestly thought, 'it must just be the lighting and makeup...' but you are honestly even hotter in person! How does it feel to be a recognizable sex symbol?"

"Funny, you should ask that... it's kind of the reason I (flew all the way to Atlanta and) called you. I've got some decisions to make... but some issues I need to work out, first."

"Okay, do you want to start with the decisions or the issues?"

"Oh, we'd better start with the tough stuff. I think I've got a sex addiction, Liz."

"Well, I believe there is a great deal of truth to the expression that 'the first step is admitting you have a problem'... but with that said, addicts are rarely the first to diagnose their problems. What makes you think it's an addiction."

"I've been having random, meaningless sex with virtual strangers for years, in the past year, while I've been in a committed relationship. I'm not doing it for any physical pleasure, and when I'm done I hate myself. But I can't stop."

"Okay, so far, I would agree you've got a problem. What's happened that you want to change?"

"'Change' is the word. I'm ready to start living."

"A lot of people would kill to have your life, Ronnie, flawed though it may be."

"I know. And you know that fame is over-rated. I know you can't name names, but I'm not your only celebrity client. If Emmys and luxury cars were the keys to happiness, you'd be out of business. I want the rest of it... I want love... I want to help people... I can't do it... like this. I ended my relationship yesterday... well, sort of... she left... and I was honestly relieved... but only for a moment. I'm afraid to go to work."

"Why?"

"It just sounds so stupid. It's really sad and sick, actually."

"You know I've heard worse than anything you've got going on now."

"The random sex... happens at work mostly... in the studio... with the production assistants and interns... all those bright-eyed girls full of so much promise... They come in for a few weeks to put TRRS on their resumes... and I don't know. Am I one of 'those men'? Do I leer at women? Do I give off something that says 'if you let me deposit my pain inside you, I'll put in a good word for you upstairs'? If I do, I don't mean to... but it's like they come in there expecting me to perform... Seriously, I've actually considered whether I should sue for sexual harassment! It's becoming a nightmare. But I'm telling you, if it started because of something I've done, it wasn't intentional. I don't want to live like this anymore."

"Have you considered just telling the next one 'no,' just turning down their advances?"

"Every day."

"Does it happen that often?" Liz tried not to sound horrified, or amused, or aroused. The reality was, there was really only so much harm Ronnie could actually do. He couldn't get anyone pregnant; and it was unlikely that he could spread or contract anything incurable. Still, she respected him for recognizing his behavior was inappropriate.

"Practically... there was a dry spell a few months ago..."

"Okay, what was going on in your life?"

"I don't know... I wasn't in a relationship. Rachel and I had split up for a few months."

"Did you discuss your relationship status with anyone?"

"No. Not directly, I guess. You think I've been doing it because I'm unhappy with her?"

"I guess we'll know soon enough, since you're not together; but I suspect it's probably more deep rooted than that. Are you as friendly and outgoing in person, around the studio as you are on your show?"

"You mean do I flirt? I guess I've been called 'friendly' before. But that's part of the job, isn't it?"

"Do you think, perhaps, you've blurred the line between your real life celebrity and the real man?"

Ronnie was quiet for a long moment. "Thank you for that."

"For what?"

"You know... 'the real man'. You knew me when..."

"I did, but seeing you and acknowledging you as a man isn't something I have to remind myself to do, Ronnie. You've done it. You're there. I think the real question is whether you see it. I know we haven't spoken in a while, and I want to talk some more; but what I think is happening is that you've somehow taken on behaviors that 'feel manly' to you, in spite of how unnatural they are to your true character. I can't wait to see what you can achieve, when you stop acting like a man - or at least the man in your head - and actually start just being one... Why did your girlfriend leave, by the way?"

"I told her I wanted to come out as transgender."

"Wow. Did you mean it?"

Ronnie chuckled. "What do you mean 'did I mean it'?"

"I mean, are you really ready to do that, or did you tell her that because you knew she would leave you, if you came out?"

Ronnie's smile faded. "Wow, Doc. That's harsh."

Dr. Keaner smiled at him. "I'm sorry, Ronnie, but I think you've come back to me after all this time because I get you, right?"

"...Right. Okay, I think it's a little of both... I've been praying about it for years... sort of. Really, it isn't even something I have to pray about. God keeps telling me it's something I need to do. It never goes away. And, honestly, I don't get it. Rationally, it seems like the most reckless, destructive of all possible maneuvers. I look in the mirror and I see a man, if I don't look below my shoulders... But, then, I put on a suit, and the world sees me as a man. Women throw themselves at me... and expect me to do manly things to them. On the inside, I feel like a man... in a good way. So I keep asking myself, 'what could I possibly have to gain from telling the world that I am not what I appear to be?'"

"What answer do you get?"

"That it's not entirely about me; but ultimately, when I come clean, I'll be happier."

"Did you explain it to your girlfriend like that?"

"No, we'd been through that before. All she sees is that, if the world sees me as something less than a man, she'll be seen as something less than a 'straight woman'."

"And you didn't care enough about her to do what would be easier for you both?"

"It doesn't feel easier for me, and I really... " Ronnie looked sad for an instant before he could finish.

"What?"

"I could never get over the fact that she never seemed to want to understand why I might need to come out."

"You think she's selfish."

"Oh, I know she is. And I completely understand that we all are in some ways. It just really bothered me that she never even tried to get it."

"Were you in love with her?"

"I don't think so."

"Well, that's good."

"What do you mean you don't want to do it anymore?" Shawn stared across the table at her best friend and biggest client.

"I mean, I want to take a break." Ronnie took a sip of his coffee and sat back.

"Ronnie, you're not some kid. You're a friggin' Emmy-award-winning talk-show host! You can't just walk away! You're not asking to take a semester off while you hitchhike through Europe." Shawn tried to black out the images of her impending financial destruction.

"You're right. Let me clarify. I'm not *asking* to do anything. But I am done with the show when this season is over."

"What the hell am I supposed to tell the network? You've got a contract."

"I do. And according to that contract, the worst they can do is not pay me for the shows I won't be doing, and keep me off the air on any other network for the duration of that contract. No problem. I don't want to be on television anymore. That works out quite nicely."

"What is going on, Ronnie?"

"I don't know. But I know I can't go back. You know they've got something else they can stick in my slot next season. I will not be missed."

"Okay, you're obviously delusional. Are you also suicidal?"

"Of course not. I just need to take some time and work out some personal things... away from the spotlight."

"And the summer hiatus isn't going to be enough time?"

"I don't know. I doubt it."

"So what are you going to do for work?"

"I'm thinking about writing, actually putting my journalism degree to work." It may have sounded like he was speaking hypothetically, but Ronnie actually had a plan. "I've never actually worked in the field before. Behind the scenes of the people who come on my show are real people, with real stories to tell. And I read pretested anecdotes. I'm a fraud. I want to find out if I have any actual talent."

"By becoming a cub-reporter?"

"No, by writing about real people and sharing their stories."

"You can't just walk away. Just give me a second to think, okay... ... Let me pitch it to the network and get you an assignment somewhere. You'll have a staff... you've already got access..."

"No. I'm not gonna run around the country waving that stupid gold statue at people. I'll work with standard credentials, or I'll sit on my couch and blog about the traffic in Atlanta."

"Fine, can I set up a meeting for you?"

"No. But you can feel free to do whatever - correction... almost whatever - you have to, to keep me from getting sued. And if it keeps you all blinged out as well, so be it... But make no promises... and I am not signing anything until August; so please don't ask."

(deep sigh) "You're an impossible, diva-bitch, and you're going to give me a stroke... Seriously, Ronnie, what's going on? Are you okay?"

"Yes, and thank you for asking. Honestly, I've really been looking at my life lately, and I just don't think I want to be... whatever it is I've become... anymore. I know, if I just let nature run its course, the machine will chew me up and spit me out soon enough; but I want to leave with my soul intact."

"Wow. You're really serious. Okay. Well, as your friend - not your agent; because as your agent, I think you suck - but as your friend, I'm very excited for you... and proud of you. Very few people have the balls to walk away while they're on top."

"Thanks. I think you've got great balls, too..." Ronnie winked, and Shawn rolled her eyes before squeezing his hand and holding onto it.

Ronnie threw on khakis and a button-down shirt and smiled at himself in his full-length mirror. It had been a year since he'd left the show and moved back to Atlanta. He loved working as a journalist. And while he hadn't exactly been nominated for a Pulitzer, yet, he was finally getting recognized for more than his swagger. He was even looking forward to being back in Georgia. People there had long since stopped asking him about the show and why he wasn't on the air anymore. He was just another reporter, and free to be just that... and whatever else he was feeling those days.

Then he remembered his task for the day, and frowned as he approached the courthouse. Most people were there for the accused, Robert Nichols. Another handful would be there for the victims. He was there, despite what he told his producer; and not just because of his personal feelings about her father, but also for *her*. He'd dropped everything else he'd been working on, when he heard the trial of the former bishop, Robert Nichols, was about to start. His memory of the man's sermon, nearly twenty years earlier was still fresh in the back of Ronnie's mind. It always had been, as he considered what he was going to do with his life, and how he could help counteract the evil in the world that continually lashed out at innocent bystanders, like he was then. He'd made the connection immediately, when he met her. She was the right age. He knew Kevin Rivers had grown up near Atlanta. As soon as he heard her say they were neighbors, he checked it out and confirmed that the beautiful, and newly single, Gabrielle Nichols was the daughter of the hypocritical, homophobic, hate-spewing mega-preacher. She was so lovely. He wondered how that were possible. More than that, somehow, he sensed the winds of change were about to blow; and for some reason, he wanted to be there to protect her.

"But how can you protect someone who doesn't even know you're alive?" He wondered if Gabrielle would remember him. They'd only met briefly, at her ex-husband's, new husband's American Music Awards' celebration. He thought he'd seen her smile at him before she left... but he couldn't move. She was so beautiful, and he wasn't ready yet. As he watched for her and considered what she must be going through, his jaw tightened. He could barely believe she was here for the trial. Talk about brave... He remembered meeting Michael on his show, and liking him instantly. Ronnie prayed that Michael would get the answers he needed, and if necessary, the justice he was seeking; but he wasn't personally invested in the bishop's guilt or innocence, necessarily, and tried not to draw any conclusions. He wanted to know about the woman, the daughter, sister, friend. Anyone else, most family members in cases like this distance themselves, especially in cases involving clergy, or abused children. This one had both; but in all of the preliminary proceedings, she'd been there, sitting quietly in the back of the courtroom, smack dab in the middle. It was hard to tell who she was there for. Was she sitting in the back in support of Michael, but not wanting to let her father know; or was she there for her father, and avoiding being recognized and harassed by the press? It didn't matter. Either way, it told him something about her character: that she was devoted, selfless and very brave; and he wanted to know more.

Ronnie considered again why he cared. How was he any different than the droves of vultures who'd camped outside the courthouse and their homes? "Because she's one of the victims." Barely a day went by that Ronnie didn't think about Hugo, and its aftermath. He'd become obsessed with the ones he called 'the forgotten victims', like his siblings, and especially his father. People mourn with the people who are directly harmed; and they vilify the accused, long before a verdict is heard. But who remembers to pray for the daughter whose heart is broken? He saw firsthand the damage a rapist can do to an entire family. It was sometimes worse than what was done directly to a victim. Even in death, there is mercy;

but how do you live with the guilt of not recognizing the danger in time to stop an attack? How do you watch your child struggle to put his life back together or make sense of what happened to him? How do you look your husband in the eye, knowing the monster was your brother? How do you live with your wife knowing you blame each other for a thousand different things? Ronnie could easily imagine what Gabby was feeling. If her father was guilty, who was she? If Michael were making it all up, what happened to the boy she grew up with and loved? Ronnie realized that she must also be there because she needed answers, no matter what the cost; and that told him she was a fighter. "Oh God, I love this woman!" He thought to himself before shifting his focus back to the immediate present.

He hung back away from the crowd. They were all waiting for Michael and the other victims to arrive. He watched the street, not knowing from where she'd come. He sighed deeply when he saw her. He hated approaching her like this, but there was no other way. She'd already started screening her calls. He didn't know what he would say, and he closed his eyes for a moment before walking toward her. He had to walk quickly to keep pace with her.

"Ms. Nichols, I understand you're also tied to the victim in your father's case. Who are you here in support of?"

"That would be an excellent question, if I were answering any."

"I understand. Please give me a call when you're able to talk." He handed her his card. She took it, noticing his hands, and then looking up briefly for the first time to see his face. She recognized him instantly, but didn't say.

17

THE TRIALS OF BISHOP ROBERT NICHOLS: PART ONE

*G*abrielle stood outside the doors to the courtroom for a long while. She wasn't waiting for anyone; she just hadn't decided where she would sit. She wasn't sure who she was there for, her brother and lifelong friend, who'd finally found the courage to face his abuser, or her father, the man accused of the abuse. The impending arrival of this day had tortured Gabby for a year. She prayed it would be easier, that by this day, she would have chosen a side. She loved her father. She had always been 'daddy's little girl'. She knew he wasn't perfect; she didn't want to believe he was a monster. That was the problem. As much as she loved her father, she loved Michael. Her father had treated him like a son practically their whole lives. Michael was her brother, and she believed there was some truth to his story. There had to be. Regardless of how this trial ended, Gabby had already reasoned two things: Something had happened to Michael Anthony Lawson, and no one was closer to him than her father, Bishop Robert Nichols. The bishop spent more time with Michael than he had with anyone else, she and her mother included. Michael spent more time with the Bishop than he did his own mother, before she disappeared. What seemed so innocent and noble twenty-five years ago now looked sinister, seemly…evil. Was Michael confused? Had the years of drug abuse and undiagnosed mental illness finally taken their toll? His suicide attempt was clearly a cry for help. But, just because he wrote things accusing her father of abusing him, right before taking a lethal dose of tranquilizers didn't make them true. Or was it as simple as it looked in the light of day? Did Gabby's father 'take' a fatherless child from his mother, brainwash and manipulate her into thinking the boy would be loved, nurtured and mentored, only to molest, rape and abuse him well into adulthood? And if he was capable of that, who was he? If her father was a monster, who was she?

Gabby had always felt more like her father's child than her

mother's. She didn't know why that was, now. She certainly knew her mother loved her; but Gabby had never understood her mother or her motives. She seemed like such a good woman. Everyone said so. How could she not have known? If she did know, how could she have turned a blind eye all those years. Why was she unwilling to stand by his side now?

Gabby glanced at her watch: two minutes past the last time she checked, and five minutes before the trial would start. She needed to get in there. She said a quick prayer and opened the door. She scanned the room. That didn't help. Everyone else was in position, exactly where she expected them to be. Kevin and Kyle sat to Michael's left, a few rows behind the prosecutor's table. Her mother, now Phyllis Richmond, sat holding Michael's right hand. Gabby wasn't surprised. Her mother had been calling her for weeks, as much for support as to help her daughter prepare for this day and the trial ahead. Phyllis didn't need to wait for the trial. She knew what she knew, and that was enough to walk away. She'd made her decision to finally protect her children.

Even seeing them huddled together in agreement, the choice just wasn't that simple for Gabby. Finally, a door at the side of the courtroom opened and Robert Nichols walked slowly toward the defendant's table, accompanied by his attorney. He looked small, old and frail; but he held his head high, not making direct contact with anyone. Gabby waited to see if he would look at her, but he did not. He just sat staring straight ahead. Gabby looked away to where Michael and the rest of her family were sitting, closed her eyes in a quick moment of prayer, and walked over to her father's side of the courtroom. She stopped by the table to let him know she was there, and then took her seat just behind him. Gabby took a deep breath and turned her eyes toward Michael and the others. Michael turned to look at her and nodded with a slight smile. He understood.

Assistant District Attorney, Craig Martinez, stood slowly and walked to the center of the courtroom. According to his resume, the law school standout was not qualified to try the case by himself. But the district attorney, Chris Porter, who'd recruited him in his second year, assured Craig that, if he came to work for the county, his first order of business would be to put Nichols away. Martinez and Porter were part of the same 'secret' fraternity of former members of the bishop's youth mentoring program; and as far as they and their brothers were concerned 'The Bishop' was to be considered 'Public Enemy Number One' until they found a way to 'put him down'.

"The prosecution will prove that over a period of twenty-five years the defendant, Robert Nichols, raped and molested at least five young boys and, in several instances, coerced them into maintaining 'relationships' well into adulthood. The defendant would have you believe these extra-marital relationships with men, who have since reached the legal age of consent, were completely platonic until the boys were of age, and then, they became consensual; but only as part of his faith's traditions. Expert testimony will show that these relationships are indeed the natural progression of a lifetime of abuse and manipulation by a diabolically charismatic and powerful man, who used his position in the church and community to lure children into his lair of control and sex, in plain view of thousands of people. Witnesses will testify to the fact that these once innocent boys thought of the defendant as a father-figure and spiritual leader; and despite his claims that nothing sinister ever went on, the intimate details of these relationships were a closely guarded secret, hidden from their parents, the defendant's wife and countless parishioners. You'll hear from a man who spent most of his life under the control of the defendant. You'll hear how, as a young boy, he was coerced from the guidance of his mother, molested, then raped, for years, and brainwashed into carrying on an affair with the same man who preached every Sunday about the plague of homosexuality; only to be cast aside when he no longer served the defendant's deviant purposes. The evidence will prove beyond a shadow of a doubt that the defendant is a dangerous predator who fed on the lives of children. You'll be sickened by their stories, not because of their graphic nature. The victims in this case were not bludgeoned or mutilated. But the tales you are about to hear of intense psychological abuse, distortion and perversion of faith practices, deeply intense and hypocritical brainwashing and manipulation will, if you have ever trusted a person of faith, or care for even one child, will disturb you to your core."

The Defendant's side was what you'd expect a corrupt Black church leader's legal team to be: old, White, expensive and experienced in representing criminals, without regard for their guilt or moral failing.

"Bishop Robert Nichols has been a well-respected, even revered member of his community, literally, his entire life. He was born and raised less than twenty miles from this very courthouse. He has dedicated his life to the church, and has sacrificed a great deal to lead thousands of men, women and yes, children to what he calls 'spiritual wholeness'. He is known as much for his service to community and steadfast advocacy of traditional American values as he is an entrepreneur and teacher. People who have known Bishop Nichols for decades will testify to his character as a responsible and caring citizen of humanity. The State will try to convince you that Bishop Robert Nichols is a monster and that somehow thousands of people turned a blind eye to unspeakable atrocities committed against children and his faith community. But witnesses will show that Bishop Nichols is just a man, no more flawed than any other, yet more likely to be the scapegoat for lives wasted; simply because he sacrificed his own life and privacy and became a public figure. You will learn the real motivation behind this witch hunt. And you'll ask yourself whether your generosity and commitment could one day be misconstrued and twisted to paint you, your life and your work in such a vile and heinous light."

For weeks, Gabrielle sat and listened as young men who apparently attended her church but she'd never seen, were sworn in, and testified in front of their families, strangers and the press. They spoke candidly, through tears, and often with heads bowed, about the intimate details of their encounters with her father. It was horrible. Looking at them, you got the sense that Robert Nichols had a type: fit...intelligent...from broken homes...beautiful. "But these boys were all in their teens when this happened." Gabby tried to rationalize. "If it's true, it's disgusting, but it's not a crime, is it? The legal age of consent in Georgia is sixteen; and they aren't even saying they had sex with him, just that he paid to keep them around. 'Juan' even said that he didn't even think anything was wrong with it for a long time..."

"Until he started demanding that I not wear clothes in his presence." A strikingly handsome, almost pretty, twenty-four year old man of Hispanic descent spoke softly into the microphone.

"And did you go along with that?"

"I did. You didn't question the bishop."

"When did you start to question him?"

"I never did, really. I just got out. I went away to college...just in time."

"'Just in time' for what?"

"The bishop started acting weird...er."

"How so?"

"He demanded that I and sometimes another guy give him massages."

"Did he just say, 'massage me'?"

"No, he'd sit us down and talk about 'the struggles of leadership', and how hard it was to run a church. Then he'd read some scripture and take us into the room."

"What room?"

"A room through the door in back of his office in the church."

"Did you ever have sex with him there?"

"No, he made us have sex with each other."

"And what would he do?"

"He'd just watch...and then when we were done, he'd beat us and scream bible verses at us."

"Did this happen to you more than once?"

"Yes. He said he was trying to cure us, and he'd keep doing it until we no longer desired to... 'live like demons'."

"Why did you keep going back?"

"I'd known the bishop for years, since I was a little kid. He was always nice to me and my mom. I loved him. I just knew that whatever he was telling me to do was for my own good, that he wouldn't hurt me, or lead me astray. I thought it was part of the program."

"What program?"

"Southern Baptist Scholars Youth Training for a New Lifestyle Academy." Chuckles sprinkled the courtroom. Even the witness smirked a little.

"I'll have order in this courtroom or I'll clear it!" The judge remained composed.

"My apologies, Your Honor. Darian, why is that funny?"

"After a while, people started saying the program acronym, SBSYTNLA, stood for something else..."

"What was that?"

"Send Bishop Some Young Tail Now, Lord! Amen!"

"And were you still a part of this program when you heard these rumors?"

"I was."

"But you stayed. Why?"

"I didn't have anywhere else to go. It was either 'camp-homo-porn-star' with the bishop or a gang; and my brother and two of my cousins were killed last year. They started recruiting me and the bishop stepped in. He said I only had two options. I could leave him for the gang, and be dead or in jail inside of six months; or I could stay with him, get a real education, work out my deficiencies, and go on to be something great. I kinda thought I could just walk away and not do either, but while I was still in school, the gang stuff was intense. There was a lot of pressure to commit to one of the three gangs that basically ran my school. But, I couldn't do that to my mother; and the bishop promised me that, if I stayed with him, they wouldn't mess with me. And they didn't."

"Are you a homosexual?"

"I honestly do not know."

"How can you not know?"

"I don't know if I feel the way I do about men because I just do, or because I've been conditioned to respond sexually to them. I loved the bishop. I love my brothers from SBSYTLA. "

"Are you attracted to women?"

"I don't know. I think I am, but..." Chauncey paused for a long time.

"I know this is hard to talk about in front of all of these people, Mr. Clifton, but please continue and speak clearly into the microphone."

"I feel wrong, like because of the things I did, I could never be good enough to be with a woman. The bishop said he would cure my desires, but all he did was taught me how to have sex. If anything, I feel like he turned me gay. I was so scared and so shy, when I came to the camp, but after a while... being with the others was all I ever thought about. And it wasn't just the sex. We got really close. I talked to them about everything."

"Did you ever talk to the bishop, or try to explain your feelings?"

"I did a couple of times. I'd leave him messages to call me, or send him texts saying I needed to talk. He said his door was always open to me if I needed him. But, he'd always reply that he'd see me at the next session and in the meantime, I should 'retire, reflect, and read.'"

"What did that mean to you?"

"That I should find a quiet place where I could be alone right away, think about our sessions, not anything in the outside world that might cause me to question my commitment to my training, and read the strategy."

"What's the strategy?"

"It's an outline of his plan to correct us of impure thoughts. It contained scripture that condemns what we were doing and pages about aversion therapy."

"What is aversion therapy?"

"The bishop explained it as a system where 'if the proper action is taken while a man is in the midst of the act that needs correcting, at the precise moment of fulfillment, he would eventually begin to loath the act, and himself, whenever he had those thoughts.' But he said it was important that we not stop on our own, because we could easily get our wires crossed and just remain stuck in the lifestyle. He said we had to be supervised at all times, and if we ever made a mistake and gave in outside of the program, we were to confess to him immediately."

"Did you ever deter from the program?"

"No, but one of my 'mates' did."

"And what happened when you confessed to the bishop?" A tearful young man sat with shoulders slumped and his head bowed so low you could barely see his face.

"I told the bishop that I wanted to leave the camp. I explained that I really was gay and that I didn't want to be cured."

"Why didn't you just stop going?"

"I loved the bishop and I wanted to make him understand, to stop the sexual part of the program; because I believed it was doing more harm than good. I believed he loved me and would listen."

"What was his reaction when you told him?"

"He wouldn't talk to me over the phone or in his office. But he told me he was very happy that I'd come to him, that he was proud of me and the man I'd become. He said since I'd be missing graduation, he wanted to take me on a trip to celebrate my 'advancement'."

"Where did he take you?"

"To this day, I still don't know. We flew on a private jet to some island. There wasn't even an airport. We got off the jet and were greeted by some guy who drove us to a cottage in the jungle. There wasn't even any electricity."

"When you arrived, did you still feel like you were going to celebrate your independence with the bishop?"

"He was still being nice to me, but no; I was scared. He was talking all crazy, like he knew I'd be the one to figure it out first. He gave me champagne; and then I didn't remember what happened after that, but I later found out that we had sex, and I was there for three days."

"You say you had sex, but you don't remember it? How did you find out?"

"When we got back, a week later, he called me into his office and showed me the video tape."

"And you recognized yourself?"

"Yes."

"Were you conscious?"

"Yes, but I looked like I was high, and even seeing it, I don't remember any of the things I did."

"Did he rape you?"

"I don't know." Micah fought back tears. "I wasn't fighting him... I was doing everything he told me to willingly. Even when I looked to be in pain, I didn't speak....I did things to him, too."

"Did he say why he showed you the video?"

"He said that he was disgusted with me. He was ashamed of me; and if I ever told anyone anything that happened at the camp or on the island, he would use it to destroy me and my family. And if I didn't swear to God right then and there that I would never tell a soul, he would kill me and my mother and make it look like an accident or a gang hit. He showed me clippings of murders in the last twenty years that had been dismissed as gang related, as though he wanted me to believe he were really responsible."

"Did you believe him?"

"I had no other choice but to."

"But you got out of the SBSYTNLA for good?"

"Yes."

"Your Honor, the State requests a break and asks that we may call our next witness when we resume tomorrow."

"I agree that we could all use a break. Ladies and gentlemen of the jury, I remind you again that you are not to speak to anyone, including and especially the press, regarding this case. Try and enjoy your evening. We'll resume at nine a.m. tomorrow. Court is adjourned."

Gabby practically ran out of the courtroom and down the stairs. A swarm of reporters were on her heals shouting questions. She was thankful she'd left her car right out front. She glanced at the parking tickets tucked under her windshield wiper and turned on the wipers and fluid until they were soggy, pasty globs of goo and no longer recognizable. She'd beaten all of the hounds, weighted down with their corded mics and out of shape cameramen, to their cars, and was safely around the block and in the hotel parking deck, before they even had their equipment loaded. Inside the deck, she sat and sobbed. "It doesn't have to be true. Daddy's lawyer's said, those boys had motivation to lie. They just want money, and now that it's out there, that he's fighting them back, they have to see it through. They could just be lying now to keep from being arrested, or to have their lies on record for a civil trial. It doesn't have to be true."

18

GABBYLAND

"*T*hese packages arrived for you this afternoon, Mr. Reynolds. Will you be needing anything else this evening?" Ronnie shook his head but didn't look directly at the clerk. He just leaned against the counter and stared into the bar. He couldn't take his eyes off of her. Was she alone? If she were, it was surely by choice. She was in the darkest possible corner in an exclusive hotel. "She wants to be alone." Ronnie smiled to himself and turned toward the elevator. She watched him walk across the lobby and into the elevator. His heart skipped a beat as their eyes finally met and the elevator doors closed.

Inside his room, he hung his garment bag in the closet and tossed his briefcase aside, forgetting for a moment that his laptop was also in there. He also forgot the urgent message to call his producer as soon as he checked in. Instead he brushed his teeth, washed his face and left the room. He breathed deeply as the elevator descended the twenty-two floors to the lobby. "Maybe she's gone." His heart raced as he realized she was still there. He noticed instantly that she'd removed her jacket, revealing her delicately sculpted shoulders. Ronnie shivered a little as he approached the table. "What'd she do that for? Like those legs aren't distracting enough?"

"May I join you?"

She didn't look up. "I can't talk about the trial." Not exactly a 'yes', but he sat anyway.

"Why on earth would I want to talk about that?" He smiled innocently at her.

"You seemed pretty adamant earlier." She turned her head slightly in his direction.

"I was doing my job, Ms. Nichols. As far as I'm concerned, you're as much a victim as the accusers in this case. Besides, I've been wanting to formally introduce myself since Kyle's party."

"Oh yeah, I forgot..."

"Thanks." Ronnie held his left hand to his wounded heart. She watched him. He had nice hands, long, slender fingers, manicured nails and no jewelry.

"I'm sorry, there was a lot going on that day. Of course I remember you, Ronnie Reynolds. I meant I forgot that we'd already met prior to your shoving a microphone in my face today."

"Again, please forgive me. I'm paid to get the big story."

"I'm not the story. There is no story. I wish everyone would just leave us alone. It's just family stuff."

"You may not think so; but your support of your father is courageous. Where does that come from?"

"I told you, I can't talk about the trial."

"I'm not talking about the trial. I'm talking about you. How are you doing it?"

Gabby rolled her eyes and held up her glass. "I drink a lot." Actually, she hadn't had anything stronger than a single glass of wine in her therapist's office, in almost a year, since just after her divorce, before her mother called and told her about Michael and her father.

Ronnie chuckled and stood to leave. She was clearly in no mood for company. "Okay, that's my cue. Enjoy your evening, Ms. Nichols."

"It's Gabby." Her smile stopped him in his tracks and took his breath away, but he kept his cool. He smiled back and held out his hand.

"It's a pleasure to make your acquaintance...again, Gabby." He sat back down and signaled for the waiter to bring two more of whatever she was having.

"Are you following me?"

Ronnie chuckled again. "Not intentionally, I promise. The network made my reservation. I'm waiting on my house to close, but they needed me back here sooner. Are you staying here?"

"Yes."

"I thought you lived here in Atlanta?"

"You know I do, and apparently so does every other reporter in the Southeast. I can barely get down my street, let alone inside my house."

"I'm really sorry about that."

"Please don't tell anyone I'm here."

"Scouts honor." Ronnie held up three fingers and Gabby chuckled.

"What?"

"How could you possibly have figured out I was a girl scout already; and what possible relevance could that have to my father's trial?"

"Uh... none, I didn't." Ronnie's face grew hot. He watched Gabby sip her drink and stare passed him into the lobby. She wasn't thinking about his silly hand gesture, just wondering what was happening to her life. Ronnie stared at her face. She was lovely, with Barbie-doll features carved in Hershey's milk chocolate and natural curls pulled back into a loose twist at the nape of her swan-like neck. No one that beautiful should be so sad. Ronnie knew something about sad.

"Whatever." She seemed to be retreating into that dark place again. Ronnie didn't want her to go. He remembered their original meeting and his conversation with her ex-husband's new husband, his hero, Kyle Rivers-Tye.

"Well, a Girl Scout never forgets, " he said. Gabrielle turned her gaze slowly back to Ronnie.

"I'm listening." After the year she'd had, nothing surprised her anymore. Ronnie searched her face and immediately saw the sadness in her pretty eyes turn to softness. She was a friend.

"Where should I start?"

"How long were you a scout?" They both giggled.

"Daisy to Cadet, so I guess a little more than nine years."

"Ha! I was an Ambassador! I'd still be a Girl Scout if I'd had a daughter." She continued to giggle as she reflected briefly on her childhood. Then she was quiet again.

"What is it?"

"I am surrounded by... otherness..." She took a long sip of her drink. "I'm sorry...it's just that I'm starting to feel like Alice."

"In Wonderland?"

"Yeah."

"You're just magnetic, that's all; special people are drawn to you. I think that makes you pretty special, too."

"Whatever." She stared into her empty glass.

"Why so bitter?" He meant that in the kindest, most sincere way.

"Wouldn't you be if..."

"If what?" Ronnie listened intently, while he watched a reporter from a competing network enter the lobby.

"If the only people you'd ever been attracted to were gay and you weren't?"

"Oh. Yeah, that might bring me down a bit, I guess." Ronnie signaled for the waiter and paid for their drinks. "May I escort you to your room?"

"No thanks. I already know great sex is no indication of one's actual sexual identity."

"Wow. Um, I just thought that you might want to get out of here before the lights and the mics start coming out..." Ronnie gestured to the blond checking in at the desk.

Gabby blushed. Even in her altered state, she knew she'd stuck her foot in her mouth. "Oh. Thank you." She took his hand and he walked her quickly across the lobby and into the elevator.

"What floor?"

"Yours." On her feet for the first time in a couple of hours, the four glasses of bourbon began to kick in.

"Um...I would love to, but if she saw you with me, she'll have no trouble finding you in my room. There's a scandal neither of us need."

"Ooh. You're smart, too." Gabby twirled toward Ronnie, released his hand and wrapped her arms around his neck. Ronnie felt another familiar rush and breathed deeply. For the first time ever he was grateful for his...otherness. A million feelings washed over him, as the most beautiful creature he'd ever seen pressed her body against him; ironically, most of them not sexual.

"What floor, Gabby?"

"Oh, yeah..." She still didn't say, as she reached in her bag for her keycard and slipped it in his shirt pocket, letting her hand rest there.

He breathed deeply. "Gabrielle. Where are we going, Sweetie?"

"Don't call me that! My son's father calls me that when he's mad at me. Shit. So does my father. Don't call me that. Are you mad at me?"

"No. Of course not; but we've been standing in this elevator for five minutes now. I can't get you to your room, if I don't know what floor you're on."

"Oh. That's easy. The penthouse, silly."

"Of course...but why in the world were you down in the lobby?"

"I didn't want to be alone up there. I'm lucky you showed up, huh?"

"No, I'm the lucky one." Ronnie used Gabby's keycard to press the button to the penthouse.

Gabby continued to cling to Ronnie during the express, yet painfully slow ride to the top floor. The doors finally opened and Gabby stumbled slightly into the palatial suite. She seemed completely unfamiliar with her surroundings, but managed to find the phone and called down for a bottle of champagne. Ronnie just watched her. He just wanted to be sure she was safe, then he was leaving. He didn't want to take advantage of her or let her do anything she'd regret. He was relieved that she was hiding out and wouldn't be calling anyone else for company. He was even more relieved when she kicked off her stilettos and climbed into bed with most of her clothes still on. He walked to her bedside and pulled the covers over her shoulders.

She reached up to him. "Don't go. You're nice."

He held her hands and smiled down at her, pointing to the couch at the far end of the suite, through the open bedroom door. "I'll be right over there." Before he made himself comfortable, he called back down to cancel her bottle of champagne. "That's the last thing she needs."

Ronnie sat for a long time watching Gabby before trying to sleep himself. Completely inebriated, she even slept like an angel. No snoring, no drool, no tossing; just the occasional whimper. After several of those puppy-like sounds, he considered lying next to her, even stood to go to her, but then he thought better of it. Wide awake, she was more than a little amorous. No telling what she would do if she stirred and found him in bed with her. And while variations of this moment had played in his head since the moment he first laid eyes on her, he knew this was not the moment. He wanted her, in a million different ways, but drunk and likely to press charges in the morning was not one of them. Besides, he knew it was the bourbon talking, not Gabrielle Nichols. As he became aware of his protective instincts kicking in and overriding his urges, Ronnie felt more masculine in that moment than he had in any of his way too many sexual encounters. Was this the moment his therapist eluded to, when he would 'stop acting like a man and just be one'? His mind wandered and he slowly drifted off to sleep.

Gabby woke in the middle of the night. Still a little tipsy, she looked around and tried not to panic. She watched Ronnie Reynolds sleeping on the couch, recalled the hours before she fell asleep and instantly checked to make sure she had clothes on. She was still wearing her dress and panties. She didn't remember anything happening. If she'd had a blackout, it would be her first. She relaxed a little as she watched him, feeling like a girl again. The only thought she could articulate was "he's so damn cute." Not 'fine' or 'sexy' like Kevin. Ronnie had a quality Gabby could not put her finger on, even as she lay across the bed watching him sleep. In his classically handsome face there was softness, something sweet. The voice was perfect, strong, more alto than tenor, but still, masculine, sultry. And those hands! Gabby closed her eyes for a moment and remembered Ronnie's touch. She let her mind and her hands wander down her own body as she imagined his hands. She sighed as she reached her hemline, which had drifted from just below her knees to the top of her thighs. As soft as it was, the sound she made woke him and he silently bolted upright.

"I didn't mean to wake you." She pulled the covers back over her hips hoping he hadn't noticed where her hands had been.

"I didn't mean to fall asleep." He stood, stretched and walked toward her. Gabby squeezed her thighs together. "I should go." She realized she should see him out and tried to get out of bed and stand without looking like complete trash. She tried to ignore the heat...

She finally made it to the door, and wondered for a moment why he was leaving. Then she wondered why she cared. He was one of them. "Thank you."

If Gabby weren't perfection, Ronnie didn't have a clue. "What for?"

"For keeping me company and for not...for everything."

"It was my pleasure, really..." He paused before turning to the door. "Would you like to have dinner with me tomorrow?"

"Well, the trial is just getting started. I don't want..."

"I understand. I'm sorry I asked. Good night."

"No. Wait. I want to, Ronnie." She touched his bare forearm. Bliss.

"Then meet me - here, somewhere else. I don't care. Just tell me when and where." His sudden burst of enthusiasm startled them both, but only for a moment. He smiled down at her and held out his hand. She stared at it for a long time before taking it. He pulled her toward him, and kissed her slowly. In the second before it happened, she thought "no! I haven't brushed! Yuck!" But as their lips met, the world went away along with her protest. She reached for his face; it was baby-smooth. He caressed her curls and stepped back slowly until his back found the door, pulling her closer to him. She inhaled his scent and sighed deeply. She pulled away slowly. "I'm sorry, I shouldn't have."

"But you did. How did you?" She wasn't angry. She was confused.

Ronnie stared at her. "I don't understand."

"Aren't you gay? How can you kiss me like that, if you don't love women?"

"I never said I was gay, Gabby. And I assure you, I adore women." He reached for her arm and pulled her in again. A little more sober now and a lot more confused, she kissed him back, reluctantly this time. Ronnie thought it would really be okay if the world ended in that instant, and resolved not to move from that spot on the wall. That moment, that kiss, was enough. When Gabby reached for his hands and guided them to her waist and let go, so did he. "I'll see you tomorrow? Eight o'clock?"

Gabby opened her eyes and sighed. But without his touch, the spell was instantly broken, and she returned to the real world. "I can't promise, but I'll try. My brother's supposed to testify tomorrow. I expect it's going to be a very bad day."

Ronnie nodded slowly. "I can imagine. Let me keep you company. I'll even bring dinner. Call me and let me know what you're in the mood for."

"You're very sweet. Why? How do you even have time for all of this? Shouldn't you be working?"

"I do have things to do. They'll get done. I'm taking a break from the show, though, and just freelancing mostly. I've got access to a crew, but there's no pressure..." Ronnie closed his eyes for a moment. No pressure, just his whole world: the woman of his dreams; a trial and a story that could change his career and his life, and a decision to make.

"What?"

He opened his eyes and smiled at her. "That's all. I'll see you tomorrow." He touched her hair and backed into the waiting elevator.

19

WONDERLAND

*R*onnie exited the elevator on the twenty-second floor, scanning the hallway. It was three in the morning and very quiet. If he went to sleep right now, he could get in three hours and still get in his morning run before he needed to be at the courthouse. Three hours sleep would only make him cranky; besides, he couldn't sleep. He thought he might never sleep again. He listened to his messages. "Crap." There were twenty-five of them since that afternoon. His assistant wanted him to know that she'd found out that Bishop Robert Nichols' daughter was staying in Atlanta in the same hotel. He was actually relieved he didn't get that message sooner. He really didn't want to stalk Gabby. What exactly did he think was going to happen here, anyway? He lay across the bed looking at the ceiling, imagining her smile. "It's too soon. You're not ready."

Was he ever gonna be ready? He'd been preparing for this event for the last decade. He'd prayed about it every day. The money was no longer an issue and he'd done all the research. He'd done ten times the required counseling and life work. In twelve weeks Veronica would finally, and in every way be…gone. He should call and cancel dinner. Tell her that she was right and they could see what happened after the trial. But that would be a lie. He wanted to see her now, to hold her now; to be there and protect her from the others. But how can he protect her and not be alone with her? He could be alone with her... just not touch her. He needed to hold back, tell her he just wants to take things slow, get to know each other before things go too far. They'd already gone too far. "It was just a kiss... like the Hope Diamond is just a rock. That's it! That's how you slow things down. That kiss was so amazing and so profound that you're terrified of what comes next, and you don't want to rush or ruin things. So we have to go slow.   Slow is good. In twelve weeks you'll take the trip you've been planning for ten years, and two months later you'll return and make love to ... the reason for it all."

Ronnie flashed his press pass and slid into the press box. He spotted her immediately. She was petite, but she looked positively tiny sitting there alone on the row reserved for defendants'' supporters. He risked life and limb, or at least his iPhone and credentials, to let her know he was there, that she wasn't alone. Gabby frowned when she felt her purse vibrate; but the mom in her wouldn't let her ignore it. Her face brightened immediately.

RONNIE: Good morning Beautiful. How do u look so refreshed?

She turned discreetly to see him sitting behind her and to the left. He winked at her, and she turned to face forward again, grinning at her phone.

Gabby: I should ask you the same thing.

Ronnie: Just popped in 2 c u - Im gonna sneak out n take a nap!

Gabby: No fair!

She shook her head as she typed back, and giggled.

Ronnie: JK kidding. Ill be back here all day. Have u decided what ud like 4 dinner?

Gabby: Surprise me.

Ronnie: Seafood?

Gabby: Love it.

Ronnie: Done. Here we go...

The bailiff called the court to order.

Ronnie arrived at the penthouse at precisely eight-fifteen. He didn't want to appear too eager. He'd already had flowers and wine delivered. He picked up the food himself from a friend's restaurant around the corner from the hotel. He was not risking this evening on room service.

She buzzed him up and met him at the elevator looking exquisite in jeans, bare feet and a baby doll tee. She'd piled her curls high on her head with what looked like a chopstick. "Wow, when you said you'd bring dinner, I expected pizza."

"No you didn't." He walked passed her, put his bags on the table and turned to kiss her, 'hello'.

"Hi," she replied sweetly. "So what do we have here?"

111

"Only the best seafood Portofino south of Manhattan."

"Yum! How did you know?"

"Let's see. You didn't blink when I said 'seafood'; so I figured you liked it all. Lobster is way too pretentious for a first date, and makes for awkward takeout..." He pulled out her chair and looked pointedly at her ass. "...And you clearly are not afraid of carbs."

"Hey!" She giggled.

"And you are not offended. Those jeans are the opposite of conservative. Thank you, by the way."

Gabby went from slightly flushed to blazing, but she kept her cool. "You're welcome." As he opened a bottle of white wine and poured, she checked out the bags and plated the food thinking 'here is a man who knows how to bring home dinner'. "This looks wonderful. Why do I get the impression you've done this before?"

"What, delivered a meal?"

"No, this 'seduction by numbers' thing you have going on." Gabby was nothing if not direct.

"Ouch. And I thought I was following my instincts."

"You know what I mean."

"Yup. You mean I brought you dinner because I read it in some book on how to bed snooty women."

"Hey!" This time he giggled. "I mean you've done this all in such an elegant fashion that it almost looks staged, rehearsed."

"Fair enough. I can find something good in that. Do you want to know the truth?"

"Absolutely."

"I have never brought a beautiful woman dinner in her penthouse suite before; but I do have a fantasy that begins something like this." Ronnie winked at her and turned his attention to his plate of pasta.

They ate in silence for a while, sizing each other up. Gabby had already surmised that Ronnie was polite, chivalrous and well-bred. She knew from watching his career throughout the last year that he was professional, sensitive and kind. She was curious as to why he wasn't doing his show anymore. His coverage of her father's trial looked like a demotion to her; but so far, he appeared to be legitimately on assignment. She'd share her professional advice on their next date, if they had one. She needed to watch him eat to know how much further things would go. She did have a soft spot for southern boys, and Ronnie was born and raised not too far from there. But in the two years she'd been single, she'd had more than her fill of pretty men with bad table manners. She cleared him to 'level two' when he used his spoon to twirl the angel hair without dripping, or slurping the pasta from twelve inches above his plate. She was looking forward to their second date when he used his napkin and chewed without smacking. "So, this fantasy of yours...do tell."

"Oh, no. You know what they say about birthday wishes; if you tell them, they don't come true."

"When's your birthday?"

"Yesterday."

"Okay, now you're lying." Gabby shook her head and laughed.

"Na uh." He reached in his jacket pocket, pulled out his wallet and flipped it open to his driver's license. He'd turned thirty-five on the day before.

"Wow. Nice pic. Happy belated birthday!"

"Thank you."

"You're welcome. So, when's the party?"

"What party?"

"Your birthday party, silly. Aren't you going to celebrate?"

"My birthday? Nah. It's just another day. I celebrate life daily... Wow, did that sound as obnoxious out loud as it did in my head?"

"Only if you didn't mean it, literally. What's so special about the way you live, Mr. Reynolds?" She held her glass and leaned back in her seat.

"Are you really asking me that?"

"Yes, I am."

"Well, let me think about it for a moment."

"You mean 'make something up'."

"Ha! You are brutal! I love it! Actually, there's a good start. Let's start with you."

"No, this isn't about me; this is about you 'celebrating your life'."

"Exactly. I'm talking about how I've become someone who no longer waits for birthdays... "

"Or invitations..." She rolled her eyes at him.

He ignored her. "... to go after something I want. When I met you a year ago, I thought you were the most beautiful women I'd ever seen, and I told myself that one day I'd..."

"You'd what?"

"I'd not wait for an event or a holiday or the perfect moment to kiss you."

"But you never called me. You were waiting for something. Thank you, by the way."

"You're welcome. Fate. That wasn't the right time, for either of us, I suspect. I was seeing someone, actually. And you'd only recently divorced, right?

"Right. But still you waited."

"No. I got myself ready. Don't misunderstand, I have not been sitting around pining away after you. I just realized in that moment that, if and when we met again, I was going to be ready."

"I don't understand."

"Of course you don't, because I'm not being very clear at all. I'm sorry. Let me try again. I've always been painfully shy."

"That's not possible. You accost people, dig into their personal lives, for a living."

"I do, but it's my job; it's not who I am. I know how to turn it on, but I don't let people in. No one knows me, Gabby."

"Okay, you're shy." She took a sip of her wine and braced for the inevitable letdown. It was coming. His yammering on about being 'shy, special, different...' was not going to work on her.

"Debilitating so, believe it or not, but I hid it well. But when I met you... " He didn't speak for a long time and instead just stared passed her.

"Well, thank you for dinner, Ronnie. We'll have to do this again soon." She stood and walked toward the door; and when she passed him, he touched her hand. She stopped and let him take her hand. They were otherwise still.

"Gabby I need to tell you something. I need to tell you who I am." She looked into is green eyes and wanted to run, but she couldn't move. She knew in that instant that whatever it was big.

She didn't want to know; but she also didn't want him to leave, and he was determined that he was going to tell her.

"You don't have to tell me. I really like you, Ronnie. I don't need to know. Can't we just be light?" She was getting nervous.

"See, that's just it. The old me wants to do exactly that. But I know what that gets me. You are so much more than...I want you to know me starting from where we are right here. I can't risk what happens if you don't."

"Okay, now I'm confused and scared." She pulled her hand away and walked to the couch. He watched her until she sat and looked at him. He stood and walked toward her, never taking his eyes off of hers. When he finally made his way across the room, he knelt in front of her, took a deep breath and kissed her slowly. Every fiber of her being responded to him, and she moaned before pushing him away. "No! Stop that! Don't make me feel like that, and tell me you have something to say that will make me not want you anymore! What is it? Are you married?"

"No."

"And you're not gay?"

"Gabrielle, has a gay man ever kissed you like that before?" She thought about that and laughed out loud.

"No! Actually, he never kissed me like that. No one has ever kissed me like that. Please stop torturing me." She pressed her nails into his forearms and he closed his eyes and bit his lip.

"Who's torturing whom?"

"Whatever, I'm not the one with the big announcement. Just tell me, please."

"Can I show you?"

"I don't know, can you?"

Ronnie smiled at the grammar lesson and the challenge. She made him feel invincible. "Actually, I can. May I?"

"Yes, please." With that he held her hands and kissed her again, this time laying her back on the couch. They made out for an hour. He watched her face before sliding his hand down her body to unbutton her jeans. She held her breath but did not speak. The work was already done, and the moment he touched her, she released her breath and wave after wave consumed her. He watched as she trembled and he gently reached inside her for the source of her pleasure. She moaned and clenched his fingers, trying not to scream. With his free hand, he pulled her jeans away and starting from her throat, slowly worked his way down her body until his mouth met his favored hand. She gasped, wrapped her legs around him and tugged at his short black curls. She cried and moaned for another hour, until she finally begged him to stop. "No more! Please. I can't. Oh my God!... Okay, you told me. Get out!" He pulled his hand away and rolled onto the floor below her, laughing.

"And what did I tell you?" He made rude smacking sounds as he licked his fingers.

"That you're a nasty, horny, bastard - and a selfish one at that"

Way to happy to be offended, Ronnie played with her hand as it dangled from her position on the couch, kissing first the palm and then each of her fingertips. He held her hand in both of his for a long while, massaging it lovingly. When her breathing slowed, he pulled her up so that she was sitting and he was kneeling in front of her. She self-consciously pulled her t-shirt down and moved to look for her jeans and panties. He pulled gently and kept her from leaning. "You don't need those, do you?"

"Yes, I do. It's only fair."

"And what's fair about you wearing those tight-ass, low-rise jeans and no bra?"

"I'm a girl. We're allowed to be sexy." She giggled.

"I see. What about men? What are my rights?"

"Oh, now you want to know what you're allowed to do? Service the needs of sexy women?"

"And have your needs been met, m'lady?"

"Uh, yeah, I told you, you can go now." They both giggled. This time, she leaned forward and kissed him deeply.

"Ooh!"

"What?"

"You like it!"

"I don't know what you're talking about. I was just being polite."

"Oh, I see. Thinking about returning the favor perhaps?"

"Exactly." She smiled innocently at him.

"Well, not exactly."

"Oh, here we go again!" She bit his lower lip and scooted close enough that she could reach his buckle.

His bliss was instantly replaced with terror. "Gabby, wait."

"I want to. We don't have to... I just want to touch you."

"And I want you to, but..."

"But, what Ronnie? What are you being so mysterious about? I've seen penises before, at least two of 'em, anyway... I want to make you feel good."

"Trust me, you already have. You do. That's not my issue." He closed his eyes and prayed silently. She watched him until he opened his eyes. Her expression was pure joy, not sex at all. She wanted to know him. He stood in front of her and unbuckled his belt. They both held their breath. "Close your eyes."

"O-kay." She obeyed his odd request, and he reached for her hands as his pants fell to the floor. He squeezed her hands gently, took another deep breath and slid her hand inside his boxer-brief. She smiled instantly at the bunny-soft curls and released her breath as her petite hand slid deeper. She caught her breath and stopped. She opened her eyes, but did not pull her hand away. He looked down at her. She wasn't horrified or disgusted. She looked curious. She moved her hand further still, and gasped when she reached softness like her own. She pulled her hand away and looked slowly at the shapely, hairless legs in front of her. She stood still and bristled when he reached for her. He stepped back slowly and moved to pull up his pants. "No... Please don't move," she whispered. She stared at his face. He was clean shaven, with delicate features, and no Adam's Apple. How did she not know? She stared into his eyes, as if asking permission, but still didn't speak. He guided her hands to his collar. Her hands trembled as she slowly unbuttoned his shirt, revealing a classic white tee. She pulled it away. Her eyes widened. "He's got knockers?" Wonderland. He held his breath as she found the Velcro closure and began to unwrap him. Tears rolled down his cheeks and his breath quickened. She cried with him. "I don't understand. Why are you crying?"

"Why are you?"

"You're so beautiful." Her hand still trembled, as it climbed up his torso to his perfect breasts and rested. They giggled nervously and spoke simultaneously. "Wow." She lifted her face and he bent to kiss her. She finally took her hand away, only to wrap her arms around him. The sound that escaped him was sweet and soft and she squeezed him. "It's okay."

"Really?"

"Better than okay". She reached for his hair and melted into him, then she led him by the hand to the bed.

"Don't you have questions?" Ronnie asked as they lay facing each other.

"Oh, thousands... I just don't know where to start. Help me? Wait. This is what you wanted me to know, right?" He blushed and closed his eyes. When he opened them, she was smiling at him.

"Yes. This is it; no pun intended."

"Don't do that. Don't make jokes like that."

"Why not? I've heard them all. I've actually got some really good ones. They don't bother me, Gabby; and I think it's empowering to own what others try to use to hurt you."

"Okay. Just let me get used to this before you take your little show on the road, please."

"Is this something you think you can get used to?"

"I don't know. I'm still trying to wrap my head around it. Maybe trying to think it through is bad idea. I just never imagined... Wow. I had no idea. I couldn't have guessed if my life depended on it. Oh my God!... You told me you were a Girl Scout!"

"Yes, I did." He laughed with her.

"Wow. Okay. What's your real name?"

"Well, my legal name is Ronnie; you saw my driver's license. But my birth name is Veronica."

"Veronica." Gabby whispered and reached for his hair.

"Please don't, Gabby. I'm not her anymore. I never felt like her. I tried. I did everything little girls are supposed to do, and I sucked at and hated all of it."

"But I bet you were a beautiful little girl."

"I guess I was pretty; but I never felt feminine. I've been trying to explain it to my mother my whole life, hoping that she'd finally admit that something went wrong, that I wasn't meant to be a woman."

"How does she handle it?"

"She tries, but she won't replace the pictures of me as a little girl with who I am now. I know she loves me, but she does not understand."

"And your father?"

"Has been amazing from the beginning; almost like he did know." Ronnie looked away. "And my brother and sister have been awesome, both of them. It's funny, I guess because I'm the youngest, they never had any expectations of me. They just let me be me, and love whoever that is. My sister has actually been helping me do the research."

"That's awesome. What research?"

"For my reassignment surgery. I'm scheduled to have the first part done in twelve weeks."

"The first part?"

"Getting rid of these things..." Ronnie pointed at his breasts. "I'll have the rest done in a year or so..."

"And then you'll be...?"

"And then I'll be a real live boy!" Ronnie's grin made them both giggle. Then Gabby raised her hand and waited to be called on."

"Yes, Gabrielle."

"What's wrong with the way you are now?"

"I'm not a man. I mean I am; but I'm a man stuck in this ridiculous body."

"There are women, and men by the way, who would give anything to be stuck in your body. It's a beautiful body. And from what I can tell so far, you're more man than any I've ever met. Wait, I'm not the best reference, actually. My ex-husband's gay. Well... I guess he's manly enough... but I would never have known, if you hadn't told me. I think I thought you were gay... but that's just because you're so... metro... Is that a bad thing?"

"No, I guess that's what I was going for. I've never thought I could pull off rugged." Ronnie closed his eyes, enjoying Gabby's kisses, as she explored his face. "So, thank you, but... I want more. I want the whole experience."

"Like what?   What are you missing?"

"Being able to pee standing up, for one."

"Oh, I can do that!"   Gabby laughed.

"Okay, Gabe, have you ever given a blowjob before?"

"Can I plead the fifth?"

"Permission to treat the witness as hostile, Your Honor? How long were you married?"

"Eight years."

"And how long did you date before then?"

"Practically forever, but officially, from the time I was fifteen; with about a four year break while we were in college."

"Yeah, you've given a blowjob."

"Hey!" Gabby pulled her pillow over her head.

"Oh stop it! You did it because it is a perfectly natural thing for a man and his partner to experience. I want to know what that feels like."

"I bet it probably feels similar to what women feel, you know except for the sucking part. An orgasm is an orgasm. Don't you think?"

"I wouldn't know."

"What do you mean you wouldn't know? I've heard you leave the building several times just with me. Were you faking?"

"Of course not! Are you kidding me? I've never felt so...wow. I never really liked being on the receiving end, that is."

"That's amazing."

"Not really. I don't like to be touched like that anymore; and the women I've dated... Let's just say, that hasn't been our dynamic. I present myself as a man. There are no expectations of reciprocation."

"But you used to?"

"Actually, no, never... well, once... and I didn't like it."

"Oh. Well, I guess that's okay... but..."

"What is it?"

"I like being able to reciprocate."

"So you've been with women before?"

"No!" Gabby buried her face in her pillow. "But you're not a woman... right..."

"Right...wow...You're something else. How are you so cool

with all of this, Gabby?"

"I don't know. Trust me, people who know me wouldn't believe it either. I'm as blown away as you are. Just don't be surprised if I don't remember any of this in the morning."

"I'll be devastated, to say the least; but thanks for the warning. And they obviously don't know you."

"Seriously, wow, Ronnie. This is a lot. Why are you telling me? Is this standard first date material?"

"Of course not. I've only ever told one other person. Before her I was in a long term relationship with someone I've known most of my life. She knew me as a girl."

"What happened? Why aren't you with her?"

Ronnie was quiet for a long time as he thought about his first love. "We were, are, the best of friends, but... believe it or not, and if you ever meet her, I'll deny that I ever said it, but I think we're too much alike. Once we got over the kid stuff, the exploration and figuring out who we were, we just weren't compatible. She's what you call a 'stem'..." Ronnie waited while Gabby raised her eyebrow. "Combination 'stud' and 'fem'. Basically, she's a very aggressive lesbian. That's not all stems, there are a million variations. For instance some studs can be downright docile, and they're only butch in their appearance. Shawn is the opposite. She looks like... well, like you, actually... but she really thinks and acts like a man."

"So your problem was... intimacy?"

"No... everything. Yes, sex was a problem. It was a constant power struggle, and not in a good way... But the relationship was awkward too after a while. I'm a Scorpio and she's a Leo..."

"Yikes. So basically, when you weren't having sex, you were fighting."

"Yeah, well, and when we were. So, enough about..."

"Wait. So do you still talk to her?" Gabby tried to get the information without sounding jealous.

"I kinda have to. She' s my agent."

"No way."

"Yup."

"Oh boy."

"It's actually pretty cool. We were just meant to be friends.

Once we figured that out..."

"Okay, and since her?"

"Oh, well, I've only ever been in one other committed relationship. That was Rachel. That ended about a year ago. We were together for about two years."

"Why did it end?"

"She broke up with me when I started talking about coming out."

"As a woman?"

"No, as a trans man. She didn't want me to tell anyone. She figured I kept it a secret from her, I should be able to hide from the world."

"Whoa."

"Yeah. It was never going to work. It was my fault. We started off wrong. I didn't trust her enough to be honest with her from the beginning; and when she found out, it was over... for a while, anyway."

"How long did it take for her to find out?"

"A few months."

"What? How?" Gabby sat up in the bed. Ronnie pulled the blanket over his chest.

"I just didn't let her see me."

"Oh. Ohhh! But you've got breasts...and no...and a..."

"It's easier than you might think for a man to have sex without taking his clothes off. I just always found a reason to keep a shirt on; and well, I always had equipment."

"Do you have it now?"

"No. I threw it all away when we split."

"I'm so confused."

"They make fantastic prosthesis these days. I was always packin'. For a while, I wouldn't be caught without... my manhood."

"So when did you stop?"

"About a year ago, when I met you."

"Coincidence, right? I didn't have anything to do with that."

"Yes and no. Actually, it was Kyle."

"Come again?"

"Your wish is my command." And with that he slid under the covers and she erupted in giggles as he kissed her thighs.

"Stop it! Seriously, what did Kyle have to do with your suddenly leaving home without your manhood?"

He popped his head out of the blankets. "Not that, silly. I told him I was trans. He's a hero of ours, you know; and he asked me if I'd come out to anyone. I hadn't, but I'd been thinking about it. For some reason, I've wanted to. I told Rachel and she broke up with me. It really was an incredible relief, despite how it turned out. And then I thought about you. And I realized that I really, really didn't want to lie anymore, ever again. I didn't really think in a million years that you would want me; but I decided then and there that I wouldn't risk losing someone else that I loved by lying."

"That's the most flattering thing anyone has ever said to me. Wow. But, I still don't get why you're flying without a net." They both laughed.

"That's exactly what it was! Keeping eight inches on me at all times made it really easy to fake it. It was too big a temptation. Before I met you, I couldn't ask a woman out for coffee, but I could meet her in my dressing room, anywhere, and screw her brains out. That was easy, and addictive...and soul-deadening. I started to feel like I was dying just a little bit every time I did it. "

"Did you do that while you were in a relationship?

"Yup, and for years before."

"But you stopped."

"I'd been clean for three hundred eighty-five days, yester-day."

"You're lying."

"Nope."

"Why fall off the wagon now?"

"And miss my shot at my dream girl?" He kissed her tum-my.

"But we didn't have to have sex."

"You're right; and by some standards we haven't."

"But by yours?"

"It's been the most amazing, exhilarating experience of my life."

"So you don't miss whatever you get from...your equip-ment?"

"Surprisingly, no. I could do this forever. Wow. Did I say

that out loud?"

"Yeah." She ran her fingers through his hair. "Don't get me wrong. I feel like a princess. You're amazing; but..."

"What is it, Baby?"

"I can't believe I'm saying this, but I don't think I'm selfish enough. I don't want to just lie here and have you serve me. I like to give back."

"Well, do you dance?' He chuckled.

"Ha ha. And, yes. I guess I'm saying I want to do more."

"And when I'm fitted with my shiny new man-parts, you can."

"But what if we, you, don't like it... more than without? What if being made love to as a women is better for you?"

"I'll never know."

"Why do you keep saying that?" She straddled him and slid down his body and began to grind slowly against his underwear.

"What are you doing?"

"Just checking things out." She reached forward and tried to slide her hand under his t-shirt.

"Baby, please. Really, I told you, I don't need that."

"Well, a very wise man once told me, 'it's not about need'." She stopped grinding and kissed his face. "You said you wanted me to know you. I think it's going pretty well, don't you?" She kissed his throat and collar bone and let her hands rest on his stomach.

"Um... yes?"

"Do you want me to stop?"   He breathed heavy.

"... No."

"No, 'don't' or 'no, don't stop'?"

"No, I want you to know me." She kissed his cheeks and lingered for a long time before pulling off his shirt, revealing full, perfect breasts. She breathed deeply. She'd never actually touched another woman before. The light from the open window illuminated their bodies and she marveled at the contrast of her milk chocolate against his creamy olive tan. Gabby tried not to rush, kissing each erect rose-colored nipple slowly, softly and finally sucking just hard enough..."

Ronnie moaned and ran his fingers through her hair. Gabby played there until she felt Ronnie's hips move below her. "I don't know what to do, " she whispered against his belly. Ronnie held her hand and guided it below his waistband. Gabby slowly slid the briefs off and tossed them aside, and kissed the tops of Ronnie's thighs. He stiffened and she hesitated. "I can stop. I'm sorry." Gabby crawled back up the bed.

"Are you kidding? Oh baby. I'm sorry. I... I'm seventeen all over again. Okay, this is the opposite of manly"

"Stop it. You said, no labels, right?"

"Right. ...I think I'm scared. No one has touched me there in a very, very long time." The words were out before he could stop them. He'd never admitted that to anyone, not even Shawn. But for the first time in his life, he wanted real intimacy, not just physical pleasure. Gabby understood.

"Not even you?"

"Actually, no."

"Maybe we should start there?" Gabby took Ronnie's hand and kissed and licked his fingers and slowly guided his hand. She took her own free hand and slid it between her legs. She closed her eyes and kissed him while rubbing the back of his hand until it rocked back and forth on its own. When his rhythm and intensity matched her own, she released and returned to his breasts and rocked slowly against his thigh. She came first, hard, and clawed at his arms, still suckling his right breast. Her sounds were really all he needed and he exploded releasing a sound neither had heard before. It was distinctly feminine and made Gabby grin with satisfaction. Her hand slipped down and she gasped. Ronnie grabbed her hand as if to pull it away. She nuzzled his breasts like a kitten, until he purred and his hand fell away. She rubbed him gently until he moved against her hand and exploded again and again and again.

20

TALK AMONGST YOURSELF

*G*abby hummed and talked to herself in the shower, as she reflected on the previous forty-eight hours. "Mmm. But, now what? He's a woman. No, he's a man, who was born a woman? But, he feels like a woman. How do you know? 'Cause I'm a woman. So what does that make you? Oh, gee whiz. I am not tellin' Kevin." Speak of the gay ex-husband...and the phone rings. She let it go to voicemail and lingered a little longer. "Really, Gabby? Can you date a woman? Well, I wouldn't really be dating a woman; Ronnie's a man. Right. Ronnie is a man. Apparently, nobody knows Ronnie's not a man. But he feels like a woman, and you really like it...Ooh, you nasty. But he's so pretty. I'm so confused."

She turned off the shower, moisturized and exited the bathroom wearing only the towel on her head. She practically fluttered to the window to open the curtains and let in the mid-morning light. She'd been gloriously naked for two solid days, no need for modesty now. Besides, who was going to see her all the way up here? She grabbed a bottle of water, her phone and laptop and lay across the freshly made bed. "Oh, how I love on-demand maid service."

She checked in with her office. All was well on the work front. Her newest clients were behaving well; well, as well as could be expected. They hadn't gotten arrested, yet. She got all tingly again recalling her latest professional triumph. She'd landed personal representation deals for all five of the Atlanta Shakers' newest starters. Her weighty commissions of their ridiculous salaries would be well earned, but it was worth it. She could cut back on her workload a little, learn to delegate more. Although it had not been part of her master plan; she'd done it because she loves them both, but representing her ex's new husband was the smartest thing she had ever done professionally. Her work for him helped earn him an American Music Award, a mainstream gospel recording contract, and real airtime on gospel radio. His career was soaring, and hers took off right along with it. The professional management world was all abuzz over what she was able to do for the talented, but humble, gay, Canadian preacher. Who was she to point out that it was all God, and a little bit of the artist himself? That labor of love did for her new PR firm, almost instantly, what took her years to do working for Tillman &Pharr (T&P). Allowing their son, Ethan to live with his dads in Canada gave her time to focus on her clients; and in less than two years, she was earning more than her highest paid client-athletes. Work-life was good.

Home-life was...complicated. After leaving T&P, and surrendering the farce that was her marriage to Kevin, there was no need to keep the house in North Carolina. It was actually more cost effective to buy homes in New York and Atlanta than it was to rent hotel rooms. Sure, she was successful, rich by some standards, but she wasn't stupid. She just hoped she'd be able to return to the house in Atlanta, eventually. Since news broke of her father's trials for child molestation and rape, and fraud and tax evasion, the press wouldn't leave her alone. Her dad was safely tucked away in a prison cell, unable to make bail or receive visitors, and shielded daily from the press.

Her mother had divorced him immediately, and made it more than abundantly clear that she would not be speaking to anyone about their forty-two year marriage, church business, or Michael...and the others. Every board member, staff member and virtually all of the two-thousand congregants of the church he'd pastored for over thirty years distanced themselves, as more and more charges were filed and victims stepped forward. Gabby was the only person to appear in support of her father. She wasn't there because she believed in his innocence; that was for a jury to determine and ultimately for God to judge. She was there because he was her dad and, whatever other sins he might be guilty of, he'd never been anything but good to her. He'd seen her through a lot, and she would not abandon him. But she wasn't going to talk about it. It wasn't news worthy, or anyone else's damn business.

She rolled her eyes at Ronnie's assertions about her 'courage'. "What the hell does he know about courage? Oh. Right. Actually...nope. I'm still confused." She rolled over and slid her hand down her torso, getting ready to reenact the high points from her trip down the rabbit hole, when the phone rang again. She picked it up. It was Kevin, and so was the call she missed while she was in the shower. He never called unless something was wrong. "Hey, KJ, what's going on? Is EJ okay?"

"That depends. We're on our way home, now. Gabrielle, who the hell is Tre Aiken, and why does he think he's my son's father?" Gabby choked and gagged on her water and dropped the phone.

Ronnie used the guest key to let himself into the penthouse. It had been a very, very good two days. But, somehow, Gabby had forgotten he was coming back.

"Hi." Ronnie watched her as she threw things into a suitcase she'd laid out on the bed. He couldn't kiss her because she hadn't stopped moving. "Are we running away together?"

"No." She ignored the sentiment. "I have to get to Toronto. I have to get to my son." She never looked at him; she just kept tossing things into the trunk. Having added what looked like months' worth of underwear, two giant bottles of shampoo and conditioner and fourteen pairs of shoes, she closed the bag. She turned to the closet and tossed a garment bag and four suits on the bed. In the split second that she finally faced him, he saw that she'd been crying. She looked terrified.

"Gabby. Stop. Please tell me what's going on."

"I can't stop, Ronnie. I have to get to the airport and see if I can get on a flight. Now."

"Don't worry about that. I can get you on a plane; and I will, as soon as you tell me what's going on...please." He finally stood in front of her, blocking her path to her luggage.

"I can't. Please, just move, Ronnie. I have to go." She still wouldn't look at him. He turned toward the door. The very thing he'd feared all along - that kept him from coming out to other women before her - was actually happening. She said it might. She'd was fine when he left, but now, she was really going to great lengths to get away from him.

"Okay." He stood watching her before leaving. "I really thought you were different." He couldn't help it. He had to say it out loud. He was devastated.

"What?" She whispered as she turned to him. Her voice was hoarse from crying. "No. Ronnie, no! This isn't about you! I have to go! I've done something horrible, and I have to make it right." He stared at her. She really did seem genuinely upset. She was actually freaking out a little.

"You've done something horrible...to your son?" This really wasn't about him. He softened his shoulders a little. He'd been standing taller, trying to make it out of there without letting her see him cry.

"Yes; not just my son, to everyone...Please, Ronnie. I can't do this right now, but I promise it's not you. I...I really like you. I'm sorry." She walked toward him and touched his face. But it felt like 'good-bye' to him. Then she let her hands fall to his chest, her forehead rested there and she began to sob. He wrapped his arms around her, and held on until she could speak. He sat her on the bed and got her a glass of water.

"What's happened, Baby?"

"I can't tell you? It's too horrible. It's too much."

"Excuse me? You're telling me, 'My name is Veronica, but you can call me Ronnie' that you have a secret too big and too horrible for me to handle? And did you forget that we're here because your father, the bishop, is accused of molesting your brother? We've got 'too much' and 'horrible' covered. Has Kevin done something? Please don't tell me it's Kyle."

"No! They're the best parents in the world. They are Ethan's fathers!"

"Is someone disputing that?"

"Yes."

"Who?'

"Ethan's real father."

"Oh. Well, that's okay. You just need a good lawyer to tighten up your custody stuff. I know a guy." Ronnie didn't get it.

"You don't understand. I lied. Ethan isn't Kevin's, and now his birth father has come out of nowhere and is demanding custody!"

"Whoa. Okay." There was no way she would make up a tale like that. "Did he know you had a baby?"

"No."

129

"How do you think he found out?"

"I have no idea. The only thing I can think of is that perhaps he saw us all on TV last year. But why now?"

"How do you know all this?"

"Kevin just called. The asshole actually showed up at their house. Ethan was there with his nanny!"

"Did he talk to him?

"No, Heather sent him away and called Kevin and Kyle immediately."

"Oh boy. How is Kevin?"

"About to spontaneously combust. He doesn't believe it's even possible."

"Is it?"

"Yes."

"Oh boy. Okay, let's get you to Toronto..." He kissed her temple and rubbed her back while he called Libby, who now worked, conveniently, for Air Canada. Gabby's flight would leave in two hours.

"That was impressive. Thank you." Gabby couldn't think straight. She could easily have called her assistant and had her book a flight; but she was barely able to articulate what was happening to Ronnie. She couldn't handle another person right now.

"No need. This is exactly what 'friends and family passes' are for...I didn't even ask...do you want me to come with you?"

"No. I couldn't ask you to do that. You've done enough. I have to come right back anyway. Court resumes Wednesday. Will you still be here when I get back?" She wrapped her arms around him.

"Counting the seconds." He looked at his watch. "We have to go, Baby. He looked at her luggage on the bed. "How long were you planning to be gone?"

"Just two days...Oh, I guess I overdid it a little. I'm a nervous packer. And a girl can never have too many pairs of shoes." She tried to be light.

"Right...but if you could cut that down a little, I could give you a lift to the airport."

"Is your trunk full of bodies?" She squinted and smiled at him.

"No trunk." He walked to the closet and found a bag that would fit. "You do not need fourteen pairs of stilettos for a two-day trip, anyway."

"You don't know what I need." She put her hands on her hips and rolled her neck.

"Really?" He grabbed her wrists and kissed her, savoring the mixture of salt and mint. He liked that, too; but vowed in that instant that he'd never be responsible for the tears. When he let go, she wobbled a little, before she started filling the smaller bag with her essentials.

"Fine." She finished and sat on the bed, as if waiting to be rewarded. He stood in front of her and she held her breath.

"Let's go." He grabbed her bag and kissed her on her fore-head. She stood and grabbed a pair of heels from the pile of discarded travel items. "No, those won't work." He looked in the closet and found a pair of black, cross-trainers, size six. She frowned at him.

"This had better be good." She slipped on the sneakers, tossed her heels in her purse while he grabbed a lightweight leather jacket from the closet.

He held her hand in the elevator; and she looked up at him when they skipped the lobby and went straight to the parking deck. "I don't trust my baby to valet parking."

"O-kay..." Gabby thought Ronnie was fun, and so far she felt safe with him. Then she met 'his baby'. "I beg your pardon?" She stared at the shiny orange motorcycle and two matching hel-mets. "I'm not gettin' on that. And I'm definitely not wearing one of those." She pointed to the enemy of women and stylists every-where.

"Do you have a car here?" He grinned at her.

"No, but I have a car service on speed dial." She smiled back.

"That's silly, and we don't have time." He strapped her bag to the rack on the back of the large bike. He put on his helmet and helped her with hers, taking extra care to tighten the chin strap. Then he hopped on, started it up, and turned to her, holding out his hand. "Come on, baby. I promise I won't go too fast."

She needed to get to Canada. There was no time for this

nonsense; besides, if she died in a fiery crash on her way to the airport, Kevin wouldn't be able kill her. "Why don't I believe you?" She ignored his hand and hoisted herself onto the back of his motorcycle all by herself. As she wrapped her arms around him, he smiled to himself. He was impressed, but not surprised.

She squeezed him tightly as he maneuvered swiftly, but carefully, through the traffic in downtown Atlanta. She smiled behind her helmet, forgetting for a moment the real world and the very big mess that was waiting for her. They made it to the airport with time to spare and had no trouble at the counter. "Please tell your sister I said, 'thank you, so much'."

"You can thank her yourself when you meet her."

"I'd love to. When will that be?"

"Soon. We'll arrange something when you get back."

"If I get back."

"Don't do that, Gabby. Everything's going to be okay."

"Okay. I'll try. Thank you, Ronnie." She kissed his cheek. He'd come as far as he could.

He kissed her slowly. "Hurry back."

21

WHERE'S A TERRORIST, WHEN YOU NEED ONE?

*G*abby settled into her business-class seat thinking, "wow, I wish I had a sister..." When Libby said she could get Gabby on the next flight to Toronto, she assumed it would be coach. As the flight attendant approached to get her beverage order, reality and then guilt began to set in. "I'll just have water with lemon, please, thank you." She didn't want to drink, and in fact, considered she may never drink again. She didn't really believe it was all the champagne she had on the night (she'd convinced Kevin) that Ethan was conceived that set off the spree of lies, that led to this day; but it probably didn't help. "Face it, sistah, there is a lot more going on with you than a little too much Dom every now and then." Gabby had known what she was doing when she tossed her condoms in the trash before she left California. She knew what she was doing when she waited exactly four weeks from the night of their reunion to tell Kevin she was pregnant. She needed to give him enough time to get his head around the idea, while leaving enough time to safely have an abortion if he could not. "He sure did come around a lot faster than I expected him to." It took Kevin a little more than twelve hours to call her and propose (well, sort of); and he never questioned her after that. Perhaps that's why she never questioned him, and why she let him off the hook so easily when he came out. Gabby really had always suspected Kevin was gay, she just accepted that he'd made a choice not to be. "Huh. That's funny. Homosexuality is not a choice, but one can indeed choose not to be... But what kind of choice was that?" She knew they'd been living a lie, and the only truth to their life together was Ethan. Her baby saved her life. Over the years, she convinced herself that he saved Kevin's too. What might he become if she didn't step in and give him a family? "You're an idiot!" Gabby lived for nearly eight years knowing she'd taken away Kevin's choices. And when he came out to her, she realized instantly that what she'd done was far worse than what he had actually done, which was simply fall in love. She never thought she'd ever be strong enough to tell him the truth. How could she tell him that the child he'd given up control of his life for wasn't his, that she'd planned the deception from the beginning? "No!" It was punishment enough living with the fact that the only man she'd ever loved didn't love her more than he loved another man. She could face the world knowing that truth; but she could not look at the man she loved and tell him the son he loved was not his. "Oh God, please help me. I don't know what I'm going to do, but I'll do whatever I have to do - whatever You want me to do. Just please, don't let that man take Kevin's son from him."

Gabby exited the terminal and looked around, trying to determine where the nearest cab stand would be. Before she found it, Kevin found her. She'd texted him before she boarded the plane. He and Kyle had already booked their flight back when he called her. They'd been waiting for her for an hour. Kyle was getting the car. The nausea returned when she saw Kevin's face. Fortunately, she was all puked out.

"Kevin, I can explain."

"The only acceptable explanation will be that he's lying or crazy; but you wouldn't have flown here if either of those things were true, would you?"

"No."

"No, what, Gabrielle; he's lying or crazy, or you're not here?" This was really going to be bad.

"He's not crazy."

They walked outside just as Kyle, the angel of perfect timing, was pulling up. He got out and gave Gabby long hug. "Hi, Gabby."

"Kyle, I'm so sorry."

"It's going to be okay. Everything happens for the good of those who believe, Gabrielle." She smiled at him and thought, 'how come when he says my name, I don't think I'm about to be grounded or stabbed?'

Kevin, Kyle and Gabby rode in silence to the couple's home in Toronto. They entered through the garage, and Kyle grabbed Gabby's bag and followed them inside.

"Mom!" Ethan flew down the stairs, across the living room and flung himself into Gabby's arms. "What are you doing here?"

"Would you believe I came all this way because I needed one of your hugs?"

"No."

"Well, I did. And I'm good now. I'm going back right after dinner." She teased.

Ethan laughed. "Hey Pops. I thought you guys were going to be gone til next Friday."

"You heard your mom. We needed hugs." Kevin squeezed him tightly. "And meat! Whatcha cookin' for dinner?"

"My parents are nuts... "

"Com'on kiddo, help me cook while your mom and P1 talk." Kyle rubbed Ethan's head and directed him to the kitchen.

"Can I use your new knife?"

"Uh...no."

Kevin and Gabby went upstairs to the guest room. "Gabrielle, please tell me this is some horrible mistake."

"I wish more than anything in the world that it were, but it's not. I'm so sorry."

"Who is this guy?"

"Someone I was dating just before we got back together."

"Did you come to New York to trick me into marrying you?"

"No! It wasn't like that. I loved you. I wanted us to be a family. I never wanted to be with him, and when I thought I was pregnant, I ran to you. I didn't even tell him. And I was going to tell you. I kept saying I would tell you. I wanted to tell you."

"Well, what happened?"

"It was like you said, everything was different than we thought it would be. I expected you to be sitting around waiting for me to make your life complete, but it was already full. Your career was soaring. You didn't even need my help with that. You didn't need me. You weren't the quiet little boy I grew up with; and I was no longer the prettiest girl in town. I didn't have anything special to offer you, except nostalgia... I thought you would say you couldn't do it. I was prepared..." She held her head in her hands. "... not to even have the bab..."

"'The baby?...You mean 'Ethan'. So you're telling me that you were thinking all of these wonderful things about me, that you loved me, and needed me, and didn't think I needed you... but you thought that you could tell me you were having my child and there was a chance that I might not want him? You get how that doesn't make any sense, don't you? You can't say you knew me and remembered me to be this wonderful person, but you didn't really know that I wouldn't tell you to abort our child! Did you consider what might have happened if you told me the truth, that he wasn't mine?"

"I didn't want to think about it. I decided that wasn't even an option. If you weren't going to be his father, he wasn't going to have one. I wouldn't have had him. There was no other option."

"Don't you think I deserved the right to choose for myself?"

"Of course, I do, KJ. I know what I did. I know what I took from you... I know how wrong I am... and you know I know. Think about it..."

Kevin was silent for a long time. "Is this why you reacted so calmly when I came out?"

"If you call that 'calm', yes. I think so. I was still afraid. I knew I'd lost you; but I didn't want Ethan to lose you, too."

"See, you're doing it again. You're telling me you lied to me because I'm good, but you kept lying because I might have walked out on a child I love and have raised for ten years because of some DNA. You truly are insane."

"Kevin, please. I'm not trying to justify why I lied. I know there is no reasonable explanation. I get that it doesn't make sense. I'm just trying to be as honest as I can now. I'm so sorry. I'll do whatever I can to make it right."

"What if it can't be fixed, Gabby?" A tear streamed down Kevin's cheek. He didn't really care about how they got there. He was hurt and scared and lashing out.

"I'll do whatever I have to. It has to be okay. I won't let that man take your son away from you. Just tell me you still want him."

"I'm going to ask you for the last time to stop saying stupid shit." Kevin shot Gabby a look she'd never seen before. It said what she'd feared, that he hated her and she'd done something unforgiveable. She shut her eyes quickly as the tears poured silently.

"Oh God, please help me." She prayed silently and reached for his hand. When he didn't pull away, she squeezed it tightly and spoke with her eyes still closed. "KJ, I don't know what to do or say right now. For most of our lives you've been my best friend, and I promise you the only man I've ever loved. I lied to you because I was afraid, and I was selfish and stupid; but I did it because I couldn't imagine my life without you. I kept lying because I couldn't bear... not just Ethan losing you, but my losing you. Your love and friendship, sharing that amazing tiny human with you have been...I don't know who I am without him...and I know he wouldn't be here if not for you... please forgive me. Please, tell me what you need me to do to make this right."

Kevin listened with his eyes closed and didn't let go of her hand. He prayed more than he listened. Being angry at Gabby wasn't going to help them. He opened his eyes and watched her. "Why does he look so much like me?" He asked softly.

"Because he's your son, Kevin. The details don't matter. Do you have a lawyer here in Canada?"

"Not one who can handle this. I can get a referral."

"Let's start with this guy." Gabby pulled out the piece of paper Ronnie had given her. "He's a friend of Ronnie's and he specializes in family law."

"Is he good?"

"Sounds like it, he graduated second in his class from Harvard Law School."

"And he's licensed to practice in Canada?"

"He's from here."

"Okay. Let's start with... Aidan Crawford." Kevin stood up and turned toward the door.

"Okay." She stood slowly and followed him until he stopped and turned back to her.

"I do forgive you, Gabby. I'm just scared."

"I know you are. I'm... Thank you."

"I love you." He hugged her and cried and smiled, accepting for the moment that they would be okay.

22

Where Am I?

"*H*old it together..." Gabby whispered to herself as she spotted Ronnie waiting for her in the airport. "We're going slow..." if by slow she meant one of those NASCAR pace-cars... They'd spoken every night for hours during the week she was in Toronto, about everything except the current issue of her son's paternity. Once she arrived in Canada and assessed the situation, and Kevin and Kyle were only concerned with fixing the mess with their family intact, as opposed to destroying her, she was able to do what she did best, multi-task. She really was excited about Ronnie. "He's so amazing..."

"Mmm." He greeted her with one of those long, slow kisses that made her knees wobble. "Hi," was still all she could say, when he kissed her like that.

"See, I told you, you'd make it back in one piece... and more beautiful than when you left."

"Wow! An 'I told you so' and a compliment in one tiny sentence...you *are* good." She teased.

"You aint seen nothin' yet." He winked at her, effortlessly slung her carryon over his shoulder and took her free hand. He watched her as she moved from side to side, attempting to hide the full-size bag that she apparently purchased and filled during her six day trip to Canada. He let her roll it all the way to the car, and finally shook his head and chuckled as he tossed it in the trunk of his orange (to match the motorcycle) '68 Mustang.

When he saw her visibly relax, so did he. "So, is Aidan working out?" The one thing Gabby and Ronnie discussed and agreed on about her situation was that it would be best to keep it quiet. She'd devoted a large part of her career to protecting some of her most famous clients from public paternity disputes. She'd worry about the damage to her credibility later. But she was thankful that she didn't have to contact any of her own professional allies, yet.

"He's wonderful, thank you. We filed a temporary restraining order, keeping Tre away from us, until we can get to court. Aidan's already prepared the counter documents. He says it is highly unlikely that a judge will give Tre even partial custody, considering our history and how solid Kevin and Ethan are." As she watched the rain outside the passenger window, her voice trailed off.

"What is it, Baby?"

"I still can't believe I did that to him. I can't believe I lied to him for ten years... I ruined his life."

"Is that what he said?"

"No. He said he forgives me, but..."

"No buts. Believe him. Accept it. Forgive yourself." Ronnie spoke firmly, as he squeezed her hand.

"I can't. What if we get a judge who had something like this happen to him, and he wants to make an example of us?"

"Stop it, Gabrielle. Did you love Kevin when Ethan was born?"

"Yes. I'd never stopped loving him, until I had to."

"Does he love Ethan?"

"Oh yes, he couldn't possibly love him more... I mean if he'd known... He just... He's such a good father, Ronnie."

"I believe that. Aidan will make sure the judge gets that, too. Do we have a court date, yet?"

"Ha! Yes, the same week my dad's trial is supposed to end!"

"Oh, boy. Okay... so we've got about eleven weeks to pray and prepare."

"Yes... but can we start tomorrow?" Gabby sounded very small; and when Ronnie looked at her again, he saw her wipe away a single tear. He reached up and stroked her hair.

"It's going to be okay, Honey. Hey, are you ready to see my new place?

"Absolutely!"

"Good, it could use a woman's touch."

"Well, we're in trouble; because my gay ex-husband did all my decorating... even my silk plants are dying."

"Note to self, call Trevor ASAP." Ronnie chuckled.

"Wow! Ronnie it's beautiful. How did you do all this so

quickly? You've done more in a week than I've done in the two years I've been in my house."

"I had a lot of time on my hands... Have you really only been gone a week?" He kissed her neck and pulled her by the hand further into the spacious, but somehow cozy, living room. "Are you hungry?" She shook her head. "Would you like a drink?"

"Surprisingly, no..." She suddenly stopped moving and stared at him. He stood in front of her and stared back, touching her hair.

"Do you want to skip the rest of the tour and ...?"

She interrupted his question by placing her hands on his chest before resting her head there. He held her hand and led her slowly upstairs. They undressed each other slowly without speaking, until Ronnie stopped at his boxers and undershirt.

"Baby..."Gabby ran her nails down the length of his arms."I need to feel your skin..." She whispered as she kissed the palm of his hand.

"I know. You will." He kissed her while guiding her back onto the bed. It hadn't been an aberration, or the wine, or their individual angst. Their lovemaking was magical. Gabby purred and cooed as she melted under Ronnie's touch. Her sounds excited him, as he moaned and hummed in response until... he felt it coming and pried her hand out of his hair and held it tightly. Otherwise he did not stop, his mouth working skillfully, lovingly...

"Ronnie!" she gasped as the tremor began from her core and radiated to her toes and the ends of her curls. She continued to scream as he pretended nothing had happened at all. She was not 'there' yet. She was quiet for a moment and released his hand, all of her strength gone for the moment. He continued to hum and explore the newness he'd created between her legs. Normally, she'd be moving to reciprocate; but she was far too pleased to be polite, so she closed her eyes and continued to ride the waves. She found the strength to move again, when he reached inside her. "Oh... yes... oh... oh..." She rolled her hips and contracted compulsively. "Baby... please... I ..."

"Shhhh..." He pressed his palm against her and plunged deeper, never taking his mouth away... and she screamed... When he was satisfied that they had arrived at the first stop on their tour, he pulled his hand away and lay beside her.

"Mmm..." was all she had the strength to say as he kissed her, taking care to leave some of her sticky sweetness on her lips. She smiled at him and whispered. "You are just plain ... nasty..." she giggled, and thanked him by licking her own lips. Completely satisfied, for the moment, he smiled and rolled onto his back, pulling her to his chest.

An hour later, he woke her with gentle kisses on the back of her neck. "Mmm..." She rolled over and touched his face. "Hi."

She wasn't expecting it, but it was a most pleasant surprise. It was warm and thick and just a little bit too much. His strokes were long and deep until, there was no space between them... and he moved slowly... rolling more than thrusting. She wrapped her legs around him, locking him in, and he released one soft low moan... He searched her face as she parted her lips and twisted her face from agonizing pleasure. When she opened her eyes and saw that he was watching, she smiled and moved harder against him. He closed his eyes, lowered his body and buried his face in the crook of her neck. When he started to thrust she cried out in pure joy. Holding both of her hands above her head as they moved, he whispered. "Can you come with me?"

"Yes..." Her reply was small and sweet, as she arched her back and tried to brace for the explosion. She was only a little startled, but pleasantly surprised at the gentleness... This sound, too, was distinctly feminine and, again, made Gabby grin with delight. "Wow." She whispered.

"Wow?" He asked.

"Wow and... daaamn, but yes... wow..." She giggled as she gently caressed his breast. He closed his eyes and smiled at her touch, completely at ease, and totally sated.

And so, they continued for the next two days, taking short breaks for snacks and showers, when they thought they were finally ready to leave the house. They even made it to the door once. But as Gabby bent over to zip a sleek thigh-high boot, for Ronnie, the notion was abandoned.

"Tell me again where we're going." He smiled and watched her, leaning against the dining room wall.

"You said something about a walk and wings...? I'm really

just..." He walked toward her and backed her against the door in the foyer. "... doin' as I'm told."

"Yeah right..." He kissed her while he slid his hand up her thigh and under her skirt. He held her there for ten minutes, pinned to the wall, with her arms above her head and her panties around her knees. She opened her mouth, but no words, not even an 'ooh' when she exploded in his hand.

"Are you hungry?" He asked casually, as he kissed her tummy before pulling down her blouse.

"I don't know..." Her whispered answer surprised Gabby and she giggled. "I'm not really sure this is all really happening... I guess if it's a dream, I don't need to eat..." She whispered between soft kisses on her neck and shoulder.

"Oh. It's real... Don't move..." Gabby remained in the foyer, but slid down the door to the floor, blissfully confused. Ronnie really hadn't drugged her, at least not in an illegal, creepy kind of way, anyway. He'd just somehow lulled her into a completely sub-missive hypnotic state. When he returned, he pulled her to her feet and undressed her again where she stood, leaving a pile of very expensive rubble at his front door. He'd stripped back down to boxer briefs and a sports bra.

He lay her on her stomach, on a pallet he'd created in front of the fire, in the middle of the living room floor. She smiled and gazed at him through heavy eyelids. The scent of the warm oil brought her back. She remembered this place, her boyfriend's new house (that he'd called in favors to move into almost a full month early, to spare her any more hotel rooms; that is, if she wanted to stay with him). "Oh..." She felt a vaguely familiar sensation as his fingers worked skillfully between her thighs and up between her cheeks. She did not speak, but tensed slightly. Ronnie noticed but didn't stop. Instead, without warning, but gently, carefully, slowly, he plunged two fingers deep inside her. The sound that escaped her was low and guttural and she immediately relaxed her body.

"Yes." He whispered her answer back to her. Using his fingers to prepare the way, pulling them out, and then pushing slowly inside her. She cried as he moved slowly at first, then deep-er and faster.

"Do you like it?" He knew the answer. She dug her knees

in with her chest pressed against the floor, and her hips slightly raised. "Oh my God!" He groaned as she pushed back against him. Gabby cried softly as he pulled her fully up to her knees and stroked her gently at first, then harder and faster as they exploded together. He pulled away and collapsed on top of her, with most of his weight on his side.

"Oh my God..." It was a whisper.

"Do you know where you are, now?" He giggled.

"I think so."

"Well?" He teased her.

"Home." She reached for his hand and held it to her heart.

"Wow... mmm... Okay, now can we please get some real food?"

"Absolutely!" They laughed and took their time getting up, showering and finally going out into the world.

23

So Says the Poet Taylor Swift

*G*abby was beside herself, and for the first time in her life, happy not to be in control. She stared across the table at Ronnie, suppressing a grin.

"What?" Ronnie asked as their food arrived.

"You. You're just so... hot... and sweet... and oh my God, wow! How did I get to be so lucky?"

"Uh, no. I'm the lucky one. You are just reaping the benefits of many, many years of therapy." Ronnie was only half kidding, and deliberately left out the years of random sex that led to his present-day studliness. He'd congratulate himself privately on triumphantly bedding the hell out of his dream girl; but he couldn't relax just yet. He'd almost been here before. Sex was the easy part. He could somehow sense what a women needed physically; but he would never acknowledge that it was because he was biologically a woman himself. He didn't like to be touched like that...Well, at least he hadn't until Gabby. He was more worried about what would happen when the novelty wore off. Surely, it was bound to. Eventually, she would start treating him like one of those fucking machines, the same way the others did. There's no way she would still look at him like that a year from now, or twenty years from now, especially if he stayed in that stupid body. "She's a straight girl who thinks I'm an impressive lay 'for a girl'."

"Oh, stop it." Gabby didn't know exactly what Ronnie was thinking; but she could see his wheels turning and sensed, from the wistful way he was still looking at her, that he was thinking about and referring to his otherness. She didn't know how else to address it, except to do what felt natural, and be honest about what she was feeling every step of the way. "I think you're beautiful, ALL of you. Accept that, and eat your chicken."

"Yes ma'am." Ronnie sighed deeply and smiled at her. "Wow."

They ate light and didn't drink. When Ronnie suggested

they stop by the opening of a friend's club, she panicked. "You don't think a club opening is a little risky right now?"

"Trust me, no one will recognize you in here." He assured her, as he greeted the bouncer who waved them in.

They sat in the parking lot for a minute longer, as Ronnie sang the last few choruses of Taylor Swift's 'Mean', with passion and sincerity. "Is this what I think it is?"

"If you think it's a gay Country / Western bar, yes, you are correct." He chuckled and started talking loudly so she could hear him. "Trevor's new boyfriend owns it. I'd told them I didn't think I was going to make it, but..." He pulled her arm gently, and twirled her toward him. "... I'm feeling energized... feel like dancin'." He breathed into her ear and she melted. "Unless you'd like to go home..."

Gabby thought, "home, the parking lot, a large stall in the ladies' room... YES!" but said instead, "I'd have never pegged you for a country music fan."

"Well, I grew up country and classic R&B. But this music has been my religion. It's got it all, 'lovin', livin' good-hearted women, family and God...'" He half sang the lyric to his favorite Trace Adkins song. "I've been living in the world... Don't get me wrong, I love all music, but I couldn't do what I do on gospel music alone; and R&B doesn't have enough heart for me anymore. But country... you give me a situation, and I'll give you a song to get you through it!"

"Okay..." Gabby smiled and shook her head as she tried to come up with a scenario. When she couldn't, she went with the obvious. "What about mine?"

"Too easy... 'Jesus, Take the Wheel'. Just let go and let God have it, Gabrielle. Tre showing up was your icy highway. You and your baby will be fine." Ronnie pulled her close, as he leaned against the bar, and kissed the top of her head. He squeezed her and brought her back to their game, before she had time to think any more about the real world. Now 'com on, you can do better than that..."

"Okay, I've got one... cheatin' boyfriend..."

"Duh, 'From a Table Away' by Sunny Sweenie' or 'Before He Cheats' also by Carrie Underwood... The country princess knows all about the heartbreak... 'Cowboy Casanova' and my all-time favorite, 'you suck and I'm sorry I wasted even five minutes of my life on your sorry ass!' anthem, 'Undo It!'" He laughed and Gabby grinned. She wondered if he knew or cared that his 'love of all things Carrie and Taylor' was the opposite of manly. Watching him, she quickly decided she didn't care one bit.

"Okay... okay... falling in love..."

"Depends... what stage are we talkin' about: at first sight, thinking about it or forever...?"

Gabby laughed out loud. "You are a nut... all three."

"At first sight: 'Farmer's Daughter' and 'Good Directions'... Figuring it out: 'Our Song' or 'God Bless the Broken Road'.. or 'Love Like Crazy'... Ooh, broken heart: 'These Days' by Rascal Flatts."

"You're just making this stuff up!" She leaned into him and giggled.

"Whatever. You'll see. Dance with me..." He starting pulling her toward the dance floor where the cutest pair of fifty-ish, butch lesbians in the world were teaching the latest line dance.

"I don't know the steps."

"You probably do... it's basically the Wobble but... sexier..." Ronnie winked at Trevor, who'd come over to greet them and give Gabby a complimentary cowboy hat. She eyed it for a moment suspiciously.

"It's new, honey. We don't play with hair around here, okay." Trevor snapped and reassured her. She shrugged before putting it on and posing. Ronnie put his hand to his heart, before taking hers and finding a spot in the enormous crowd. Of course, he was right. She definitely had some country in her. He backed away from the dance floor and watched, as she and the other curvy girls swayed and teased to 'Honky-Tonk Badonkadonk'. When the song was over, she fell into his arms laughing. It was the most fun she'd had in years. Ronnie smiled down at her, and she pressed her back against his chest, reaching up to run her fingers through his hair. It was time to go.

Gabby was confused when they drove into the entrance of her neighborhood on the opposite side of town from Ronnie's house. Ronnie sensed her concern. "I thought we could sneak in and get some of your things." It was after two a.m. on a Saturday night, and as far as anyone following the trial knew, she wasn't back in town yet.

She gave him directions to her house and shook her head thinking, "oh, I am so marrying you!" She only said out loud, "beautiful, smart and sneaky..." as she handed him the key to open the door. Inside she turned off the alarm and pulled off her shoes. He followed suit and looked around her large, but sparsely decorated living room.

"I warned you." She laughed pointing to the bare walls.

"You did.... What do you like? We can go and pick out some things tomorrow, if you'd like. I'm told I have a decent eye."

"Whatever. Your house is gorgeous, unnaturally so..."

"I beg your pardon?"

"You know exactly what I mean. Neither a tomboy nor a straight man should be able to put a place together like that. You've apparently got some weird decorator gene."

"Well, I've been called a mutant more than once." He chuckled.

"Exactly..." She smiled back, as she dragged suitcases from her enormous walk-in closet and laid them open on the floor. He just smiled and waited for instructions.

"Do you want some of these photos from the living room?"

"Yes, thank you. Not all of them, just a couple... the one of me and EJ together, and one of him by himself. The one with him in his tux from his dads' wedding is my favorite."

"Now, that, is a handsome kid."

"Yeah..."

"What is it, Baby?"

"Everyone has always said he has my smile, but otherwise, he looks like Kevin."

"That could still be true, Gabrielle. He probably does walk and talk just like him. He's probably picked up all of his facial expressions, even his mannerisms. It happens with kids who are adopted all the time. I've done shows where you couldn't tell the adopted kids from the biological ones. That's how big a role nurturing and environment play in the development of a child. If the two of them still agree that EJ is Kevin's son, then he always will be. Nothing a judge says is going to change that in any real way. Even if the worst happens, they're not going to stop loving each other. Please don't worry. I know it's going to be okay." He walked over to her and pulled her into his arms.

"Why are you so sure?" she asked as she wrapped her arms tightly around him, resting her head on his chest.

"I don't know. I just am." Ronnie did know; he just didn't want to say. He had an uncanny sense of discernment about some things, all things that didn't directly involve him, actually. He knew when people were good, and when something bad would happen. He believed that only good things were in store for Gabby and her family from now on. What he didn't know was how deeply involved he would be. He already knew he loved her, had loved her since they first met. But on the surface, her life was utter chaos; and he was a pleasant distraction from it all. How would she see him when the dust settled? Would she still want to be with him, when the trials were over and he wasn't protecting her? Would she love him, when his transformation was complete? And if she stuck around for that, would she demand that he kept his truth a secret? Ronnie wanted so much to just relax and enjoy what was happening. He was falling in love for the first time in his life. He'd dreamt about it, and it was indeed more amazing than he'd ever imagined... and a little scary.

"So..." Ronnie batted long dark lashes at Gabby. They were sitting at opposite ends of his bed like preschoolers in a game of duck-duck-goose. They'd put her things away and undressed for bed. Neither was sleepy, and they were both feeling a little worn out from their second two-day marathon.

"So..." She smiled back at him, wearing a loose cami and boy-shorts.

"So, I was thinkin'..."

"Oh, boy..."

"Now that you know..."

"Know what?" She asked sincerely.

"All my... business..."

"Oh! Yeah! Now that I know..."

"Are we okay?"

"You're kidding, right? We are more okay than I've ever been in my entire life."

"So you think this is something you can do?"

"You mean you and me? Absolutely!" She hesitated for a moment. "But..." Ronnie braced himself for the letdown, the conditions, the list of places they could go and people who could know about them, about him. "Maybe we should stop having sex, and get to know each other a little better?"

"Huh? Is that all?" Ronnie visibly relaxed.

"Well, yeah. Sex is the easy part, really... isn't it? Don't we want to know if we actually like each other with our clothes on?" There it was. She said it, and he believed her. She really didn't care about the other stuff at all. She was just a 'good girl' trying to be with a 'nice guy'.

"I was planning to just keep you naked and locked in the house, actually. With all of today's technology, you can work from home, can't you?" He crawled across the bed to kiss her now outstretched leg.

"See! That's what I'm talking about! When you touch me, I can't think straight. I need to figure out how to function in the world again. Do you know I actually forgot a couple of times that I have a son, with questionable parentage, mind you, a business to run, and a father on trial?"

"Well that's a good thing, right?"

"No, that's an amazing thing... except..."

"What?"

"I'm afraid you might not be...human; and I really need you to be real, Ronnie. Everything is moving so fast. This pace doesn't scare you?"

"Not at all. Everything about you feels right to me, Gabrielle."

"How can that be? My life is a mess."

"People are messy."

"But..."

"But what, Baby?"

"It's all too much for even me...My father's trial... Ethan's dad. And I did that! I told a lie that could potentially and permanently insert a monster into my son's life, and separate him from the only father he's ever known. How are you just ignoring that? I lied to him for ten years. How are you just ignoring that?"

Ronnie took a deep breath and kissed her tummy, before resting his hand there. "Because people make mistakes. You said yourself Kevin forgives you. If he can't judge you, I'm certainly not going to. It doesn't even matter how it's all come out. All that matters is that you're dealing with it; and when it's all done, your family is going to be stronger. I just want to be around to see it. And I am horrified by the charges against your father, and my heart is breaking for Michael and the others, but I'm thankful that we are where we are today; and I'm not going to over-analyze it (anymore), or run from it. I've never been so excited about anyone... ever. I'm not scared, not now...And as for the physical part..." He breathed deeply again, taking in her scent. "My need to be close to you isn't about sex at all, and if that's what's confusing you, I can fix that. What's happening for me is something else. I've never wanted to be connected to anyone the way I need to be connected to you. I've never felt safe; but with you, I am literally exposed and... it feels amazing."

"So you're saying you're okay with us taking a couple of steps back?"

"Hmm... wow... That's what you heard, huh?" He chuckled and it made her tummy wiggle. "I'm saying I understand that you're scared, but I'm not. And to be quite honest with you, the one thing I have never done willingly is 'step back'. This, what's happening between us, isn't like any other time for me. I made love to you...because I love you. There. I said it. But I knew I loved you almost instantly; so I've had some time to wrap my head around this whole thing. I know things are really moving fast, but it feels good to me. I have no regrets, not a single one. If I said now that I'm gonna try to keep my hands off you, I'd be lying. And frankly, I think you're just talkin'; but if you really wanna torture yourself, there is a beautifully furnished guestroom across the hall." Ronnie paused and slowly marched two fingers up her thigh, while she considered his solution to her problem.

150

"Has anyone ever told you you're a jerk before?" She asked with her eyes closed, as he pulled gently at her panties.

"Only every person who's ever tried to convince me to do something that made no sense, without any real logic or reason."

"Arrogant jerk!"

"Yup, that's exactly what they call me," he whispered, before kissing the top of her thigh and flinging her panties across the room.

24

COUPLE'S COUNSELING

*D*r. Keaner suppressed a grin. She'd been thinking and talking to her husband about retiring for two years. But that was also exactly how long, off and on, she'd been counseling Gabby, and she just couldn't bring herself to abandon her before she was ready. Gabby had come so far, from the angry, self-loathing, guilt-ridden and battered, psychologically, if not physically, shell of a woman she'd been; to the kind, honest, genuinely confident and strong person sitting before her. "You look like you've been well." Liz smiled and waited to see why Gabby suddenly needed to see her a week earlier than their normal monthly session.

"Better than well... better than...ever, I think. It's been a great week." She smiled. "Great couple of months, actually. There's some stuff going on, though." Gabby briefly summarized what was going on with Kevin and Ethan and the 'paternity thing'. Dr. Keaner looked concerned, until Gabby breathed deeply, sunk back into the couch and smiled.

"Oh my God!" Liz couldn't help but smile back at her. "You're in love! Is it Ronnie? Wow!" It had been about a month since her two favorite patients started dating, and it was driving Liz mad not being able to tell either that she was seeing them both. The moment she'd figured out that Gabby's 'Ronnie', and Ronnie's 'Gabrielle' were both hers, she searched frantically for some loophole in the medical ethics laws that would allow her to tell them. There wasn't one. "Damn HiPAA!" As long as they were seeking counseling separately, she was stuck. And likely always would be; because while they each had things personally that they were still working on, as a couple, they were...fantastic, and so far, good for each other.

"I didn't know I could feel this way! I've been a mess my whole life, not that anyone else could tell. To everyone else, I, and my life, looked perfect. But he has seen me... he sees me, at my ugliest. He sees past the fear and the bitterness and the arrogance. He actually likes me, when I'm not sure what to do. And when I am 'good', and I feel like 'my old self', 'Gabby, Ruler of Empires', he still likes me! I can do no wrong! And it's not to say that he thinks I'm perfect or right all the time. He just wants to see it ALL, and he's seen me through a lot. Sure, I've had you, and Nikki, when Kevin left me... correction, when Kevin and I split up, and through the beginning of this nightmare with my dad... But Tre showed up at a time when I thought I was finally going to be okay; and suddenly, it was like someone was trying to destroy me. I know I wouldn't have survived, maybe even the day, that first day, without him. I know, I had you. But do you know what I mean?"

"I do. Counseling is just a place to talk things through. It isn't a magic shield, protecting you from all hurt, harm or danger. Life gets through and sometimes it hits hard. But give yourself some credit, too, Gabby. This 'Ronnie' of yours," Liz wanted to scream inside, "does sound healthy and good for you; but you've done most of the work to getting to him on your own. For instance, you just said 'when Kevin and I split up' for the first time since I've known you. You get it now, don't you?"

"Get what? That I'm not some controlling, manipulative monster who deliberately tried to destroy a wonderful human being and use him for my own evil purposes?" Gabby chuckled.

"Uh...yeah..." Liz squinted at Gabby and laughed.

"And that I'm actually as much a victim of my father's evil and my mother's cowardice silence?"

"Yes..."

"Oh, yeah...I do get that. Why didn't you tell me sooner, by the way?"

"Because I didn't have to tell you just now. You figured it out on your own. If I'd tried to tell you, would you have believed me?"

"Probably not...Oh. Oh!...Whatever. Shut up. You're not that smart." Gabby smiled until her cheeks hurt, while Liz just shook her head and glanced at the clock above Gabby's head. If she could just get her to linger, just fifteen minutes longer, as she usually did, 'they' might actually run into each other in the lobby. That wouldn't be so bad, or even unethical. She knew neither of them were keeping the fact that they were in therapy a secret. "Oh, look at the time!" Gabby suddenly popped up, her usual glass of red wine untouched. "I've got a conference call with my attorney...like now; and I want to pick up some things for dinner with my sweetie. We take turns cookin' dinner. Is that not the cutest thing ever?"

"It really is. Is that new for you?" Liz sounded very interested, but still spoke slowly.

"Kevin and I ate out when I was in Charlotte, and we had lots of room service in New York. We never had 'normal' family meals together. And everything with Ronnie is like that...new, and special, but somehow very, very ...easy." Gabby beamed, with her hand on the door.

"I can't wait to hear more, Gabby. Are we moving up a week, or was this a one-time thing?"

"No, we can put it back next month, I think. I just wanted to get in while everything was still fresh, you know with the paternity mess."

"Well, again, it sounds like you've got a handle on it all. I will see you in four... no five weeks."

"Thanks, Liz."

"You're welcome, Gabrielle." Liz chuckled to herself. Gabby missed it! Liz never called her 'Gabrielle'. Only Ronnie did that. As soon as Gabby was out of Liz's office and on the elevator, Liz rushed to the window to see if they'd collide. But she hadn't heard Ronnie yet. Her office was only on the second floor, and she could usually hear the motorcycle he usually drove to their sessions. She looked up at the clock again. Ronnie was always prompt, but never early. Liz actually pouted, as she saw Gabby's black, convertible Mercedes pull out of the lot, and onto the street. "Dang-it!" She laughed as she heard Ronnie, and then saw him coast in from the opposite end of the parking lot.

"Well, you're certainly in a good mood." Ronnie, looked suspiciously at his therapist. "Do you have something you'd like to share, before I tell you about my awesome, fantabulous, spectacularific existence?" He grinned at her.

Liz thought, 'Yes! Ooh! Pick me! Pick me!', but said instead, "just happy to see you so happy, Mr. Reynolds. What's new?

I take it all is well on the romantic front."

"All could not be better. Actually, all *that* is so good it's a little scary. It's not so much that Gabrielle is perfect; it's just that she's perfect for me. Even when things should be a mess, or we should be pulling away from each other... For instance, she's got this 'paternity thing'." Ronnie watched as Liz's eyes grew wide. "I know, right? You hear 'paternity' and you think what kind of woman has a 'paternity thing'; but it's not like that. Anyway, she should be falling apart at the seams... but she's not. She's facing it head on. She's not trying to run from it, or me. And she's not trying to hide it. She didn't even have to tell me. It's all happening in Canada! If she hadn't told me, I'd have never known. But I have so much respect for her, and her honesty, and her courage. And she doesn't need me, or my help; but she's letting me help her. I know it's early, and a part of me wants to run away and wait to see how this all plays out, and then see if we can have anything. And she said she tried to do that in the instant she found out about it all, but we can't wait. It's like the first time, for both of us... I've found someone who wants all of me, and exactly what I have to offer, at precisely the moment that I'm available to give it, and nothing else that's going on seems to matter."

"Would it sound too much like 'I told you so' to say I'm not the slightest bit surprised? I take it she knows all about your plans?"

"Huh. Yeah. She does. And even that's amazing. Gabrielle is a 'notoriously straight' woman. Her father is, rather was, a prominent Black Southern Baptist preacher. Before 2008, she was a Republican, for crying out loud! So, when I told her, and I told her almost immediately...our first date, actually... she didn't bat an eye. But that's not the most amazing thing. I've never had a problem 'getting women'; or keeping them, for that matter. The thing that gets me is everything she's done and said since I told her. Not only does she not care that I'm 'technically' a woman, but she also doesn't care whether or not I transition. And not only does she not care that I'm a woman, or whether I transition; but she also doesn't seem to care whether anyone knows! That's always been the thing. I always had to choose. With my first girlfriend, I had to be a lesbian; with my most recent ex, and all the random conquests in between, I had to be a man. Gabrielle doesn't say, 'walk like a man'. She doesn't care *how* I walk, as long as I walk beside her." Ronnie sat back and shook his head in disbelief.

"That is amazing. But, you don't trust it."

"It's not that I don't trust it. It's just that I've spent so much of my life planning to change...waiting for the day when I'd be 'made whole'..."

"And now?"

"I feel pretty darn whole, now. And I always said that, that feeling would have to come from within, that it wasn't something someone could give me. God had to do it. And I thought, allowing me to walk this path, and ultimately transition, was part of what God has planned for me. That that's why what happened, happened. I always believed that there was some divine purpose for the storm. But if it's not so I can overcome everything that happened to me and become the man that *he* and everyone else said I wouldn't be, then I'm not sure now what the purpose is. I mean, sometimes I think I get it." Ronnie was quiet for a long time.

"What do you come up with?" Liz tried to ease the answer out of him.

"I know I'm supposed to help people. I know I'm supposed to write. I even think that there's a reason I've been thrown into such a public life. You know how hard this used to be for me."

"Yes, I do."

"But I have trouble pulling it all together. I don't see how the storm fits into it. Could it have been just something that needed to happen to get me out of my mom's house? See, I don't think God would do that. I don't think God would allow me to be hurt like that, and destroy my parent's marriage, and my brother, and take so much away from my sister...all of us... if something BIGGER and meaningful weren't meant to come of it." Ronnie stared at Liz, who was uncharacteristically quiet for a long time. Their session had actually been over for more than twenty minutes; but Liz wasn't expecting anyone else. She glanced at the clock and was actually glad their time was 'officially' up.

"Ronnie, you know I deliberately avoid discussing patient issues in the context of faith, my own or yours. But since our time is up," she winked at him. "I can say that I agree with you. I do not believe God would allow you to come through, all that you have, without some extraordinary plan in mind, just for you. And professionally speaking, I've never met anyone better equipped to do and achieve the extraordinary. And as a person of faith, not as a doctor, I have to tell you that, as extraordinary as transitioning surgically would be, even though one has to be psychologically qualified to do so, I believe there is something even more special set aside for you to do than that. Perhaps, in addition to; but this trip you have planned for, a month from now? is not the most amazing thing you will do, not by a long shot."

"Thank you, for that, and for sharing your personal beliefs with me." Ronnie smiled at the woman who knew him better than almost everyone. "It's funny you should mention the timing. I did at least delay the surgery. I was supposed to go in four weeks. But with the trials, and Gabby, I couldn't leave right now. I can't leave her. But I didn't cancel it. I just moved it to June. I think the dust should be settled by then. And perhaps, between now and then, I can figure out what I'm supposed to be doing with my life."

"I have no doubt you will."

25

TIME HEALS

"*M*ama, this is Ronnie."

"It's a pleasure meeting you, Ms. Richmond. Thank you so much for agreeing to speak with me. I really appreciate it, but I am sorry that you're going through this."

"Thank you. Gabby said you weren't interested in talking about Robert. I'm going to hold you to that."

"Yes, Ma'am. As I mentioned to Gabby, I'm more interested in talking about the people most of us don't consider at times like these, the family of the victims, and the of the accused. It's unfortunate that in this particular instance you're both."

"We are. And you must realize how hard it is being recognized as the wife or daughter of a child molester, of someone who lied to thousands of people for... decades. Why are you so interested in us?"

"Well, I know firsthand what tragedy to a child can do to an entire family; and I think the world needs to see how women like you and Gabby soldier on through the worst of times. I think it will give people who may be going through something similar the hope and encouragement to go on. It's really hard to say... I just know that my family could have benefited from seeing you and Gabby survive what's happening to you... I'm sorry I can't explain it better. I just feel it's important."

"I understand... May I ask what happened to your family?" Phyllis motioned for Ronnie to sit.

"I'm gonna get some coffee." Gabby excused herself. She knew the story Ronnie was about to tell, and just couldn't bear to listen.

"I was attacked by my mother's brother when I was thirteen, on the day Hurricane Hugo hit Charleston, South Carolina. My brother and I were with my grandmother in Marietta for the summer, and my sister was away at college."

"I'm so sorry..." Phyllis squeezed Ronnie's hand.

"I'm okay. I've always believed that everything happens ultimately for the good of those who believe. It took a lot of counseling and prayer, but I honestly believe I came out a stronger person than I would have been had it not happened."

♪*Everything that happened to me that was good...*♪ Phyllis sang softly...

♪*God did it!*♪ Ronnie answered. "And I'm not saying that God made that happen to me. Evil comes from the Devil, but when the choice was made, God stepped in and saved me... and used what was done to me to set me free from what I believe was a worse fate."

"But things were not so good for your family?" Phyllis asked as Gabby returned with a tray of refreshments and sat next to her mother. Phyllis watched Ronnie's eyes sparkle at the sight of her daughter.

Ronnie took a deep breath. "No, my family fared far worse. It was almost as though they were raped and beaten. None of them were ever the same. My grandmother died, I'm told of a heart attack brought on by the stress of living with a monster she was afraid of. My brother has been in and out of rehab and hospitals for repeated overdoses. Neal told my father that the attack was his fault, that 'he' had been talking about me before our grandmother put him out of the house, and he should have known not to leave me there..."

"Do you feel that way?"

"Absolutely not! Neal is only eighteen months older than me. He wasn't my bodyguard, and there really wasn't any reason to think Scott would have laid a hand on me. He was an addict and he snapped...And if Neal had suggested for one moment that he needed to protect me, and not the other way around, I would have laughed at him. I was so cocky..." Ronnie's face lit up with a boyish grin. "But Neal... he was so smart, and so talented. When he wasn't playin' basketball, he was reading... actually, I'd seen him more than once with a book in one hand and a basketball in the other. But after that day, he was never the same... My mother has barely been able to look at me since it happened. But she and I had our own issues before... I was not a typical teenager... I wasn't easy... but she didn't know how to help me. Sure she took me to a counselor for years, but she never got to know me. I have to admit, though, that is the one thing that may have been the same with or without the storm. Wow." Ronnie was quiet for a long time... then a tear rolled down his cheek.

"What is it?"

"It's been over twenty years... and it never occurred to me...My mom lost me, her mother, her husband, her brother and at least half of one of her two remaining children all at once. And I've actually resented her." Ronnie sat back on the couch and cried. Phyllis watched as Gabby went to his side and stroked his hair.

"Oh my God." Phyllis reached for tissue and wiped her own eyes. "Is she still alive, Baby?" Ronnie sat up and wiped his face.

"Yes, Ma'am. She is."

"Then it's not too late. What's her name?" She asked so she could remember to pray for her.

"Annette Reynolds... no, Grey, Annette Grey; she divorced my dad when he went to prison."

"For killing her brother?"

"Well, he didn't kill him... and he got out in less than five years, but yes."

"And her brother?"

"Was murdered in jail, but not before being raped and castrated. He actually lived in there for thirteen years."

"How do you know all that?" Gabby hadn't heard that part before.

"I didn't tell you my dad was in the same prison? Somehow, dad got there first and by the time Scott got there, they knew he was coming. Dad never had to lay a finger on him. Word got out that Scott was the man who raped his thirteen year old daughter and left her for dead. Even the guards wouldn't protect him."

"Please God, no..." It was barely a whisper, but Ronnie saw Gabby's face and remembered why they were there, and simultaneously forgot he'd just met her mother an hour earlier.

"Oh Baby, I'm sorry." He pulled her close while she cried. "I know. I know. No, Gabby, that doesn't have to happen. You said yourself; they've had him in protective custody all along. They won't put a man your father's age in with the general population. He'll be okay, Gabby." Ronnie looked at Phyllis, but didn't let go of Gabby's hand. "I'm sorry, Ms. Richmond. The last thing either of you need to hear are horror stories about prison. Can I move on to your story?"

Phyllis took a deep breath and smiled at Ronnie. She liked him as much in person as she had on his show. "Did he just say that he used to be a girl? God is truly amazing!" she thought before picking up her coffee. "I can't imagine what you need from us, but I'm willing to try if you think it would help. I can see it's important to you. Did you always know you'd go into ministry?"

Ronnie looked puzzled for a moment. "No ma'am. I knew I needed to help people; but I never thought of it as ministry."

"Well, as someone who's worked in the church for forty years, and in the world my whole life, I can tell you that you do not have to be in a church, or associated with one, to minister to people if your goal is to serve God and improve people's lives."

"Thank you, so much for saying that. I never... Wow." Ronnie looked at Gabby who squeezed his hand and smiled at her mother. Ronnie took a deep breath and thought, "I love these women..."

Then he tried to regroup. "Let's start there, with your ministry. What have the immediate effects of the trial been on your personal ministry?"

"It's been painful, sometimes ugly; but I've actually stayed with the church. As you can imagine, almost everyone left right away, and stayed gone for almost a year. But the people who stayed and prayed with me, prayed for me... helped me rebuild."

"Because you were already an ordained minister... had you had an active pastoral role in the church before?"

"Oh no, and I traveled and ministered under the title 'Evangelist', because our church didn't begin ordaining women until ten years ago. And when they did start, he wouldn't allow it."

Ronnie shook his head. "How has all of this affected your relationship with your daughter and the rest of your family?" He winked at Gabby.

"We're actually closer." Phyllis smiled. "There was always something between us before. You know about fathers and their little girls... But we've finally realized how much we need each other. It didn't happen automatically, though. We both went into our own protective shells for a long time. I had so much guilt... and shame!"

"Can you talk about that?"

"Well the guilt is obvious, really. Why didn't I see it? How many lives could have been saved if I hadn't ignored the things that I did see? If I'd only been stronger and stood up to him when things didn't feel right... What made me stay thirty years longer than I should have?"

"Thirty, really?" Gabby asked. She was thirty-five.

"Gabrielle, from the time we were married, your father and I were barely more than roommates until you were born, and then that stopped again almost as soon as you got here. It was like he'd fulfilled his manly obligation by getting you here, and then just... From then on, we were just platonic partners... not even partners... we weren't equal. It was his show, and I was supporting cast. Outside of the local church, we led very separate lives. And I've cried and cursed at the idea that he was only able to get to Michael because no one cared where he was or what he was doing. He didn't even have to be convincing. No one cared. That's where the shame comes in... when I had to really look at who he was, the man I married and gave forty years of my life too... If he was all of those evil things, and I'd only ever been his wife, what was I now?"

Ronnie shook his head and smiled. "You've clearly made it through that storm. And I think I'm here because you need to tell people how you did it..."

Phyllis smiled back at him and pointed upward. "You know, and I know, God did it. At every turn, with every door I knocked on, every time I opened my eyes or walked outside... God sent me a sign... God told me that even as an old woman, I was first and foremost, HIS child. He told me that the battle for my husband's soul was His and not mine; but what that man did to me, was distract me from what I was called to do. Yes, I served, but I served as less than half of who I am. When I stopped hiding my light and stepped into the fullness of ... not who my husband told me I could be, but who God told me to be... I was literally born again. And I am not wasting one single day of what is left of this

162

new life. I tell the truth, based on what God tells me, not what that man wanted me to believe. Oh, baby..." Phyllis looked at her daughter, "I am so sorry. I'm so sorry I wasn't stronger for you."

"Don't say that, Mama. I used to blame you. But I don't, I promise. I'm starting to believe more and more... Ronnie, and Kyle, won't let me forget, that everything happens for a reason, and ultimately for the good of those who believe. If one thing about my childhood had been different, we wouldn't have Ethan. If I hadn't married Kevin, he wouldn't have met Kyle, and I wouldn't have met Ronnie." She beamed at him. "I'm not saying we're perfect and everything is fine, but I know we're better and stronger... if for no other reason than what you said, 'we're closer', and as much as I pretend that I don't, I do need you... and my heart is breaking for Daddy and Michael, but I am so happy to have you 'back' in my life!" Gabby moved to where her mother was sitting and hugged her as she cried happy tears. Ronnie sat and watched and tried not to cry anymore himself. When they settled down, he stood up.

"I can't thank you enough for talking to me, and being so open. It truly was more than I asked for; and I know that it will bless someone. Your faith and courage are remarkable, Ms. Richmond."

"No, I'm just doing my best to be obedient, honey. But you know something about courage yourself, don't you?"

"Ma'am?"

Phyllis laughed and held each of their hands, as they stood on either side of her. "Let us pray. Heavenly Father, thank You so much for Your many blessings, and for Your promise that You will never leave nor forsake us, as long as we do our best to walk in Your will and Your way. Thank You for giving me back my precious baby, and for keeping her safe and happy and strong. Thank You God for sending her love! Thank You for Ronnie. Please continue to protect and keep him and bless his ministry, Father. Let the world see nothing but the beautiful child of God whom You've called to do Your work. Protect his heart from hardening, as he has to walk through evil to get to light. Please put a fence around him as he continues his journey. And finally, shield us, Your children, from all hurt, harm, and danger and bind the enemy who would seek to rob, kill, destroy and distract, as we know that there is so much work left to do.   I ask these things, Father God in Your Son's name, and I thank You in advance because we know that it is already done. Amen."

"Amen." Ronnie and Gabby said together, as the three of them stood still in their circle and cried and laughed.

26

THE REYNOLDS' MYSTIQUE

*"**H**ey Ronnie... This is your brother, Neal. Give me a call when you get this message. Hope everything's okay with you. I miss seeing you on TV. Bye."*

Ronnie listened to the message again. Neal sounded... good. He made a mental note to call him later and turned his attention back to Gabby.

"Your mom is incredible. Ya know, I've been wondering how you turned out the way you did... you know..." He hesitated.

"It's okay to say it, Ronnie..."

"I don't want to judge..."

"With my father being a hypocritical, false-preaching, child-molesting, rapist monster?"

"Um... yeah... sorry..."

Gabby smiled at him. "Thank you."

He rubbed her leg. "I'm not sure what for, but you're welcome?"

"For seeing me... for loving me through all my crap. I have taken my mom for granted my whole life. Daddy was always this bigger than life character, so big that she disappeared... but she didn't. She's been there. I don't know how she survived living with him, or how she's getting through this. I know they aren't together anymore, but just the knowing... Even if he's somehow found not guilty... he's really not a very good person, is he? My mother, of all people, has no reason to lie about him now. She gave him forty years of her life... the things she said he did... what she saw and kept to herself..."

Gabby closed her eyes and lowered her head. She took a deep breath before speaking again. "I have to confess, part of me wonders what was in it for her, why she stayed as long as she did... but mostly, I just wish we were closer, that she'd let me help her."

"Well, like she said, 'it's not too late'."

"Yeah. She's been doing all the reaching out. I guess it's

time I tried to meet her half way."

"That's my girl..." He smiled at her before kissing the palm of her hand. "...speaking of half way... remind me to call my brother, please."

"Of course. Was that call earlier from him?"

"Yeah. He says he needs to talk."

"Are you worried about him?"

"I guess he sounded okay. It's just been a really long time. We've never been really close. Growing up... well, there were two phases... First, I was his annoying baby sister. I followed him around everywhere. Then I decided I wanted to be just like him and my dad. He was so smart and cool. I didn't know what it was then, but later I referred to it as 'the Reynolds' Mystique'. My dad and Neal had this thing, this way about them that my mom and Libby, as much as I love her, just didn't have. I've spent my whole life trying to be like them, to measure up... Anyway, 'phase one' was this little girl who idolized her big brother... at least that's what it looked like to him. But when I knew I was different... not a girl, it put even more distance between us. I thought he'd like me more, you know, think I was cool, too; but... he was never mean to me..." Ronnie was quiet for a long time as they sat in the driveway. "After the storm... Actually, it was just before, which is how I know it wasn't because of, when I really started to feel confident in who I was, he seemed to like me just a little bit less. He didn't want to hang out with me anymore. He used to have friends over and let me play basketball and board games with them... Remember 'Risk'? They used to have these marathon games of 'Risk'. Four of his friends would come over, and they'd spend all day... I remember one time, Mom spent the entire morning cooking ribs and mac-n-cheese and greens - Mom, can throw-down in the kitchen...for a White woman - anyway, she'd spent all day cooking, and they'd spent all day working up an appetite playing Risk and two-on-two and, when she went out for a couple of hours, Neal and I and his friends ate every bit of it. I've never seen her so mad, not even when I gave my whole summer wardrobe to my girlfriend... " He chuckled.

"What'd she do?"

"There wasn't really a whole lot she *could* do, but scream.

It's not like we could cook. She couldn't even yell at our friends. Like she could never say anything to Shawnee. She'd never take the clothes back, or point out that ribs and all the cheese that went into her macaroni were expensive. My goodness, we were some bad-ass kids! And she was... my mom put up with a lot... Anyway, that was the last time I really felt like 'one of the guys'. After that... well, Hugo was in 1989, and the 'Great Mac-n-Cheese Debacle' was that Spring before school let out... Is it sad that that's my fondest memory of my brother?"

"No. Actually, it sounds like all of your memories of him are fond. Just sounds like that's the most memorable. I think I'm a little jealous. I wish I'd had a sibling to get in trouble with. Our house was a very lonely place for me. Michael was my father's. God that sounds so awful now... But it wasn't like either of them were there for me, even though, when speaking to me about Michael, my dad would always say 'your brother'. It used to sound like he was offering Michael up to me like some kind of gift or peace-offering. Like he was a brand-new puppy, and not the son he spent all of his free time with. I do love Michael like a brother. You really can't help but love him, if you know him at all; but it was different. I get it now. He wasn't really part of my family. My dad wouldn't allow mom or me to ever really get close to him. It was more like having a permanent houseguest. And even living next to Kevin, I always felt lonely. I'd have loved to have a sister... or a 'real' brother.

"Do you want more kids?"

"If I wanted one now, I'd have to adopt. I had a partial hysterectomy just last year. But I did, for a long time want more children, at least one more. But, Ethan's almost ten. That window is closed for him. Another child would be more for me than him. I don't want to be selfish, like my father was. If I can't give him a real sibling, I don't want to *take* anything from him either. I want a real relationship with him."

"You *do* have the 'relationship' part working. You know that, don't you? He adores you, and 'the dads'. I had that with my dad. I wish I'd had it with my mom. But, I bet Ethan wouldn't have things any other way."

"My only prayer is that I don't screw him up. He's... amazing, Ronnie"

"Well, from what I can tell, you're all doing a fine job." Ronnie smiled lovingly at Gabby.

"Do you want kids of your own?"

"Huh..." Ronnie leaned back and smiled slightly. "Really?"

"Uh, yeah... I think we're having 'the talk', aren't we?"

"Wow. Yeah, we are. Okay... I've never admitted this to anyone, not even my therapist; but, yeah, I want kids. That was the only 'female' fantasy I ever had. I actually wondered what it would be like to... be a mother."

"Not a father? Huh... wow." She smiled back at him.

"Not too weird for you?"

"What would be weird about that? You're a woman, Ronnie. It's the most natural impulse in the world to want to bring life into the world. I get that some women just don't have it…"

"And some of us suppress it..."

"Why is that?"

"I can't speak for anyone else... but for me... even though we're talking about the most natural thing in the world, the concept is scary. Everything that goes along with it. Think about it. Just the basics...sex... I have never wanted to have sex with a man before. So right there, I've eliminated the possibility that that would happen for me accidently."

"Do you think it's because of what happened to you?"

"I don't know. I was already sexually attracted to women before it happened. But I still had this longing. And after, there was no way I was ever going to be able to do that. And after a while, it just became something that I had to just let go. It wasn't like I could say, 'I'm a man; and oh, by the way, I'd like to have a baby'." He shook his head. "And then it wasn't an issue anymore. I..." Ronnie closed his eyes trying to block out a tear that threatened to fall. Gabby squeezed his hand tightly and waited. "Sometimes I think the storm was God's way of telling me it's okay to be who I am. When I was told that it was likely that I never would be able to get pregnant, I took that as permission to let 'her' go. 'Veronica' was of no use to me... like this."

Gabby closed her eyes and fought back tears of her own. "...I don't... I want to say something... but I don't know how... or if I should."

"It's okay..." Ronnie wiped his face. "We're having the talk, remember?"

"I know that I don't have a lot of experience, not just with women, but experience in general. I've lived a pretty sheltered life. But, when I hear you talk like that, it makes me so sad. I know I will never fully understand how or why you've chosen to be less her and more him, and I don't know how much this bothers you... but I still see her. I'm sorry. I hate to break this to you; but it doesn't matter to me what you wear or drive, or how you..." She dug her nails into his thigh through his jeans. "... I still see glimpses of her... more than glimpses... sometimes she's *all* I see. And I feel so special and honored that I get to... know her and love her. And what makes me sad is that you don't love her... or that anyone ever let you believe that she wasn't beautiful, however she decided to walk in the world. I don't care what pronouns you use. I see you. I love the man you are 'in the world', but I still see the woman, functioning uterus or no, and I love her too. I know saying all of this must really be messing things up for you... and I'm s...."

Ronnie interrupted her by kissing her softly. "Shhhh..." He pressed his forehead against hers gently. "I get it. It's okay." He looked down at the clock. "Wow. We've been sitting here for an hour."

"Wow." Gabby repeated, not sure what else to say. Ronnie's kisses always made her feel good. She'd never noticed it was a ploy to shut her up before. She felt self-conscious and insecure, wondering if she'd offended him. "You really do need to learn how to shut the hell up, Gabrielle." But weren't they trying to have an honest, mature relationship, free of all the games and lies they'd had in their previous relationships? Gabby didn't want to be one of those women who manipulated Ronnie and used him, and told him, or let him believe he could only be ... 'one thing'. And she'd learned the hard way that concealing her own true feelings was a mistake as well. "I love this man and I love the woman someone convinced him he had to destroy! Why can't he be both?" She followed him quietly into the house.

Only five minutes after arriving at Ronnie's dad's for brunch, Gabby had to excuse herself to take a call. The men took advantage of the break to resume their ongoing chess game.

David laughed at his son. "Oh, man you've got it bad!"

"What are you talking about?" Ronnie tried to be cool.

"Oh, like you've brought any of your thousands of other women here to meet me."

"There haven't been thousands; officially, there have only been three."

"Whatever, I've only ever met one. She's pretty. And she seems smart enough. What does she see in you?" David teased his son.

"Hey!" Ronnie pretended to be offended. "Actually, I'm still trying to figure that out. She certainly doesn't need me...or my money. You know who she is right?"

"No. Is she an actress?"

"No, she's a publicist and agent. She represents half the NBA and NFL." If his dad didn't recognize Gabby from the papers or television as 'Bishop Robert Nichols' celebrity-agent daughter', Ronnie wasn't going to bring it up. David was a gentleman, and the least judgmental Christian Ronnie had ever heard of; but Ronnie didn't want to start a conversation they'd have to end when Gabby walked back into the room. And he had a self-imposed, unspoken rule about discussing her father, except when absolutely necessary.

"That is impressive. And seriously, she seems to be crazy about you..."

"Almost like it's too good to be true?" Ronnie said mostly jokingly.

"No, Chip... I'm not saying that... I just don't want to see you hurt... Does she know?"

"Actually, she does. I showed her right away..." A devilish grin crept across Ronnie's face, as he recalled their first few days together.

"Whoa. TMI."

Ronnie kept laughing. "Hey, you asked."

"Yeah, but..." David chuckled, then got quiet. "You talked to your mom lately?"

"I called her last week, but I had to leave a message. Libby says she's okay. She finally got her to move in with her."

"Really? Why'd she need to do that?"

Ronnie hesitated. At thirty-five years old, he still held out hope that his parents would get back together. He actually didn't know that his father had resumed supporting his mom almost immediately after getting out of prison, even though, she refused to him. What Ronnie did know, and didn't get, was that in the twenty-two years since Hugo, she had never even dated another man. Apparently, Annette Gray was still stubborn, more than a little bit crazy and, in her own crazy way, still very much in love with her ex-husband. At least that's what Ronnie hoped was going on with her. He worried about her, especially while he'd been away. Libby said she'd never really seen her smile since the storm. "I don't have all the details, Dad. I think she just needed to get out of Marietta. You should call her and ask her."

"I tried that, Ronnie. She doesn't want to see me."

"You said you tried ten years ago. Things have probably changed since then. How's the saying go 'time heals all wounds'?"

"How often have you seen her? Yeah, don't answer that. What makes you so wise?"

"Countless hours of prayer and therapy..."

"Oh yeah..."

"And have you met my girlfriend?" Ronnie sat back and grinned.

"Naw, that's not you, that's dumb luck." David laughed. "I'm just saying... no way you could pull that off on purpose..."

"You're probably right. You jealous, felon?" Ronnie laughed.

"Hell yeah...Girl!"

"Hey, sometimes it takes a woman... check mate."

Gabby returned to a chuckling David and a blushing Ronnie. "Oh, my...Do I need to go back outside?"

"No, Baby, I was just giving Dad a little dating advice."

"Oh. Ooh. Wait. Don't listen to him, David. Everything he knows about women he learned from an outdated library book! Remember our first date?" She giggled as they stood to go into the kitchen.

"Yes, I do, and because I'm a gentleman, I'll pretend that I don't." Ronnie whispered in her ear and kissed her neck, before following David down the hall.

"I can hear you! Seriously, I know you think I'm a lonely old man, and I've got to get my jollies any way I can, but these are images I do not want in my head!" David shook his head. "Gabby, do you have children?"

"I do. I have one amazing son, Ethan. He's almost ten."

"He really is a great kid, Dad. He reminds me of Neal: athletic, super smart, funny... and he cooks, and plays guitar."

"Yeah, well you and your brother are a lot alike. He came by the other day. He said he was going to give you a call. Have you talked to him?"

"No, but we're going to be back, next weekend, baby? I'll try to get up with him then."

"You need to do more than try, Chip. He misses you."

"He's got a funny way of showing it."

"Why do you say that?"

"I'm not exactly what you call 'hard to find', Dad. I sent him tickets when I was doing the show. Neal has been to see Libby three times in the last year alone. How is he suddenly missing me?"

Gabby frowned at her vibrating phone. "I'm so sorry. Please excuse me again."

"It's fine, Baby. Tell Chris I've got his back," Ronnie said referring to Gabby's latest superstar in crisis-mode.

"Ronnie, how much have you spoken to your brother since I went away?" David looked at his son across his dining room table.

"Not much. He sort of changed."

"Hold on." David got up from the table and went into his den. Ronnie heard the sound of boxes being shuffled around, and then his father returned with a stack of envelopes. He handed the bundle to Ronnie.

"What's this?" Ronnie stared at the letters addressed to his father in prison. He knew the address well, as he'd written him himself at least once a week for almost five years.

"Letters from Neal, mostly about you. Chip, your brother has been tormented for years, decades, really, feeling like what happened to you was his fault."

"No. How? Why?" Ronnie held the letters delicately in his hands.

"He thinks he didn't protect you. If he'd been looking after you..."

"But Dad... Neal was just a kid, too. He couldn't have known that mom's brother was capable of something like that."

"That's what I told him, but... "

"Why are you showing me these? Why are you telling me this now? Why not a long time ago?"

"I thought I was sparing you more pain, by not telling you that your brother was unhappy and guilt-ridden over something that happened to you. You had enough to deal with. And frankly, I thought I could handle it. You know. When I got out I tried to re-connect with him as soon as I could. But he was a grown man by then. If he needed me, he wasn't saying so. He'd see me and talk to me, but... I thought he was ashamed of me, that I'd gotten locked up, after everything I told him. We talk, but he's never been the same. But last week, he was different, and the last couple of times we've talked, he's only wanted to talk about you, not Libby and not your mom. He's hurting, Chip; and I can't reach him. Please call your brother. I'm worried about him."

"I will. I promise.

27

APPLES, TREES... AND HATE-MONGERS

*T*he next day, Gabby and Ronnie drove forty minutes to the other side of Atlanta to Libby's house. Gabby was nervous. As they pulled into the cute neighborhood of large homes on tiny lots with tree-lined sidewalks, Gabby realized she'd never had to meet anyone's mom before. She grew up with Kevin, his parents were like second parents to her. No one in the time before or since Kevin was marriage material. Ronnie said they were just going to stop in and see Libby, but he warned her that his mom might be there.

His nephew, one of sixteen year old twins, met them in the driveway. "Superstar!"

"Spiderman!" Ronnie greeted the young man with a man-hug. Connor more closely resembled his uncle than either of his parents.

Gabby smiled to herself when she finally got it. "He really does look like a sixteen year-old-boy!"

"Connor, this is my girlfriend, Gabrielle Nichols."

"It's a pleasure to meet you, Miss Nichols." Gabby was impressed at how quickly he made the switch from playful, adoring nephew to polite young man.

"Please, call me Gabby, Connor. 'Miss Nichols' makes me feel old."

"Yes ma'am." He smiled and lead them into the house. Gabby opened her mouth, as if to stop the 'ma'aming' too, but thought better of it. She'd never let her son get away with less.

The rest of the Miller family slowly made their way into the family room of Libby's pretty home. First Cameron, the physically identical, but in every other way opposite twin, surfaced from the basement, greeting his uncle with the same enthusiasm. Libby, who Gabby had already met came downstairs, followed by her husband, Lonnie, a giant, black bear of a man, with a warm smile and easy laugh. He hugged Ronnie and squeezed Gabby's hand. "I've heard a lot about you, Gabby. Did Ronnie tell you that before

he ran off to Hollywood and became famous, he was the bass player for the hottest band in Atlanta?" Lonnie asked as he set his guitar
case down.

"No, he didn't..." Gabby stared at him.

"Yup. I've been waiting seven years to say this... We're gettin' the band back together!" Ronnie grinned and looked at Gabby,
as if asking permission.

"What are you looking at me for?"

... Ronnie, Lonnie and the twins set up in the garage and
made not entirely horrible music for Libby and Gabby until a gray,
Ford F150 roared into the driveway. Annette emerged from the
driver's seat looking slightly haggard, but otherwise still very pretty. She stared into the open garage. She knew her son-in-law was a
musician, but last she heard, he hadn't been playing. She looked
around to see who belonged to the new Mercedes taking up her
usual spot in the driveway. She smiled when she saw who looked
like Neal from the back. She thought, "he must finally be doing
well for himself". He looked good, maybe a little fuller than she'd
like, but at least he was eating well. He had a full head of dark
curly hair. Everyone was smiling. "What a nice surprise." Her eyes
moved quickly to the far side of the garage to a pretty woman, who
looked more like Shawnee than any girl she'd think of as 'Neal's
type'. And then he turned around. Ronnie's face lit up when he saw
his mother. It didn't matter that she just stood there speechless. He
was happy to see her, happier than he ever imagined he would be.
He walked slowly toward her.

"Hi Mom." He smiled at her, waiting for her to recover
from the shock of seeing him in person for the first time in more
than ten years.

"Ronnie?" She whispered more to herself than to him. She
knew it was him, but... He was so handsome. He looked so young.
Her beautiful baby girl was now an incredibly handsome, and completely believable, man. She shouldn't have avoided images of him
when he was doing his show. She would have been impressed.
Libby told her, but she didn't believe it were possible. "Oh my
God... my baby..." She wrapped her arms around him and cried.
When she pulled away, she continued to stare at the son she'd never
acknowledged. She looked back and forth between Ronnie and

Libby. It was fascinating. If you didn't know, you could tell they were siblings, but Ronnie looked more like a younger, lighter version of his father than even Neal did. She just stared at him and smiled through her tears.

"Mama, this is Gabrielle."

Gabby quickly wiped her face and wiped her hands on her jeans, feeling silly and very, very happy. "I'm sorry. It's so nice to meet you, Mrs..." Gabby hesitated. She couldn't remember Annette's maiden name.

"Call me, 'Annette' or 'Anne', Gabrielle."

"Thank you. Then please, call me Gabby?"

"Hi Gabby." Annette giggled nervously and squeezed Gabby's hand back. "Wow, I run out for an hour to get my mani-pedi on and come home to a full-blown reunion and jam session! Elizabeth, why didn't you tell me? I would have gotten my roots done. Gabby, I assure you that I'm usually better prepared to receive visitors than this."

"Oh lord, Mama; you look fine. Ronnie and Gabby just called and then showed up. Does the rule about calling three days in advance really apply to your own children?" Libby rolled her eyes and patted her belly.

"I'm just saying. And please stop chastising me in front of company. I don't care if this is your house."

"I'm not chastising you; Ronnie and his girlfriend aren't company, and this is your house, too. Now, quit it. It's too hot."

"You see how she treats me, Gabby? She's been like this for the last three months. You'd think she's the first woman to ever have a baby. She's always complaining and fussing about something, her feet, the heat, how fat her ass is gettin'."

"Watch it, old woman."

"Says the knocked-up forty-one-year-old..."

"Uh! Ronnie, please take your mother to dinner so I can put bugs in her bed!"

"Oh my! Okay... That's a good idea. Baby, do we have time?" Ronnie looked at Gabby to see if she was okay. He knew they had no plans.

"Of course, but can everyone come? Y'all are so much fun. I grew up an only child... kind of."

"That's right...Aren't you Bishop Nichols' daughter?" Cameron, the untrained twin, blurted out.

"Cam!" His parents and brother shouted in unison.

"Sorry."

"It's fine. Cameron. Yes, I am the only child of Bishop Robert and Phyllis Nichols, and trust me, there is little that you can say or ask that I have not heard."

"But you won't be hearing any of that here." Ronnie kissed her on her forehead. "Is everyone ready to go?" Ronnie asked looking around the garage. The Miller's and Annette all scrambled to change for dinner, while Ronnie and Gabby waited and cooled off in the kitchen.

"So, that wasn't so bad, right?"

"Are you kidding? She's delightful. So real and funny. And she's so happy to see you, Baby."

"Yeah... I don't know what I was worried about."

"Time heals..."

The family giggled and told stories about the Reynolds siblings for hours over dinner. Back at the house, Connor pulled out an old photo album. Gabby gasped and pointed at pictures of Ronnie during his various hair stages.

"Have you ever had a bad day?" She teased.

"Oh, God yes!" Annette offered. "Do you want to see my pictures?"

"No." Libby and Ronnie answered together, quickly, in unison, but somehow, gently.

"Fine." Annette sat back and sipped her evening cocktail. "Gabby, I bet you were an absolutely lovely child. Poise like yours doesn't happen overnight."

"Thank you! I'm just happy to be able to leave the house without pantyhose on. I wasn't allowed to wear jeans growing up... or pants for that matter."

"Ha!" Libby laughed. "So, your mom was crazy, too?" She winked at her mother who finger signed what looked to Gabby like 'Lard butt.'

"No, my dad, actually. I needed to be in my Sunday-best at all times. 'Appearance is very important, Gabrielle.'" She shook her head and frowned, as she lowered her voice to mimic the bishop.

"Hmph." Cameron grunted and looked away.

"Gabrielle, please excuse my grandson. He seems to think that being a homosexual gives him license to make people uncomfortable." Annette wrapped her arm around Gabby's shoulder. Gabby shot Libby and Ronnie a look of surprise and panic. Ronnie stared daggers at his mother, until she removed her arm. Libby just shook her head and waited. Cameron did tend to lean a little toward the drama, but he was far from obnoxious. He also knew how to defend himself. He squinted at his grandmother in a gesture that could not be mistaken for eye-rolling, but was the clear opposite of contrition.

"I do apologize if I made you uncomfortable, Miss Nichols. It's just that your father has been running around this city, on TV... everywhere, telling people that 'God hates fags'. I've known my whole life that I'm gay, and that it's not a choice. I've been watching him, for at least as long as I've been allowed to listen to radio or watch TV independently; because I want to know what's going on 'out there'. And watching and listening to him, it's as though *he*, not God, hates me! And now there are all these boys and men coming forward saying that he...I'm sorry that you just wandered in here with Uncle Ronnie, expecting a quiet family gathering, but you're as close as I can get to him. Do you know why he's been saying all of those things if... Even if he never laid a finger on any of them, he's surrounded himself with young, attractive gay men. They must have believed he cared about them, even liked them, more than he wanted them to change. How could he have partnered with the likes of racist Jon Hamilton Jr. to destroy and condemn us? How can he call himself a man of God and preach such venom about people he claims to love? Isn't it his calling as a Christian to love ALL people, including me?" Cameron stared at Gabby with tears in his eyes.

Gabby felt her face grow hot. She'd never heard it put so simply. No one had been bold enough to question her, at least not since Ronnie had become her personal shield. And even then, other reporters were only concerned with her belief in her father's guilt or innocence, not the greater questions. Not even in the indictment or the opening arguments had the duplicity been so clearly laid out. Being a pompous hypocrite wasn't, after all, an actual crime. Her father was finally being called to answer for what his accusers believed they could prove in a court of law. But this beautiful boy was asking the questions that she, her mother, and thousands of congregants should have been asking for decades. She knew what her father would say: 'I hate the sin, not the sinner.' She knew how absurd, and just plain untrue, a statement that was. She wasn't going to lie to this young man and his family. He deserved better than that. She stared at Ronnie, until he was about to speak, and stopped him. She didn't want to be rescued. She closed her eyes and prayed for the words. When she opened them, she walked over and sat next to Cameron.

"Wow, Cameron. How old are you? I... I wish I knew the answers to your questions. More importantly, I wish I'd had the courage to ask them myself. I can't speak for my father. You know that. But I can say that I'm sorry that I turned a blind eye to the hate that I did know he was spreading. Even if he stands before his God and hears that what he believed to be true is right; and I don't believe for a second that he will, he's been wrong...every day of my life. He has no right to judge you, or to teach me or anyone else to. And while I have felt that way for a long, long time, I've never been more convinced, or convicted than I am right now." She touched his cheek. "I can only speak for myself; but, to the extent that my silence...and my cowardice has caused you pain, and I see that it has, I'm so deeply sorry." Cameron hugged Gabby as they both cried. When they let go, she smiled and sighed deeply. "I want nephews!" she pouted.

"Looks like you got 'em." Ronnie smiled and winked at Libby.

28

SHADES OF GRAY

*A*s Gabby anticipated, it had been a variably 'gray' day. Not for weather, but for Ronnie. The built-in organizer in her head, for better or worse, color-coded everything, including, and in retrospect, unfortunately, Ronnie's varying degrees of gender. But at least she kept it simple. Boy days were black. Ronnie looked good in black. On a solid black day, she swooned like a teenager, and he gave her butterflies with just a glance. On a white day, (well white-ish, Ronnie was never all girl), Gabby floundered a little. When Ronnie was more girl than boy, Gabby wasn't sure of much of anything, except that she was a stone-cold lesbian. But she felt off balance everywhere else. Sexually, she couldn't get enough of...her; but outside of their bedroom, Gabby couldn't be led by a woman. Still, she couldn't decide which she liked best. Fortunately, she didn't have to. One-hundred percent days at either end of the spectrum were few and far between, and Ronnie typically stayed a heather-gray, a little more masculine than feminine, but not hard. Gabby thought she could rest in the peace of a solid gray day forever. And as they lay on the couch with her head on his chest and her hand tucked under his t-shirt, she purred. He smiled, smelling her hair and enjoying the softness against his face. It had been a good day. He'd been worried for nothing.

"Your mom's really nice, Baby. I don't know what you were so worried about." Gabby said lightly about Annette.

"Oh trust me, you stick around long enough, she'll show you. She's just waiting for the right moment." Ronnie's tone was similar, but with a hint of warning.

"You don't think you're being a little paranoid, Ronnie?"

"Are you saying you think she's right?"

"I'm just saying, what would be wrong with softening a little to appease your mother?"

"Whatever. Come here." She didn't answer or move, she just lifted her face slightly to kiss him. He kissed her deeply, harder than she expected, and he held her arms firmly, pulling her closer to him. "Thank you," he whispered when she'd done what he'd asked. He pulled her tank top over her head as he kissed her. She smiled and sighed, reaching for his t-shirt, but he held both of her wrists in one of his hands.

"Baby, I need to..." It was usually all she needed to say to get him to take his shirt off so she could feel his skin.

"No." He'd never told her 'no' before. "You don't 'need to', Gabrielle. You want to." He released her hands and she let them rest on his chest.

"Ronnie? Honey, I didn't mean it like that..."

"It's okay. I'm fine." He slid his hands up her torso to her breasts. He rubbed them and pulled gently until her nipple reached his mouth. He sucked hard and she arched her back and moaned. He held her there for a moment, as she straddled and ground against his stomach through her pajamas. He tugged at her bottoms, until she slipped them off and tapped her hips, directing her to stand so he could sit up. He pulled her back onto his lap facing him. Her skin felt like silk beneath his fingertips. She pressed her naked body against his fully clothed. She rolled her hips against him and rubbed her full soft breasts against his face. He ran his nails down her back and kissed her throat. Gabby held her breath. He knew what she needed. She closed her eyes as he caressed her hips. It would just be a moment more... He lifted her from his lap and laid her roughly on the couch. She smiled until he stood up and looked down at her. His expression was 'black'. She held onto his right hand, pulling it to her mouth and sucking his fingers, paying closest attention to the two she needed. He watched as they disappeared inside her pretty mouth. He smiled as she moaned and slid her hand between her legs... but he refused to give her what she wanted. He walked away, leaving her naked, and more than a little confused, on the couch. She clutched a pillow to muffle a fake scream. After a moment, she followed him into the bedroom. He was in the bathroom with the door closed. He never closed the door unless... Moments later, he emerged strapped. She smiled and reached up to touch him. He bent to kiss her and held her hands, not letting her touch him. She whimpered into his mouth. Ronnie didn't speak. He just walked slowly toward the bed, forcing her backward. When they reached the bed, he spun her around and pushed her shoulders forward, bending her over. He didn't need to touch her; he knew that she was ready. Gabby closed her eyes and held her breath. It was thick and unusually cool, but satisfying and she held her head back, as he stroked her deeply. Ronnie closed his eyes, and let her sounds wash over him. She was vocal, loud, vulgar. The only time she cursed was when he was fucking her. It wasn't his preference. He liked her sweet, playful, even, on rare occasions, in control. But he wanted to remind her that he could go there, and take her with him. He tortured her for hours, bringing her to the brink and stopping before she could soar. He let her rest. She was, after all, his Angel Gabrielle; he'd die before hurting her. And he showed her by massaging her tender flesh with his lips and tongue until she was ready for him again, but only until. And again he'd lay her on her stomach and press deep inside her until she pushed back and began to rock against him.

"Ronnie please..."

"Please what? Do you want me to stop?"

"No."

"What do you need?"

"I don't know." She lied. She was afraid to say. She vaguely remembered what she'd said hours earlier to get herself in her current state. She didn't dare tell him again that she needed to touch his skin, and taste him and feel the softness of his breasts against hers... to rub pert nipples against her lips. He'd kill her in some freakish..."Freakfest!" "Baby, please! Whatever I did... I'm sorry! Please let me..." Gabby moaned into the mattress. Her tears real by now, she arched her back slowly, and looked over her shoulder at him, hoping that he'd take pity on her and give her what she needed.

"Okay." He sighed deeply and kissed sweat on the back of her neck, as he slowly pulled away and out. He stopped and rested his head on her back, pressing his chest against her hips. He teased her, rolling his knuckles in the ceaseless wetness. She moaned softly, as he finally slipped his middle and index fingers deep inside her. "Do you want me to go and get it?" he asked knowing that from there she could have finished on her own.

"Yes." He smiled and kissed her cheeks as he raised up to work her. She groaned and her sounds became sweet and light, as she cried and moved against his hand. "Ronnie!" Her explosion radiated from his hand and through his body, and seemed to go on forever. Gabby sobbed softly until finally she fell asleep.

29

SAY MY NAME

*R*onnie couldn't sleep. He got out of bed, lugging the heavy dildo and its itchy harness back into the bathroom. He was too disgusted with himself to care for his equipment, and tossed it in its case at the back of the linen closet unwashed. Already, he recognized his behavior as so contrary to his own character and love for Gabby that it scared him. "What the hell was that?" He sat on the edge of the tub, miserable. "No, seriously why did you do that?" He had no repressed fantasies about controlling her or depriving her of... anything. And if part of him had decided to step over to the dark side and become a masochist, he was going to need to check that; because, frankly, he sucked at 'bad ass'. "No, my friend, that was not a good look for you, at all... Yeah, well she didn't seem to mind... much." That was actually true. He peeked into the bedroom and watched Gabby sleeping soundly. To her, it was just... sex; and it was different because, although he was almost always the initiator, and always assertive, he'd never been controlling or aggressive. He hadn't been punishing her; he'd punished himself. He'd spent the entire day, as he had every other, just waiting to be alone with her. He lived for her touch, for her kisses, the way she made him feel...whole, masculine...beautiful.

"Dummy." He looked up and saw his reflection in the mirror from the waist up; and surprisingly didn't rush to cover himself. He stared for a moment before standing and walking across the spacious bathroom to the mirror. It had been a long time since he'd done that, just really looked at his own naked body. Deliberately looking himself in the eye had become a daily practice, something he and Neal learned from their dad. Actually, it was Neal who first talked to him about it, the first year their dad was away. Neal shared the lesson with Ronnie as a check of one's 'spiritual fitness', without consideration of gender at all, so it never occurred to him to have routine face-to-face talks with himself naked. And before the storm, and especially after, he was just more comfortable with his clothes on. Besides, in his head, the order made sense: shower, get dressed, brush your teeth, check yourself. Most of his life, except for his dark 'it's good to be the king' phase, he fared pretty well. In his head, 'clothes made the man', so, typically he liked what he saw. But as he stared at his reflection and allowed his gaze to lower slowly, something was different. The most surprising thing to Ronnie was that, he wasn't displeased with himself or even what he saw. He shook his head and chuckled. "You know she's gonna get you back, right?" He actually smiled, imagining what she might do. He looked up again at the face of a man who knew he was loved by an amazing and exciting woman. And while he barely recognized himself from the neck down, the face was reassuringly familiar. His eyes were still a brilliant green, not black as they felt earlier. They actually did look, to him, intelligent, kind and...happy. He closed and opened them slowly to look down again. "Hmph." His neck was long, elegant, actually. His shoulders were broad, but not too muscular. He turned his body slowly from one side and then the other, holding the tummy that was only a few hundred crunches away from being rock hard. He liked his arms the best. They were well defined, but not overly cut. Facing front again, he took a deep breath. His breasts were, as Gabby repeatedly reminded him, perfect. "Hmph." He didn't stay there long, he kept his hands by his side, and didn't dare go farther south. Instead, he looked back up, leaned just slightly toward the mirror again and nodded. "You're okay."

But he still wasn't sleepy. His mind was racing and he replayed the day in his head over and over again. It had been a good day, actually one of the best ever, except no Neal. He washed up and went to his office and found the letters his father had given him. He stared at the envelopes for a long time, before putting them back in a fireproof cabinet. He didn't need to read them. He needed to call his brother. It was nearly five a.m., but he knew if he put it off he wouldn't do it at all. Neal answered right away and recognized Ronnie's voice instantly. He didn't care about the hour; he was glad Ronnie called, and asked if they could meet in Macon around noon. Talking to his brother gave Ronnie enough comfort that he thought he could finally sleep, so he crawled back into bed, pulled Gabby close and slept for a few hours.

He slid out of bed Sunday morning without waking Gabby. Again, he passed the mirror check, but in the light of day, he still had a few mixed feelings about the night before. "It was sex. It felt good, sort of." But he knew it was malicious. He watched the woman he loved sleeping and sighed deeply. However assholy he may have been, there she was. ♪I got-a roof over my head, the woman I love layin' in my bed, and it's alright, alright, alright... alright yeah...♪ He sang his favorite Darius Rucker song to himself as he tiptoed into the kitchen.

Gabby was awakened by the smell of coffee, and the comfort of Ronnie gently kneading the small of her back. He closed his eyes and smiled to himself when her lips curled in a sleepy smile. "Good morning," she said sweetly with her eyes still closed.

"Good morning, my love. I'm going to meet Neal in a few hours. I made coffee, French toast and bacon. Do you want it now, or would you like to sleep in?"

"Mmm. Have you showered yet?"

"Nope. I was waiting to see if you'd want to join me." Gabby pretended to try to lift her arm and giggled. "Okay... hop on." Ronnie gave her a piggyback ride to a waiting tub. She sighed as he lowered her into the piping hot bath and slid in behind her.

"Mmm. This is nice." Gabby smiled, as Ronnie twisted her hair into a knot on the top of her head and ladled soapy water onto her neck and shoulders.

"I'm glad you like it." He kissed her wet shoulder.

"It is a wonderful and most unexpected surprise."

"I know..." Ronnie whispered, with a hint of remorse in his voice.

"Yeah... Baby... Were you mad at me? Are you?" She asked out of deep concern, not anger.

"Why do you ask that?" Ronnie tried to play innocent. He was prepared for retribution; but he actually hoped it might be physical.

"Um, because you've never just ... fucked me before... and well, I ... I don't think I'm qualified to do my job anymore, you know, having lost my last bit of brain matter somewhere around the fourth or fifth round. Don't get me wrong, it was fun; and I don't have to go to the gym this week, but..."

Ronnie blushed. "I'm sorry. We're probably gonna need counseling over this, but I heard 'your mother's right' coming from the woman I love, mostly because she is, in every way, the opposite of my mother, and I kinda lost it. After spending just a couple of hours with her, and then hearing you say you like me better softer, I kinda freaked out."

"I didn't say that, Baby! I don't feel that way. I like you, I love you, however you decide to walk in the world, all man, all woman, black, white or gray..."

"Huh?"

"Oh, nothing..." Gabby quickly changed the subject. "I do have a question, though…"

"Ask me anything."

"Why do you always call me 'Gabrielle'?"

"Huh? Okay, I didn't see that coming... I don't know." Ronnie was quiet for a moment while he considered her question. "Okay, well, first of all, that is technically your name, and I think it fits you. It's a beautiful name, and you are to me, the most beautiful woman in the world. Do you know what it means?"

"You know what? I don't. I've never liked it, so I never bothered to learn the meaning."

"It's Hebrew for 'God is my strength.'

"Wow!" Gabrielle giggled.

"Exactly. You're my 'Angel Gabrielle'. You're the strongest person I know. I felt that before I knew what your name meant..." He wrapped his arms around her, suddenly feeling very foolish. "I'm so sorry, Baby... about last night. I just got scared. It felt like...something else...like you were saying you wanted me to be...someone else. And I think there is a part of me that is afraid that you'll lose...whatever it is you see in me, if I don't...maintain."

"You're kidding me, right? Because that sounded like, you're afraid I won't respect you if you, every now and then, start acting like the woman you actually are! Okay. Here's the thing. I'm not in love with your 'persona'. I'm in love with YOU. You are my... everything. I think what I was saying is that you really do 'have it like that, now'. But if you wanted to lighten the mood, you could play along... But, I get it! Your mom needs to accept who-ever shows up wearing the Ronnie suit. And I know she's going to figure it out. She sees you, Honey. She can't miss you. You don't have to try to be more or less anything anymore, for me or your mother or anyone else. When you smile, when you walk, it's your world, Baby."

"Wow. You really are my angel. I know that sounds like... but... I know I wasn't half of whatever you're talking about before you. You give me wings. I love you so much. I just don't wa..."

"Shhhh... You're my EVERYTHING... And you cannot mess it up."

30

LET IT BURN

*N*eal sat on the porch thinking about when he and Ronnie were in school. He was constantly defending Ronnie. Neal's teammates and other boys his age never seemed to stop making rude comments about his little sister, about how pretty she was and how 'one day, my boy's gonna let me tap that!' The day Bobby Johnson, his former best friend, said that in front of everyone in the locker room was the first time Neal got suspended for fighting. Bobby later apologized, but they were never the same again. Nothing was ever the same again. Ronnie was just in the eighth grade; and when guys saw her and his older sister at his games, Ronnie was dressed like a boy. There were tons of pretty girls at the games and around school who actually liked boys. It would be a long time before Neal figured out that the reason they messed with Ronnie was because they knew they didn't stand a chance with girls their own age. It hadn't occurred to him that it was all just talk; that the boys he grew up with weren't evil or dangerous. They were just dumb kids doing what boys do. Still, he didn't like it. Ronnie was his baby sister. She looked up to him; and at school, and with their dad away at work, it was his job to protect her. But it was a hard job, one he looked forward to getting a break from.

He prayed the summer between his sophomore and junior years would last forever. At home and at Mona's house were the only places he felt like he could relax. Ronnie would be safe around family. She spent most of her time avoiding their mom and locked up in her room with her best friend, Shawnee. No danger there. It was about the same at Mona's. There weren't any girls around, but the only boys were younger than her, or related to them. Scott was more like an older cousin than an uncle. Sure he was stupid and kind of a redneck, but at fifteen, Neal didn't know that blood relatives could be just as dangerous as total strangers. He'd have never left her alone that day, or that night. If he'd have seen the signs, he would have made their mom come and get them out of there. How did he not see the signs? How could he ever look at her, or him, again after what he let happen? How could his dad ever love or trust him again? "He'd left me in charge! I was the man of the house!" Neal had said as much to his father, in letters and later in person; but no matter how his father tried to reassure him that it wasn't his fault, that he didn't blame him, and was fairly certain Ronnie didn't either, he never got over it. Not a single day went by that he didn't remember and wish he had that day to do all over again. The memories of that day, more than twenty years earlier, were as fresh as the tomatoes and green beans that still grew in the family gardens.

Ronnie pulled into the circular gravel driveway and said a prayer before getting out of his jeep. He was glad Neal was on the porch. He hadn't been in that house in twenty years. He wasn't sure what his reaction to it would be. Neal slowly pulled himself out of his rocking chair. It made Ronnie smile to see his big brother. "You know you are too damn young to be sitting on this porch in a rocking chair!" Ronnie laughed at the image of Neal whittling on their grandmother's front porch.

"It's been a long summer out in these fields. Somebody's gotta pick the beans." Neal chuckled.

"You have not been playing farmer out here for the last twenty years!"

"Naw, I haven't. This is actually the first time I've been back here in a while. Libby's boys have been tending the fields. I just came to check the place out. Libby didn't tell you Mom's sister Jackie died? This house and land are ours now."

"Who'd Mona leave it to?"

"All three of her kids. After they died it was to go to their kids. Mom doesn't want to have anything to do with it, not even as a rental. But the tax bill is still in Mom's name and she can't afford not to pay it."

"I hear ya. So what do you wanna do with it?"

"I thought I'd let you decide."

"Why me?" Ronnie knew the answer, but this was as close to a real conversation as he'd ever had with his brother. He wanted to hear the words.

Neal looked away. "I thought because of what happened

here... you'd wanna help me burn it down." Neal looked mischievously at his younger brother and Ronnie smiled back.

"Sounds like somethin' I've wanted to do for twenty years; but isn't arson a felony?"

"Actually, yes, it is; and insurance fraud is also a felony, but this decrepit castle has no mortgage. We certainly won't be burning it for insurance and according to our mother, it's ours. There is no law against setting your own house on fire in a manner that doesn't endanger anyone else... I think. And we're smack dab in the middle of five-hundred acres of farm land. I checked it out. And I got the volunteer fire department on speed dial... just in case..."

"You're serious!"

"As first communion on Easter Sunday, bro."

"Hmph."

"What? You don't want to?"

"Naw. It's not that. I've just never heard... You never called me that before. I thought you... I thought you were calling to tell me how I screwed your life up..."

"What? Ronnie! Oh wow." Neal sat on the stoop next to Ronnie and didn't talk for a long time. "Ya know, I can actually see how you could think somethin' like that."

"You were the only boy and then... I just took up so much of everyone's time and energy."

"No, I didn't resent you, Ronnie. Nothing that happened was your fault. It was the world, Scott, kids we went to school with..."

"What?"

"I know I never told you. You weren't supposed to know about the danger. I was supposed to protect you. But you know even while you were figuring it all out, and wearing my clothes, guys knew you were a girl. That's how they saw you. Me too, for a long time. And you missed all of it, you know, coming into manhood kinda late, but teenage boys are assholes, man."

Ronnie laughed out loud.

"Seriously, I got in fights on a regular... I thought, tryin' to keep those knuckleheads away from you."

"I had no idea."

"Of course you didn't. You weren't supposed to know. I

was just supposed to protect you... And I didn't..."

"But you were just a kid, Neal. He was our uncle. You couldn't have known."

"I should have known."

"Please stop saying that."

"I've been asking God to let me have that day back every day of my life since."

"That's kinda stupid, by the way... Oh my God. Stop it! Stop doing that. I don't! Was it horrible and scary and ...? I really do believe I died more than once that night. But I... Neal, this is going to sound crazy, but, next to something that's happened pretty recently," Ronnie smiled to himself thinking about Gabby "it was the best thing that ever happened to me. No. I know that sounds sick, but Neal I was so miserable. Mom was riding me every day about being a damn debutant... I don't think I would have survived another year in that house, if something hadn't happened to make her back off. I wouldn't wish what did happen on anyone, but I think it saved my life. It wasn't just about the clothes; it was living with her and having her not see me. Even if I'd stayed a girl, can you imagine the kind of... she'd have completely lost her mind if she'd realized that, as a woman, I'm a lesbian. Do you know how nuts our mother is - that *this* is actually a more preferable alternative to homosexuality?!" This time Neal laughed out loud.

"Yeah, she is kinda crazy. You think I should tell her I'm bisexual?" He asked with a straight face.

"Oh, gee whiz... only if you have to. I'm telling you, I aint seen her in a while before the other day, but I don't think she's ready. Seriously, Neal. I'm happy. I'm good. My life is amazing. Please don't waste another second of your life mourning mine. I honestly don't know how my life can get any better... But..."

"What?"

"It hurts me to know that you've been unhappy... Ya know, I wanted to be you. Is this why you barely made it through your senior year, why you didn't go to college?"

"Yeah, but I'm getting it together. I'm actually enrolled now; but ya know, I still don't know what I want to do. Isn't that crazy? My whole plan centered around playing basketball and going to college, but I never really thought about what I would do after that happened. And when it didn't happen, I was really lost. Don't get me wrong, I've been working... but I've just been working... just living with no direction or purpose. I'm still waiting to see what I wanna be when I grow up. I gotta tell you though, seeing you, knowing that the you I'd been seeing on TV wasn't some act, that you're really okay, I think I'm gonna be okay now, too."

"Whoa, happy to hear that, but trust me, the me you saw on TV *was not* okay..." The brothers filled each other in on the last two decades of their lives until they noticed that they had only a few hours of daylight left.

"You been inside yet?" Ronnie asked Neal, who stood up and looked at the door.

"Not yet. I can wait til you're gone if you want. I just wanted to see you, Ronnie."

"It's okay. I'm okay. I'm glad you called me. It's been too long. You sure we can't get arrested for this?" Even having come to terms with what happened, Ronnie was still a little afraid of his grandmother's house.

"If you want to let it burn, I will call the sheriff and confirm your famous mug doesn't end up on the six o'clock news."

"Still the big brother, huh?"

"Always, Chip."

Ronnie smiled. "Let's do this." They stood for a long time before entering after unlocking the door. They each had equally horrific images to brace themselves for. Sure, Ronnie was attacked, but it was Neal who'd found her. Aunt Jackie had only been dead for a month. Libby's twins never came in the house when they tended the gardens, so it had been closed up in the summer heat for a while. Even with the new wood floors and the stale smell of gardenias, Ronnie could still smell Scott's sweat and beer. Neal watched him, trying to stay just close enough. When they made it to Ronnie's old bedroom, Neal waited in the hall. Ronnie pushed the door open slowly. The bed was still there, and made up to be a pretty guestroom. Ronnie held one of the posters and squeezed his eyes tightly. He said a prayer of Thanks for his life and specifically that he lived through the storm. He prayed for Neal and thanked God for bringing them back together. He'd felt like he'd been living with a hole in his heart for twenty years. He was functional, maybe even successful, but when he thought of his brother, he never felt quite right. As he turned toward the door, and saw Neal in the doorway, he finally felt at peace. Neal watched him with tears in his eyes. Ronnie took a deep breath and sighed. "I'm really okay, Neal."

31

TWO GAY DADS AND A RAPIST
WALK INTO A COURTROOM

*R*onnie squeezed Gabby's hand before she walked slowly across the small courtroom to the witness stand. Kevin and Kyle looked on, as they all silently sent prayers her way.

"Ms. Nichols, isn't it true that as soon as you learned of Mr. Rivers' success in New York, that you hatched a plan to make him marry you?!"

"Of course not! I loved him!"

"But you knew he was gay?"

"No, he didn't come out until much later."

"But you already stated that you did know, that you've always known."

"You're taking that out of context! My point was that Kevin is a good man. He was trying to do the right thing!"

"The right thing based on your lying and manipulations?"

In a low voice, "I wanted EJ to be Kevin's."

"But you knew he wasn't?" There is a long pause "Ms. Nichols, please answer the question."

"Yes."

"And you withheld that information hoping that if he thought you were carrying his child, he would marry you?"

"Yes."

"No further questions, your honor."

"Redirect?" Aidan approached and stared reassuringly at Gabby.

"Ms. Nichols, how long have you known Mr. Rivers?"

"Almost thirty years, most of our lives."

"Did you just wake up one day and decide to trick him into being a father and marrying you?"

"Of course not. We were childhood sweethearts. I loved him. When I thought I was pregnant, I panicked. I hadn't even decided that I would keep the baby by the time I came to New York. I didn't even see a doctor. I just wanted to see him. When I saw him and he still loved me... I wanted the life we'd always talked about. I know it was wrong; but I knew he would be a good father."

"And has he been a good father?"

"The best."

"How is that possible with his career being in New York?"

"He found other ways to be present. When he was home, he did everything - midnight feedings, diaper changes, play dates. We even scheduled EJ's checkups around his schedule. He only missed the mundane stuff, really. And when EJ could talk, they talked every day. Kevin knows Ethan better than anyone, even me. He's his best friend."

"And when he came out to you and told you he was going to marry Kyle Tye? You had an opportunity to make things right. You could have separated and kept Ethan from him."

"No. I could not. Kevin is Ethan's father. I couldn't take him away from him. I wouldn't. I ..."

"What is it, Ms. Nichols?"

"I owed him. I know that that lie, even though it gave him a son he adores, it took things from him. It took his choices. I took years of his life that he might have lived differently. We'd never have gotten married if not for Ethan. He came to me and told me the truth. I couldn't punish him by taking away his son, ever, but certainly not after what I did to him."

"Since your divorce and Mr. River's marriage to Mr. Tye, what's happened to Ethan?"

"EJ lives with his dads in Toronto. He spends holidays with me and we meet when I fly to New York for work, at least once a month, and now we talk everyday - sometimes for hours."

"Does he seem happy to you?"

"Oh, yes. He loves Kyle, and church and the theater. He's always been different. He has access to culture and the arts that he didn't have in North Carolina. He's a straight 'A' student. He sings and plays the piano. He was okay at home with me; but he missed his dad. Now, he's really happy."

"And it is your wish that you be able to share custody with

Mr. Rivers and Mr. Tye."

"Yes, it is my wish that my son continue to live with his fathers, Kevin and Kyle Rivers-Tye."

"And what about his birth father, Mr. Aiken?"

"What about him?" Gabby asked innocently.

"Why not him?"

"I don't believe he really wants Ethan."

"So you didn't tell him."

"No."

"Was he abusive?"

Gabby hesitated. "Ms. Nichols, please answer the question." The judge prompted.

Gabrielle shifted in her seat. "Yes, when he drank."

"Did he hit you?"

"Yes."

"Were there any witnesses to this abuse?"

"I called the police twice, and once had to go to the emergency room. I had a broken rib and my face was..."

"Your Honor, I'd like to enter Exhibit B. This is the photo taken by hospital staff when Ms. Nichols was admitted on May 9, 2000."

"Did you leave him after this?"

"I didn't have to. We didn't live together and he disappeared so he wouldn't be arrested."

"When did you see him again after this?"

"Nine months later, in February of 2001."

"Did you have sex with him?"

"...Yes."

"Was it consensual?"

"Objection! The attorney for the defense is trying to suggest that my client assaulted this witness!"

"I'm trying to establish the circumstances surrounding the conception of Ethan Rivers, your honor."

"Overruled. You may answer the question, Ms. Nichols."

"I didn't want to, but I was afraid."

"But you didn't press charges?"

"I was afraid. And embarrassed. I graduated Magna Cum Laude from Stanford University and here I was being treated like ...

trash by... I couldn't tell anyone."

"But you did tell someone?"

"Yes... my father."

"And what did you tell him?"

"That I thought I was pregnant."

"And what did he tell you to do?"

"He said I'd better make KJ marry me."

"You didn't tell him that the baby wasn't Mr. Rivers?"

"I did. He said it wouldn't matter, that Kevin loved me and would do the right thing."

"How could it be the right thing, if you hadn't been together in years, and you knew the baby you were carrying wasn't Kevin's?"

"My father is a... was a Baptist preacher from Georgia. He's very, very 'old school'. As far as he was concerned, when I lost my virginity to Kevin, I became his responsibility."

"So, at twenty-four, after being raped by the plaintiff..."

"Objection!"

"Withdrawn. At twenty-four, facing an unplanned, unwanted pregnancy, you consulted the only man you really trusted to guide you, your father, and he advised you to tell your boyfriend the truth, and his response was to take responsibility for you and your child?"

"Yes."

"Did you ever tell Mr. Rivers that Ethan wasn't his?"

"No, because as far as I'm concerned, he is."

"So you've had no contact with the plaintiff before he showed up at Mr. Rivers' home, unannounced, demanding to see a boy who didn't know he existed?"

"Leading, Your Honor."

"Withdrawn. Ms. Nichols, what was Mr. Rivers' reaction when you admitted that Ethan could possibly not be his son?"

"Disbelief. He was devastated. When he could finally speak to me, we met for a family meeting, he, Kyle and I. I begged his forgiveness and asked that I be allowed to help make it right."

"Did he ever indicate that he did not want Ethan?"

"Absolutely not! His only concern was that Ethan could be taken away."

"Did he ask you what you wanted?"

"He did, and I told him I wanted things to stay the way they'd been, for Ethan to stay with him and Kyle."

"Did he ask for your help?"

"Yes."

"And you've given it willingly?"

"Yes, whatever I have to do."

"Ms. Nichols, who's paying Mr. Rivers' attorney fees?"

"I am."

"Are you doing so willingly?"

"Absolutely."

"No further questions at this time Your Honor; but we'd like to reserve the right to call this witness again."

"So noted. We'll take a twenty minute recess and be back by eleven o'clock."

Gabby had returned to her seat, and stood the second the gavel hit the bench. She turned to the left to avoid Kevin, who sat next to her on her right. They'd barely been speaking since Tre showed up. "Gabby..." She didn't stop or answer Kevin. She still couldn't really face him; but she was determined to do whatever she needed to get that man out of their lives and away from their son.

Ronnie noticed the exchange, nodded to Kevin and went after Gabby. She'd covered fifty yards of marble before he caught up with her. He touched her shoulder just before she got to the stairs. "Baby. Stop. Where are you going? You have to get back in there."

"I know, I just need some air. I can't face them. I can't face you. I knew it would be hard, but..."

"It's fine, honey. You're doing a great job. It's all going to work out. There is no way a judge is going to give that man even visitation, let alone custody."

"But..."

"But what? All you had to do was tell the truth. You did that."

"Sure, after lying to him for ten years!"

"I told you I forgive you, Gabrielle." Kevin and Kyle appeared behind them. "You were really brave in there, really. Thank you so much." Kevin opened his arms and she walked reluctantly toward him. When he wrapped his arms around her, she let go and began sobbing.

"I'm so sorry, Kevin." He could barely make the words out, except for their familiarity. She'd barely spoken to him except to apologize and beg his forgiveness since he found out. And he'd long since given it. He knew what a manipulative monster her father was, and how easily she could have been led to lie. He believed her when she said she wanted him to be the father. What she didn't tell him was anything about Tre or that he'd been abusive. "If you'd have told me, maybe we could have fought for legal custody ten years ago; but I think the outcome would have been the same. I love you. I love our son. However he came to be in this world, he's my son. Please try and let go of...this. You're ugly when you cry." Ronnie and Kyle both just shook their heads.

Gabby punched him in the arm then rubbed it. "Thank you." She looked pointedly at Kyle.

"Everything happens the way it's supposed to, Gabrielle." Kyle smiled at her.

"Amen." Kevin and Ronnie said in unison.

"Okay, let's get back down there."

"Mr. Aiken, why are you here?"

"I got a call from some attorney that I had a son in North Carolina, and I wanted to see him."

"Who did the attorney tell you he worked for?"

"Gabby's father."

"Did you think it was odd that she wasn't calling you herself?"

"No. The lawyer said that the bishop said she'd lost her mind and had let some faggot run off to Canada to raise my kid." Aiken's attorney visibly cringed. He was hoping to avoid putting the man on the stand because he figured he'd say something stupid.

"And had you known about Ethan, would you have attempted to contact him, even if Mr. Rivers weren't a homosexual?"

"Well, sure. He's my kid; so I guess so, yeah."

"No further questions, Your Honor."

"Mr. Aiken, how many phone calls did you receive from Mr. Nichols' attorney?"

"I don't know. A few I guess."

"Wasn't it exactly three?"

"Maybe."

"Did you ever discuss money?"

"I don't remember."

"Your Honor, I'd like to present copies of two cashier's checks for fifty-thousand dollars each, payable to Mr. Aiken, from an account in the Cayman Islands, that was found to belong to Robert Nichols. The dates and the amounts on the checks correspond with deposits made to Mr. Aiken's account, and were each made one day after Mr. Aiken spoke with Mr. Nichols' attorney. The records being handed to you show a third call was made, but no corresponding deposit. Mr. Aiken, was one-hundred thousand dollars the agreed upon amount for you appearance here in court?"

"No. The money wasn't for me to show up in court. It was to help me take care of the kid."

"So, you're saying it wasn't incentive to fly all the way out here from California?"

"Well, it helped. But that's not why I did it."

"And why did Mr. Nichols give you the money?"

"...I told the lawyer that I hadn't worked in a while, and I didn't think I could get out here...and even if I did, I didn't know that I could take care of anymore kids."

"And what did the lawyer say to that?"

"That I didn't have to take care of him. I just had to show up. As long as it could be proven that I was the kid's real dad, they'd give him to me. He said that after a while, someone would come and get him."

"Did he say who would come and get him?"

"I just assumed he meant the bishop. He said the bishop would be traveling, but as soon as he was done with his church business, he'd come and get his grandson. They just needed me to get him; and since he's mines, I figured, why not."

"No further questions, Your Honor."

Gabby hadn't actually exhaled in months, but she resumed visibly holding her breath when Judge Terry entered the courtroom.

"This case is particularly puzzling to me. I don't think I

have all the pieces. Mr. Aiken, I find your timing conspicuous, and
your motivation sketchy at best. Ms. Nichols, I find your judgment
to be questionable; but I believe you've acted in the best interest of
your child, at least since your divorce. There is an overwhelming
amount of evidence that suggests removing Ethan from the care of
his fathers would be both unnecessary and harmful to his development. With that said, the law is the law, and Mr. Aiken is legally
entitled to have a chance to know his son. My issue however is the
absence of Mr. Aiken's name on the birth certificate or a paternity
test. Do we have the results from the test yet?" Judge Terry spoke
directly to her clerk.

"I'm told they're ready and are being sent over by messen-
ger. They should be here any minute."

"Your Honor, neither party is questioning that Mr. Aiken is
the biological father." Aiken's attorney offered.

"Then no one, but me, will lose any sleep over the results. I
want definitive proof of paternity, before I make any decision that
will affect the life of this child. Anyone with objection to that had
better keep it to themselves. Let's break for lunch. Hopefully we
can resolve this matter when we resume at two o'clock." She
banged her gavel.

"Gabby, is there any way at all..." Even at the eleventh
hour, Kyle tried to remain optimistic.

Gabby was quiet for a long time. "I want with my whole
heart for this to be some big stupid expensive mistake, Kyle... but
the math doesn't add up."

"You told me he was premature." Kevin's comment was
more a hopeful reminder than an accusation.

"I know. It's what I kept telling myself. But..." Kevin
walked away and sat on a bench with his head in his hands. Kyle
started walking toward him until Gabby touched his arm. She
walked over and sat on the bench close to Kevin and took his hand,
now damp from his tears. "Ethan is your son, Kevin. I don't care
what the test says. We brought that child into the world, and no
court is going to tell me I have to share him with that ... Neander-
thal... I will do whatever it takes. I promise. I still know people. I
can make that fool disappear for at least another ten years. By the
time he shows up again, Ethan will be a Senator." Kevin giggled

and wiped his eyes. Gabby pulled him close and hugged him.

When the judge finally entered again at two-thirty, she looked stern, and a little annoyed.

"I have the results of the test, and my ruling. In the Province of Toronto, I have the discretion of awarding custody to non-biological parents; but I frankly do not like to do so. I was prepared, in this instance, however, to exercise my judicial power and order that the minor child, Ethan Rivers-Tye, remain in the joint custody of his mother and fathers, with supervised monthly visitation by the plaintiff, at his, or his benefactor's expense. I am happy to announce that I don't even have to do that. According to these tests, and I had the lab run them more than once, there is a less than one percent chance that Tre Aiken is your son's father, Ms. Nichols. What I think you'll all find more interesting than that... a second set of tests show a ninety-nine percent chance that Mr. Rivers is actually Ethan's biological father. Court is adjourned, and might I add, may God bless and protect your family."

32

THE TRIALS OF BISHOP ROBERT NICHOLS: PART TWO

*G*abby felt no anxiety about going to the courthouse for the second round of testimonies. She didn't hem and haw about where to sit. There was nothing to consider. As far as she was concerned, 'that man' was lucky he was in protective custody. She eased past the reporters with Ronnie by her side. He was off-duty.

"Ms. Nichols. Are you going to testify on your father's behalf?" Ronnie held up his arm to shield Gabby from the cameras, until she stopped walking.

"No. I'm here in support of my brother, Michael Lawson." And with that, she proceeded up the stairs with her head held high.

Michael's testimony was excruciating, not just for Michael but for everyone. Kevin and Kyle had already heard most of it at least once. But it was particularly difficult for Gabby and her mother to hear. They sat holding onto each other tightly, but tried not to look away from Michael. They needed him to know that their hurt and shame was 'that man's' fault and not his.

"State your name, please."

"My name is Michael Anthony Lawson."

"Mr. Lawson, can you tell the court how and why your relationship with the defendant started?"

"I don't know why it started. I didn't really realize anything was wrong until I was about ten and he started actin' weird."

"What do you mean by weird?"

"He was always telling me I needed to keep the things we did a secret. He kept telling me I was special and spending time with me made him happy, but if anyone else knew...some people would be jealous and we wouldn't be able to anymore."

Even though he was testifying of his own free will, and on his own behalf, it was still very difficult for Michael, who was normally an outgoing and communicative minister of God, to describe his relationship with 'the bishop'. The Porter was having trouble concealing his frustration with his own witness.

"Mr. Lawson, I know you've had to say these things out loud before, but not in front of this jury. I understand it's very difficult, but they need to hear you say what happened to you."

"We had sex."

"Can you be more specific please?"

"Um. No. Not really. It was sex."

"Anal sex?"

Michael shifted in his seat. "Yes."

"Oral sex?"

"Yes."

"How old were you when the sex started?"

"I was twelve."

"And were you, as a twelve year old boy, on the giving or receiving end of this sex with the pastor of your church?"

"Objection, Your Honor! Relevance?" The attorney for the defense stood quickly.

"I'm curious myself counselor. What's your point?" The judge tilted his head.

"Your Honor, the defendant is charged with child abuse and rape. The rape is cut and dry; but if you'll give me a little leeway, the jury will hear how the abuse and manipulation continued well beyond the plaintiff's childhood."

"Let's hear it."

"Thank you, Your Honor. Mr. Lawson, as a twelve year old boy, were you on the giving or receiving end of the anal sex you had with your pastor."

Michael closed his eyes. "Receiving."

"Did it remain that way throughout your relationship?'

"No."

"When did it change?"

"When I was about sixteen."

"Your roles were reversed?"

"Yes."

"And how long did it continue."

"Until about two years ago."

"So as an adult, you were involved in a sexual relationship with the defendant?"

"Yes."

"Was it consensual?"

"I don't know."

"Mr. Lawson, I apologize again. I don't understand. How could you not know whether it was consensual. You know what that means don't you?"

"Of course I do; but it started when I was six. By the time I was old enough to choose for myself...I loved him. I loved being with him."

"Did he tell you he loved you?"

"Yes. Always, from the beginning."

"Did you ever consider that you should stop?"

"I did. I started to realize I'd never had a life. I'd never been anything but his...I'd never been anything. I saw Kevin and Gabby and other people my age living and moving on, having families and relationships, careers, and I wanted to have a life, too."

"Did you know by then that there was something inappropriate about your relationship with the bishop?"

"Of course, I did."

"Why didn't you say anything? Why didn't you go to someone in the church?"

"I was ashamed. And I was scared. I didn't want to be alone. When the bishop was around, things were pretty cool. I got to go places. I always had nice clothes. I was afraid of what would happen to me if I told anyone...I didn't really want it to end."

"So, how did it finally end?"

"I don't know... we just started spending less and less time together. He still did things for me, but I didn't go anywhere with him."

"When did you stop traveling with him?"

"When he moved me to New York... when I turned eighteen. He said I was old enough to take care of myself. But he continued to visit me monthly, until his last trip to Africa two years ago."

Michael returned to his seat without looking at anyone. He just sat and stared straight ahead, thinking perhaps it would have been better had he just died. It was almost as though he'd said the words out loud. Kevin and Kyle, Phyllis and Gabby all responded as though he did, as each found a way to touch him, until they could get him safely out of the room. Ronnie's heart broke as he watched his new family hurting so deeply. But he also felt a tremendous amount of pride at their courage. Michael didn't have to testify. None of them had to be there.

Atlanta, Georgia may be two thousand miles from Hollywood, California, but with its three professional sports teams, blend of urban style and Southern charm, it has been a magnet for famous people and their families for decades. Few people in 'The ATL' are ever caught off guard when they see someone they've only seen previously on the field or stage, or in movies and television. But when the Georgia-born, Grammy, Dove and NAACP Image award winning gospel singer, turned superstar, Richard Richmond, entered the courtroom and walked the long aisle toward the witness stand, to testify for The Prosecution, the crowd of hundreds, mostly church-folk, who knew the artist through his recorded music and sold-out concerts, released one very loud and collective gasp. And then they were reverent again, because after all, they were in a courtroom, and there was a judge on the bench, and there was at least one man of God in the room. Actually, Kyle sat, uncollard, just behind Michael, and chuckled to himself at the irony. He was among the less than one percent of the people in the room who knew why Richie was there.

"State your name, please."

"My name is Richard Travis Richmond."

"What is your occupation?"

"I'm a gospel singer and songwriter."

"How do you know the defendant?"

"He was married to my aunt, Phyllis Richmond. I lived with them for a short time, when my mother died."

"Do you recall how old you were?"

"I was seven years old."

"And how long did you live with your aunt and her husband.?"

"Only a few months. Maybe three."

"Did you leave to live with other family?"

"No, I went into foster care. I was in and out of foster care programs until I was eighteen."

"Was it your choice to leave the Nichols' home?"

"Yes, it was."

"Why would you leave a comfortable home, with two parents for foster care?"

"I didn't like living there."

"Did you know why, at the time?"

"Yes."

"Why?"

"My aunt's husband used to come to my room at night..."

"What did he do?"

Richard was quiet for a long time. Then he spoke quietly. "He'd get in bed with me, undress me and touch me... and make me do things to him."

"Did you ever tell anyone?"

"Just the social worker who placed me. I told her I didn't want to go back there. I didn't tell her why at first; so she thought I was just missing my mom. When I told her what was happening, she said she couldn't do anything to him, because it would be hard to prove. But she wouldn't send me back."

"How have you remembered this all these years?"

"Some things you never forget. And I started receiving counseling years ago, to deal with some issues I've had stemming from that time in my life. I actually went and saw copies of my records, just to be sure I hadn't imagined it all. But my case worker at the time had actually written it all down. Whether she could have done anything about it or not, she made sure my complaint was documented."

"Why are you telling the court all of this now, Mr. Richmond?"

"Because that man got away with abusing me. He was allowed to do it then because the world doesn't value the word alone of a small child, and for most of my life, I was too ashamed or afraid to say anything. And that's why he was able to get to these other boys. It has to stop. He has to be stopped. Perhaps, if it's hard for people to believe these young men, for whatever reason, someone will believe me when I tell you that, that man," Richard pointed directly at the defendant, "used to crawl into my bed, do things to me, and say that 'that's what men do.'" There was another

collective gasp from virtually everyone but Michael, the other witnesses and Michael's family. They weren't surprised by Richard's
appearance in court, either.

33

THE JOURNALS OF PHYLLIS RICHMOND

*R*onnie thought back to his first talks with Gabby, at the beginning of the trial. She'd claimed not to know where her courage came from. But as he watched her mother take the stand, to testify against her husband of forty years, he had no doubt which of her parents Gabby most closely resembled.

"Ms. Richmond, How did Richard Richmond come to live with you and the defendant?"

"Thirty-five years ago, my sister, Carol, was ill, she later died; but before she did, she asked me to look after my nephew, Richie. He was seven. I never actually saw anything, but Richie started having problems. He started wetting the bed and acting out. I thought it was because he missed his mother. A few months later, the social worker who'd placed him with us said that they'd need to do an investigation, because they needed to rule out the possibility that he was being abused. I told Robert what was happening, and he said that he wasn't going to be treated like a criminal for taking in a troubled child who needed a home; and if they wanted us to prove we were fit, they could find somewhere else for him to go."

"Did you communicate that to the social worker?"

"No. I was going to, but first I asked Richie if he wanted to stay with us. He said, 'no' without hesitation. I was so heartbroken that I didn't ask him why. I knew he meant it, so I dismissed it as 'grief'. Social Services removed him from our home the next day."

"What was your husband's response?"

"He really withdrew from me. He started sleeping in one of the guest rooms and taking trips alone. We stayed married, but we were basically living separate lives."

"How long did that go on?"

"Objection, Your Honor! Ms. Richmond's testimony after her nephew was out of her home is not relevant to this case!"

"Permission to approach?"

"Approach. It's unusual for the defendant's spouse not to be heard in instances like this counselor. What's your beef?"

"This witness was introduced as a corroborating witness, specifically to address statements made by Richard Richmond; and essentially had nothing to say accept that she didn't see anything! The State is attempting to enter new testimony. If Ms. Richmond truly had something relevant to say, separate from her testimony about previous witnesses, she should have been introduced weeks ago."

"I'm inclined to agree..."

"Your Honor, the defense opened this door. Phyllis Richmond lived with the defendant for more than forty years. She can speak not only as a witness to the suspicious relationship the defendant had with Richard Richmond, but also to his character. The defense has offered his forty year marriage and long-standing ties to the church as evidence of his impeccable character. Consider her further testimony a rebuttal to those 'facts' entered into evidence as well."

"Very well. Objection over-ruled."

"Thank you, Your Honor. Ms. Richmond, I'll ask the question again: After Richie left your home, you stated that your relationship with you husband was even more strained, and he moved out of your marital bedroom. When, if ever, did that change?"

"About five years later."

"What changed?"

"We decided to start a family of our own. He moved back, and within a year, I gave birth to our daughter, Gabrielle." Phyllis looked lovingly at her daughter.

"How did Robert Nichols respond to the birth of Gabrielle?"

"He was happy to be a father. He was good to her; but he seemed disappointed that he didn't have a son. I even suggested that we could try to have a boy, but he refused. He just went back into his own world."

"Did anything else ever happen that would lead you to suspect your husband might be having inappropriate interactions with young boys?"

"Not right away, that I ever saw directly... but... I wondered why he seemed so preoccupied with lesbian and gay issues. There is actually very little in the bible that speaks of it; yet, it was a large focus of his ministry."

"Objection, Your Honor! The Bishop Robert Nichols' objection to homosexuality no more suggests he's a pedophile than yours or mine would! Again, I challenge this witness on the issue of relevance!"

"Counselor, my opinions about homosexuality are, certainly no matter for this court, and I'll warn you to keep me out of your analogies. Mr. Smith, if you have a point with this witness, please hurry up and make it."

"We are almost there, Your Honor. Ms. Richmond, did you agree with the part of your husband's ministry that publically condemned homosexuality?"

"No, not at all. I believe that what people cite in the bible about homosexuality has nothing at all to do with what goes on between two loving people who happen to be of the same gender. All sex, for instance, outside of marriage is a sin, and he never spoke about fornication or adultery. They are and were much bigger threats to the institution of marriage."

"Did you share these views with your husband?"

"I attempted to on a few occasions, in the beginning."

"And what was his response?"

"Anger. Sometimes violence."

"Toward you?"

"Only once."

"Do you recall why?"

"He'd just come home from a trip to…Jamaica, I believe, and was suddenly very excited about organizing a march to ban homosexuality..."

"You mean, 'marriage rights for homosexuals'?"

"No, homosexuality in general. He wanted to have sodomy laws reinstated and even get lesbian and gay centers and collegiate organizations shut down."

"Did he explain the urgency?"

"Not exactly, he just said that the focus of his trip was to find a plan to 'rid the society of the sickness and plague of gay sex'. I've never forgotten the words because he kept shouting them at me."

"Do you recall why he was so excited, with you in particular?"

"I'd questioned him when he came in about Michael. He'd gone with him, and I was asking Mikey if he had a good time." Phyllis began to speak softly. "He said, 'yes' but he wouldn't look at me, and went up to his room and stayed there. When I asked Robert what was wrong with Michael, he said he was behaving like a 'spoiled, ungrateful brat, because he was never satisfied'."

"Did you know what he was referring to?"

"Not really. I know that Michael had been very excited to be going on this, his first church trip, and he was always a very polite, sweet and respectful boy. It surprised me to hear *anyone* describe him as 'spoiled' or 'ungrateful', especially someone who knew him as well as Robert did, and I said so."

"And what was your husband's response?"

"He slapped me in the face for questioning him."

"Did he ever hit you again after that?"

"No."

"Why?"

"Because I never questioned him again."

"Ms. Richmond, do you recall the circumstances under which Michael Lawson came to live with your family?"

"Michael's mother.... had been the choir director for our church for several years. She was devoted to the ministry and spent a great deal of time in the church. Michael, Gabby and Kevin were always together and Robert suggested we help her out by letting Michael spend a lot of time at our house when his mother was working and not at the church. Then one day, she said she needed to go away for a little while, and asked if we would keep him with us until she returned."

"Did you have this conversation with her?"

"No, Robert told me... but I didn't find it odd because he was at the church every day. It just seemed like it would be easier for her to speak with him directly. As pastor of the church, most people went directly to him with their problems."

"Did she ever return?"

"No."

"Did you ever know why?"

"No."

"Did you ever legally adopt Michael?"

"No. I never brought it up for fear that he'd feel abandoned by his mother. Most of the time, he was very happy living with us. He had his friends, Gabby and Kevin, and he did seem devoted to Robert. He called us 'Mom' and 'Dad' for fifteen years.

"When did you first hear that your suspicions about your husband were true?"

"Objection, Your Honor!"

"I'll rephrase. Ms. Richmond, when did you first learn that Michael Lawson was accusing your husband of molesting him?"

"When he showed up at my home to tell me, two years ago."

"Did you believe him?"

"Yes."

"Why?"

"Because I always felt in my heart that there was something not quite right about their relationship. Robert kept it so secretive; and Michael became so timid around me, all of a sudden."

"Why didn't you do anything, when you saw the change in him?"

Phyllis paused for a long time and wiped away tears as she looked at Michael. "I was afraid of him... And I couldn't prove anything. I never traveled with them, and for years, they traveled almost constantly. When they were home, we stayed busy and out of each other's way. I think I convinced myself that it was my imagination, that it was just to awful to be true."

"Did you love your husband, Ms. Richmond."

"No. I wanted to feel the way I did when we first met; but he changed right away, almost as soon as Gabrielle was born. He was cold and distant, very arrogant, and sometimes, just plain mean."

"Why did you stay as long as you did?"

"It's how I was raised. I was taught that you stay together. You don't walk out. It's what we taught the women in our church, as well. If I left simply because I no longer liked my husband, I'd be a hypocrite."

"So, why did you finally file for divorce?"

"Because I believe Michael, and Richie. Richie's told me since then what happened to him, too; and I know it was a very long time ago... but some memories are just too awful to forget. I may not have seen Robert put his hands on those boys, but I remember what they were like before they came to us. They changed around him. They were never bad, but it was as if they'd been touched by something evil. Like a light went out inside them. Sure, they looked fine. Michael stayed with us for twelve years, and he did his chores and his homework. He said his prayers. He sang in the church choir... and he followed my husband around and sat at his feet with more love and devotion than I've ever seen. To think about it now, I know it didn't feel natural. I knew he was different from other young people. Kevin and Gabby were respectful, well-behaved; but they had each other, and other friends. I might have dismissed it because so many of the other boys in our church, especially those in the mentoring program, were a lot like Michael... rambunctious at first and then... different... quieter.

The minute I saw Michael's face, that day he came to see me, I knew what he would tell me. I couldn't stay married to a monster. I may have been able to stay, if it meant my own suffering, but not at the expense of a child. I believe that he hasn't loved me in years, if ever, and he stayed because of what it would look like for a man of his stature to get divorced. My biggest fear and regret is that, had I left him sooner, or stood up to him, he might not have gotten away with it for so long. He used to say that I was lucky to be married to him. But I know now that being married to me lent him credibility and believability, while he traveled all around the world do and saying all those evil and hateful things. I might not have been able to stop him, but I wasn't going to let him hide behind me anymore."

"Ms. Richmond, you'd been married to Mr. Nichols for more than forty years. You're talking today with a great deal of clarity and detail about some things that you say happened more than thirty-five years ago. How can you recall it all so clearly?"

"I've kept journals, that I write in almost every day, since I was sixteen years old."

"Have you been referring to those pages lately?"

"Yes."

"And do they specifically reference the incidents you've shared with us today?"

"Yes."

"And have you submitted these journals to the prosecution willingly?"

"Yes."

"Your Honor, at this time, I'd like to enter into evidence the journals of Phyllis Richmond. They have been inspected and verified by an independent analyst as being authentic and written during the time periods she stated here."

Michael shut his eyes tightly, trying to fight back tears, knowing that it was finally almost over. The closing arguments were a formality. There was really nothing left to say. The family, including Gabby, Ronnie and Richard, spoke quietly just outside the doors to the courtroom, discussing what to do while they waited for the verdict to come back. "The D.A. said it could be a couple of hours or several days." Phyllis reminded them as she invited them all to wait at her home for the call.

But no sooner did she say the words did an assistant fly out of the courtroom. "The jury is back!" It took them all of twenty-five minutes. Apparently, there was some debate about sentencing. The jurors voted unanimously to sentence Nichols to death; problem was, they weren't charged with the sentencing, only his guilt or innocence.

"We find the defendant guilty on all counts, Your Honor; but we were wondering if we could possibly add more."

"Thank You. The jury is excused." The judge suppressed a giggle. "Sentencing will resume tomorrow morning."

The family gathered again outside the courtroom. Phyllis and Gabby held Michael while he cried. Kevin, Kyle and Richard stood by and tried not to burst into song. Ronnie looked on, and said a prayer of Thanks that he too, lived to see that day, and that moment.

34

TWO-SPIRITS, UNICORNS
AND OTHER MAGICAL CREATURES

Ronnie gave Kyle a long hug before they settled into oversized rockers on the back porch of 'Mama Rich's modest country home. Ronnie was nervous. He'd been in therapy for years, trying to sort out a multitude of feelings: the abuse in his childhood, his gender issues, his habitual abuse of sex, and most recently, his decision to make the change. He felt like he was ready. His therapist believed he was and had even signed the necessary paperwork, stating that 'Ronnie Reynolds is an intelligent, mentally sound individual who has done all of the necessary work to..." He'd discussed it with Gabby more than once, but admittedly not in great detail. And he'd finally really prayed about it. He'd told himself he'd been praying all along; but had he? Why did the answer seem to be different lately? For the first time since he made the decision to have gender reassignment surgery, God's answer to him didn't seem so clear. So, before Kevin and Kyle left for Canada, Ronnie asked Kyle for a moment alone. "Thank you for seeing me."

"No need to thank me. You're family. It's good to see you outside of all the mess we've had going on. But, how is work?"

"Work is good. It's funny, *TRRS* was my dream job. Journalists work as correspondents for decades trying to get behind a desk or sit at the big round table..."

"But it wasn't good for you, huh?"

"It really wasn't. I love the story behind the headline. This trial, for instance. I'm not there for the accused; I'm there for the victims. I want to tell their stories. People need to know that this is happening, that it can happen in their churches, to their children..."

"It's sad and scary, but true. I have to say, I'm happy that you're out in the world and not wasting away behind some desk, too. But don't knock network television. If not for that show, we'd never have met. And you wouldn't have met Gabby."

"You are absolutely right."

"So, what's going on?"

"Right to the point, huh?"

"Well, you said you needed my help?"

"I did, didn't I?"

"You did."

"Did you mean what you said to me when we met, about not being able to tell I was trans?"

"Absolutely, I would have had no clue, if you hadn't told me you were born a woman."

"I guess that's a compliment..."

"Considering that it is your goal to be seen as a man, I think so."

"Can you tell I haven't... done it?"

"It?"

"The reassignment."

"Really. Wow. And you're planning to?"

"I've been planning it for quite some time now.

"Okay. I assume you've done the necessary counseling and research."

"Of course. But..."

"What is it?"

"May I ask your opinion on the whole thing?"

"You may, Ronnie, but I think my opinion is irrelevant. Something like this is between you and *your* God."

"I know, and I thought I had a handle on it, that I was clear..."

"What's different?"

"Gabrielle, for one thing."

"Yeah, Gabrielle will make you rethink some things." Kyle smiled and shook his head, thinking about the woman who'd become his sister, more than 'his husband's ex'. Ronnie grinned back at him.

"Well, she's different; you know...I'm different with her. She makes me feel good, like I don't have to hide...or be anything more than I am."

"She's comfortable with you in your own skin."

"And *I'm comfortable* with her in my own skin!"

"Sounds like a match made in heaven to me." Kyle continued to smile.

"But..."

"You spent years planning to do this, and now you feel like God's telling you 'no'..."

"Yes."

"Wow." Kyle nodded his head.

"I'm still having trouble with what the Bible, God, says about transgenders."

"You're referring to the scriptures. This really is hard for me, Ronnie; because I know the scriptures. They are some of the same scriptures used to persecute homosexuals. So my answer to you is similar to my answer to myself. I believe it's all about interpretation. While I believe the Bible is the living Word of God, I also believe that the Word was revised with the birth and resurrection of Jesus Christ. I believe that it is important to look at each passage in context, and consider the time in which they were written. The Bible is the Word of God, as interpreted by man; and man has a long history of getting it wrong. Slavery, racism and the roles of women are just a few examples."

"But you have an opinion."

"Ronnie, my opinion is just that, *my* opinion. It's not relevant to you and your situation."

"But it would help me to hear it."

Kyle took a deep breath. "It's complicated. I believe that God made each of us individually and with a divine purpose. I believe that everyone's journey is unique; that even identical twins will walk separate paths. If we meet someone who can walk along with us, we are blessed, indeed. I think transgendered people have a very specific purpose in the Kingdom, and their journeys are perhaps the most complicated and painful of all. It's one thing to suffer everything you have to, to say, 'I'm gay'; but it's something entirely different to say, 'I was born in the wrong skin.' That requires a kind of courage and sacrifice that is almost unfathomable."

"You said it. You said the thing I've feared. You said what I've felt most of my life, and I've said a thousand times. 'I was born in the wrong skin.'"

"And you fear that because..."

"Because to say that is to suggest that God made a mistake! To say I was born in the wrong body, and then go out and correct it, is arrogant and blasphemous!"

"Not necessarily, Ronnie. Not if you consider it's all part of the journey. Only God can judge your walk. Only you know what God tells you about who you are. It's just really important that you listen."

"I have been listening, but now..."

"Do you think the answer has changed?"

"Does God do that? Change His mind?"

"I believe that God gives us what we need to help move us along; and knew before we were born exactly where our journey will end."

"But what do I do, Kyle?"

"Oh, no!" Kyle chuckled. "You are not leaving that here! That over there is your journey. I cannot, will not, tell you what you should do!" He stopped smiling. "Because I can't, Ronnie. I'm not God! I can't judge you. I thank God that I can't, and that I'm free to mess up and be forgiven, and start all over every day."

Gabby wrapped her arms tightly around Ronnie while he slept, but lay in bed wide awake herself for a long time. Ronnie noticed she hadn't turned over, as she normally would have, after a while.

"What is it, Baby?"

"I'm still so confused."

"What exactly are you trying to figure out?"

"If you're an 'other', what does that make me?"

"Well, who's asking?" Ronnie tried not to get defensive. He'd had this conversation before, sort of... Gabby really was quite unique.

"Just me, because it's no one else's business." She played with his hand and he kissed her forehead.

"Good answer. Let's try and figure it out together. When you see me, what do you see?"

"I see a man. That's easy... Wait, you're talking about with your clothes on, right?"

"For now, yes... Okay, now, without."

220

Gabby took a deep breath and hesitated.

"It's okay, Baby. I want to hear it."

"Okay, when we're out or even, actually at home, just around the house, I still see a man. You're just so damn cute... But here, like this... when you're not all suited up, I see a woman, a strong, athletic, incredibly beautiful woman. I know... but I can't help it. I think you're so lovely. I love your body, your softness... I love absolutely everything about you."

"Wow."

"Yeah... but Baby, you say that like it's some revelation. And that makes me sad. I don't understand how anyone could love you, and look at you and not see; or better yet, actually see you, and not love you..."

"I present myself as a man, Gabrielle. There are expectations; and in this body, I fall short, pun intended, of a lot of those expectations."

"But... it wasn't like that with us."

"Because I told you right away, and gave you an opportunity to get to know me and decide..."

"Okay. So, are you okay with the way I see you... and the way we are together... you don't mind that I see you as *equally* male and female?"

"I can't believe it, but I can honestly say, 'no', I absolutely love everything about the way you love me." He closed his eyes, as she kissed him sweetly.

"Okay, so if you're both male and female; and we're both okay with that, what does that make me?"

Ronnie chuckled. "Oh! Well, that makes you a unicorn, of the rainbow variety!"

"Huh?"

"You, my dear would be the rare, but entirely authentic, truly bisexual woman. And I am the luckiest man/lesbian in the world!"

"So, what will I be when you emerge from your chrysalis and become a beautiful boy butterfly?"

"Oh, well then you'll just be an ordinary, straight girl." Ronnie chuckled again, before he realized how unappealing that sounded.

"Hey! I don't wanna be ordinary! I wanna be a unicorn!" She whined. "Seriously, Baby I love you so much." She sat up. "Doesn't this change anything for you?"

"I've been trying not to think about it; trying not to make my transition about you or us. I've been in transition my whole life. I never imagined that anything like us would happen for me. I mean I did, I just thought it would be... after. You truly are the woman of my dreams; but I always dreamt I would find you as a man! I have fantasied for at least a third of my life about making love to you as a whole man! And while, I can't imagine anything more wonderful than what we share now, I'm afraid of not finding out, and blaming you for making me stay like this."

"But aren't you afraid that it won't be right, that it won't feel as good? That you'll regret having done it?"

"Of course I am, but not more than I am afraid of *not finding out.*"

Gabby started to cry, as she slid her hand down Ronnie's tummy. "I love Veronica. She's my friend." She was touching him there, but to Gabby, 'Veronica' was much, much more than his beautiful, perfect breasts, or the softness between Ronnie's legs.

Ronnie closed his eyes. "She's quite fond of you... too..." He moved slowly against Gabby's hand, as she followed it with her mouth.

"We have an understanding... I keep her secrets... she keeps mine..." Gabby whispered before she kissed her friend sweetly. Ronnie moaned softly and bit his lip. He tried to keep his eyes open, but as Gabby worked instinctually, as always, he closed his eyes and cried. He felt more connected to her than he ever had to anyone ever, and the feeling only grew stronger. Gabby reached up and searched for his hand. She held it tightly and began to cry and moan along with him. When she could tell he was close, she grew quiet again. She didn't want to miss it. Ronnie's explosion was quiet but visible. His body vibrated gently, as wave after wave rolled over him. He sighed and then panted, trying to indicate that she could stop, that he needed her to. Gabby refused and instead just increased her intensity. She licked and sucked and bit gently until... again... and again... Finally... she rested her head on Ronnie's thigh. "See, I am a unicorn." She said almost to herself, but

Ronnie heard her and pulled her back up to him.

"You are the most beautiful, most magical creature... Thank you." Gabby kissed him deeply and deliberately, so he would taste himself on her lips and tongue. Ronnie moaned again as she slid back down his body.

"You don't understand. I'm only special because you are..."

Ronnie watched, almost outside of himself. She was so beautiful. But what he noticed most was how happy she was, how happy she'd been since they'd been together, even with everything she'd been through with her father, and then Ethan. She'd always been beautiful, but now she glowed - all the time, not just here. Gabby read his thoughts and whispered, "It's you. You... all of you... please, Baby..."

They barely spoke in the morning, as they showered and drove to the airport. Gabby made casual conversation over breakfast with Neal, who insisted on going with Ronnie to Montreal, and tried not to cry. And when it was time for them to board the plane, she didn't ask him again. She just held him tightly and held his face in both of her hands. She loved him. She wondered if she said it often enough, or if there was something else she could do to show him. It didn't matter. She didn't have to say it at all. Ronnie could feel it. He stared into her beautiful eyes. She was trying so hard to be strong. He hadn't seen that look in her eyes since they started dating. She smiled and she held him and kissed him... but her eyes... "I'll call you as soon as we land."

"Okay." She clung to him and spoke into his chest.

He pulled away slowly and lifted her face. "I love you, Gabrielle."

The dam broke before she could get the words out as her tears poured. "I love you, too... You know that, don't you?"

"Yes..."

35

ALL HAIL THE QUEEN

"*H*ey. What-cha do-in?" Nikki sang into the phone, in her normal voice, the one she reserved for her closest gal pals. Normally, a call from Nikki would have perked her right up. But Ronnie had only been gone a couple of hours, and already, Gabby was barely functional. It was a struggle to even answer the phone. She was so sad, and scared, and not at all sure how she was going to make it through the next ten weeks. She smiled a little to herself; her best friend did have the best timing.

"Nothin'." Gabby sounded small.

"Why so glum?" Despite everything she'd been through, Nikki hadn't heard Gabby sound like that in at least a year.

"No reason. What's up?" And Nikki was absolutely certain that wasn't true; so she was immediately glad she'd called.

"Can you get up here by noon tomorrow? I suddenly have to make an appearance at the Broadway Legends' luncheon, and I need a hot date."

"And there are about fifty available women, who actually *want to* date you, just fifty feet from your office door."

"Yes, but they all work for me; no one knows you, and I don't want a real date. Oh, stop playing hard to get. It'll be fun."

"Why are you even attendin' a 'legends' luncheon, anyway? You're old, but you're not that old."

"Because I'm on the selection committee... bitch." Nikki actually uttered that last part under her breath.

"Oh." Gabby giggled. "Okay. Pick me up at the airport...in an actual, standard size - luxury is okay - automobile, please."

"Tease." Nikki groaned, getting the clue that Gabby didn't want to reenact her last trip to New York, the one that jump-started their sisterhood, and Gabby's acceptance of her own 'otherness'.

"Molester." Gabby quipped.

"Yo'daddy."

"Ow-uh." Gabby whined.

"Too soon?" Nikki asked, with a touch of sincere remorse.

"Uh, yeah! I still haven't even talked to the creep, yet."

"Are you going to?"

"I don't know. Right now, I can't think of anything to say, but... 'die!'"

"Ooh...Yeah... You should probably put a little distance between you for a while."

"You've got a point. I'll call you back with my flight info."

"Thanks, doll."

"No, thank you, Sissy."

Just ten hours later, the women were curled up on Nikki's comfy couch, getting caught up. Gabby'd had so much going on the last year, between her father's trial and the paternity scare-miracle, that she and Nikki hadn't really talked much about Ronnie. Nikki sat patiently, plying herself with mimosas, in preparation for the crow she was inevitably going to have to eat. She prided herself on having the most acutely tuned gaydar in New York. She was never wrong. Still, she liked Gabby, in fact, loved her, enough that she was genuinely happy for her. So she just nodded silently as she choked on her defeat, while the 'madly-in-love, but some-how-still-hurting, one who broke her winning streak', went on and on about the most wonderful man in the world.

"Ronnie is... Ronnie is something else. He makes me feel...not just beautiful, but special, like there is no other woman in the world like me. In one instant, I'm a princess; protected, all power, no responsibility. At night I'm The Queen: still pampered, protected and powerful; but... okay, I'm a good Southern Baptist girl, and I know better than this, but don' t knock being worshiped 'til you've tried it. It's like that song, 'When a Man Loves a Wom-an'! That's how he makes me feel...Ours is NOT a partnership of equals. I'm The Queen! Do I respect him? ... I do."

"Why? How?" Nikki asked, as though she didn't believe it were true or even possible for a woman to feel that way about a man.

"Because he's smart and sexy and strong and confident. He only chooses to submit to my every whim. I see it. It's fun for him. He's sweet and fun and capable. If he were any more perfect, I wouldn't be able to stand him. Whatever it is I need, whenever I need it, he's right there giving it to me. It's amazing."

"Sounds too good to be true. What's the catch?"

"There's no catch. He's perfect."

"Gabby, please. You would not be sittin here with me, drinking mimosas at nine a.m. on Saturday, if everything were fine."

"Yes, I would!"

"Yeah, actually, you would...you should definitely see someone about that... but you wouldn't be trying to convince me of how perfect your new boyfriend is. You'd be with him. Where is Prince Charming, anyway?"

"Out of town."

"Following a story?"

"Not exactly."

"Visiting the wife and kids?"

"That was just plain, bitchy, Nikki. No!"

"Well?"

"I can't say."

"But it's big enough that you're not with him, and you're trying to convince yourself, and me, that he's perfect."

"He's actually not perfect. He snores like a bear; and sometimes he leaves the toilet seat up." Gabby smiled to herself. She actually even liked Ronnie's snoring.

"Uh huh. Spill it."

"I can't."

"But you want to."

"I don't."

"Liar."

"Nikki, promise me. You can't tell anyone, especially not Kevin."

"Oh, I'm gonna fly to Canada as soon as you pass out!"

"Bitch!"

"Seriously, Sweetie, what is it?"

"Oh geez, how do I put this? ...'Ronnie' is short for 'Veronica'..."

"Oh, is that all?"

"Wait for it..." Gabby counted down in her head.

"Hey, you ARE gay!"

"Uh, no... I'm a unicorn!" Gabby giggled.

"What the... uh... oh nevermind. But she hasn't done it yet, has she?"

"No, HE hasn't... Damn it, Nikki, you can't do that! There is no way you'd know, if I didn't tell you.   Please!"

"I'm sorry. I'm just messing with you. You're right. I would have had absolutely no idea. Wow."   Nikki took a long sip of her drink and mumbled under her breath. "That explains a lot."

"Hey! I heard that! That explains what?"

"Nothing."

"Don't make me put my drink down."

"Oh, I wish you would. Seriously, I was just thinking that explains why I always found Ronnie so damn sexy."

"I'd scratch your eyes out, if that weren't so true."   Gabby squirmed a little in her seat, fanning herself.

"So, really he hasn't done it...? Is he gonna do it? But he's got the tools. What am I talking about? Hell, I've got tools. I've always said that 'a real man has nothing on a lesbian with a loaded backpack'."

"Not a lesbian, Nicole; but you're right about that.   Oh *my* God."

"So he's off where exactly?"

Gabby was quiet for a long time.   "Montreal... doing it."

"No way."

"Yup."

"Um, why do you look so sad?"

"I don't know.   We talked about it.   I think I'm just a little afraid of what it will be like after." Gabby put her drink on the table and wiped a tear from her cheek. "I really do love him ex-actly the way he is."

"Does he know that."

"Yeah, and he says he understands."

"Does he let you touch him?"

"Of course, why wouldn't he?" Gabby asked innocently, and actually sounded a little offended.

"Um, because most male-gender-identified females won't."

"Whatever. I needed to know." Gabby stated matter-of-factly.

"Damn. You really are The Queen."

Gabby blushed. "Really?"

"Think about it, Gabby. Ronnie is a man. Actually, he's so *not a woman* that he's going to get his feminity removed, permanently. There are women who don't think of themselves as anything other than women, who wouldn't let even another woman touch them. Not all, but a lot of butch women. Wow. He really does love you. More importantly, he must have really trusted that you love him."

"I really do, Nikki." Gabby continued to cry.

"What is it, Sweetie?"

"What if it's not the same?"

"Um, Gabs, you do know that boys and girls are different, don't you? It's not going to be the same."

"You're a jerk. You know what I mean. What if I don't like it? I love making love to him now, the way he's been. I wouldn't change anything about it. I don't want it to change. I don't want him to change."

"Did you tell him?"

"Kinda... I think so. Well, maybe not in so many words. Actually, not in words at all, I think. I don't remember. The last few days have been kind of a blur." Gabby grabbed her drink again, before she closed her eyes, and thought back to their last night together and smiled.

"Oh my God! You ARE lesbian!"

"No, I'm not... well, maybe... okay, fine, sometimes...on Tuesdays... and Fridays... and every fourth Sunday?" Gabby held her glass affectionately in both her hands, and looked down sheepishly.

"Whatever. I guess we'll see for sure when he comes back with his shiny new man-stick and no vajajay."

"You suck!"

Nikki spit out her drink. "Ah!... But the question remains, will you?"

"I hate you, and I'm going home!" Gabby laughed.

"No, you're drunk and you're taking a nap before we go to that dreadful thing."

"Oh, yeah." Gabby stretched her legs across Nikki's lap and

tried to sleep.

36

HAPPY FATHERS' DAY

*G*abby sat in her living room staring out the window. Spending the six of the eight weeks Ronnie'd been gone in New York with Nikki was actually the best idea Nikki'd had since they met. The house was so quiet with Ronnie gone. She missed his humming, and cleaning, and the incessant busy-ness that drove her a bit nuts in the beginning, but she grew to love. Once they'd settled in and each got back to work, she realized that she was actually living with someone for the first time in her adult life. Her relationship with Kevin was more like an endless string of long weekends than a marriage. As she thought of what she'd like to do for Ronnie for their one-year anniversary, she was also very deliberate about giving Thanks for that broken road that brought them together.

She loved Ronnie so much in fact that, after considerable prayer and counseling, she actually tried to find the blessing, or at least some semblance of understanding about *all* of the things that brought them together. She knew she'd come a long way in the last few years, but she wondered if she were finally strong enough to stand up to *him*. It was time to face her father. She'd defended him, against her own conscience, if to no one else, her entire life; and stood by him, literally, through the worst of times. She'd sat in those courtrooms for months, listened to the boys, Michael, Richie, her own mother... She wanted to honor him, to not judge him, the way he had everyone else. And she told herself over and over that she could still love him, because he'd always been good to her. But with Ronnie away, the house was too quiet; and she'd been replaying Tre's testimony over and over in her head. The trials had been over for months. She told herself that she just wanted to focus on her work and Ronnie, before he left; but the truth was, the reality of what her father had actually done to her, and her family, was so painful that she'd blocked it out. But she'd figured out in therapy that she didn't like that about herself, and had been working very hard to not bury her emotions. It didn't matter that no harm was done, and Ethan never knew there was even the slightest chance that he could be taken away from his dads. She knew, and she needed that man to know that she knew, what he tried to do to her.

He approached her smiling... "There's my girl!" He noticed her tears right away. "Don't cry, Babygirl. Everything will work out. My attorneys have already filed an appeal." He spoke reassuringly of his two, consecutive life sentences.

"Why? There isn't any basis for an appeal. You did do those things to Michael, and Richie. Even if you never laid a hand on Michael... you manipulated him. You used him. You manipulate and use everyone."

"Watch who you're speaking to like that, Gabrielle."

"What are you going to do to me, Daddy? Send a monster after my son?" She asked slowly and watched for his reaction. He looked wounded at the accusation that he might have done something wrong, but not surprised or guilty.

"Now, Gabrielle, I did that for you and Ethan. You obviously didn't know what you were doing when you signed whatever you did! If you were in your right mind, you'd have never let Kevin near Ethan!"

"So, you're saying *I'm* crazy? That the only reason I would share my child with his father would be because *I've* lost *my* mind? Are you so old and crazy that you'd forgotten that you were the reason I lied to Kevin in the first place? I can't believe I didn't see you. You truly are the essence of evil. Well guess what? Ethan is Kevin's son."

"Just because you and those men say it, doesn't make it so." Apparently, the pit bulls he'd sent after her child hadn't bothered to tell him they failed. Perhaps because there was no money left to pay them.

"As usual, you didn't hear me. The judge ordered a paternity test. Ethan has always been Kevin's. It's over. You don't have anything left to touch us with. But I do have a question. Why do you him so much? I know you pretended to love him... that alone should have been a sign. It even seemed weird back then. But you resented him even before he came out... Did you...?" Gabby watched her father's face, and saw as he tightened his jaw and he avoided her eyes. "No! Tell me you didn't!"

"I did not! I never laid a hand on that boy!"

"But you wanted to. And he knew it... That's why he never liked you..."

"He avoided me because he knows I knew what he would be! He pranced around like he owned the world and the laws of man and nature did not apply to him, even as a child! Aaron and Tresa did that boy an injustice, not teaching him to walk like a man. That's why he left you!"

"You're a fool. Our marriage ended because it was based on a lie."

"Is that what he told you, when he left you and your son to be an abomination? He turned his back on God and the way he was raised! He disgraced our family! That child needs to be raised by his blood, by a real man!"

"Like you? So what about Michael, Daddy? Why didn't he turn out okay? Who's to blame for all his pain and misery? His mother left him with you! Don't answer that! I only need to look in the mirror to understand. I'm as messed up as Michael, maybe even worse. At least you taught Michael to hide his pain, and keep it to himself, instead of spreading it around like so much toxic waste."

"You're ungrateful! I treated you like a princess!"

"You taught me how to lie and to judge people! It's a wonder I have anything good in my life at all! How can you not see all of the people you hurt - me, Michael, Mama, Kevin, our son, the thousands of people of God who trusted you?... And the whole time... throughout the trial... I just kept telling myself...'he's your daddy, Gabrielle; he's never been anything but good to you...' I tried so hard to believe that. I tried to block out the lies you told me; the ugly way you taught me to treat people, how you had me thinking I was better..."

"You are better!"

"No! I am a child of God! I am flawed and selfish and messy... but I am beautiful because God loves me... just like He loves Michael and Kevin - all those people you told me were less than me... just like He loves you! I thank God that there is a God, and I can get up and walk away from here, knowing that you're in His hands, and I'm no longer in yours! I came here prepared to for-give you, because I know that's what my God wants me to do. But for the first time in my life, I'm not willing to lie to please you or make you happy. I know that if I pray, if I ask God to help me forgive you... for what you almost did to me and my son... He will... but I'm not ready! I won't ask for that! I want you to rot here. I want you to be afraid and alone... and damn it... abused! for what you did to us... for what you did to my mother... and I know you're sick... and death would be merciful... but I want you to live... just long enough that you come to realize all of the hurt and harm you've done." Gabby stood and walked away, as her father watched her, for the first time in his life, speechless.

She managed to hold it together until she got to her car. She cried and cursed the whole way home. She cried for two whole weeks. And she absolutely refused to pray, until the day Ronnie was to come back. She sat in the middle of their bed squeezing a pillow. She wanted to be happy. She missed him so much. She cursed her father some more for the trouble he'd caused, for bringing Tre back into their lives and interrupting her mostly wonderful life. "He ruins everything he touches!"

"Does he really, Gabrielle?" The Holy Spirit interrupted her fit.

"Yes, he does!" She yelled, defiantly.

"Like what?"

"Well, there's Michael for one."

"I've got Michael."

"Well, there's that man he brought into our lives! And even before that! He made me lie to Kevin!"

"No, Gabrielle, you lied because you wanted Kevin, and you wanted the life you had together. And if your father hadn't led you astray all those years, you'd have never known Kevin, or had Ethan."

"My father was not part of some master plan! He's evil!"

"Perhaps, but EVERYTHING works for the good of those who believe. You just keep believing. It's time to forgive him, Gabby."

"No!" She screamed at God. "I meant what I said. I want him to hurt. I want him to suffer."

"No you do not, Gabrielle."

"But it's what he deserves."

"Who will his suffering help?"

"Me! Michael, my mother... those other boys!"

"Those boys are all grown now; nothing will bring them back or restore their innocence. But, I can restore their hearts. How will Robert's suffering help anyone?"

"We will know."

"How can knowing your father is being hurt help you? What will you do, wake up every morning and think about him being tortured? That's not living. You and Michael and Phyllis are supposed to live, now. You leave the justice to Our Father."

"But I can't! I want him to burn! I want big mean disease-ridden Aryan Racists to do unspeakable things to him!"

"No you don't." The Lord chuckled.

Okay, fine. I don't. But...

"Why not?"

"Because he's my father..."

"And..."

"And I love him."

"As I love you..."

"Unconditionally..." Gabby conceded and wiped her tears.

37

WHY WAIT?

*A*nd as soon as she stop crying, her phone rang. Actually, it sang to her. ♫*He builds me up; he gives me love...More love than I've ever seen...*♫ Gabby thanked God again before she ran to answer Ronnie's call.

"Are you home? I thought you weren't getting in until ten." It was six in the evening.

"I caught an earlier flight. But, I can go find something to do, if you'd rather I not come home right away." Ronnie's voice was... Gabby closed her eyes and smiled, and forgot to respond.

"Actually, I'm kinda going through withdrawals. Can you meet me?"

"Absolutely! Where? When?"

"Well, it's Friday night, right? Same bat-time, same bat-station..."

"You're having karaoke withdrawals?" Gabby squinted and thought 'oh, no he di'n't!'

"Eight weeks is a really long time, dontcha think?" Ronnie teased.

"Hasn't it been more like twelve?"

"No. It's only been eight. Are you gonna meet me?" Ronnie whined now.

"Are you asking me to?" Gabby decided to play along and play hard to get.

"Oh. Okay. Baby, I miss you... And I know that when I get home, I'm not gonna wanna, or be able to, leave you for at least as long as I've been gone. And as much as I miss holding you, and kissing you... and the way you..." Ronnie moaned into the phone. "I also miss how much fun we have on our Friday nights... and I think it would be a really, really good idea if we shared a meal, and I built up some strength, before we locked ourselves away for days and days, and weeks and months... So, would you please meet me at the spot at eight-thirty?"

"Well, since you put it like that, I guess I can..." Gabby grinned into the phone.

"Thank you, Baby."

"You're welcome."

"K. Bye."

"B...?" Gabby stared into the phone. "Oh, no he did not just hang up on me!" She laughed and tossed the phone on the bed and ran to shower and got dressed.

The karaoke bar on the corner of Peach Lane and Peach Cocktail Road had been their date-night spot for months. Between the trials, Gabby's clients, Ethan's visits and Ronnie's work, they actually had to start scheduling time together. Much to her surprise, Gabby looked forward to those Friday nights at The Silver Spur almost as much as she did their still, or at least what had been their red-hot... she tried not to think about how their love making might change...

She'd never been brave enough to sing by herself in public before; but Ronnie had been right, as always, and after the first time, she was hooked, and very, very good. Ronnie was still full of surprises. Gabby shouldn't have been surprised that he had a wonderful singing voice, but she was. He was so good and so popular that it made her blush. And it wasn't just because people recognized him from his show. He was actually just that good, and when he approached the stage, there were whistles and cheers throughout the bar. There were even a few "we missed you, Ronnie's" from the large crowd of regulars. He waved as he hopped onto the stage, smiling, but feeling uncharacteristically nervous. As always, he looked at, and sang only to, Gabby.

♪*Hey, whatdaya say girl, let's do something crazy?*
Been putting it off, you know what I'm sayin!♪

This time, the crowd, directed by Trevor, especially those who knew the song, waited until he finished the first verse of the popular Rascal Flatts song to go wild... and when she looked confused, a guy at the table next to her pointed to the stage and said, "he's talkin' to you, honey! Listen!"

♪Why wait another minute for
somethin we shoulda done yesterday?
I know a little church with a preacher
who can hook us up right away
Love don't need a reason
Baby, I don't see how I could love ya
any more than I do today
So whyyyyyyyhy wait?♪

Gabby just beamed up at Ronnie and shook her head laughing. When he saw her smile, he leapt from the stage, tossing the mic to the DJ for someone else to finish his song.

"Well?"

"Really?"

"Uh, yes! You can't sing any Rascal Flatts song unless you are truly heart broken, in love, or fully intending to follow through. I think they have it written in their licensing. Will you marry me, Gabrielle?" He actually got down on one knee (closeted germaphobe that he was, he put down a napkin first), right there in the middle of the bar, and pulled out a ring.

"Absolutely, yes!" Their bar friends hooted and howled and cheered and raised their glasses, as she confirmed her answer with a kiss.

"Wow! She said 'yes'!" Ronnie shouted, just in case the kissing wasn't clear enough. "Let's get outta here..."

"But we just got here!" She yelled back, still holding his hand and smiling.

"Yes, but the song said, 'why wait?'."

"You mean you want to get married... NOW?"

"Uh, yes, now. ♪I know a little church with a preacher who can hook us up right away...♪ He sang to her with a grin.

"Where?"

"Toronto."

"Kyle?"

"Why not? Ethan's there. One of my best men is there. We can buy a ticket for whomever else you'll need. Let's just take a break from it all and just do it. Your clients are quiet, right...?

Vegas would be faster and simpler; but I thought you'd want family around. Besides, Kyle and Kevin are kinda expectin' us to call and say we're on our way..."

"You told them?"

"And I have your mom and Michael on standby."

"Oh my God!"

"Do you still mean 'yes'?"

"Absolutely! Let's go!" She kissed him again and then practically skipped toward the door.

In the car on the way to the airport, Ronnie made two quick phone calls. "She said, 'yes'. We'll be there around midnight." was all he said to each unknown person, before he returned his attention to his fiancé.

"Do you need to call anyone?"

"Wow. Let me think. Um, Shelly?"

"Oh, that was her. She and Tiana are kinda in on it, too. They'll see you in the morning. Do you need any other attendants other than Ethan, Kevin and Nikki?"

"You got Nicole Vanderpip to agree to be a bridesmaid?"

"Only because I promised her she'd be the only one on your side in a dress."

"But what about Libby?"

"She is directing and reading, and she said, and I quote: 'too damn old and too damn pregnant to be a damn bridesmaid!'"

"Okay, Lib, but why all the hostility? They make really cute maternity dresses now..." Gabby giggled at her future sister-in-law. "Gosh. I should call Claire and Joy; but they probably hate me." Gabby said, referring to her two, she assumed former, best friends, and the only attendants from her wedding to Kevin. She'd said she wasn't running; but she practically left skid marks in Charlotte, when she'd left three years earlier, and the girls only found out after she'd been in Atlanta for six months, that she was gone, and her 'perfect marriage' was over. Gabby still felt guilty about not trusting her friends more, but she was working on that. "Oh, well. We can have them down for the weekend when we get back. Let's do it!" She immediately let it go and tried to wrap her mind around what was happening.

Gabby had been rambling for one-hundred-forty-nine

minutes of their two and a half hour flight to Toronto; and then finally, in a moment of calm, she turned and looked at Ronnie. "Baby, I can't get married in two days...or whenever you've masterminded this whole circus to happen. I don't have a dress."

"Are you sure?" He asked softly, as the pilot announced their descent.

She just stared at him. "What did you do?"

"I don't know. Maybe I didn't do anything. I guess you'll just have to trust me... or marry me in... *that.* Yeah, that will do. What you're wearing now is just perfect, actually. You can say, 'I do', buck-neked, if you wanna. But we're here now." He grinned at her.

"Okay, now you're starting to scare me." She was only half kidding.

"Do you want me to pull everyone back and slow down?" He wasn't kidding at all. Nor was he really concerned. He actually did know she trusted him.

"No!... I love you! You're just... Wow... I don't know if I can take any more surprises tonight, Baby. Did you actually buy me a dress, in addition to doing *all* of this other...madness?" She giggled.

He blushed and laughed. "Sorta... Well, maybe... I guess we'll see in a moment, won't we?"

"Oh my God! You are insane!" She laughed as she slid into the limo at the airport. Ronnie stopped talking to her for the short drive from the airport to her hotel, and just stared at her and held her hand tightly. At the hotel, he checked her in and escorted her to her suite.

She gasped when she saw them: not one dress, but six, all beautiful, all distinctly different, and all seemingly in her size. "How did you do this?" She looked from the dresses and back to Ronnie with tears in her eyes, afraid for a moment to walk all the way into the suite.

"I had lots of help. Remember when Trevor had you try on those dresses for that celebrity fashion show? He was just trying to get your measurements for me."

"So there's no celebrity-spouses fashion show?" Ronnie shook his head. "Good. Oh my God..." She just stood in the doorway staring at the beautiful gowns.

"Try one on, baby."

"I'm afraid to. Is one of these really a Mimi Chavez original?"

"Can you tell a Mimi Chavez from a six-hundred-dollar knock-off from the Bridal Barn?"

"From six-thousand feet away!" He knew that was true. He'd been given dozens of up-and-coming designers to choose from, but everyone he asked assured him that Mimi would be Gabby's first choice.

"Well, in that case; yes, if you can spot it. And I think there's also a Christian Siriano in there..."

"No! Can I wear more than one?"

"Do you wanna get married in all the different places we live?" He laughed. If she'd said 'yes', he'd have made it happen.

"No! I want to marry you tomorrow, wearing... that one!" She pointed to the dress farthest away from the door.

"Wow, I'm glad I didn't bet you anything."

"Is that it?'

"Yup."

"No way."

"There's a note."

Gabrielle, congratulations! You're a very lucky woman! Ronnie helped us design this gown especially for you, 'for the most beautiful girl in the world'! I hope you love it. One of my assistants will meet you in Canada to make sure it fits perfectly. Best wishes for a happy and long life full of blessings! Mimi

Gabby let her hand drop and the note fall to the floor. She stood and looked around the room Ronnie'd had turned into a bridal boutique, and could no longer suppress the tears. "When did you do all this?"

"I started planning a few months ago. I went to pick up the dress... two weeks ago?"

"So... when I thought you were off getting your new boy

parts...?"

"I was... most of that time, but then I was in New York, and Toronto planning our wedding."

"How'd you know I was gonna say 'yes'?"

"What?" He walked slowly toward her.

"You heard me. How'd you know I'd say 'y...'" He pulled her by the arm and kissed her slowly... and waited. She let out a long sweet sigh. "Oh, yeah... right... Oh! Okay. Wait. We have a problem. I can't try these on by myself and you can't help me. You can't see me in the dress I choose."

"Even if I helped make it?" Ronnie sounded confused, and slightly concerned.

"Uh, yeah... even if you helped make it, Smarty... It's bad luck, Honey."

"Seriously?"

"Baay-beee!" She whined.

"Okay, okay... Ladies..." Suddenly, Libby, Shelley and Tiana, Claire and Joy, Nikki, and Gabby's mom emerged out of the closed bedroom. Gabby burst into tears and was instantly enveloped in their love and support.

"...So, you'll pick a dress, and shoes, and jewelry... and tomorrow night we'll have a rehearsal dinner, and the following morning, Trevor will be here to do your hair and makeup; and then at four p.m. in the afternoon, Kyle's gonna hitch us up...in front of God and e'rybody."

"Really?"

"Yes, Baby I told you, everyone is on board. Have we forgotten anything?"

"And Ethan knows?"

"It was kinda his idea?"

"What?"

"Well, when I asked him if I could ask you... the day you introduced us, he said 'definitely and it should be a surprise'. I told him if his brilliant idea got me dumped, I was gonna kick his butt; but he convinced me you'd love it. Then he reminded me that Kyle had been teaching him stuff, and 'he'd like to see me try'."

"Wow."

"Yeah, that's what I said..."

38

NASTY HEFFAS

"*S*hawn Pearson, Best Person" Shawnee held out a tiny, manicured hand.

Nikki reached for it slowly, taking time to thoroughly check out the stunning, and completely bald woman attached to it. "Nicole Vanderpip, Maid of..." Nikki was interrupted by Shawn's burst of laughter and accompanying cosmo-sloshing.

"Did you say 'Vanderpip'?" Shawn giggled.

"Yes. Yes, I did." Shawn's smile was contagious, even at Nikki's expense. She stared at the pocket-sized 'stem', who was somehow a sexy, studly version of the bride-to-be, and shifted slightly on her heels. *"How has Nichols not told me about her?"*

"I'm so sorry." Shawn tried to pull herself together. "I'm being a bitch. I can usually contain myself til the third date or so. It's just... funny."

"It's okay." Nikki went back to looking bored and pretending not to have a sense of humor. "I get that a lot." She lied. No one had ever been bold enough to laugh directly at her before, about anything... except maybe Kevin.

"You don't look like a 'Vanderpip'." Shawn stepped back and stared her up and down, literally undressing the smokin' hot, forty-ish, Broadway executive with her eyes. Nikki felt exposed. She liked it. "You should definitely change it." Shawn continued, biting her expertly glossed bottom lip.

Nikki squinted at her thinking "damn she's cute", but said out loud, "make me an offer," as she handed Shawn her empty glass.

"I'll be right back." Shawn assured her. She turned away, vowing not to look back, but thinking "oh, you know she's watchin."

Shawn found Libby and Gabby by the bar, catching up with Claire and Joy, and squeezed in between Gabby and Libby's giant belly. "How did you not tell me about her?" Shawn whispered loudly.

"Because she eats people!" Gabby whispered back the warning just as loudly. "And I don't mean in the way you'd like... ya nasty heffa..."

"Oh, my!" Libby laughed and took a long sip of her cranberry juice. "The gays are so much fun!"

"It's never too late, Libs. Com'on over to the dark side." Shawn pretended to leer at her fake sister. "But the offer expires after your water breaks. Pregnant women are so damn sexy!"

"Uh!" Libby gasped and shook her head laughing.

"See! Nasty heffa. Go get eaten." Gabby laughed and waved in Nikki's direction. "On second thought, you two were made for each other."

"Lawd, please let death come slowly!" Shawn turned from the bar with a drink in each hand and proceeded to walk away, before Gabby plucked one of them out of her hand and sat it on the bar.

"You're cut off. My baby's gonna need you tomorrow." She winked at her friend.

"Yes, my queen." Shawn winked back and marched happily toward certain death.

"Ughhh... Gotta pee again... Be right back, Sweetie." Libby waddled away to the ladies' room for the twelfth time.

Gabby pulled out her phone and began texting frantically, while Claire and Joy were distracted by the 'entertainment'.

Gabby: *Save me!*

Ronnie replied instantly: *Whats wrong?*

Gabby: *Ive entered the 7th circle of hell!*

Ronnie: LOL - *Huh? What? Strippers?*

Actually, Shawn had arranged a much more unique outing for her bachelorette party.

Gabby: *Yuck! No! Worse! Shawnee and Nikki!*

Ronnie: *Noooooooo!*

Gabby laughed out loud at Ronnie's text.

Ronnie: *Somebody's gettin' fired.*

Gabby: *I told Shawnee she was gonna get eaten alive.*

Ronnie: *Oh, Im not worried about that one. Shes scrappy...*

Gabby: *LOL - Can I come home now?*
Ronnie: *What home, Baby? We're in Canada*
Gabby: *Where are you staying?*
Ronnie: *KKs BnB* (Translation: Kevin and Kyle's house.)
Gabby: *Like I said, can I come home now?*
Gabby perked back up.
Ronnie: *I miss u 2. Less than 24 hrs...*
Gabby: *Wont make it that long - Im sneaking out...*
She grinned as she typed.
Ronnie: *No*
Gabby: *Bye...on my way...*
Ronnie: *No.... will come 2 u - 1 hr...*
Gabby: *I love you! Hurry!*
Ronnie: *I luv u more*

"While I'm certain that this exact fantasy is playing daily on a continuous loop in Ronnie's head, it aint gonna happen. I'm not that drunk." Gabby teased, as Shawn began to make herself comfortable in Gabby's suite. She'd spotted Gabby sneaking off, and immediately abandoned their other guests, and most unwillingly, Nikki. Shawn was taking her 'best person' duties very, very seriously; well, mostly.

"How much more drunk do you need to be?" Shawn laughed.

"Get out." Gabby chuckled.

"Okay, I'll be right outside." Shawn conceded and made her way to the door.

"You will not."

"Watch me. Wait. Give me that chair."

"Oh, no you are not getting ready to camp outside my door!"

"Oh, yes, yes I am."

"Why? What do you think I'm gonna do?" Gabby asked innocently.

"Let me see your phone."

"Why do you need my phone?"

"Fine. Go to bed."

"Ughhh...You suck." Gabby pouted and flopped on the bed.

"Just doing my job, Your Highness."

"Thank you, Shawnee." Shawn smiled at her, as she dragged an uncomfortable looking chair just outside the door.

No sooner did she sit down, did Shawn glimpse Ronnie bouncing off of the elevator and heading down the hall. He stopped when he saw her, and tried to retreat into the elevator, hoping she hadn't seen him.

"I see you. You're not getting in there." She said as loudly as she could without actually yelling down he long hall.

"But..." Ronnie looked sheepishly at Shawn, when he'd finally made it to her.

"Uh, no. How are you even here? Who's supposed to be watching you?"

"I think 'Plan A' was Aidan; but he, of course, got wasted. So I slipped out while he was getting a lap dance."

"Lap dance? You had strippers and didn't call me?"

"Well, see... what had happened was..." Ronnie recounted the story to the tune of the theme song from the Fresh Prince of Bel Aire, complete with dance moves, circa 1990; until Shawn laughed so hard she fell out of her chair. While she was picking herself up off the floor, he tapped lightly on the door to Gabby's suite. As she was opening the door, Shawn pounced on him and pulled it shut, keeping Gabby from opening it far enough that he could get in.

"Seriously, if I break a nail, one of you is walking down the aisle with a black eye. Now would you, please, just go to your separate quarters, and let me do my job."

"Just one kiss?" Gabby whined through the door.

"Okay... fine, one kiss..." Shawn said, as she and Ronnie both rushed over to the door and waited for Gabby to open it. "Oh, you think she's talking about you? Oh, hell no."

"I hate you." He shot daggers at his best friend, and shook his head to wipe away the image he got of the two of them making out.

"I know. Do you wanna see what we did tonight?" Shawn asked loudly.

"Noooooooo!" Gabby screamed.

"Then tell him to take his happy ass back down to your

baby-daddies' house, or I'm breaking out the pictures."

"You would not!"

"Tell her."

"Um, Baby... what'd you do tonight?" Ronnie grinned at the door.

"Ya know, Baby, I'm really very sleepy, all of a sudden; and you know, if I don't get my twelve hours, my eyes get all puffy. You've done all this work; I wanna be pretty. Maybe you should let me get some sleep."

"Wow. Really? Is it that bad?" Ronnie whispered to Shawn.

"If you get her away from the door, and promise not to try and punk me again, I'll let you see!" She whispered back loudly.

"Deal." They did their secret handshake. "O-kay. Call me before you go to sleep, Baby?"

"I'm gonna jump in the tub, and then it's straight to bed. As soon as my head hits the pillow, I'll call you."

"Okay." Ronnie walked down the hall and actually got on the elevator. He returned fifteen minutes later with a six-pack and a huge platter of chili-cheese fries. "Let the show begin." Shawn cued up the photos from earlier that night, and traded her iPhone for the plate of cheesy goodness. Ronnie giggled and blushed through the mayhem. "I cannot believe you took my fiancé, my straight, pregnant sister and a friggin' Broadway producer to an erotic, lesbian fight club."

"Oh, but I did!" Shawn grinned and licked chili from her fingers.

"They do seem to be enjoying themselves." Ronnie turned the phone to rotate the image.

"Told ya... nasty heffas... Oh my God...especially, Libby! I always knew she was hidin' something."

"Stop! My eyes! It burrrns!"

"So, you still gonna marry her?" Shawn winked at him, as he reached his fork into what was left of the container of fries.

"Oh, I'm trying to figure out how to move the ceremony up a few hours..." He spoke with his mouth full, and grinned.

"Wow." They said together.

"See! I told you, you were a lesbian!" Shawn teased, knowing full-well what the actual distinction was between her and

Gabby; and how Gabby and Ronnie functioned much more naturally than she and Ronnie ever could have.

"Uh, no... I am absolutely NOT a lesbian...okay fine... maybe a little... but only on Tuesdays... and Fridays... and every fourth Sunday... Besides, I told you that labels are for cheap junk mail campaigns...and cans of soup." He quipped.

"Damn. I'm too drunk to tell if that is amazingly profound, or really, really corny." She beamed.

"Me too. I think it's probably a bit of both." He chuckled

"Seriously, Ronnie, I'm so proud of you, and so happy for you, I'm actually a little pissed."

"I beg your pardon?"

"See, I've got this speech to give tomorrow; and *every time* I practice it, I start crying like a little...girl."

"You are a girl, dumbass."

"That is so not the point...Wow, you're still a jerk..."

"Only when I'm right..."

"As I was saying..." Shawnee paused, realizing that, perhaps if she said what she needed to, to Ronnie then, she'd make it through the speeches. "I know a lot, don't I?"

"You know everything, Shawnee; more than anyone, including Libby, and my therapist... except Gabrielle." They sat on the floor in the hallway and were suddenly quiet, as he reached for her hand. Before Gabby, Shawnee was the only person who knew how often, and how close, Ronnie had come to not making it; not just through the storm, but for many years after. He didn't even talk about it in therapy. It felt like failure to him, lack of faith. He was going to counseling, when he could no longer go to church, to work through and push passed the despair. But when the nightmares wouldn't stop, and when years after it happened, he could still feel the pain, hear the voice and smell the filth; he more than once, wanted to, and prayed that he could...just die. He believed with his whole heart that the attack did not 'make him'; but what it did do was make it harder, seemingly impossible, to get back to 'her'. Although he admitted to absolutely no one; not Shawnee, not Gabby, not even God, he had believed that 'Veronica' was dead. And he asked, more than once, if it would be okay, "Since I can't be what anyone else wants or needs me to be, can I please go, too?" But, over and over, the answer was always the same:

God said, *'No. I have a plan and a purpose, uniquely designed for you!'*

So, each morning after 'a bad night', Ronnie called or found Shawnee and shared his miracle with her. She always thought it was odd that Ronnie told her. But it seemed the most natural thing in the world to him. As far as he was concerned, no one else was strong enough, except his dad; and Ronnie couldn't bear bringing that kind of pain back into his dad's life. More than that, he felt that no one needed the blessing of his testimony more than his best friend. He'd been her safe harbor from her verbally abusive mother for years before the storm. He knew, even while it was happening, that he'd left her 'alone' for a while, while he fought to get back. Before he moved away, he'd sit and watch her walk home alone. Only years later, when they lived together in Atlanta, did she finally tell him about the fights at school, and the bullying... and the drunken beatings she endured for years, when she stopped hiding from her mother, but still refused to leave her. In Ronnie's eyes, the pretty little girl, who grew up to be the smokin' hot tomboy who managed his career, and would see him safely down the aisle, was every bit as amazing (only in a way that made her the perfect match for someone else) as his bride to be. As he sat holding Shawnee's hand, thinking about all they'd been through, and what was getting ready to happen, he said a silent prayer of Thanks for the gift she'd been to him, practically his entire life.

"I kinda thought that." Shawn continued. She sat straight up and turned to look at him, before wiping a tear away with her free hand, and then resting her head on his shoulder. "You made it, Ronnie. You're getting ready to marry the woman of your dreams, in the fairytale wedding you've been planning since we were ten. Did I ever tell you how really 'not masculine at all' that is, by the way?"

"Oh God! Will you let the stereotypes go for like five minutes, please?!" He nudged her and smiled.

"It's really hard. Actually that's not even 'lesbian-like', either! What the hell *are* you?" She giggled in a loud whisper. "Seriously, you're finally going to have it all. And I honestly can't be happier; or think of anyone who deserves it more. I'm so excited about tomorrow... and I really can't wait to see what happens when the show resumes...and you're at like one-hundred and ten percent."

"Wow." Ronnie didn't say anything for a little while. "Thank you so much, Shawnee... I love you, so much. You know, there is a part of me that knows, 'God Did It!'; but there's another part that believes I wouldn't have survived without you. I can't imagine what my life would be without you...By the way, you're fired."

"Whatdahell?!" Shawn sat up and squinted at him.

"I know, right... Well, not right away, but when my contract expires at the end of this season, I'm really done. I just want to write. I don't need an agent for that. Besides, we've decided that when we get back from our honeymoon, I'm going to come out."

"And what on Earth does that have to do with the rising cost of condoms?"

"You are so damn dumb, I don't know what to do! It means, you little freak, that finally, *The Ronnie Reynolds Show* will be over."

"And again I say..." She paused for effect, and he chimed in with song...
♫...Rejoice!♫

"Shut up." She hated arguing with him. Even drunk, he was faster than her. "How does your coming out change anything?"

"Um, the network will pull the show, for lack of ratings...and probably sue me for being in breach of some stupid morals clause."

"First of all, you're an idiot. And secondly, I'm you're agent, so you don't have a morals clause. I killed that bitch ten years ago. I told them if they wanted a friggin' boy scout, they should have shopped for their talent at a Walmart in Nebraska. But since they had indeed acknowledged that they'd just discovered the brightest star since JFK, you should have at least as much freedom to screw up as he did."

"Aw... Thanks, Shawnee. JFK was a womanizer, who our own government feared would be so powerful, they had him shot in the head, by the way."

"Allegedly, you're welcome, and my point exactly."

Shawnee said without an ounce of humor.

"Ooh, I must really be drunk, because I honestly do not understand the words that are coming out of your mouth!"

"I'm saying you got the gig because you're amazing. You kept it because you're real, and people *genuinely* love you. And those same people are going to still love you, when you stop being a pussy and... tell them you were born with one!"

"Ew! You are certifiable. There is no way..."

Shawn didn't even let him finish. "I will bet you a million dollars I'm right." And she was serious.

"Aw... you're so pretty..." Ronnie shook his head laughing at her.

"What?... No, seriously, I am a little drunk. What'd I miss?"

"That's a sucker bet. If I win... if I come out and America demands my head on a platter, the network will fire me, I will be sued for fraud, and I'll have nothing to give you... If you win, I'm just gonna quit anyway, and I still won't have a million dollars to give you."

"Ha! Wow! I'm really not that drunk... If I'm right, you do the show for two more seasons, and you continue to pay me my commission, plus a million dollars for making me think this damn hard."

"Whatever. It's never gonna happen. And when you lose, I want your T Rex:" He added referring to her three-wheeler.

"Not that I care; cuz I'm right; but it's too small for you. I had it modified... and it's purple!"

"Purple just happens to be my wife's favorite color. And yes, you are a dwarf... conveniently enough, so is the wife."

"I'll take your stupid bet!" She shook his extended right hand. "And... Oooh! I'm tellin', Gabby you called her short!"

"She already knows. I bought her stock in Manolo Blahnik as a wedding gift."

"Does she also know you're an arrogant jerk?"

"As a matter of fact, she does!"

39

I TOLD YOU SO!

*G*abrielle and Ronnie's holy union was even more amazing than either of them ever imagined it could be. Everyone they loved was there, including all of each of their families, their closest friends, and on the front row, Dr. Elizabeth Keaner. Ronnie finally put her out of her misery just before he left for Canada, explaining that he and Gabby figured it out their first few days together. They trusted her, but agreed it would be easier for each of them to get what they needed from her, if she didn't know. She forgave them instantly, when she received their wedding invitation, in the form of a phone call from Ronnie. She announced her retirement to them at their reception.

Gabby clung to Ronnie and watched their family and friends interacting. The man of her dreams, had given her the wedding of theirs. It couldn't have been more perfect, had she planned it herself. And she was still crying happy tears when Kevin walked over to say, 'I told you so!', and pulled her onto the dance floor.

She returned to find her mother holding Ronnie's hand. "Oh, I'm so happy! Please tell me you'll let me throw a blessing and reception in the Atlanta church when you get back!"

"Wow, Mommy! Really? You don't think that would be uncomfortable?"

"Why Gabrielle? That's God's house, and you're my only daughter."

"And we'd like to finally throw you a real shower." Claire chimed in.

Gabby smiled at her sorority sisters. "I just knew you guys were through with me." She laughed to herself that she'd known them since high school, and it had never occurred to her that they were actually a couple, until they announced their own wedding would be six months later.

"More hurt than angry, but it's all good, now." Joy explained. "We're always gonna pray for you, whether you're speaking to us or not. And we'll be in the front row of your children's, and grandchildren's weddings, too."

Gabby tried not to cry and hugged them, as Ronnie just watched, feeling a little overwhelmed himself. He had to reel it in when Ethan walked over, stood in front of him, and held out his hand.

"See, I told you she'd say 'yes'."

"You did. And thank you again for the excellent advice."

"So, what should I call you?" Ethan asked more out of curiosity than concern, as he leaned against the wall next to Ronnie.

"What do you want to call me?"

"Will you still feel like a 'dad-type person' if I just keep callin' you 'Ronnie'?"

"Absolutely. What should I call you?"Again, just more small talk.

Ethan watched his mom with her best friends; and waved to his Grandma Phyllis, both sets of his dads' parents, and his new grandparents, Ronnie's mom and dad. They were really nice. And although, he didn't know a whole lot about why his mom's dad wasn't there, he thought it was really cool that Ronnie's mom and dad hadn't stopped holding hands the whole time they'd been in Canada. Ethan liked the way 'Granna', as Annette asked to be called, looked at 'Papa Dave'. It was kinda the same way his dads looked at each other, the same way his mom looked at Ronnie. Ethan had never seen her so happy.

"Well, Mom calls me 'Ethan', or 'EJ' and 'Squirt', and 'Ethan-Jerome' when I'm in trouble; but I hate that. The dads call me all that too... and 'Son' a lot. I figure that's a dad thing, right? Well, you make my mom really happy; so I guess you can call me 'Son', too."

40

RONNIE 8.0

"*R*onnie..." Gabby sighed, tugging at his undershirt, indicating that she needed to feel his skin.

"I know, Baby." He was nervous. He'd thought it all out so carefully, the reveal. What better moment than their honeymoon? He took a deep breath and kissed her before guiding her to sit on the bed. In the low light of their cottage, it was hard to see much. Gabby really wanted to hop up and turn on all the lights, but tried to contain herself. Ronnie closed his eyes in a quick moment of prayer and pulled the shirt over his head. Gabby tilted her head slightly at the sports bra but didn't say anything. As he reached under his arm and unzipped it at the side she thought she understood. A compression garment would make sense after a mastectomy and pectoral reshaping. But as he pulled the bra away and let his arms fall to his side, she gasped. Her eyes shot up to his face and then slowly back down his body. His once full C-cups were not gone, just reduced to a tight and perky B. Gabby couldn't move. She just sat there as the tears begin to pour. She smiled and laughed as he walked slowly toward her. She put her hands on his tiny waist and pressed her face against the brand new rock-hard abs. She walked with her fingers up his long, newly-sculpted torso to her smaller and just as beautiful old friends, letting her hands rest there.

"Thank you." She whispered against his skin. "You're so beautiful." She said through tears before taking one erect nipple in her mouth. He lowered his head to watch her, enjoying her kiss until she tried to move her hands lower. He took her hands and laid her back onto the bed, still wearing his boxer-briefs. She honestly didn't care about the rest. She loved him, however he'd transformed himself, but she knew deep down she needed something of the woman to remain. She'd have been happy if the surprises and the physical part of their honeymoon ended there, expecting that he'd be too sore to perform. But as had become the norm, Ronnie exceeded her expectations. He did things with his mouth and hands that no 'anatomical man' had ever done, as he again and again reminded her that she was beautiful and loved. She drifted in and out of euphoria for hours, as he pulled her back each time she felt recovered enough to take over. Finally, in a brief moment of clarity, she spoke. "Baby, please let me touch you." He didn't answer, he just held her hand to his heart, as they lay facing each other under the covers. He stared at her face, and she stared back lovingly. A tear rolled down Ronnie's cheek and he closed his eyes tightly trying to stop it. Gabby kissed it and held his face in her hand. "It's okay," she smiled referring to the fact that he'd been making love to her for hours, and while she heard the familiar sound of his climax, she'd seen no sign of an erection. She assumed it was too soon.

"That's not why I'm crying, Gabby."

"Okay... Talk to me." She whispered softly and held her breath.

"What did I ever do to deserve you?"

"You love me." She released her breath and kissed him sweetly.

"I do." He smiled at her and closed his eyes again. He held her hand, kissed the palm and slowly slid it down his torso. She closed her eyes and smiled, enjoying the ride down, trying not to move too quickly. Her smile grew when she reached the soft curls... but then she froze and the smile was gone. Ronnie held his breath. She reached further down into what had become her favorite playground, the paradise she'd thought was lost.

"Uh!" She gasped as she rolled her fingers in the damp fur. She didn't know which way to go. She stared at him as he still held his breath. "You didn't?"

"No, I didn't."

"Baby, why? Was it because of me?"

"Yes…" Gabby started to cry.

"Ronnie, I'm sorry! I shouldn't have said anything. I just wanted you to know that I love you, that I'd love you no matter what! I don't want... I don't want you to resent me..." she began to sob.

"Oh, Baby, no! I did it because of you, but I mean that in the best way in the world. I suddenly realized I didn't need to do anything else. With you, for the first time in my life, I feel complete and wonderful just as I am. I can't imagine anything more exquisite than what we are together. You make me feel like I don't need to be anything other than what I ..." Gabby kissed him before he could finish, and slowly slid her hand back down. She squeezed him and let her fingers slip in and out of the wetness there. He panted as she quickly returned a small portion of the pleasure he'd been giving her. As he purred softly she moaned and went in search of the source. She found it and spent days there as he eagerly submitted to her hands, lips and tongue.

"Hey!" Gabby opened her eyes and squinched up her face. She'd been so tickled to be reunited with Ronnie and her old friends that she almost forgot why he'd been gone for eight weeks. She was more curious than worried, as she suspected at least part of his time away from her was spent planning their wedding extravaganza. Still, she required transparency. Ronnie stirred next to her and walked his fingers up her arm. She moved like a cat, bolting upright, knocking him flat on his back and landing on his chest. "Pinned ya!" she laughed. She'd been wanting to say that out loud since she first saw *The Lion King*, and wanting to try that particular move since her night out with Shawn and the girls just twenty-four hours earlier.

"Whoa?" Ronnie chuckled and tried to wrap his arms around her waist, but she grabbed his wrists and held them above his head. He closed his eyes and smiled as she scooted forward so her knees kept him from putting his arms down.

"So... Baby..."

"Yes, My Beloved?"

"Ya know... you left me in Georgia... by myself... for ten weeks under the impression that you were getting some long-planned and wholly unnecessary... modifications..."

"Well, actually, it was exactly eight weeks, I came back early; but yes, I did."

"You did leave, or you did get modifications?"

"Well, the first is pretty obvious." He laughed, enjoying her weight on top of him. "And the second I'd be more than happy to show you, if you'd release me from this super-hot, sex-ninja hold you've clearly been practicing. Remind me to send the girls gift baskets, by the way."

"No."

"I beg your pardon."

"I'm not letting you up. Spill it."

Ronnie chuckled and tried not to grin as he easily rocked his arms loose and tickled her feet until she backed up. What Gabby lacked in strength, she made up for in determination, and quickly repositioned herself and held his arms at the biceps.

"Fine. Okay. Actually, you've experienced part of the modification already." She giggled as he half-heartedly tried to lift his arms. "As I was saying, if you'll get your lovely ass off my chest, or at least allow me the use of my arms, I can show you..."

Gabby sat up slowly, sliding her hands from Ronnie's arms and to his chest. She looked down. The girls were still there, just perkier. "What?" She asked impatiently.

"I've been working out?" He flexed well-defined biceps.

"Clearly. You look uh-mazing. But if you're telling me you snuck away to Montreal, Canada to lift weights, I'm gonna kick your ass for real. We just spent ten grand on a home gym!"

"We?"

"Okay, I, but you said you wanted it."

"I do. I love it! And it's gonna come in handy. Did the guy come and install the mirrors yet?"

"No. Stop stalling!"

"Okay. Okay. But you really do have to let me up."

"Okay." Gabby pouted. "I'm starving. Do you want anything?"

"Just water, please." Ronnie kissed her on her forehead before walking into the bathroom and closing the door. Inside, he took his time. A lot of time and effort, not to mention money, had gone into this moment. He didn't feel right praying about sex; but in keeping with his recent practice of 'praying about everything', he asked for proof that he'd made the right decision. "Please, let this be 'enough' for both of us?" He stood in front of the mirror. "Not bad..." By the time he returned, Gabby was sitting in the middle of the bed with two bottles of water and a tray of fruit. She clumsily tried to discard a half-eaten strawberry without looking at the tray.

"Uuh... Oh!" She held her hand to her mouth, suppressing her genuine surprise. "What's this? Ronnie 8.0?" She scooted off the bed and rushed to stand in front of him, as he held his Superman pose.

"Something like that. See... 'enhancements'." He reached for both of her hands and bent to kiss her.

"So. I really, really, really hate to ask this, but..." Ronnie finally regained his breath enough to speak.

"Don't bother. A million times better than 'the real thing'! Oh my God!" Gabby reached down and gave her new best friend a squeeze and gentle tug. "Can you feel that?" she breathed into his neck.

"Oh, yes." He closed his eyes and rolled his head back.

"How?"

He rubbed her hand as she held him before taking it and sliding it down the underside of the completely realistic shaft. It seemed to go on forever, but did actually come to an end. Gabby gasped when her fingers met the familiar feminine folds and bunny soft hair she'd enjoyed just hours earlier and she realized that 'the end' was somewhere, apparently deep, inside her new husband.

"Na uh."

"Uh huh."

"Wow. So, when I do this..." she stroked and pulled gently "you can feel me?"

"Yes."

"Is it good?"

"It's fantastic."

"And when I..." Gabby proceeded to demonstrate and verify almost every possible interaction and watched with glee as Ronnie responded. She even tried to fake him out, just in case he was bluffing for her sake. But when she said "how's this?" and hadn't done anything, he called her on it.

"You didn't do anything that time, Honey." He chuckled and pulled her on top of him. "Baby, I can feel you, everything you do. I can feel how wet you are, and I felt tiny tremors the first, second and third time you came."

"Ha! You missed two!" She teased as she kissed his breasts and prepared to try her favorite position. He moaned as she slipped the thick and supple tip inside her. She moved slowly at first, determined to take it all in. As she found her rhythm she began to bear down, pushing deeper inside him. She didn't know. He had considered, but not fully realized what the choice of that particular prosthetic meant for them. Ronnie hadn't been penetrated, beyond the shallow fingering he allowed, in twenty years. Discounting the rape as the horrible accident, not sex, he was a virgin. Gabby looked down at his face, saw what looked like panic and slowed to a near complete stop, but did not pull away. "Oh my God. Baby, I'm so sorry."

"No." He pulled her forward to kiss her, but pressed her hips down. "Don't stop."

"Are you sure?"

"Yes... It feels good. Are you okay?"

"Oh, I," she slid down again hard, "have never been better." Gabby rolled her hips gently until Ronnie began to rock against her again.

Gabby collapsed next to him and screamed into a pillow. He fumbled for her hand and held it tightly, needing to stay connected just a while longer.

"So."

"So?"

"So, that's what I was doing in Montreal for the past eight weeks."

"Because there's a special super-bionic, custom-tailored, amazing-dick factory in Canada?"

"Yes, yes there is."

"Oh, man I love this country!"

41

NOW, FREE SOMEONE ELSE!

"**B**aby, are you sure you're okay? I mean, not having done it?" Gabby asked.

"Yes! I prayed about it. I thought about it. And all I could think about was how amazing it is to be with you. I wouldn't trade the way we are together for anything in the world. Are you sure you don't want to be with 'a whole man'?"

"Don't say that. Don't ever say that again. You are all the man I will ever need."

"I believe you. I can hardly believe you're real, but I believe what you tell me. I can feel it. Speaking of telling... I'm ready, Baby."

"Really? Are you sure? Wait a minute. Why tell now, Ronnie; now that there is no way anyone would ever know?"

"I know... and you know... and God knows. There is someone out in the world who needs to see me and know that it's possible to make it through everything I've been through; not Hugo, but the transition, what I went through with my family, the struggles with relationships, finding myself... all of it... Someone needs to know it's possible to change and be whole and happy, and accepted, and successful."

"And you think your story is a successful one?" Gabby teased as she nibbled his earlobe.

"If for no other reason than this one right here... Hell, yes..." He pulled her on top of him and kissed her slowly. Gabby sighed sweetly as she pressed her naked body against his torso. "Wait." He stopped kissing and looked into her eyes. "You're okay with me coming out, publically... like on the show and everything?"

Gabby suddenly became very serious. "On one condition."

"Okay." Ronnie braced himself. Whatever it was she needed, he would do.

"That I can be there with you when you do it..."

Ronnie fought back tears. "I don't think I would be able to do it any other way."

The studio was standing room only for the final show of the season. Everyone was there, Ronnie's parents and siblings, his friends Kevin, Kyle and Michael; Mama Rich and Ethan...The network had been building up the hype all season long, that there would be a big surprise at the end of that, Ronnie's last, season. Ronnie could hardly believe that they'd actually made it to the last show without having to tell what the big reveal would be; but Shawn insisted that it would not happen, unless they trusted him enough to tell absolutely no one, including the network, before that live show.

"My guests today are men and women, by choice, or some would say, divine intervention, who identify as 'Transgender'. It is an honor to share their unique stories with you." Ronnie introduced his three guests, as each of their photos was highlighted. After the audience had met and spoken with Dawn, Aidan, and Harriett, a fourth photo appeared. The photo of a beautiful baby girl, in a pink chiffon gown, was replaced with Ronnie's photo from *People Magazine's* '100 Most Beautiful People' cover.

"I was born Veronica Anne-Alise Reynolds." A collective gasp was quickly followed by silence, then whispering, then silence again, as people stood... and then thunderous applause. After it died down, a tearful Ronnie kept going, thanking the audience for their support, and explaining that "I've been in one state of transition or another most of my life, from my earliest memory. I don't remember when this picture was taken." Ronnie looked at his mom on the front row. "But I remember what must have been Halloween just a few years later? I wanted to chop all my hair off and go trick-or-treating as my dad!" The audience giggled. David beamed. "But it was never my intention to deliberately deceive anyone." Ronnie didn't explain that he hadn't actually gone through with the surgery. That intimate detail, like those truths about his guests, and every other transgendered person, was no one's business but his and his wife's.

Ronnie's wasn't the first show to introduce transgendered

people; but he was the first celebrity to come out at the apex of what had been a long and successful career. That left room for some very real and relevant questions. Gabby stayed very close to him. She'd promised herself she wouldn't speak unless called on, but she held his hand tightly. Ironically, the first question went to her.

"My question is for Gabrielle. So, what does that make you?"

"Lucky!" She waved her ring. "... Seriously, it's very simple for me. I love 'Ronnie'... who just happens to be both male and female... but he refers to himself as 'he' so I classify myself, when I'm required to, (she winked) as straight."

"Ronnie, why are you doing this now? Did something happen?"

"Honestly, God only knows why I'm really doing this now... but I'm doing it because it was finally more uncomfortable hiding than being real. I got to the point where I felt like a fraud talking to people like my guests today, and my brothers Kevin and Kyle Rivers-Tye, who've been out in the world fighting a real war for my rights, as well as their own. It wasn't just a feeling, actually. I *was* a fraud. Sitting at that desk every night with brave, honest people, and not standing up and saying 'you're my brother, and your struggle is my struggle' was... I think my nephew would use the term 'hypocritical, punk-ass...', but I'll just say 'cowardice'. And, by the way, I apologize."

"But you could have gone on forever, and no one would have known."

"I knew."

"Of course, but why's that such a big deal now?"

"I didn't want to wait until after I retired. That sounded and felt too much like hiding. It's not something I'm ashamed of. In fact, I don't think that people who choose to keep their identities private do so out of shame or embarrassment at all." His guests nodded. "For me, it actually was more about fear. I think when you make a choice like ours... No. I think *when I* made the choice, because I can't speak for anyone else, it was because it was easier for me than the alternative. From my earliest memory, I felt inadequate as a girl, as a woman. More than that, I felt wrong. But I did feel

masculine; and that didn't feel wrong at all. My guests have described similar and different experiences. There are degrees. The
one thing I've yet to hear is 'shame'. But the fear is a different story.
I remember, vividly, the fear of not being loved. My whole family
is here with me today; and I am so blessed and happy to have their
love and support. But getting here was not easy for all of them."
Ronnie was careful not to call his mom out. "I remember the fear of
loss...that someone I loved would not accept that I was so different,
sometimes just because of what they assumed my difference said
about them. I lived with, first the fear of being abused, and later the
actual abuse, by someone who didn't understand, and so he tried to
destroy me... because I was different. I spent most of my adult life
afraid that I'd lose the life I thought I'd created for myself. I expected, until very recently, that people and things would gradually
fall or be peeled away."

"And I have to say this. I believe that on some level, most
of the things people fear in life are irrational. Most of us will likely
never encounter half of the things we fear most. If you're afraid of
flying, you can choose to stay on the ground. If you're afraid of the
water, you can learn to swim. But when your fear is of how you'll
be received... just walking around in the world, being who you
are... To my knowledge, no one has ever died from 'the fear of
something' alone. But people have been killed, by their own hand
and others, over things we fear and don't understand. And *that's not
irrational*. It's real. How do you escape that? Well, again, I can only speak for myself; but it was the revelation, that I would never be
able to escape what I or anyone else is afraid of, that finally got to
be too much. I'd never be able to escape it, so I had to overcome it.
I was kinda hoping that if I just walked into the water, and didn't
actually die, I would win! If I lose absolutely everything else," he
turned and looked at Gabby, knowing he would not lose her; "I've
got nothing left to be afraid of. And yes, I know how selfish that all
sounds. But I also know that there is at least one other person in the
world who needs to see me being just a little bit selfish and more
than a little bit brave. And if that one boy or girl hears me, and
chooses to live, not just a better life, or an alternative life, or a trans
life, but *whatever* their life is, it was worth *anything* that I might
lose…and *bigger* than whatever I might be afraid of."

T. Randall Jones

42

IT'S CALLED A MIRACLE, DUMMY!

*G*abby flew up the stairs two at a time. She couldn't make out what exactly was going on; but Ronnie was practically screeching at her to come upstairs. She'd almost dropped her tea on her way to her downstairs office. She'd never actually heard him raise his voice; so, she couldn't get to him fast enough, as she heard him literally freaking out. She found him in the master bath. That alone was a pretty sure sign that something very serious was wrong. There was no way she should have been able to hear him a whole story away at the opposite end of the house.

"I'm here, Baby! What's wrong?" She asked breathlessly.

"What the hell did you do to me?" He sat on the toilet, pointing to a pair of blood-stained boxer-briefs about six feet away from him.

"Whoa." Gabby stared wide-eyed, as she processed what was going on. "Hey!" She frowned for a minute, as she realized that he saying it was her fault he seemed to have suddenly started his period at thirty-six years old. Then, just as quickly, she chuckled, until Ronnie shot daggers at her.

"Oh, Baby..." She tried desperately not to giggle. "No, really. This isn't funny at all." She tried to think of very bad things, but couldn't. Instead, she just looked at him lovingly.

"Honey, is this what I think it is?" Seeing her face, he calmed down immediately.

"Yeah, I think it is... Oh my God... You've got a period. What are you gonna do?"

"Get rid of it." He said without an ounce of humor.

Gabby hesitated and then said, "Well, of course." but thought "Are you sure?"

Ronnie sat back on the toilet. "Will you make me an appointment, please?"

"When do you want to go?"

"Now."

"O-kay." She left the bathroom and began shaking her head and smiling again as soon as she was out of his sight.

They drove in silence to Gabby's ob./gyn. Ronnie had stopped getting regular physicals two decades earlier. Deep down, he knew it was probably not the smartest thing to do. But the entire process was, as one would imagine, just way too awful. And since he'd never actually had a period, foolishly he assumed all was well, that those parts just didn't work anyway. They didn't bother him, so he didn't bother them. They had an understanding.

Dr. Lillian Taft arranged for the couple to meet her in her office, on a Saturday afternoon. Gabby held Ronnie's hand while he recounted his (not entirely unique) history, specifically the part about believing his uterus had been destroyed twenty years earlier. They did an ultrasound and a pelvic exam; and to his absolute horror, and Gabby's curious delight, everything appeared to be completely normal.

"But why hasn't he had a regular period before now?" Gabby asked, seeing that Ronnie was too dumbfounded to speak.

"While this is certainly unusual; actually, I've never seen it, the combination of the initial trauma and the subsequent stress could have triggered a hormonal imbalance. The history you had sent over indicates that your testosterone levels, which we all have, by the way, have always been elevated, and your estrogen pretty low. Studies have shown that in biological males, those levels begin to naturally reverse when a man is in love. But there is no real medical explanation as to why it's happening to you now. In biological females, the opposite happens: testosterone levels go up and estrogen comes down. It's nature's way of helping us relate to one another. Have you ever done any kind of hormone therapy, Ronnie?"

"No. I did the research, and I was afraid of the side effects."

"Well, between the three of us, I'm happy to hear that."

"So, what are our options?" Ronnie was slowly coming back.

Dr. Taft smiled patiently at him. She wasn't a specialist. This wasn't even a terribly interesting medical finding; only a bit odd. And if she didn't adore Gabrielle Reynolds, she might be bothered by the disruption to her day off. Still, she was just amused. The man sitting in front of her, whom she recognized as an Emmy-winning talk-show host and journalist, was indeed a fully-functioning, biological, actually, only postpubescent woman. Her natural compassion for people allowed her to empathize with him; but beyond the obvious, she failed to see what all the fuss was about. In fact, she just thought it was, as her son would say, 'wicked-cool'. "Ronnie... May I call you 'Ronnie'? I'm not sure what you're asking. There is no medical reason to *do* anything. Are you in any pain?"

"No."

"Excellent. Gabby, you know the drill. There are excellent over the counter products for menstrual cramps, bloating, headache... If you'd like, I can provide birth control pills to regulate your cycle; but aside from that, I would just do what you've always done. Leave your body alone. Don't attack it, and hopefully you will slip quietly into menopause without any drama...." She paused to look again at the lab work she'd put a rush on. "Your pap is normal, you won't need a mammogram for, looks like, four years..." Ronnie groaned and Gabby smiled sympathetically, wondering if she should ever mention that now that his breasts were smaller, his mammogram was probably going to suck even more. "Make an appointment for a year from now for a follow-up, unless you have problems before then... Or, if you'd rather, schedule your appointments together under Gabby's name...."

"You don't think he needs to see a specialist?"

"Not unless you start taking testosterone, which again, I highly advise against. Otherwise, and I apologize in advance for how this sounds, you're just one of the girls; and an extremely healthy one at that."

"Thank you, Lillian." Gabby stood and extended her hand.

"You're very welcome, Gabby. Ronnie, it was very nice meeting you. I'm a huge fan. Thank you so much for calling me."

"Thank you. And thank you for seeing us." He said sincerely, instantly receiving the message that, to his new ob/gyn, a little blood in his boxers didn't make him any less 'Ronnie Reynolds'.

To Gabby's delight and Ronnie's...okay, slightly bitter delight, the only thing that relieved his menstrual cramps was orgasm therapy. For three months, she watched the calendar and watched Ronnie's mood change; and then, like clockwork, he'd spontaneously start baking. But the double-fudge, chocolate on chocolate cake, with chocolate chips stopped working after 'day one', and he was still visibly uncomfortable; and he absolutely refused to take Midol.

After a warm bath, and what had quickly become their 'day one' ritual, mutual masturbation, Gabby slid out of bed, over to one of three bedroom closets, the one that held her hats and shoes. "I thought you might still be fussy, so I picked up something for you..." She presented him with an elaborately wrapped package. "Happy 'Just Cuz' Day!"

"Oh boy. I'm scared. It's probably a damn..." Ronnie shook the box gently and attempted to guess its contents. "...assortment of the latest and greatest feminine hygiene products..." Ronnie was pretty bitchy until at least 'day four' of the longest 'normal' period (eight days) Gabby'd ever heard of.

"Oh stop. Open it."

"What in the world?" He held the chorded appliance quizzically.

"It's a massager."

"Is that what they told you? Cuz it looks an awful lot like an industrial-strength vibrator to me."

"Potato-po-Ta-to... Lay down." Gabby kissed him sweetly while, gently shoving him back onto the bed. "Wait." She grabbed a bottle of warm lubricant and, keeping it on low, began pressing gently against his ever-so-slightly bloated abdomen. When he moaned softly, and his arms slipped to his sides, she moved slowly lower, until he parted his legs slightly....

"I hate you." He said as he curled up on his side and wrapped his arms around her.

"I know, Honey." She giggled and kissed his forehead. "You're welcome."

Six months after Ronnie's first period, and two days before his thirty-seventh birthday, he was still acting as though his official induction into womanhood was the worst thing that had ever happened to him. And considering all that Gabby knew he'd actually been through, it was, frankly, starting to get on her nerves. She moved noisily about their bedroom, putting away laundry and dusting; two things that he typically did, except when he 'was a girl'. When she was finished, she opened the blinds and sat at the foot of the bed, gently rubbing his leg. "Baby, get up. We're going to church."

"Are you mad? Why?" Gabby hadn't been to church herself in over three years. For Ronnie, it was going on three decades.

"To give Thanks? Heathen."

"'Thanks' for what?"

Gabby shot Ronnie a look that would have burned a whole in him, had he not had his head buried under three layers of covers. "Among a million other things, your period...."

"Oh, you have lost your mind. Are you high?" He slowly wiggled out from under his blankies.

"Nope, never been more lucid, as a matter of fact. Seriously, Baby. It's time. You've been moping around this house for months; and I've been walking around you on eggshells every twenty-eight days..."

"More like every twenty-four..." He grumbled.

"Oh, shut up! I've had enough, now! I've kept it to myself long enough; and I think it's giving me an ulcer. How can you not see it?"

"See what, Baby?" Ronnie sat up. He'd never seen Gabby so upset, at least not at him.

"The miracle!"

"Oh... No... Still don't get it... What miracle, Angelface?" He couldn't look at her and be unhappy. In fact, he'd only been sleeping through his periods because she'd been letting him. All she'd ever really needed to do was what she was actually doing then, come and talk to him. The only thing that really got to him was that the whole bleeding thing was the literal opposite of masculine; and he'd insisted on being treated like a man. How could she respect him when he was binge-eating, superplus tampon wearing basket-case for eight days a month?

"You're an ass!"

"Pretty lady cussin' at me 'bout miracles, say what?"

"Oh, am I cussin'? So sorry. Okay, let me try again. Baby, this," she rubbed his belly, causing him to purr in spite of himself, "is God! I saw it instantly. And that's funny, cuz you know I usually don't get spiritual stuff right away... But your period starting now, after all this time, is not some curse. You heard Lillian. It's not even medically, interesting... It's a miracle! You said yourself, you'd only ever had one truly feminine desire... to have a baby. Before six months ago, you believed, and it looked as though, that was physically impossible. And we found out that there is a possibility that you could actually have this most precious thing, which you thought you'd lost! This is God...GIVING IT ALL BACK, BABY!"

"Do you really believe that?"

"I don't understand how you, of all people, do not believe that!"

"But why, now?"

"I don't know why, Honey. I don't know why what happened to delay the start of your womanhood happened at all. I will never understand why God allowed something so horrible to happen to a soul, not just a woman, so beautiful. But God did; and you're the most amazing man, AND the most beautiful woman, I've ever known. And when you told me that day that the only thing you wanted, that you could not get back, was to have a baby, I wanted to find 'him' and kill him all over again. I wanted to slap the doctor who convinced me to remove my own uterus; because 'there was a slight chance' it might give me problems later! I was gonna make him put it back in, so I could have our baby for you! I was so angry at God, for you!... Oh, wow..." Gabby sat on the bed for a moment staring at Ronnie, who stared back at her in awe. She truly was something else. She squinted and tilted her head... and then started to giggle.

"What is it, Baby?" Ronnie was fully awake now, and watching and listening to his Angel Gabrielle, he was starting to believe.

"How much have you thought about not transitioning since you made the decision?"

"Hmph. Not much at all, really. Wow."

"Really, not even since you started?"

"No. Except for the stupid cramps, and the whole 'men don't have periods thing' playing in my head, it really hasn't been that bad, actually. I think I'm just mortified because I thought I'd escaped this whole thing. But now I realize it was nothing to really run from. I'm sorry I've been such a baby."

"Oh trust me, Honey; I really think I understand. I was afraid to say anything. I thought you were upset with me, that you blamed me for talking you out of doing it. If you had..."

"No. Stop right there." He pulled her close. "I'm so sorry, Gabrielle. I need to say this; and then I'll really be okay if we never talk about it again. You didn't talk me out of it. I don't think I ever truly wanted to. It was just what made sense... for someone else. I was living as a man. I didn't need this body, or so I thought; and I could afford to do it."

"You don't have to apologize, Baby. I actually think I get it. I believe this is your reward for not doing it."

"Okay. Now *that* I don't understand. You said you didn't think it would be 'a mistake' to have the surgery; you just liked me the way I am. Why would God reward me for not doing something I shouldn't have been doing in the first place?"

"I meant every word of that! I believe with my whole heart that transitioning is absolutely the right choice for some people. But I bet most men who transition never fantasized about being mothers; and you did!"

"I do, actually."

"Still?"

"...Yes." He said softly through a tearful smile.

"Wow. God is good."

"All the time..."

"Get up. We have to go to church."

"Yes, ma'am, we do."

43

THE JUDY TORRES SHOW

*A*fter the wedding, the 'big reveal', every major magazine cover, and countless awards, Ronnie was emotionally, exhausted, and frankly, tired of talking about himself. But Shawn and Gabby double-teamed him and convinced him that one last interview would catapult his off-camera efforts into the stratosphere. His resistance aside, Ronnie secretly loved the friendship that was forming between his wife and his best friend; besides, it was surprising how much more there actually was to say. So he allowed them to 'use him' to make the next 'brightest star since JFK' famous. He vowed that the family's interview with Judy Torres would be his last, outside of his contractual agreement to the network.

"So, I saw the show. Actually, I watched it live and then I watched it again. Did you know you were doing something no one has ever done before?"

"I think so."

"Is that why you did it?"

"No, actually. It really wasn't about being recognized, ironically. It really was, selfishly, about not wanting to be afraid anymore. But I did not understand that right away. It just felt like something I *had to* do."

"Dr. Keaner, you've known Ronnie for a long time haven't you?"

"Yes, actually. Since 'she' was ten." Liz smiled at Ronnie.

"And he's not your only transgender patient?"

"In my forty year practice, I've treated dozens of gay, lesbian, bisexual and transgender people."

"Have you been able to cure any of them?" Judy knew exactly what she was doing.

"Thankfully, no, I have not. There is nothing to 'cure'. In fact 'Gender Identity Disorder' was recently removed from the American Psychiatric Association's (APA) Diagnostic and Statistical Manual (DSM) and replaced with the terms 'gender incongruence' or 'gender variance', because 'gender variance is not a psychiatric problem; it's a natural human variation that in some cases requires medical attention and support.' And I personally believe that it is society that needs 'curing'. We've been conditioned to see and treat each other according to our genitalia. It's absurd, really, when you think about it, even if you choose to look at it spiritually, as I do. Say you believe that God made us in 'His' image. I think most people would agree that God is not flesh and bone at all. God is Spirit, not even neuter, but possessing all of the positive and good attributes that can exist in each of us, emotionally, psychologically, sexually and physically. So, why is it such a stretch to accept that those attributes exist in us in more than two possible combinations?"

Judy paused while the studio audience applauded for the doctor's concise and insightful explanation of 'what's wrong with the world'. "Annette... 'Mom'... Ronnie's not the first person to talk about how coming out saves lives, and helps strengthen families; but he is the most famous celebrity to come out as being transgender. And I watched you most closely as he explained why. Can you talk about what all of this has meant to you as a mother?"

Annette looked at Ronnie lovingly, and he smiled and nodded his head. "I'm a country girl. I grew up in a small town about eighty miles outside of Atlanta. The most cosmopolitan thing I ever did was fall in love with a Black man. And it was a big deal when David and I met in 1968. I think it is what literally killed my daddy, but I didn't care... Well, just look at him. Look at my children! Anyway, it was a really big deal; but only in the beginning. I was never asked to stretch much further than not being a racist. I never had to consider what other differences people might have. I'd never known any gay people, and gender identity was just ... well what's that? But I, we, were blessed with three beautiful children; and I counted myself among the luckiest former beauty queens in the world that two of them were these absolutely gorgeous baby girls. Oh, I had all these plans! We were going to take Georgia by storm! I had poor Libby twirling a baton like a pro at six. But she hated those itchy dresses, and she was, still is, smart as a whip; but literally, the nicest person in the world. Even as a child, she didn't have a competitive bone in her teeny tiny body. I had to accept the fact that my Elizabeth was never going to be a pageant diva. Our Neal came out one-hundred-percent boy, all 'rough and tumble' and super athletic. He was his father's son. So by the time 'Veronica' was born, I thought 'this is it!' Not only was she stunningly beautiful, with her silky curls and emerald green eyes, but she was a fighter from Day One. But she was only interested in fighting with *me,* probably because no one, but me, ever messed with her. By the time she could walk and talk, I couldn't make her wear pink panties, let alone anything trimmed in lace. And I walked around scheming and planning... and I prayed about it! That's right, I did. I got on my stupid knees and prayed to Baby Jesus that my beautiful baby girl would just stop being so damn stubborn, and be what I wanted her to be! She was too pretty to be a tomboy, or a lesbian. What the hell is a Transsexual? I ran home one day having looked up something called 'gender identity disorder' and showed it to David. What'd you do, Honey?"

"I threatened to leave your crazy butt, if you didn't leave my baby alone." He rubbed her hand.

"He did - threaten that day - not leave. And it didn't stop me. I pushed and pushed and pushed. I wanted my baby, all of my children to be successful, and I was determined that you couldn't be different and be successful. They had to conform. They had to fit in. I pushed my baby away from me. He was gone long before he was taken. And even having survived that, having lost so much, my mama, my brother, my husband... "I thought I still have 'Ronnie'." I even determined that I would call 'her' 'Ronnie'... not because that was the name he'd chosen for himself, but because I thought I could appease 'her' into doing what I wanted 'her' to do, and being what I needed 'her' to be... Until he had to leave me. And I watched as he tried to become a man, without his father, and with what amounted to the 'opposite of help' from me. He only had Libby. My intolerance and selfishness harmed her, too. She had to give up so much to be the parent I refused to be. And I was so busy feeling sorry for myself, that I basically forgot Neal even existed. Not really, but I wasn't present. All because I couldn't allow them, Ronnie most of all, to be who he needed to be, the person he believed God made him to be. And as I look back now at everything I was afraid of, at why I resisted, it was because I was just... ignorant. I can say it now. All it means is that there are things you just don't know any-thing about, right? I didn't know, because no one had ever tried to tell me, before I had a child who needed me to 'get it' right then and there. I'd never seen anyone like my Ronnie on television, at least not that I know of. I'm not saying I have an excuse. I'm saying that I believe that Ronnie's story could save a family a lot of hurt and misunderstanding. I believe it could save a child a lot of pain and loneliness. If I'd have known just one other real person who's life was good, even though they were so different... or perhaps *because* they were *so special*... I might not have made such an ass of my-self." Ronnie burst out laughing and stood to hug is mom, while the rest of the family laughed through their tears.

"Congratulations on your Pulitzer!" Judy beamed at Ronnie.

"Isn't that wild?"

"No. It's not really. I saw the documentary. It's amazing. What made you go there, instead of following the pack and focus-ing on the accused and the 'main victims'?"

"Don't give me too much credit. I was doing that, 'follow-ing the pack'. Actually there were two things that got in the way. The first was Gabrielle. I can say it now; but I abandoned my cov-erage of the trial to be with her. I had to choose between writing about her father and getting to know her. Once I realized I had a choice, it was easy. I couldn't be a rat reporter. No offense, guys. I had the ultimate conflict of interest. I was in love. But the most pivotal event in determining what I would report on was my first conversation with Evangelist Phyllis Richmond."

"Your mother-in-law?" Phyllis smiled at Ronnie and he blushed.

"Yeah... When I met Mama Rich, Gabby and I were still just dating, in the early stages. She didn't know me. She had no reason to trust me. I was just some guy who was trying to get in good with her daughter; or worse, just another reporter. It took knowing my story for her to share hers and begin to trust me. And as I was telling it, as I talked about my mom in particular, and eve-rything she lost when I was raped, I started looking at what they all lost, my siblings, my dad. In a lot of ways they suffered more, be-cause they had to suffer in silence. No one thought to take my brother and sister to counseling beyond that initial week. It was years before anyone noticed that my brother was devastated... guilt-ridden, suicidal. He'd been a star athlete and an honor student, and we were all too broken to notice that he was falling apart; or more importantly that there was something that could be done about it. They chalked it all up to him being just another Black kid without a father. 'He'll be alright when the old man gets outta pris-on... or take his place.' No one considered that he wasn't part of the typical cycle; that prior to 'the storm' he was a brilliant schol-ar-athlete on his way to his choice of Ivy League schools. No one considered he might be victim of some serious trauma himself. My sister dropped out of school to take care of me, when my mother couldn't relate to me anymore. To this day, she'll say it was a labor of love, and that she wanted to drop out. But the reality is, at twen-ty-two, she sacrificed her own dreams for me."

"Was it worth it?"

"I don't know how you measure that; but she saved my life... And my mom..." He paused for a moment, and wiped a tear away. "She'd lost so much, all in that one day... me, for a while, my dad, for twenty years, her mother, her brother... And for years, all I could do was be angry at her. I even blamed her for what happened to me; like if she'd somehow been more understanding, it wouldn't have happened... But what was more important than what I realized about my family was that it was happening to families everywhere. We focus on the victims, sometimes the accused; but never on the people closest to them. I finally figured out that my life and my work were supposed to be about identifying the ones I started call-ing 'the Forgotten Victims', and sharing their stories."

"Would you change what happened to you now, looking back?"

"No. Not at all. It was bad, but it was part of the journey. Seeing my family back together, whole and happy, and even stronger than we were before...having made the most wonderful friends...and finding the love of my life, I wouldn't trade one of those people for that day. You know what they say, 'what doesn't kill you...' I did not die."

"Are you stronger?"

"Oh, yes, and happier than I ever imagined possible. I'll never know what might have been; but I honestly can't imagine how I could have gotten to where I am in this moment in my life, if everything, every painful, scary, awful thing had not happened exactly the way it did."

"I heard a rumor... care to comment for the record?" Judy smiled at Ronnie.

"That depends..." He smiled back.

"Someone said you're giving away all your worldly possessions."

"Okay, that's an... actually, more than a slight exaggeration. But I have donated my Prize money and my salary for the last two years of the show, to the foundation my family and I established. It's called the 'Veronica Reynolds Recovery Ranch', or 'VR^3'. It's a residential facility and school, in Macon Georgia, for victims of abuse, and their siblings. It is free to any family that needs a place to rebuild, and includes family and individual counseling."

"Why name it after Veronica, and not R^4?"

"I thought she deserved a life and a legacy of her own."

"So, what's next?"

"Professionally or personally?"

"Both."

"Well, I lost a bet with my agent... " He laughed and shook his head. "... so the show is coming back for at least two more seasons... "

"And personally?"

Ronnie looked at Gabby and smiled. Then he closed his eyes, and took a deep breath, the focusing technique he'd been practicing to avoid rubbing his belly in public. "We're thinking about having a baby."

TRUTH! the series Continues!

Read on to find out what happens next!

I GOTTA GO

Michael tapped lightly on Kyle's office door. "Reverend, do you have a moment?"

"One second." Kyle answered from behind the closed door as he put away his sermon notes. Then he thought, "No! Absolutely not, not if you're coming in here to tell me you're leaving!" He'd seen this coming. Michael had been through so much. He truly was a walking miracle. Still Kyle watched him struggle, not seeing his own worth. Kyle believed with all his heart that Michael was a huge part of Lvolution Church's growth in the past three years. With Kyle spending more and more time touring, Michael held the New York church together. He was more than a Praise Arts minister; he was a minister, period. Kyle was never surprised to return and hear of the worship that took place in his absence. It was more than praise. People were leaving fulfilled and, most importantly, returning to worship and serve. The 'Dr. Martin Luther King Jr. meets Luther Vandross', preaching and teaching style of the Rev. Dr. Kyle Tye was only a happy surprise to people who came to church for the spirit-filled atmosphere ushered in by Minister Michael Anthony Lawson and his eclectic ensemble of praise leaders, singers, musicians, and dancers.

Kyle was torn. He knew it was time for Michael to go. But, selfishly, he needed Michael to stay, not just for what he meant to the church, but for much more personal reasons. Kyle was afraid for Michael. He saw the life and purpose that God poured back into his friend-brother-brother-in-law when he returned to the church. It was a fear that he never spoke of. It was unspeakable, faithless. He knew, intellectually anyway, that God didn't bring Michael through all that 'He' had, to his present, shining glory, only to let him fall apart. He'd built a hedge around him in the form of his church, his family and his own renewed faith; and, He'd lifted him from the ashes and set him apart as a most beautiful example of His redemptive power.

And Michael was beautiful. He had always been, inside and out; but now, while he still looked younger than his thirty-two years, he looked more like a man and less like a beautiful boy. He stopped cutting his jet-black curls, and embraced the unruly mane that grew more up and out than it flowed down. No one seemed to really know what his true ethnicity was; he didn't know himself. But he was frequently identified as 'the big-ass Indian with the curly fro.' At six-foot six, he somehow moved with the grace of a dancer; but now that he ate real food and didn't drink or smoke, a fuller, softer form replaced his artificially thin physique. His once wild, hazel eyes were wiser, more contemplative, and quite often closed in prayer.

Kyle watched as he waited for Michael to realize he'd opened the door. When he opened his eyes, Michael smiled at Kyle and gave him a long hug. Kyle tried not to cry. This was the day. He saw Michael at least five days a week; they never hugged. "What's up, Mike?"

"Why do you assume something's up?" Michael still had the smile of that mischievous 'little boy' he'd met years earlier.

"Because you're knocking - you never knock; you called me 'Reverend' - I don't think you've ever called me anything other than 'Rev' or 'Kyle' or 'Rev-Doc'; and you're standing outside my door prayin'... " Kyle chuckled.

"I do too knock...I just don't usually wait for you to answer." If the blinds were open, and it was clear Kyle wasn't counseling someone.

"Exactly." Kyle stared at his friend and watched his smile fade.

"It's time, bruh."

"Are you sure?"

"Yes...no."

"How long are we talking?"

"I don't know. I don't think long. Ya know, Kyle, I've never been on my own before; not as an adult, anyway. It's time."

"Take it from someone who's been alone most of his life; it's over-rated, Michael."

"No, you were a monk. I'm just talking about traveling a little." Michael wasn't ready to tell anyone the details of his trip. He really was just off on a journey to find peace. He didn't want anyone to know that 'peace' might include finding his mother. He wasn't ready to discuss the variables. What if he didn't find her?

What if she wasn't happy to see him? He just wanted to try.

"You live in New York City. What's left to see?" Kyle was being a brat.

"I live in the basement apartment of my Nana's brownstone, and all I see are those four walls and the inside of this church. I thought I'd start by seeing the rest of New York City." On his way out of it.

"So you're not leaving town?"

"Yeah, Kyle... I am. But there's really no plan. Do you understand?"

"I do, Michael. I'm sorry I'm giving you such a hard time. I think I'm just jealous." Kyle wasn't entirely joking. He had been the model for structure and discipline since he could speak. He did understand; but he was too afraid to let it all go, even for a day, the way Michael was about to. Even though they'd been touring some, as part of their music ministry, he and Kevin had basically slowed down a great deal. They did finally turn the castle in Canada into a bed and breakfast and moved into a larger apartment in the city. The Toronto church was being pastored by Kyle's former associate pastor, Grace; and there were plans for a new church in New Jersey. Kyle had discovered that it was a challenge, at best, to follow his personal dreams of reaching millions through music, while also building churches on the ground. But Kevin was determined that they would find a way to do both, and grow their family. Kyle was faithful, and grateful to have such a supportive husband, however, all he heard in that moment was that his friend and his minister of music was about to go off the grid. "I'm not replacing you, unless you call me and tell me you're not coming back; and I'll find you if you do. Are we covered?"

"Yes, sir. Believe it or not, we could both be gone for months and I doubt anyone would notice in the service." Michael's smile returned as he thought of the church and the people he loved.

"Oh, trust me, you will be missed; but, I know what you mean. God does indeed run this house."

"Amen." Michael stood to leave.

"So, you're taking your church phone, right?"

"Uh, no..." Michael reached in his pocket, and handed Kyle his purple iPhone. "...But I have everything I need in this one. Do you have my personal number?" He held up the same phone in red and called Kyle.

Kyle breathed a sigh of relief as his phone started ringing and Michael's face popped up. "Okay, okay. We're good. I'm not going to freak out, I promise."

"Why would you? God's got me."

"Yes, He does." They exchanged a quick man-hug, and Kyle watched Michael glide down the hall and exit the sanctuary doors into the brilliant, summer sun...

Unholy Wars – TRUTH! the series: Book Four

Kevin and Kyle's combined ministry is soaring! Still, the executive producers of the controversial and wildly popular 'Sin Series' gospel   musicals continue to face adversity in the music industry. But, why all the drama? Neither is in need of the money or fame that comes with commercial success. It's not about bling or gold statues; it's about Kingdom building and salvation. The presumably solid, power-couple use every weapon in their arsenal to do God's work. Meanwhile, a deep, dark family secret is brought to light, pitting brother against brother on the world's largest stages.

The Promised Land – TRUTH! the series: Book Five

Longtime BFFs and friendly combatants Gary and Nikki never have agreed on the hiring philosophies of The Company. Their differing views on racial equality and social justice escalate into a battle that threatens to destroy the forty-year-old, star-building, powerhouse. Their company, friendship and lives at stake, each is forced to make tough choices as personal health issues and haunting missteps persist. Promises to past loves are broken as new love is put to the test.

Lvolution – TRUTH! the series: Book Six

Kevin, Gabrielle and fam gather together for their son's high school graduation. As the first openly bisexual class president and valedictorian of the prestigious southern Christian academy prepares to take the stage, protestors march, blaming everything from global warming to the price of gas on the world's moral decay; the greatest example being Ethan and people like him, who dare to love and live according to their truths. Ethan is not afraid. He is, in fact, surrounded by an army of family; a family born of love, that knows how fight.

About the Author

T. Randall Jones is a writer-activist, occasional poet and accidental songwriter. She writes to uplift, inspire and celebrate gay, lesbian, bisexual and transgender people of faith, and to affect positive change by telling their stories. She lives in North Carolina with her wife and their three children, and is currently working on her third and fourth novels.

Visit her website:

www.Lvolution.org/Artists/TRandallJones

www.ingramcontent.com/pod-product-compliance
Lightning Source LLC
Chambersburg PA
CBHW070840250626
47159CB00003B/867